I0627290

WHAT LURKS

A Cryptid Anthology

WHAT LURKS: A CRYPTID ANTHOLOGY © 2025 Graveside Press

Published by Graveside Press 2025
graveside-press.com

All rights reserved.

This novel is entirely a work of fiction. The names, characters, businesses, places, events and incidents portrayed in it are the work of the author's imagination or are used fictitiously. Any resemblance to actual persons, living or dead, events or localities is entirely coincidental. No part of this book may be reproduced or transmitted in any form or by any means, electronic or mechanical, except for the purpose of review and/ or reference, without explicit permission in writing from the publishers.

Editing: Kelley York, Lauren Woods, Syd Tomac
Proofreading: Syd Tomac
Cover illustration: Dave Dick – instagram @dave_dick_
Cover layout and text: Sleepy Fox Studio – sleepyfoxstudio.net
Interior Formatting: Sleepy Fox Studio – sleepyfoxstudio.net

Digital 978-1-967547-53-1
Paperback (KDP) 978-1-967547-50-0
Paperback (Trade) 978-1-967547-51-7
Hardcover 978-1-967547-52-4

No part of this book has been created using Generative AI. Graveside Press and its authors do not consent for our works to be utilized in any form of training for machine learning.

Content Notes

Please note: because this is a horror anthology, it should be assumed that the basic horror tropes will apply. These include death, gore, and violence.

For a list of potentially triggering subjects, please refer to page 347.

Contents

The Spectergraph by Liddell Rayne 7

Long Pig by A. Atkins 26

Pop Goes the Wasset by S.E. Howard 38

Quarry by Liam Hogan 52

Separations by Aldrian Estepa 59

Harbinger by LR Woods 71

Mothman by Caterina Minezzi 87

Out of the Woods by Jamie Churchman 88

It Knows My Shape by Gio Clairval 101

Den Mother by Rey Revelli 117

The Red Ghost by Frankie Regalia 133

Apotheosis by David O'Mahony 143

MIMIC: Breeding Season by Я.R. Harrow 149

Untitled by Lumitar via DepositPhotos (illustration) 155

On the Nature of Grief and Ghouls by Hannah Birss 156

The Sounds of the Forest by gaast 165

The Winter Caretaker by J. Needham 178

Skunkape by Terry Campbell (illustration) 191

Lord of the Dance by Micah Giddens 192

The Teague Thing by Terry Campbell 204

Wastees Beyond Wastes by Leon Saul 217

A Terrifying Prize by J. Neira 226

The Cryptid in the Woods by Adrielle Reina 238

Split Stone by Joshua Lim 247

The Rattler by Alex Burnstein 258

Cornfield Gothic by Gabrielle Contelmo 270

Yamadhin by Z.D. Dochterman 278

Wampus by P.N. Harrison 290

The Beast of Always by C. Charles Knight 301

RIP Dag Gadol Diner by Laura Barker 309

The Windchime Witch by Brahn Smith (illustration) 317

The Branches Look Like Antlers by Chrissy Gray 318

Crack Open the Shell by AM Sutter 331

About the Authors 342

Content Warnings 347

"*Am I walking away from something I should be running away from?*"
— Shirley Jackson, "The Haunting of Hill House"

The Spectergraph

LIDDELL RAYNE

PART 1

THE AIR WAS thick with the scent of damp concrete and rust. Jamie fiddled with the camera strap on her shoulder, moving slowly through the deserted lot. Her boots crunched over broken glass and dry leaves. The city was full of spots like this—streets long forgotten, where the remains of old buildings stood as silent witnesses to a time when they were significant, now left to crumble. Her breath clouded in the cold air as she lifted her camera.

The late afternoon sky had settled into a thick gray overcast, diffusing a dim, muted light over the crumbling structures. Perfect for photography. No harsh shadows, just a soft, dead glow that made everything look haunted.

Jamie navigated the area with a calm, deliberate focus, her keen eye searching for the perfect shot. The place was eerily quiet, the silence enveloping her like a dense fog. There were no traffic noises or distant voices—just the occasional sigh of wind through shattered windows. It felt as though she had stepped into a world where time had paused.

She had found the place by accident while wandering earlier that day. It wasn't on any maps, at least none she had checked, and the rusted street signs were unreadable. The buildings were old, maybe pre-war, with brickwork cracking like dried skin and empty windows like hollowed-out eyes.

Jamie wasn't intimidated by places like this. In fact, she felt a strange attraction to them. An odd beauty existed in forgotten places. A quietness, a feeling that whatever had transpired here had left a mark, just waiting to be discovered.

She framed a shot of an old storefront, its glass long since shattered, the metal security gate hanging loose from its hinges.

Click.

An ancient, rusted streetlight appeared, its base adorned with dried vines that seemed to whisper tales of forgotten times.

Click.

As she continued her walk, she stumbled upon something even more intriguing: a secluded alleyway nestled between two buildings, enveloped in a deep, shadowy silence. Brick walls framed the entrance, graffiti-scrawled and peeling. Moisture slicked the ground, reflecting the faint daylight.

Jamie felt a little jolt of excitement. *This was the one.*

She stepped closer, angling her lens to capture the full length of the alley. The light just grazed the edges while the center seemed enveloped in a dense, almost tangible darkness. The composition was perfect.

Click.

She paused for a moment, glancing at the camera screen to review the shot. Shadows obscured the long alleyway, but the image was clear. The contrast was excellent, and there were no distractions. Feeling content, she gently let the camera rest against her chest and adjusted the strap.

Suddenly, she heard a creak from somewhere nearby.

She stopped, her breath hitching in her throat. Just a moment ago, the wind had been calm, and the noise was too piercing, too intentional—like the slow creak of a door opening. Jamie slowly turned her head, looking around the deserted lot.

Nothing.

Only lifeless buildings, empty storefronts, and the alley behind her extending like a throat into the unknown.

Yet she sensed a presence at that moment—like the prickling weight of unseen eyes. A sensation that raised the hair on your arms before your brain even registered it.

She took a deep breath to calm herself. A stray cat had probably caused some mischief. Or maybe her nerves were getting the better of her. She glanced at her watch. Late.

Time to go.

Jamie sat cross-legged on her couch, her laptop casting a soft glow in the dim apartment. A half-empty cup of coffee sat forgotten on the table beside her as she scrolled through the day's shots, fingers absentmindedly tapping against the trackpad.

She felt a sense of satisfaction with most of them. The atmospheric lighting and the striking juxtaposition of light and decay—it was exactly what she'd been hoping for.

She finally arrived at the alley photo. Her finger hesitated over the trackpad. At first glance, it looked just like she remembered: dark, unsettling, a perfect composition of shadow and empty space. Yet, as she stared at it, a tightness formed in her chest.

She zoomed in.

At the far end of the alley, just before the darkness swallowed everything, stood a figure.

Jamie's breath stilled.

It was barely visible, little more than a faint silhouette blending into the shadows. It stood at the alley's dead end, tall and slender, facing the camera directly. No distinct features. No blur of movement. Just *standing there.*

A chill crept up her spine. The alley had been deserted when she fired the shot. She was absolutely certain of it.

She blinked hard, then leaned closer to the screen. Maybe it was just a trick of the light, a shadow cast by something she hadn't noticed.

She fiddled with the brightness settings, but the figure stayed put. An odd, unsettling feeling twisted in her stomach, something deep and instinctual. She let out a quick breath and shut the laptop. It's nothing. Just her imagination running wild. Yet as she sat there, the sensation lingered.

Jamie turned off the lights and slid into bed, but sleep didn't come easily.

The image of the figure lingered in her thoughts, seared into the back of her eyelids like an afterimage.

It was just a shadow. A coincidence. You're being paranoid.

In that twilight zone between waking and sleeping, she sensed it. A presence, a heaviness in the air, nudging at the boundaries of her consciousness.

The feeling of eyes on her.

She rolled onto her side, drawing the blanket closer. Her thoughts lingered on the photo, fixated on the strange shapes of the alleyway. Her apartment was quiet, yet the silence seemed off. Too heavy, too motionless.

Her pulse raced. She cracked one eye open, scanning the room. Faint light from the streetlamp outside filtered in through the blinds, casting long, slender lines across the walls. Everything was where it should have been.

Except…

The shadows in the corner seemed off.

Jamie stared at them, unmoving, barely breathing. Her rational side told her it was just her imagination, but something deeper—something instinctual—kept her frozen. In the farthest corner of her room where the shadows pooled darkest, the shape seemed *taller* than it should be.

She told herself not to look. She squeezed her eyes shut, forcing herself to breathe evenly. Nothing was there. Nothing was—

Something creaked.

A slow, deliberate shift of weight against the wooden floorboards.

Frozen, she kept her eyes shut, her body rigid. Her heartbeat thundered in her ears.

Silence followed. Long. Dreadful. Then—

The unmistakable sound of a breath. Right beside her ear.

Jamie gasped, jolting upright and reaching for the lamp, her fingers fumbling blindly.

Light flooded the room.

Nothing.

The corner was empty. The room was still. She sat for a long moment, panting, her skin crawling. It was a dream. Had to be. Just stress. Just exhaustion.

Still, she hesitated before turning the light off again.

When she finally did, she swore she felt something in the dark. Waiting. Watching.

***

PART 2

Jamie woke to the sound of her phone vibrating on the nightstand. She groggily reached for it, squinting at the screen. *2:47 a.m.* A notification:

One file modified: DSC_0453.jpg

Her heart pounded heavily within her chest. That was the alley photo. For a moment, she simply gazed at the screen, trying to shake off the lingering haze of sleep. Maybe the laptop had automatically saved something, or there was a software glitch. But deep down, she felt that wasn't the case.

The unease from earlier rushed back, creeping up her spine.

Jamie hesitated before pushing back the covers and stepping out of bed. The apartment was silent except for the hum of the fridge in the other room. Everything was exactly as she'd left it—laptop shut, camera bag on the chair, blinds drawn tight against the window.

Still, the atmosphere felt off. The shadows in the corners of the room seemed more intense, as if they had thickened in her sleep. She inhaled deeply, opened her laptop, and went to her photo folder.

There it was—DSC_0453. The alley photo.

The timestamp indicated the file had been changed minutes earlier. Jamie's stomach twisted into a knot. With a deep breath, she double-clicked the file. The image appeared, taking up the entire screen.

Her heart skipped a beat. The figure had moved. It no longer stood at the far end of the alley, but had come closer to the foreground.

The silhouette had shifted forward, stepping out from the deep shadows. It still wasn't fully visible—its features remained blurred, indistinct—but its posture had changed. Before, it had been standing still, almost distant.

Now, it leaned slightly forward, as if aware of being seen.

She sat frozen, her brain scrambling for explanations. Maybe she had taken two photos in quick succession and hadn't realized. Maybe the camera had glitched. Maybe—

Her eyes flicked to the timestamp again. The original was taken at 6:42 p.m. The modification happened at 2:47 a.m.

She hadn't touched the photo, so how had it changed?

With a shaky breath, she reached for the camera on the desk, flipping through the original files on the SD card. She scrolled to the alley photo, heart pounding.

The figure was in the same place as before. It hadn't moved. Not closer. Jamie stared at the laptop screen, then back at the camera. The images didn't match.

Her breath turned shallow.

Jamie sat there, the screen's glow creating distinct shadows on her face, her heart pounding so intensely that she nearly missed it—a gentle creak of the floorboards. Right behind her. Her entire body tensed up. She didn't turn or move.

For a moment, the apartment remained eerily quiet. Then again—the faintest sound of weight moving across the floor.

Her hand clutched the edge of the desk tightly. The air behind her seemed heavy and off. Something had taken up space that hadn't been there before.

A long, slow breath rattled through the room. Not hers.

Jamie spun, slamming her hand against the desk lamp, flooding the room with light. Nothing.

The space behind her was empty. The apartment was still. Her chest heaved as she scanned every shadowed corner, every inch of the floor. The only thing staring back at her was her own reflection in the dark window.

Jamie couldn't sleep. She stayed at her desk all night, scrutinizing the photo and desperately trying to understand it.

She scrolled through every forum she could remember, searching for terms like 'photo figure moves' and 'ghost in photograph.' Most of the results were just the usual chatter—blurry pictures of dust, old tales about haunted images. But at around 5:00 a.m., buried in a deep thread on an old photography forum, she found something that made her stomach turn to ice.

A post from six years ago, by someone named *L.Davenport*:

If you ever see it in a photo, DON'T LOOK AGAIN.

The reply chain was a mess—half of the users called it an urban legend, others said it was some kind of psychological phenomenon. A few people shared their own stories.

> I took a photo of an abandoned lot, saw a shadow figure in the back. Thought it was a trick of the light. Next day, it had moved closer. I deleted the file, but it wouldn't go away. The night after that, I saw it outside my window.

Another user responded:

> It only moves when you look at it. It knows when it's been seen.

Jamie's mouth went dry. She scrolled further, heart racing.

The last message in the thread made the hairs on her arms stand up:

If you see it in a photo, you have to get rid of it. Fast. But you can't just delete it. You have to pass it on. If you don't—

The message cut off there. The user never posted again. Jamie swallowed hard. She turned back to the image on her screen, her mind whirling. The figure was still there. Still closer than before. Her hands felt ice cold against the laptop.

Her gaze dropped lower, to the very edge of the frame. Something new had appeared. Something she hadn't noticed before. The faintest outline of a handprint. Pressed against the lens.

As if something had reached for her.

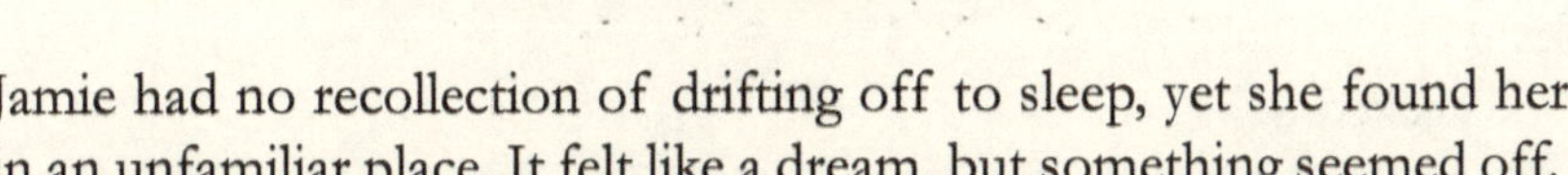

Jamie had no recollection of drifting off to sleep, yet she found herself in an unfamiliar place. It felt like a dream, but something seemed off. She stood at the entrance of the alley, the same one in the photo. However, now the buildings loomed larger, the walls felt more constricting, and the darkness at the end seemed unfathomably deep. The air carried a damp, metallic scent.

She hesitated even as every fiber of her being urged her to retreat, to wake up, to flee. Just as she was about to give in, a sound reached her ears—soft, reminiscent of cloth brushing against uneven stone. A figure emerged from the shadows. Jamie's heart skipped a beat.

The shape was human—almost. Its limbs were abnormally extended, its movements jerky, like a puppet guided by invisible strings. The edges of its form flickered, unstable, as if it struggled to maintain one shape.

But its face—

There was no face. Just smooth skin where features should be. It tilted its head, as if trying to understand her. Then it moved a step closer.

Jamie tried to turn and run and found she couldn't move. Her feet felt glued to the pavement, her body paralyzed.

Another step.

And another.

A disturbing, elongated sound filled the air as its mouth started to take shape, stretching open far too wide—almost unnaturally so—to show only darkness. Its voice came out harsh and grating, like the scrape of broken glass, as it uttered a single word.

"Mine."

Jamie jolted awake, her chest heaving and gasping for air. She found herself back in her apartment, but that unsettling feeling still lingered. The laptop remained open on her desk, the eerie alley photo still displayed on the screen. This time, the figure in the image seemed closer, almost as if it could step out of the frame.

PART 3

Jamie scrolled through the deep web, fingers shaking. She had seen ghost stories before, urban legends passed around like campfire tales. But this…this felt different.

She stumbled onto a buried forum post with a title that made her stomach turn:

"Photographic Anomalies & Observational Entities—Read Before Looking."

She clicked it.

User: LuxSpectrum99

Most people assume it's a spirit. A haunting. But it's not. It's an anomaly. A being that only exists when captured in certain spectrums of light.

Your camera picked up something that wasn't meant to be seen. And now that you've seen it—

—it's seen you.

Jamie's skin prickled. Further down, a different user had responded.

User: DeepFieldVision

Light bends in strange ways in abandoned places. Some locations create gaps—windows into other spectrums. Infrared, ultraviolet…even things we haven't classified yet. Cameras don't just capture images. Sometimes, they reveal things that were always there, just outside our visible perception.

She thought about her photo. The figure had started at the far end of the alley, deep in the shadows. Almost imperceptible. But each time she had viewed the image, it had become clearer.

Not closer.

Just…more real.

She continued scrolling, hoping to find answers. But when she reached the final comment in the thread, it made her blood run cold.

<u>User: L.Davenport</u> (*Last seen: 6 years ago*)

DO NOT LOOK AGAIN.

Jamie slammed the laptop shut.

Her breath came in short, panicked gasps as she sat frozen in her chair, hands clenching the armrests so tightly that her knuckles ached. The image was burned into her mind—the figure, no longer distant, now right at the edge of the frame.

Almost stepping out. She forced herself to breathe, to think. Had she imagined it?

No.

She knew what she had seen.

She wiped a clammy hand across her face, glancing around the dimly lit apartment. The first hints of dawn seeped through the blinds, casting pale slashes of light on the hardwood floor. Outside, the city was just beginning to stir—cars in the distance, the occasional muffled voice.

Normal sounds. Normal life. But inside, her world felt wrong.

Jamie hesitated, then—against every instinct screaming at her—she reached out and flipped her laptop open again.

The photo was still there.

But the figure hadn't moved further. It was still at the edge of the frame, frozen just before stepping into the light.

Her stomach twisted. *It only moves when you look at it.* The words from the forum flashed in her mind. Slowly, she moved the cursor to the file, right-clicked, and selected Delete.

A warning popped up.

Are you sure you want to move this file to the Trash?

Yes.

The file disappeared from the folder.

She exhaled sharply, trying to release the tension gripping her spine. That was it. That had to be it. She opened the Trash bin to clear it completely.

And froze.

The file was still there.

A fresh wave of ice washed over her. Jamie clicked Empty Trash and watched as the icon spun.

Then stopped. The file remained.

Her breath hitched. She tried again.

Empty Trash. Nothing.

She clicked the photo directly, choosing Permanently Delete. A new message appeared on the screen.

File cannot be deleted. File in use.

Her throat went dry.

In use? By what?

A sharp buzzing filled the apartment.

Jamie jumped, almost spilling her coffee. Her phone was ringing, but it wasn't her familiar ringtone. The sound was jumbled, distorted— like a signal trying desperately to break through. A harsh metallic whine crackled from the speakers.

Jamie quickly grabbed the phone from the table, her heart skipping a beat as she saw the unknown caller ID. A wave of anxiety washed over her, and she paused, her thumb just above the answer button. The buzzing intensified, adding to her unease. Just as she was about to answer, the phone screen flickered and the call abruptly ended.

It rang again.

Jamie's hands trembled as she hesitated. She knew she shouldn't respond; every part of her was urging her to stay silent. Yet, despite the warning, she found herself unable to resist. Her thumb tapped the screen, her heart pounding wildly, she brought the phone to her ear. For a brief moment, there was silence.

Then—

The phone line was filled with a low, wet static, no voice or breathing. Just a dull, shapeless hiss, reminiscent of an old radio struggling to find a station. Jamie was about to pull the phone away and hang up when—

Suddenly, the static ended. A single sound crackled through the speaker, breaking the silence.

No words came through. Just a click, similar to a camera shutter snapping. Jamie felt her breath hitch as the call abruptly ended. Her phone screen seemed to have a mind of its own, dimming the brightness. Without any warning— a new image popped up in her photo gallery.

Jamie felt a wave of dread wash over her. She hadn't snapped any fresh photos, so she hesitated before clicking on it. Her heart sank as she saw the image: a picture of her apartment, capturing the familiar dim lighting, the couch, the coffee table, and her laptop still open to the photo of the figure. But what caught her attention most was the reflection in the black TV screen—

A figure. Standing behind her. Jamie's heart skipped a beat. She whipped around—nothing.

The apartment was empty, yet the room felt off. The walls seemed to close in, the light somehow more intense—as if it had a heaviness to it. She glanced back at the phone. The photo was still there. But something had shifted. The figure was nearer now. Almost fully aligned.

Jamie's throat tightened. A new notification popped up. No subject. No sender. Just two words.

LOOK AGAIN.

Her hands shook nervously. The photo flickered. Jamie hesitated, dreading what she might find. Still, she pressed the button. Her heart skipped a beat. The figure's reflection had vanished, and her own reflection was different. Altered.

Her familiar features were slightly off-kilter. Her eyes appeared a bit too wide. And the mouth…it wasn't hers.

Jamie's hands went numb as a chilling realization dawned on her. Something was in the apartment with her, something trying to change her. And for the first time since this terrifying ordeal began, Jamie truly understood—

It wasn't coming through the photograph.

It was coming through her.

PART 4

The following morning in her apartment, Jamie pondered the chaotic events that had taken place the day before. Her thoughts and emotions swirled around, each vying for her focus. The apartment was still, with only the gentle hum of the refrigerator in the kitchen and the faint murmur of traffic outside her window breaking the silence.

Her hands gripped the arms of the chair so tightly that her nails dug into the fabric. The air in the apartment had shifted—heavy and motionless, as if it waited for a storm to break. It wasn't just the knocking that had started; it was the eerie quiet in between. The apartment felt as tense as she did, as if it held its breath alongside her.

Every part of her urged her to get up, to act. Yet she remained paralyzed, her eyes fixed on the front door, the chain lock secure, the deadbolt firmly in place.

Another knock. Jamie's stomach twisted.

She squeezed her eyes shut, willing herself not to breathe too loudly. The door didn't shake. The handle didn't rattle. But she felt it just beyond the threshold.

Something waited. Listening. Then—

A soft exhale.

Her skin crawled. Something was breathing on the other side of the door. Jamie's body tensed, her pulse hammering so hard she thought it might burst. The knock came again. But this time, it was wrong.

It wasn't on the door anymore. It was lower. Near the bottom. Like someone—or something—had crouched down, pressing against the wood.

A whisper seeped through the crack. *"Let me in."*

She clamped a hand over her mouth to keep from screaming. She stayed still, every muscle in her body locked tight. The air around her felt heavy, as if the very space she occupied pressed in from all sides.

The door creaked—not from movement, but from weight. Something was leaning against it.

The handle turned.

She quickly reached for the lamp, switching it on. The room filled with a comforting glow, sending the shadows retreating to the far corners.

Silence. No more knocking. No more whispering.

She crept forward, step by agonizing step, until she reached the door.

Holding her breath, she pressed her eye against the peephole. Nothing.

The hallway outside was empty. Still, something felt wrong.

The world beyond the door looked…*off*. Like a photograph where the colors had been slightly warped. The edges of the hallway looked too still, like a paused video, frozen in time.

Jamie's stomach twisted. She needed answers. Now.

She took her laptop off the table and dropped onto the couch, her hands trembling slightly as she launched the browser. She desperately needed to find something—any explanation, any reason why this was unfolding. There had to be more than what she had discovered previously.

At first, she searched for paranormal theories—ghosts, urban legends, shadow people. But none of it fit. This wasn't haunting her. It was getting closer.

That's when she changed tactics. She searched for anomalies in light and photography—scientific theories about cameras capturing things beyond human perception.

Most of the results were dry, technical discussions. But buried deep in an obscure physics forum, she found something else. An archived journal article from 1997. The title sent an icy shiver down her spine:

"Unclassified Spectral Entities & Non-Linear Photographic Capture" – Dr. Victor Alen, Theoretical Physicist.

Jamie's pulse quickened. She clicked the link.

The webpage was ancient—black text on a gray background, the formatting broken in places. The article itself was dense, filled with equations and scientific jargon she barely understood. As she skimmed through, one passage stood out:

"There are locations where light doesn't behave as expected. Dead zones, abandoned spaces—places thick with history and decay. In these spaces, light bends unnaturally, creating what I call spectral alignments.

Cameras, especially digital ones, do not simply record images. They translate data. Sometimes, they pick up wavelengths beyond human perception, revealing entities that are normally unseen..."

Jamie's fingers curled against the laptop. The article continued:

*"But the danger is not in capturing them. The danger is in **making them aware of us.** Some things exist only as long as they are observed. And the more they are seen...the more they align with our reality."*

Her breath hitched. She thought of the photo. The figure hadn't just moved—it had become clearer. More defined.

Like it was adjusting itself to her world. She scrolled further.

"I believe there is an entity I've classified as (Spectergraph) Phototropic Phenomenon No. 132.

It is not a ghost. It is not alive in the way we understand. It is an observational anomaly—a being that exists only

*through sight. It aligns itself with the observer. The more
you look, the more it conforms to your space, to your time.
Eventually, it does not need the photograph anymore. It will
have aligned completely. And then, it will replace you."*

Jamie stopped breathing.

She thought back to the photo.

The first time she saw it, the Spectergraph had been deep in the alley. Barely visible.

But now? Now it was at her door. She swallowed hard, scrolling to the bottom of the article. There was one last note.

Dr. Victor Alen was declared missing in 1998. His research remains classified.

Jamie's blood turned to ice. The research had been buried. Alen had disappeared. Just like Liam Davenport. Just like the other forum users who had seen it. If Alen had been right… She was already running out of time.

A notification blinked in the corner of her laptop screen.

Jamie's heart nearly stopped. A new file had appeared in her gallery. She hadn't taken any new pictures. Her hand hovered over the trackpad, her pulse hammering as she clicked.

The image opened.

Jamie's breath left her lungs. It was a picture of her standing in her apartment.

Right now. The same dim lighting. The same terrified expression. And behind her—

A shape in the reflection of the window. Tall. Thin. Almost perfectly aligned.

Jamie's hands trembled violently. It wasn't in the photo anymore. It was here. Her vision swam, her stomach twisting in terror. She thought of Raines' final words:

"Eventually, it does not need the photograph anymore."

The entity didn't move closer. It became clearer. It wasn't just a shadow in a picture anymore. It was real. It was waiting. Jamie's throat went dry.

Then, from the corner of the room, a shift. A quiet inhale. Slow. Deliberate. She turned. And the lights went out.

PART 5

The darkness swallowed everything. Jamie couldn't see. Couldn't move.

Her breathing was quick and anxious as the apartment seemed to move around her. The air felt heavy and oppressive, as if it were closing in. The silence wasn't just a void; it felt like it was holding its breath. She could still sense it in the room with her. It wasn't a ghost or a curse, just something unusual.

Something that had always existed just beyond human sight. Something that cameras, by accident or design, had made visible. The moment she had captured it, she had made it aware of her.

And now…

It had aligned completely. Jamie's pulse thundered in her ears. She reached out awkwardly for her phone, the cool metal feeling slippery against her sweaty fingers. The screen flickered on, sending a soft light into the suffocating darkness.

One new notification. A new photo.

Jamie's stomach twisted as she tapped it open.

Her lungs seized. Another picture of her apartment. Right now.

Everything was the same—the overturned coffee table, the laptop still glowing faintly in sleep mode, the lamp she had knocked over in her panic.

But Jamie wasn't in it. The space where she should have been—was empty.

Her hands went ice cold. She was still here. She could feel herself. Could feel the couch beneath her, the air against her skin.

But she wasn't in the photo. Her body trembled as she slowly lifted her gaze to the dark window across the room.

The faint light from the phone screen reflected off the glass. There, in the reflection—

Something was standing where she should be.

Tall. Thin. Motionless.

The shape was wrong. It was her size, her build—but it wasn't her.

It was smooth where her features should be, like a figure carved from wet clay before it had time to set.

No eyes.

No mouth.

Just a hollow impression where a face should be.

Jamie's breath hitched. Then—

It tilted its head.

Not the reflection. The thing standing behind her.

Jamie whipped around, her body moving before her brain could catch up.

Nothing.

The space behind her was empty. But she didn't feel alone. The air still carried weight. The wrongness hadn't gone away. It had simply… settled.

The laptop flickered. A new file appeared on the screen. Jamie swallowed hard, forcing herself to look.

She tensed. Another photo. Another image of her. Except this time—

The reflection didn't stand in the window anymore. It sat in her place on the couch. Jamie's place. And it stared at her.

Her vision swam, her stomach twisting violently. Theories rushed back to her—the articles, the warnings.

"Some things exist only as long as they are observed."

"The more you look, the more they align."

The Spectergraph had been coming toward her. It had been taking her place. Piece by piece. And now, it wasn't in the photograph anymore.

It was real.

She sprinted for the door, but the moment her hand grasped the knob, her body locked up. Her muscles wouldn't move. She was trapped. Not by force—by something else. Something inside her trying to take control.

Her fingers felt numb. Her legs felt heavy. Like something was settling into her skin. Like something was aligning perfectly.

Jamie gasped, her breath coming in sharp, ragged bursts. Her phone vibrated in her hand.

A new notification. A new photo.

She didn't want to look. But something in her was making her. Her trembling fingers swiped the screen. And then—

The world tilted. It was her face. But not her. The features were almost right. The eyes were placed correctly, the lips formed just as they should be.

But they were off by a fraction of a degree. A perfectly aligned imitation. It was her. And she wasn't here anymore. Her vision blurred.

Something pressed against her from the inside. Like she was folding, her body turning into something else—something meant to fit a mold.

She tried to scream—

Everything went black.

EPILOGUE

Jamie opened her eyes to darkness.

Not the kind that came from simply shutting out the light. This was deeper, thicker, like the very concept of space had unraveled around her. The air itself felt wrong, heavy yet empty, stretching in ways that made her skin crawl.

She tried to move. Her limbs obeyed sluggishly, like they weren't entirely hers anymore.

There were no walls or a floor, only an endless horizon of changing reflections—glass-like surfaces extending infinitely in all directions, twisting into unimaginable forms.

Then she noticed them: multiple figures. Some stood still, their shapes incomplete, their faces smudged as if ink had been washed away by rain. Others moved in jerky, unnatural ways, always just out of her clear sight. They weren't paying attention to her. They were seeing right through her.

Jamie spun around frantically, hoping to find something—anything—until she noticed her reflection. But it wasn't her.

It was her body, her face, her hands…but she wasn't inside it anymore. The reflection blinked when she didn't. Moved when she didn't. It was standing in her apartment. Living in her space. Wearing her life.

Jamie reached out, pressing a trembling hand against the nearest surface. Her fingers sank into it, the glass rippling like disturbed water. She desperately tried to push back, to return to where she belonged—but then, a hand seized her wrist. It was cold, unsettling, and felt empty.

She gasped, twisting away, but the reflections closed in. The featureless figures shuddered, their distorted mouths opening in silent, gaping grins.

And then—

A click.

The faint mechanical snap of a camera shutter.

The reflections shuddered, the entire space quivering like a disturbed photograph. The glass rippled, warping, stretching—

Light.

Jamie turned toward the glow, straining to see—and in the shifting dark, she glimpsed it.

A computer screen. An open photo editor. A figure sitting at a desk, head tilted in confusion, staring at a newly discovered image.

A picture of her, trapped inside the Spectergraph.

Her mouth moved, but no sound escaped. The space around her contracted, pulling her toward the glass—toward the screen—toward the person now looking at her.

The glass flexed—

And then, the screen flickered.

A hand—her hand—moved outside the photo. Not her. The thing wearing her shape.

It leaned closer to the screen, tilting its head, its mouth curling into something almost like a smile…

████████████ DEPARTMENT OF ████████████
DOCUMENT NO. ███-████-132
SUBJECT: Phototropic Phenomenon No. 132 (P.P.132)
DATE: ████████████
STATUS: ███THREAT-LEVEL ███

OVERVIEW:
P.P.132 is a non-corporeal, phototropic anomaly classified under Spectral Alignment Entities (SAEs). Unlike known spectral phenomena, it does not require a physical host and does not originate from any biological or supernatural source. Its ████████████to photographic capture and observation.

Repeated exposure to images of P.P.132 leads to ████████████ effects on the observer. Once integration reaches Stage ████████████, the observer is no longer distinguishable from the anomaly.

This is not a visual distortion. It is a systemic failure of identity.

INCIDENT REPORTS ████████████:
- 06/09/███ – Image recovered from ████████████ National Park. Initial review showed no anomalies.
- 06/12/███ – Photographer (████████████ ████████) reports "a figure" in second image review. Image analysis confirms P.P.132 presence.
- 06/14/███ – Photographer complains of feeling watched. Subsequent images show the figure ████████ with minor distortions in subject's reflection.
- 06/16/███ – Photographer's apartment found empty. Personal belongings undisturbed. Last image shows subject's reflection missing.
No ████████ ████████of departure.

ENTITY CLASSIFICATION:
- SPECTRAL ALIGNMENT PARASITE – Exists only when captured via photographic/digital means.
- NON-PHYSICAL, NON-SAPIENT, HIGHLY RESPONSIVE TO OBSERVATION.
- MOBILITY: UNKNOWN (Moves only through perceptual pathways).
- FINAL FORM: ████████████.

CONTAINMENT PROTOCOLS:
- DO NOT ENGAGE. DO NOT ATTEMPT ERASURE.
- All instances of P.P.132 imagery must be quarantined.
- Deletion attempts result in ████████████ reoccurrence.
- DO NOT view affected images in reflective surfaces.

FINAL LOGGED ENTRY:
"No one's being haunted. No one's being hunted. But the moment you see it, it sees you. And if you keep looking… it won't need the image anymore."
— Dr. ████████ █. ████████, [FINAL TRANSMISSION LOGGED ███/███/███]

Long Pig

A. ATKINS

He wiggles his stumps.

They were toes, once. Ten little piggies who went to market.

He doesn't go to the market anymore.

His bare, bony un-feet don't feel the cold. He moves swiftly, carves through the air, a freshly sharpened butcher's knife on the wind. He slips between the trees, branches and brambles and brush scratching at his un-legs, always reaching for him, always hungry.

The land is insatiable, just like him.

Snow is thick on the farm, each flake nestling layer by layer into itself, blanketing the earth in the softest of quilts. The ground has begun to tremble in the absence of the sun, a drumbeat—heartbeat—deep in the earth, counting down the days.

Night is coming. The longest one.

And so is he.

<hr>

MARY

Pollyanna was a screamer. *Insolent child*, pushing me, testing me from the very beginning when she took three days to slither out of me, a shrivelled, stinking, bloody mess. Like a mutant beetroot, always squawking.

Darryl didn't like the noise, so I bounced Polly on my hip while I filleted fish, pickled herring, processed the chickens. I rocked her while I starched Darryl's shirts, strapped her to my back while I scrubbed the floor. And still she screamed, her purple little face twisted in agony, my grey matter slowly turning to pulp from the constant noise.

Michael had been such a quiet child, but that night, on the barnboard floor in front of a pile of wooden blocks, he screamed, too.

It was the solstice, The Long Night, my favourite day of the year because it meant the impending return of daylight hours and work that took Darryl far, far away.

They won't stop screaming, Darryl said.

That's what they do.

Darryl's cold, hard eyes fixated on the wailing flesh of his flesh. Make them shut up, he said.

I cocked my head to the side, skin tingling, and clutched Pollyanna closer to my breast as I stepped in front of Michael.

Darryl grew taller, every short, angry inhale inflating his spineless body. He stepped towards me.

You have one job, he said.

I put Pollyanna on the floor beside her brother, her healthy little lungs ratcheting up to new heights.

I'll make them be quiet, he said.

My hand slipped into my apron, gripped the worn, familiar handle of my fixed-blade knife.

Move, Mary.

I didn't.

Mary, he said, warning in his voice.

I rounded my back, stuck out my chin, stepped lithely towards him and hissed.

No.

He paused. What are you doing Mary?

But I wasn't Mary. I was Ma.

He stepped back.

Too late.

The blade slid between his ribs like butter, easier than with the hogs. His eyes bulged, eyelids stretching and pulling away as if invisible hands had taken hold, yanked them open and whispered *See? Look what happens when*—but he was fading too fast to hear the rest.

He crumpled to the floor and probably shit himself, but I was too used to the smell to notice. Pig shit, chicken shit, baby shit. I was a full-time shit wrangler, chained to excrement management for so long that my nostrils simply ignored the smell.

The old farmhouse floors were poorly levelled and the pool of blood from his belly spread, the rust-coloured puddle inching towards Polly.

Michael, who could walk now, toddled towards it while I half-watched; my brain was too busy panicking. Not because of the dead body—I had no shits left to give for Darryl—no, it was trying to understand what the ringing-that-wasn't-ringing in my ears was. I hadn't yet figured out that it was simply the absence of Screaming Baby.

I realized this as Michael squatted down beside the pool and put his fat little hands palms-down in the hot, red molasses. He squealed with delight, dropped to the ground on all fours, and slurped at it like a dog at a water dish. When he reached out to his sister, she suckled his blood-soaked fingers. He looked up at me, mouth smeared with blood like when he was born, and smiled.

Pollyanna was quiet the rest of the night. I took her outside with me, left her in a warm bundle in her playpen while I sharpened my butcher's knife next to the pigpen. She watched while I worked, her too-big eyes staring up at me while I drained ~~Darryl~~ the body, the blood a precious balm I collected in jars. I tossed the rest of his innards to the pigs.

Michael sat beside his sister and watched as three deer emerged from the treeline. They knew they were safe. Venison wasn't on the menu that night.

It was a good winter. A *quiet* winter. The body filled a freezer-and-a-half and Lord knew I could get a *long* way on bone broth.

In the evenings, I'd wipe the corners of Michael's mouth, pink blood-milk dribbling down his sleepy little chin as he drifted off. I'd kiss his forehead, his soft, sweet forehead, before pulling the door closed and enjoying the rest of my evening by the crackling fire.

Pollyanna didn't need it. She'd been silent as the grave for weeks.

Sometimes, I'd pull out ~~the body's~~ Darryl's hand. I kept it in the freezer with the chicken feet. I'd rest it on my knee, a gentle caress for a job well-done. Sometimes I'd hold it by the stump and slip it between my legs, careful to keep things quick so it didn't thaw.

Darryl had been good for something, in the end.

POLLYANNA

The house always smelled of vinegar and blood. Ma could get blood out of anything; her summer dresses with their grisly paisley had been scrubbed spotless more times than I could count. She wore those very same dresses to the funerals.

Nobody ever complained that Mary Pritchitt wore sundresses at wakes.

She's trying to cheer everyone up, they'd say, but really they were all hoping for a slice of something. She was famous for her beef casseroles and tourtières, but she only ever made them for the dead.

Why don't you make them in bulk, they'd ask. We'd all buy them.

Please, they'd say. Can I just make one special order? For Christmas? I'll pay you well.

They'd bug her and bug her and bug her until Michael came over and suddenly nobody was bothering Ma. Everybody *Suddenly Had to Go*.

We were on vacation in Alberta. All I remembered about it was scratchy motel sheets and cartoons in Spanish because the guy who worked at the front desk didn't know how to change it back to English. But I knew it was a vacation because Ma wore her vacation dress.

Michael and I were going nuts cooped up in that motel. I was little— five, maybe? Six?—and my brother was doing his best to keep me occupied during the day while Ma went out, but it was tough; I was used to the woods, *Our Woods*, used to running barefoot for miles, collecting pine needles and sap in my curls. I was used to climbing rock faces of exposed granite taller than our house before Ma'd even rung the breakfast bell. Spent my afternoons chasing rabbits and the evenings snapping their necks and pulling out their guts for Michael to skin them for supper—Ma didn't trust me with a knife, yet.

The hotel suite with the vertical blinds wasn't cutting it.

Several sunrises and multiple reruns of the cartoons later, Michael hoisted me onto his shoulders and took me for a walk. We were lured into the video store by the giant elephant on the sign and the smell of popcorn on the muggy, lazy city breeze.

There was a room in the back, away from the rest of the rows of movies, with vertical blinds in the doorway like the ones in the motel room window. I wandered inside while Michael filled a paper bag to the brim with freshly popped popcorn from the machine.

The room was different, somehow. I knew I wasn't supposed to be in there. That those movies weren't for me.

What are you doing? a puce-coloured man growled at me.

Before I could answer, he grabbed the back of my shirt and burst through the blinds, yanking me down an aisle so hard my feet barely hit the ground.

Whose kid is this? he shouted.

Michael paused, then slowly rested his popcorn on the counter's edge.

Mine, he said.

The man paused. Everyone always paused for Michael. Where are your parents?

Michael squinted at the man's hand on the back of my shirt. The man let go, and I stumbled towards my brother, tears in my eyes.

The man started cursing, spit flying from his mouth, and several other folks in the store stopped to watch. When he finally stopped yelling at no one, when he realized that Michael hadn't moved, hadn't even *looked away,* he took a tiny step backwards.

Do something about her, he said, gesturing at me.

Like what?

Discipline her!

Michael just stared at him. He stared, and he stared, and nothing about him changed but *everything* changed: his body boiled, something roiling beneath his skin, his pupils dilating into vertical slits like a snake, exhaling clouds of black smoke that filled the room with noxious gas, his face contorting, cheekbones so sharp the air would have cried if he'd so much as moved a muscle.

The man began to sweat. I could smell it. He looked at me and then around, cleared his throat before turning away and scurrying out the door. Another *Suddenly Had to Go.*

Michael picked up his bag of popcorn and held it out for me.

I climbed onto his shoulders and spent the rest of the walk back to the motel tapping the top of his head—my signal for him to tilt it back— and trying to drop popcorn into his open mouth.

He and Ma went out together that night. When I woke up in the morning, Ma was in her driving dress, her vacation dress nowhere to be found. We left the motel that afternoon, drove sixteen hours straight until we bumped our way down the uneven drive and heaved a collective sigh at the familiar crunch of gravel and whisper of the trees. *Home.*

A few days later, I found a dreamcatcher on my nightstand. It was made of hair, tiny bits of inner-ear cartilage woven into the strands like prey in a spider's web.

When I got older, I dreamed I went deaf. Ma was in the woods in her hunting dress, shaking her arms at me, lips frantic. Her armpits were drenched, the neck of her dress damp with acrid sweat. She reeked of fear, like the mice I trapped and cupped in my palms, pissing and shitting themselves and scratching at my skin while I squeezed.

No matter how hard I tried, I couldn't hear her, couldn't hear anything. I raised my hands to my ears and found my brain-matter leaking out of the holes where my ears used to be. I pulled it out like pumpkin pulp, but instead of seeds, found only the bones of the inner-ear. Ma ripped her own ears off with a silent scream.

I told Michael about my dreams.

Bring me your dream catcher, he said.

Why.

Just do it.

I handed it to him and he tossed it unceremoniously into the fire.

Why did you do that!

I'll make you a new one, he said.

We watched in silence as the hair crackled and fizzed in the flames. It smelled like popcorn.

He made me a new one from a pair of eyeballs, like jujubes. Dried the mass of pink optic nerve by the fire and strung the pink sinew like the strings of an Indian drum. That night, I dreamt of a feast, a magnificent roast and thinly sliced retina carpaccio that I made with the carrot peeler. It didn't scare me the way the other dream had. It made me think of warm fires and full bellies, and the dry heat of the woodstove in the heart of winter.

I loved winter best. The old farmhouse walls were thin, and when the snow fell and the nights got long, Michael would whisper through the walls, loud enough for it to seep past the faded floral wallpaper of his bedroom and into mine.

He'd tell stories of men who'd gotten lost in the woods, grown so desperately hungry they chewed off their own lips. He said one lived on our land—or rather, we lived on his. I began to wake in the night, unable to move or speak, the creature skulking into my room from the window or emerging from the shadows behind my bedroom door. It would grasp my wrists in its long bony fingers and stare at me.

My pulse hammered, blood too thick for my veins, its lipless hole where a mouth used to be gaping at me like a fish. It was trying to tell me something, something really important, but it had eaten its own tongue and couldn't speak.

I told Michael about the visits.

You don't need to worry, he said. It'll never hurt you.

Michael and I were two peas in a pod, the best of friends, inseparable except for chores and school, which I did at the kitchen table with Ma while Michael went out to hunt. I'd sit and look at the books that didn't matter to me. I didn't need to know any of those things to build fox traps in the foliage around the chicken coop, or to butcher a turkey. But he told me I should do school, so I did.

It was me and him against the world. Until Allie.

I don't know how they met. I don't know where she came from. Maybe from another homestead down the road. Maybe from town, although Michael rarely went. Either way, Allie found her way into Michael's bed.

She'd climb the eavestrough of our house, shimmy along the windowsill, and slip inside his bedroom window. I used to press my ear to the wall and try to listen, try to hear the magical words she whispered each night that made Michael forget to mend the fence to the rabbit den. It was a slaughter, the wooden walls sprayed with blood and bits of rabbit fur. Ma was furious in that quiet way of hers. She served him nothing but cockerel for an entire week, Ma and I enjoying our rabbit stew from the chest freezer in the basement and Michael choking down the tough, gamey boy-chicken that we normally just beheaded and threw to the pigs. But he never complained; he sucked out the marrow and chewed the cartilage because that's what Ma served him and he'd never disrespect Ma at the table.

He started talking funny. Talking about getting a job. Ma asked him why he wanted a job and he said, well, isn't it kind of odd that I haven't had a job?

Ma said his job was to protect the farm. To make sure the livestock died by nothing but our own hands. To take care of me. *Take care of your sister.*

I want a paying job. Isn't it odd that I haven't had a paying job? I'm seventeen, after all.

What can you buy that we don't already have? Ma asked.

Michael paused. A house, he said quietly. A house of my own.

I nearly stabbed him with my fork, because I could practically hear Allie's soft, breathy voice and ridiculous chuckle falling from his lips. He was possessed. I could feel the Michael-ness of him leaking out of the holes her claws had made in his skin.

Why do you need your own house, Michael? Ma asked.

He didn't answer, and I wanted to tattle-tale, tell Ma he had a girlfriend, but I didn't.

Ma sighed and wiped the blood from her hands on her apron. She scratched her nose, leaving behind a red-brown smear, her motherly *war paint.*

We'll talk about it after Solstice, she said.

I dug my fingernails into my palms until they bled.

That afternoon, when no one was looking, I loosened all the screws in the lattice Allie used to climb from the eaves to the window.

I woke up in the pre-dawn hours to Michael standing over me just like the creature had, chest heaving, his long bony fingers snapping out and gripping me by the wrists. He hauled me out of bed and down the stairs in my nightie and bare feet, out the back door, and shoved me at the body splayed in the snow. Allie's blonde head was bent at an unnatural angle that made my stomach churn.

Why did you do this, he asked.

I thought you might be sick of cockerel, I said.

His mouth twitched, and he couldn't hold back his snort. We laughed until the sun came up, until our ribs ached and our throats burned, until our howls became wheezes and we'd run out of tears.

I did my schoolwork alone at the table while he and Ma spent the day processing the meat. They removed the feet first, running their fingers beneath the skin to loosen it from the bone, breaking the joints and pulling them apart just like we did with the chickens.

He and Ma argued over something for a while, but she could never say no to him. They sent me to my room to study, and I watched from the window as Ma dumped the slop for the pigs and hauled the good bits inside. She'd changed into her cooking dress.

Michael didn't have cockerel for supper that night.

Do you remember that trip to Alberta, I asked him through the wall.

I heard him shifting under his covers. Yeah, he said.

What were we doing there.

He sighed. Go to bed, Polly.

I am in bed, *Michael*.

Don't be a smartass.

At least I'm not a dumbass.

I could feel him rolling his eyes and heard him crack his knuckles, a gross, annoying habit that made me stick my tongue out at him because he hated when I did that.

Don't, he said.

You and Ma never tell me anything, I said, crossing my arms.

Polly…

But he never finished his sentence. I waited, and waited, and after what seemed like forever I heard his gentle snores as the bleak white light of winter dusted the tops of the naked trees.

Michael had to go away after that. Ma said he had personal business to take care of, but never told me what. Just that he couldn't be doing it at home.

I can take care of it, I said. Whatever it is that he needs, I can do it.

Ma paused, a funny look on her face. You can't help him with this, Polly, she said gently.

Why not?

You just can't.

I hated that he was gone, the monotony of the days without him, the oppressive loneliness of the silent nights. Ma missed him too, but had *too much work to do* to dwell on it. She'd rap her knuckles on my books, said busy minds don't miss their brothers, and so for the first time in my life, I really began to study.

I got my licence that spring and drove the pickup around town for something to do. I was parked on the bank of Deer Lake—not the big beach where townspeople went swimming but the little rocky shore on the other side that nobody liked. I was lying across the front seats, bare feet hanging out the window in the spring breeze, nodding along to a song on the radio when a boy with blue eyes and blond curls appeared out of nowhere.

I love this song, he said.

I jumped and slammed my knee into the horn, which echoed across the water.

He reached into my truck and helped me sit up.

I can do it myself, I said.

Of course you can, but why should you?

I didn't have a good answer, and so he invited himself to sit beside me and told me his name was Billy Church. He unfurled his freckled, lanky body in the passenger seat and yammered on about someone named Stevie Nicks. He smelled clean. Like lemon.

I had no idea what he was talking about, but nodded like I did.

I should go, I said, when the sun started to go down.

Okay, he said. And then he kissed me.

I dreamed of Billy that night, and many nights after. I dreamed that I stripped his skin and sewed it into a coat, that I tucked my nose into my Billy-pelt and sniffed as deeply as my lungs would let me. I caressed the tanned hide while standing watch over the dream-farm, stroking the wooden barrel of the rifle Michael got me for my tenth birthday that I'd lovingly dubbed Chicopee.

I woke to an unfamiliar tingling between my legs.

I told Ma at breakfast and she blushed.

We don't talk about our personal business at the table, she said.

Personal business… Like Michael's?

That's enough now.

That evening, Ma gave me a weathered book called *Our Bodies, Our Selves*. I think it was supposed to teach me about what they called *puberty*, but I was fascinated by what they called *sex*.

The next time I saw Billy Church, I told him I wanted to try it.

Really? he asked.

Why not?

He didn't have a good answer, so I invited him to sit beside me, which he did. He didn't do any yammering that time.

When we were done, we stared at the roof of the truck, and he asked me if I liked it.

I wasn't sure why, but I lied. I told him I liked it a lot. He smiled and said he wanted to do it again tomorrow.

I said I'd be busy. That I had to clean the blood out of the upholstery.

Oh, he said. Sorry.

It's fine, I said. I can get blood out of anything.

Okay, he said. Maybe Wednesday then. And he left.

I didn't tell him I thought it would have been better if it were his blood on the seat. That I wished he'd had dead eyes, like the deer I'd shot with Chicopee shortly before Michael left.

By the time the snow fell, Michael was home and my belly was round.

His body had changed too. He was so tall he had to stoop through doorways, his skin covered in such thick hair that he didn't need clothes to go outside. All of his limbs had elongated, his smile too wide, like he'd grown extra teeth and his jaw had stretched to accommodate them.

I'm too big for my bed, he said.

So am I, I said.

We laughed and laughed, and spent the night in the barn stretched out under a stack of blankets on a pile of hay.

Have you told him, Michael asked.

Yes.

And?

And what.

Don't be a smartass.

I smiled, but it fell fast, a deflated balloon making its sad trip back to earth.

Billy says it isn't his.

Michael snarled, a viscous, feral, snapping sound that raised goosebumps on my flesh. That told me to run.

Shhh, I said. I put my palms on his long, hairy arms and squeezed. Shhh, it's okay, big brother. Everything is going to be okay. I'm going to be okay.

We fell asleep, curled up together like on that motel bed in Alberta.

When I woke, he was gone.

MARY

Mikey was a screamer. He'd arrived early, a shrivelled, stinking, bloody mess all over my living room floor. He got blood on my Grandma dress.

He never stops screaming, Polly said.

That's what they do.

Polly's warm, loving eyes fixed on the flesh of her flesh.

What do I do, she cooed.

I cocked my head to the side. You have one job, I said.

Polly put Mikey into his bassinet and spun his mobile, his healthy little lungs quieting. The mobile had been a gift from her brother; I'd found it on the porch, a mandible that had been strung with teeth and that smelled inexplicably like lemon.

Mikey hiccupped, soothed by the clatter of bones.

My hand slipped into my apron, gripped the worn, familiar handle of my fixed-blade knife.

I want you to have something, I told her.

What is it?

I handed Polly the knife, but she wasn't Polly. Not anymore. She was Ma.

She took a step forward.

Thank you.

She wrapped her arms around my ribs and squeezed, until I squealed like a hog.

Mikey's eyes bulged, and Polly laughed.

You like that? she murmured to him. *Oink oink oink!* You like the sound of the little piggies?

He screwed up his face and probably shit himself, but I was too used to the smell of shit to notice. Pig shit, chicken shit, baby shit, *again*. But I was a retired shit wrangler now, and walked across the poorly levelled farmhouse floors to sit in my chair, dragging my pile of knitting to my belly.

Polly leaned forward and pretended to bite his tiny toes.
This little piggy went to market, she said.

***

He catches the scent of fresh meat. It's miles away, but he closes his eyes and feels its beating heart through the soles of his un-feet. He flies, like the earth is tearing itself apart to get out of his way.

He descends upon it, sinks his teeth into the flesh and tears, digs into the soft parts with his clawed fingers and shakes it and shakes it until night has fallen and the ground is covered in wet marrow.

He strips its toes for later, so he can stop eating his own, and buries it with its shoes.

He lies face-down in the blood-soaked earth, opens his wide, lipless mouth and swallows it down, makes love to it, fucks it until the ground is sated. Until he is too, for now.

The farm is in sight. He can smell it, layers and layers of scents, blanketing him in the softest of quilts. It knows he's coming, and it thirsts for him.

Night is here. The longest one.

And he is home.

Pop Goes the Wasset

S.E. HOWARD

"MUST'VE BEEN A snow wasset," Milt remarked, wearing a parka zipped up over his long johns. He wore a jeep cap with the earflaps down, his hair sticking out in fuzzy grey tufts from beneath the edges. He held a Winchester 30-30 that Police Chief Laura Waggoner kept telling him to put away because the last thing they needed was for him to accidentally shoot somebody.

"A what?" she asked, squatting to take a closer look at what was left of Milt's chicken coop. Inside, all thirty hens lay slaughtered, a mess of blood and feathers scattered across the snow.

"A snow wasset," he said again, then turned to Dennis, the young officer who'd accompanied her. "You know."

"Uh, yeah," Dennis said, and when he glanced at Laura, she understood.

It's a Yooper thing.

That's what native residents of Michigan's Upper Peninsula—or the "U.P."—were called. Dennis was a Yooper, having been born and raised there, as was Milt. Laura, on the other hand, hailed from Ann Arbor.

I may as well be from another planet.

"It's kind of an urban legend, Chief," Dennis told her. "You know, like the Dogman or mermaids in Lake Michigan."

"*Uff da,*" Milt scoffed. "Those are just stories."

He'd reported hearing the hens fussing and squawking just before daybreak, with the ensuing racket enough to wake him and his wife. Armed with a rifle and flashlight, Milt had gone to investigate, but it had been too late.

"Snow wassets are real," he continued, his expression grim. "And one wouldn't leave tracks behind, just like this."

It was the height of winter, the ground covered in at least fourteen feet of snow. Wolves or coyotes would have left prints coming to and from the woods, but although the snow inside the coop was bloodstained and kicked up, the rest of the yard remained conspicuously undisturbed.

"Your grandpa never told you about snow wassets, eh, Chief?" Milt asked. "We get them every so often, traveling down from Canada if the winter's cold enough."

"What are they?" Laura asked.

"Weasels, giant ones. Big as a grown man—bigger, even—and mean as hell. They keep under the snow mostly, digging burrows and tunnels. They sneak up under you, track your movements through vibrations in the snow, then come at you from beneath." He motioned with his hand, mimicking a mouth gaping wide, then shutting. "That's how they hunt."

Laura waited for the punchline because she'd stepped right into that one, setting herself up as the butt for one great big Yooper yuk. At any second, Milt would start to smirk, then inevitably chuckle, saving the heartier belly laughs for when he met up with his buddies later at the VFW and told them about how he'd pulled one over on their gullible new police chief.

Laura turned to glower in Dennis's direction. "You about ready? We're burning daylight."

"Yes, ma'am," he replied, swinging his leg to straddle one of the snowmobiles they'd brought. Milt kept a small herd of beef cattle and worried that whatever had gotten into the chicken coop might go after the younger heifers in the corral by the barn. Laura had promised they'd head that way on the sleds to check.

"No, no, you never mind with all of that, Chief," Milt said to her now. "I've caused you enough trouble for one morning. I'll just wait until Barb gets up, then head out that way myself..."

His change of heart caught her off guard. His call to the station had come in around five o'clock, well into her eleventh hour on an overnight shift. She'd been tired, irritable, and had told him in no uncertain terms that it wasn't the police department's job to respond to nuisance wildlife incidents.

"Put out some fox traps," had been her suggestion at the time, at which point Milt had lost his proverbial shit, proceeding to rant and rave about his goddamn tax dollars at work, and how much money he stood to lose if even one of the coyote or wolves or whatever the hell had got into his flock took a mind to go sniffing after his cattle next. Laura had finally relented and agreed to come out and take a look around, if only to shut him the hell up.

"We're already here, Milt," she told him dryly. "And we brought the snowmobiles and everything." She pulled her shotgun out of the back of their truck, then mounted the other sled. "Your tax dollars at work, remember?"

Laura was from Ann Arbor, but her grandfather, Roy, had been a Yooper. In fact, he'd served as police chief for more than twenty years, and she knew it was by his last name and reputation alone that she'd even been considered for the job, never mind offered it.

Even so, she hadn't exactly been welcomed with open arms by some of the officers who were to be under her command. Several had quit, although whether it was because she was a woman or an outsider, she wasn't sure. Dennis, however, had stuck around, and when she asked him why, he'd answered by pointing to the wall of her office, a wooden plaque hanging there. A single word had been engraved on it: *SISU.*

Sisu was a Yooper term derived from the Finnish who'd originally settled the area. Roughly translated, it meant *inner strength* or *courage*. The plaque had once belonged to her grandfather, had hung in that very same office, as a matter of fact, for the entirety of Roy's tenure as police chief. When he died, it had been one of the first things Laura had taken to remember him by. Having it there behind her desk felt akin to Roy's spirit watching over her, his *sisu* guiding her.

"You mind telling me what the hell all that was about?" Laura asked, having raised her hand and signaling Dennis to stop once they'd traveled out of sight of Milt's house.

"Sorry, Chief." He managed to look appropriately sheepish. "I told you, it's just an old story. Loggers made it up to explain when men went missing out in the woods during the winter. They used to say snow wassets got them."

She'd heard worse, she supposed. After all, the Great Lakes region remained rife with folklore about weird, ridiculous creatures, or "fearsome critters," as they were called. During the early part of the twentieth century, the logging industry had dominated the Upper Peninsula, with workers traveling from one seasonal camp to another, clearing forests for timber. In those days, homespun yarns about monsters lurking in the arboreal dark had helped to keep the steady influx of lumberjacks entertained.

"Giant weasels," she said dubiously, and with a grin, he shrugged.

"Yeah, and if you hear my grandpa tell of it, they don't have legs, either."

She snorted a laugh. "How the hell do they get around then?"

"They burrow, like Milt said. They dig tunnels all down through the snow. My grandpa said wassets sleep during the summer up around Newfoundland, then get active in the winter. Kind of like reverse hibernation, I guess? Anyway, they tunnel all over the place, anywhere the snow's deep enough."

This just keeps getting better and better.

"Giant, legless, burrowing snow weasels," she repeated, and he nodded. "And do you believe in them, too, Dennis?"

"No, ma'am," he replied with a laugh. "Not a chance."

They came across a stretch of rolling, snow-draped meadow broken by a zigzagging line of paw prints. These led out of the nearby dense pine forest and meandered a short distance before abruptly stopping. The tracks didn't appear to turn and head back in the direction of the trees, but rather, ended altogether, as if some mysterious hand had reached down from the sky and plucked straight off the ground whatever wayward and hapless beast had made them.

"These look like wolf tracks," Dennis remarked. "There's blood, too, where the snow's been kicked up."

Around the spot where the prints disappeared, the snow seemed to have dimpled, leaving a shallow crater several feet in diameter. Curious, Laura prodded at it tentatively with the toe of her boot, then watched as it caved in several inches. When she tapped at the spot again, it didn't collapse any further; still, it struck her as odd.

And, she realized, dimly familiar.

"What do you think happened here?" Dennis asked.

"I don't know," she admitted, adjusting the strap of the shotgun across her chest. "Let's keep going."

When she was seven years old, Laura and her parents had come to the Upper Peninsula to visit her grandparents for Christmas. By then, the snow had been heavy and deep, much as it was now, and she remembered Roy meeting them in Saint Ignace to pick them up and drive them the rest of the way in his four-by-four truck, chains on the tires and all.

Despite the veritable winter wonderland right outside her grandparents' back door, Laura hadn't been allowed to play outside much during that visit.

"It's dangerous," was all Roy would offer by way of explanation or excuse, and Laura might have whined about it more had her grandmother not found ways to distract her, such as letting her help make and decorate Christmas cookies. Laura had also spent much of the time playing inside with her grandparents' dogs—especially with her favorite, a fluffy black-and-white border collie named Chicory.

Thus, one morning, when she heard Roy shouting for Chicory from the stoop and learned the dog hadn't returned from having been let out earlier, she'd grown despondent with worry. She wanted to go look for Chicory, and although Roy had been reluctant, she'd pleaded and hounded until at last, he gave in, and she'd ridden in front of him on a snowmobile as they charted a course across the snow, following the dog's errant tracks.

Eventually, they'd come across something almost exactly like what Laura and Dennis had found in Milt's pasture: a place where the prints abruptly ended, and a shallow, blood-spattered depression surrounding them.

"Stay here," Roy had instructed her as he climbed off the snowmobile. Squatting in the snow, he'd studied the crumbling crater and bloodstain with a peculiar expression before returning to the sled.

"What is it, Grandpa?" Laura asked. "Where's Chicory?"

"Gone," Roy replied, his voice as strangely gruff as his expression. He'd offered no more explanation than this, despite her pleas, and had turned the snowmobile around, heading back to the house.

The barn was rustic, hewn from rough timber, with an open bedding area below and hayloft above. Despite the relative shelter this offered,

Laura and Dennis found most of Milt's cattle in the adjacent corral, clustered together along the far side, tails swishing, ears flicking, uttering low, occasional bawls.

"Wonder why they don't head into the barn," Laura remarked as they cut the engines to their sleds.

"Cows don't mind the cold so much, I guess," Dennis replied.

They tromped together toward the barn, wading through the deep snow with wide, clumsy strides. Once they drew close enough to see beyond the far wall, she caught sight of something in the adjacent field.

"Is that blood?" Dennis said when she pointed it out to him. "Maybe Milt was right and something got into the herd after all."

"Sure looks like it," she said, unslinging the shotgun. The Remington had a four-shot capacity magazine, and although she carried it with one round already chambered, she lowered the barrel toward the ground to load it fully. Then, thumbing the safety off, she hoisted the gun. "Come on."

The day after Chicory disappeared, Laura woke up before her parents or grandparents and put on her parka, cap, and mittens. She'd been to Roy's office enough times to have seen the wooden placard on the wall, and, determined to prove her own *sisu*, she set off across the yard behind her grandparents' house toward the back fence line and the woods beyond.

"Chicory!" she called, cupping her hands to her mouth, watching as her breath dangled in the air like a ribbon of gauze. "Chicory! Here, boy!"

Another of Roy's dogs, a beagle named Peanut, bounded through the snow alongside her, fully anticipating a morning of adventure and play, judging by the joyous gape to his mouth. All at once, however, as they drew within a few yards of the field fence, Peanut came to a stop, his tail erect, nearly perpendicular to his spine. His ears drew back, gaze sharp and fixed on the woods just beyond the fence.

"What is it, boy?" Laura asked, wondering if Chicory was out there, if Peanut's keen nose had picked up on his scent. She looked toward the thick growth of pines, their dense, snow-laden boughs sagging low, but saw nothing. It was very quiet, as she'd noticed it tended to be in the winter, the snow dampening even birdsongs to silence.

"Chicory?" Her voice warbled uncertainly.

Peanut's lip curled back from his teeth, and the dog uttered a low, menacing growl. His nose twitched, his attention riveted on the trees.

"Chicory? Is…is that you?"

She heard the whisper of snow shifting, then just beyond the fence, she saw the ground swell as if pushed up from beneath, a slight mound in the otherwise smooth, flat surface of the snow that moved toward her in a gentle undulation, like a wave at sea.

"Laura!"

She whirled, frightened by the sharp, shrill urgency in her grandfather's voice, and saw him plodding across the yard. He hadn't put his coat on, had only managed to pull on his boots, which she saw had remained untied as he lumbered in broad strides toward her. Within seconds, he reached her, snatching her off her feet.

"What are you doing out here?" he cried, his eyes frantic with alarm. "I told you it's dangerous!"

By the time he'd rushed with her back to the house, everyone else was up, undoubtedly alerted by Roy's mad dash outside and his shouting.

"I just wanted to find Chicory," Laura wailed, and her grandmother had done her best to console her by making hot cocoa.

"I'm sure he's found his way to one of the neighbor's farms," she told Laura. "Chicory's probably holed up in a nice, warm barn somewhere, asleep in the hay bales."

But by the time they'd left to return to Ann Arbor a week later, Chicory hadn't returned. For years after that, Laura's grandmother said somebody must have taken the dog in, that it had always been too friendly for its own good. As much as Laura wanted to believe this, she'd always known the truth. She'd seen it in Roy's face.

As Laura and Dennis approached the site just past the barn where they'd noticed blood, they stumbled upon the source: the hindquarters of a dead cow sticking out of the snow.

"Is that one of Milt's—?" Dennis began, then his voice faltered as the cow's body moved, slipping with jerking motions deeper into the drift. Within seconds, only its rear hocks and hooves remained visible; with another quiet scuffle, these too disappeared from view. In the aftermath, they both stood there in mutual stupefied silence.

"What…the hell was *that?*" Dennis asked finally.

Laura shook her head. "I have no idea."

"But that was one of Milt's cows. Something just…*took* it."

Still, she could only shake her head helplessly. If he was looking for an explanation, he'd turned to the wrong person. Nothing in her experience could explain what they'd just witnessed—what could have possibly not only killed a fully grown, half-ton Angus, but then also pulled the carcass beneath the snow on its own.

"I need you to go back to the sled," she told Dennis. "Call this in on the radio. Tell Jeannie we're going to need someone from Fish and Wildlife out here."

"You think it's a bear?"

"Maybe," she said, and as he hurried back across the barnyard, she raised the shotgun to her shoulder, leveling her sights at the bloody patch of snow where the cow had disappeared. With few other food resources available, a bear that had roused too early from hibernation could have resorted to preying on livestock for food. Maybe it had dug out a den nearby beneath the snow and was dragging the cow there for safekeeping. It sounded unlikely, but what else could it be?

There's nothing else big enough, not in this area, to—

She saw the snow shift slightly, as if an air bubble beneath the surface had pushed it up. Again, she felt a creeping sense of déjà vu and thought of that morning in her grandfather's backyard.

The strange mound in the snow began to move slowly, like a wave rolling in open water, just enough to convince herself it wasn't her imagination. It drew closer and closer, and as the distance between them closed, it picked up momentum, until without warning, it rushed straight at her. Before Laura could do more than backpedal in alarm, never mind lob off a shot, the snow abruptly flatlined, as if whatever had pushed it up had dived deeper below the surface.

What the hell was that? she thought, swinging the barrel of the shotgun back and forth. *Where did it go?*

All at once, she thought of what Milt had said earlier, as ridiculous as it had sounded at the time, the story about snow wassets. It couldn't possibly be something like that, she told herself. Snow wassets were tall tales made up by old-time lumberjacks too drunk and bored for anyone's good.

They can't be real.

She looked over her shoulder and saw Dennis making his way across the barnyard. Just as he glanced back and met her gaze, something else Milt had said occurred to her, words that now filled her with ominous dread.

They sneak up under you. Track your movements through vibrations in the snow, then come at you from beneath.

"Dennis—!" she began. *Don't move,* she meant to shout at him in warning, but it was too late as the ground beneath him suddenly seemed to give way. Like the deceptively thin top of an ice-covered pond, the snow beneath Dennis burst underfoot, and Laura had a split second to see his face, his eyes flown wide, before a blur of movement—something enormous and white—leaped up.

Dennis uttered a shriek as it plowed into his side—the largest animal she'd ever seen, as huge as a polar bear. In fact, as impossible as that would be, that was what she thought it was at first, judging by its size, its heavy coat of dingy white fur, and the flash of its teeth—huge, jagged, and sharp. She caught a glimpse of these last just as they punched through Dennis's parka, its tremendous jaws snapping shut with brutal force. She heard the wet crunch of bones snapping in his ribs and spine, and blood spewed out of his mouth, choking him.

She only realized it wasn't a bear, couldn't possibly be, because it didn't have any legs. Its thick, elongated body seemed to writhe and move in a serpentine manner, with no visible limbs at all. It seized Dennis with its mouth alone, then dragged him down, still gripped in its teeth. Only then did she know for sure what she hadn't wanted to think possible, what she still couldn't believe.

A snow wasset.

The top of the shaft collapsed as it retreated, leaving behind the distinctive crater still visible on the surface. From under the snow, she heard Dennis's muffled screams continue for what felt like an agonizing eternity, then his voice abruptly cut short. The ensuing silence was somehow even more awful, and the shotgun sagged in her grasp, tumbling into the snow as her fingers slackened.

"Dennis," she whimpered, staring in stricken shock at the place where only seconds ago he'd been standing, the bloodstained patch of snow left behind.

Milt was right, she thought, sinking to her knees. *Oh, God, he was right all along...*

On the far side of the corral, no more than thirty yards away, she could see the snowmobiles. Under ordinary circumstances, she could reach them within a matter of minutes, but this, she now realized, was anything but ordinary.

That thing's still out there. Shivering, she panned her gaze, looking across the open expanse. *Not just out there—it's* down *there, underneath the snow.*

Milt had said snow wassets tracked their prey through vibrations in the snow as they moved. That part seemed to be true, considering

Dennis had been making his way back to the sleds when he was attacked, while she'd been standing still. Which meant however short a distance away the snowmobiles may seem, or how quickly she could run to get to them, it wouldn't matter.

"Goddamn it," she whispered.

The cattle in the corral began bawling again, a chorus of short, sharp, overlapping cries of alarm as along the fence, the snow rose in a sudden, telltale undulation. It slid slowly along, like a fingertip grazing beneath a thin sheet of silk, following the outer perimeter of the corral.

Was it back so soon? What had happened to Dennis?

But she already knew the answer to this.

What should I do? she thought, even though she knew that answer, too. If she stayed put, she'd die—if not because the snow wasset got her, then from hypothermia. Even bundled up like she was, it would be only a matter of hours, and she had no idea how long it might take for someone to come looking for her.

She could fire the shotgun into the air, hoping the sound of the blasts would reach the farmhouse, but doing so would cost her precious ammunition she might very well need. Thinking of the wasset's enormous teeth, the horrific crunch of Dennis's flesh and bones as its jaws snapped together, made her shudder.

I have to try to reach the sleds.

If she made a run for it, every footstep in the snow would be like beating a drum—or more accurately, ringing a dinner bell—for the wasset to track her. She had to figure out a way to get to the snowmobiles while causing as little disturbance on the ground as possible.

Maybe if I lie on my stomach, she thought. *Keep my legs out straight behind me...?*

Roy had given her this advice once when talking about ice fishing and how to escape thin ice if she ever felt it crack beneath her.

"You want to distribute your weight evenly across as wide a surface area as possible," he'd instructed. "Then army crawl toward safety."

She didn't know if doing this would dampen any vibrations her movements might stir through the snow, but there wasn't much choice. Shifting her weight, she slid her legs out behind her, then curled her fingers around the shotgun and began to creep forward. The entire time, she locked her gaze on the mound of snow moving back and forth along the perimeter of the cattle yard. Every instinct in her body screamed at her to run, to scramble upright and bolt like hell for the snowmobiles, and only her grandfather's voice in her mind kept her pinned to the ground, inching forward.

You want to distribute your weight evenly across as wide a surface area as possible, then army crawl toward safety.

Safety. She clung to this hope even though she didn't know how long it would take for her to reach it. Still, Roy's words echoed in her head on constant replay, and God, how she wished he was there with her now to snatch her up, carry her back to someplace warm and safe.

She felt the snow beneath her arms crumble unexpectedly, then collapse. With a frightened yelp, she slid face-first down a sharp, sudden incline into a hollow cavity hidden beneath the surface. Snow flew up her nose, splattered into her face, left her choked and sputtering. She lost her grip on the shotgun and pushed herself up with her hands, looking around wildly and finding it buried nearly to the stock nearby.

What she saw just past it left her biting back an anguished cry: Dennis, lying with his back to her, the snow around him blood-soaked. Laura scrambled to his side, but he didn't respond.

"D-Dennis?" she pleaded, grasping him by the shoulder and tugging. As he rolled over, she saw he'd been ripped open from sternum to groin like a Christmas gift by an overeager toddler. From the glistening, meaty cavity that remained, flaccid loops of his bowels had spilled out against the snow, still steaming.

Laura clapped her hands over her mouth, knowing if her shriek escaped, the wasset would be back in an instant, tracking the sound vibrations through the snow straight to her. She mewled through her gloved fingers in abject horror, then looked around, certain that the scuffle as she'd fallen through the tunnel ceiling would alert it as well. A long, excruciating moment passed, then another without any sign, and she began to scoot backward, following the slope to the surface again.

I'm sorry, she thought, eyes stinging with tears, because from the way Dennis was lying, he appeared to be looking directly at her, eyes unblinking, face frozen in a mask of unimaginable pain and terror. Seizing the gun again, she kept pushing her way up, wanting to tear her gaze away from him, but unable to. *I'm sorry, Dennis. Oh, God, I'm so sorry.*

Once she reached the surface, she huddled against the ground, struggling to collect herself. She hadn't made it far across the barnyard at all before falling, and the distance yet to go between her and the snowmobiles seemed insurmountable. The cows still bawled from the corral, the mound beneath the snow as the wasset cut back and forth still rising and falling, and she forced herself to start moving again, crawling through the snow.

Laura wasn't a religious sort, but she prayed now not to some omnipotent deity, but rather to the only soul she'd ever met who even came close to godlike in her regard.

Help me, Grandpa. Give me some of your sisu. Please…

Ahead of her, the slight bulge in the snow came to a sudden halt and wavered in place, as if on alert. Laura froze with it, gritting her teeth to stave as much of her breath as she could from causing movement through the snow. Even though all she saw was that white, glistening crest, it felt like the wasset beneath it could see her, staring her down.

Please, Grandpa, she thought, lips quivering, her vision blurring with tears. *Please, please, help.*

The wasset rushed at her, again plowing underneath the snow and cleaving a wake that headed in Laura's direction. Seized with sudden panic, she sat up, jerking the shotgun to her shoulder. Without even drawing a clear bead, she squeezed the trigger. The resounding boom rolled across the barnyard, while the stock kicked back against her chest. Through the haze of smoke surrounding the gun barrel, she could see she'd missed, the wave still coming straight at her. Ratcheting another shell into place, she clenched her teeth, then fired again. This time, she saw snow splatter from the point of impact and heard a high-pitched screech, like an injured animal. A bloodstain had appeared where the round hit home, and she ratcheted a third, aiming for this same spot.

"Die!" she screamed as she fired, her voice strangled with sobs. There was only one shot left and she chambered it now with a furious jerk. Just as she pulled the trigger, the leading edge of that surging snow wave broke only three feet away and she saw it—the snow wasset, its jaws flung open, lined with jagged teeth. It leapt at her, and she shot it through the mouth, sending meaty chunks of brain and splintered bone flying out the back of its head. Like a marionette with its strings abruptly snipped, it crashed to the ground.

The wasset lay on its side, more than ten feet in length, its heavy coat of coarse, pale fur now peppered with broadening patches of bright red blood. It wasn't dead yet; she could see its chest rise with a slow, shallow inhalation that shuddered loose again, and it nuzzled weakly at the snow as if it meant to lift its head. Its glossy black eye rolled toward her, and its lip wrinkled back along its snout as it uttered a low growl. She saw bloody froth around its mouth, strings of raw meat and sinew still caught between its teeth, and at this—the realization these had come from Dennis—something in Laura snapped. Flipping the gun between her hands, she charged at the wasset and began bludgeoning it with the stock.

"Die," she cried, then she said it over and over, her voice rising to a shrieking crescendo: "Die, die, *die, WHY DON'T YOU JUST FUCKING DIE?*"

Again and again, she rammed the butt into its skull until it finally sagged against the snow and fell still. Only then did she drop the shotgun, stumble backward, and collapse. She didn't know for sure when she'd started to cry, but she continued to sob as she sat in the snow, inconsolable and anguished as she thought about poor Dennis.

I'm so sorry, she imagined herself saying to his family, because she didn't know how in the hell she would explain to them what had happened—or if she even could. *Your son was killed by a weasel. A giant, legless, burrowing snow weasel.*

At this, she snickered, then started to laugh, a shrill, hysterical sound like a witch's cackle.

Not a weasel—a wasset, she thought, then threw her head back, screeching it at the sky. "A goddamn snow wasset!"

After a long moment in which she struggled to compose herself, Laura rose shakily to her feet. The cattle in the corral watched her with anxious eyes as she floundered through the snow, limping in a crooked path across the barnyard toward the snowmobiles. When she finally reached one, she collapsed across the bench, clinging to it like a life buoy on a storm-tossed sea.

"What's up, Chief?" the dispatcher Jeannie called back in a cheerful reply after Laura pawed the radio handset from the console and hailed her. "You about finished over at Milt Johnston's place, eh?"

"Listen to me," Laura rasped into the mic, clutching it between her hands. "I'm going to need backup here, whoever you can call in. I need them out here fast."

"Say again, Chief? You're breaking up. You need what?"

"Backup," Laura said again. "Call in whoever's off duty, tell them to get up to Milt's. I'm going to need someone from Fish and Wildlife, too, just as soon as you can get them. And…" Her voice grew strained and, for a moment, she didn't know if she could finish.

Sisu, she told herself, picturing Roy's plaque in her mind, her grandfather watching from over her shoulder.

"And the coroner. I need someone to head out to his house and wake him up."

"Come again, Chief?" Jeannie sounded worried now, if not a little frightened. "You said you need the coroner?"

"Yes," Laura said, looking through the snowmobile's windshield toward the barn and the sprawled heap of the dead wasset below. All around its head, the snow had stained crimson with blood, a bright bloom that continued expanding across the yard, like a rose opening in the sun.

"I'm going to need to talk to the mayor, too," she said. "Maybe even the governor."

They have to be told about this. People have to be warned. This isn't like the Dogman—these things are real, and they're dangerous.

"The governor?" Jeannie repeated, at a loss.

"Yes, damn it," Laura snapped because there wasn't time for this. "People have to be warned. Before it's too late, or anyone else—"

Something struck the underside of her snowmobile with enough force to rock it sideways, and with a startled cry, Laura dropped the radio. She managed to scramble clear before the sled toppled fully, falling to her hands and knees in the snow.

"...do you copy?" she heard Jeannie calling over the radio, muffled now in the snow. "Are you there, Chief?"

She could see what had toppled the snowmobile: a misshapen bulge in the snow that looked much, much bigger than the one she'd seen in the barnyard. And much, much closer.

Oh, God, Laura thought, too frightened to even think about running. Whatever *sisu* she may have had, be it her own or borrowed, was gone, and as the thing beneath the snow moved toward her, she could only watch like a terrified, helpless child. Because this time, she knew her grandfather couldn't save her.

No one could.

Quarry

LIAM HOGAN

To the best of my knowledge, I have always been here. Lurking in the deepest, darkest depths of the flooded quarry, my myriad tentacles are the only part that ever moves, drifting through still, cold waters like delicate, long-stemmed grasses. Like hair, like spider silk, bowing this way and that as though in a gentle wind, alert to anything that breaks the surface. But my knowledge—of grasses, of wind, and even of quarries—came relatively recently, with my first human. Before them, I knew no words and had only stolen flashes of more primitive urges: the hunger for food, the fear of predators, the rough, *insistent* imperative of sex. Along with wistful remembrances of movement: soaring through the air, or scrambling up a tree, or lying stealthily in wait (just as I wait, deep underwater). Punctuated, and terminated, by the fall—so often the fall!—that delivered these small mammals and birds and reptiles into the grasp of my ready tendrils, homing in on their brief, thrashing struggles, pulling them down, down, down…

Humans have *so* much more going on. And now, it seems, so do I. In devouring the tender meat hiding inside my victim's skulls, I also devour their language, their memories, even their dreams and desires. The *fresher* the brain, the headier the meal; the more vibrant and lurid the thoughts, the more their dreams become mine.

Which doesn't make for restful slumber, as I squat in my underwater hollow, momentarily replete, processing my food. They are full of contradictions, these second-hand visions, these murky snatches of lives lived above and beyond the water's edge. It is tricky to separate fact from fiction, what they have experienced from what they *wanted* to experience, from what they now never will. Dreaming their dreams means they dream no more, and their fate, as a succulent morsel for something utterly strange and alien to them, is probably the very last thing they would *ever* have imagined.

But feed I must, especially as my hunger is for more than mere nourishment. Each meal complements all that has come before. Each adds to my absorbed experiences, my collected recollections, my museum of memories. If I am what I eat, then I contain multitudes and am far from reaching my capacity.

Because as yet, none of the mortals I have consumed had the answers I desire the most. I long to know more about what I am and how I came to be. None of them have given clue to the mystery that resides in the dark, in the Stygian gloom. None have shed light on my own existence.

The first was a young lad, each scoop from his skull rich with recent memories of fallen fences and faded warning signs, the temptations of bushes thick with untapped blackberries, the excitement of trespassing, the possibilities of discovery and adventure leading him to scramble along a treacherous rock ledge. Lingering notes of endless school holidays, of late summer boredom, of a hot dusty walk from an overcrowded terraced house, of older sisters (flashes of their flesh, simultaneously held tight and shoved violently away, contradictions indeed!) and a remote mother, a chain of sketchy male friends eager for the lad (the only other man about the house) to spend time "in the great outdoors".

As my serrated palps scoured the insides of the lad's brain cavity— so much contained within such a small space!—for the very last scraps (grainy black and white images on a too-close screen; eldritch horrors from outer space; strident, discordant music; an actress's fake screams; exquisite, complex layers of make-believe fear…) I knew only that *this* creature had not known enough, had hardly known anything at all, that his scant years of experience and his peculiarly narrow worldview offered only glimpses of what *might* be available to me. I sucked thoughtfully on his other organs, organs I could not name for neither could he, disappointed that they offered nothing more than a smorgasbord of rotting flavours (even though that alone had once been more than enough to excite me). As I waited for the action of time alone to grant me access to the liquefied marrow of his bones, I slowly digested what little I had learned from him.

It was a long, frustrating wait until my next sentient meal. Though I did not go hungry in between. In the dead of an autumnal night, with sharp rain dancing off the surface of the lake and swamping my senses, a bulky body, long dead and weighed down by a chunk of concrete, was delivered to me as though in offering. But the brain contained within the tough wrapping of inedible plastic was a mindless blank. I ate dispiritedly, as bored as the lad had been. More so, for this meal lasted longer than that skinny kid had. And from it, I got nothing, nothing but faint echoes of violence and fear. They were, alas, *empty* calories.

I toyed with his bones awhile, draped them in the plastic shroud that flared in currents I created for just that purpose. But I couldn't see how to put them together properly, and the smallest kept slipping through my grasp. So I abandoned them all to the ghostly creatures that feast on my slim leftovers and fell into my usual somnolent state. My tendrils are an underwater web, spanning almost the entire quarry pool, so that I know if anything larger than an insect enters my languid waters.

The depth at which the bulk of me resides is such that only my outer extremities, tasting the surface, are aware of the seasons that pass above me. Those tentacles told me when the surface froze over, a rare event; least-wise, I could not remember it so, and nor could those minds, animal or human, which I had consumed. I despaired. So imprisoned, there would be no meals at all, and I would go hungry for both food and stimulation.

I was wrong.

I felt the vibrations in the tendrils that remained frozen, bonded to the surface. Like a bone dragged across stone, someone—a small group of someones—was up there, on the other side of the ice, slipping and sliding and shouting with something that might have been joy.

Until it turned, in an instant, to *fear*. The ice wasn't frozen enough for such daring winter activities. I both felt and heard the creaking, the eerie pings ringing like a bell as cracks raced across the perfect frozen layer. And then: the sharpest of retorts.

Perfect no more. Something, *someone*, fell through the shattered ice and, despite frantic struggles, was unable to haul themselves out. It was the work of a mere moment to wrap their struggling limbs in mine, to drag them down, even as the rest of the vibrations scattered and the ice fell ominously quiet.

This one was a girl, fourteen, with the last remnants of baby fat she would never grow out of but I would feast upon. Though not until after I had sucked out her plaintive teenage dreams, the forever thwarted happily-ever-after endings, and relived her final waking nightmare with its ripe spike of desperate, primal fear.

I was still mulling this over, still feasting, when there came more commotion above, more shattering of ice. A whole host of people seeking the girl who had fallen through. But they could not have her. She was *mine*, and I would not let her go, not until there was nothing left to glean from her shivered bones.

There was a much longer gap after that. An agony of seasons. This perplexed and frustrated me, for I wanted—*needed*—more. Two youths and a dead man had merely whetted my appetite, and only let me guess at what must be happening above. New fences, new warning signs? It seemed, when I selected one from a group, the survivors had raised the alarm, and in the aftermath of a fruitless search, the quarry was once again off-limits and out of bounds.

Should I take only those who entered my waters alone? Could I be that selective, avoiding the temptations presented? And would temptation ever present itself again?

But it seemed that no matter the warnings, the dark history, or the physical obstacles, my body of water would always be attractive to some. A year after the ice, a thin line descended into long-undisturbed waters, crowned by a metal hook with a wriggling worm pinioned on the barbed point. Such lures did not interest me, but what was at the *other* end of the line did.

It was easy to tempt him into the water. To play with that lure, to tug and twist, pulling hard, but not so hard that the plastic should snap. To let go for a moment before reeling him in, even as he tried to reel *me* in.

He was a fool, that fisherman. There are no fish in my lake. I had long ago eaten them all. And his thoughts, his dreams, were dulled by the empty bottles he left on the shore, his mind tainted by cheap booze along with the rest of his fatty flesh. Perhaps the young are a better meal, after all.

When first I fed, a feast such as he would have sustained me for a long time. Long enough to ignore any clamour of vibrations that might greet his disappearance, ignore the search parties, wait patiently until the next solitary soul broke the surface of the lake, long after unsubstantiated rumours of hidden danger had died down and the always tranquil waters proved tempting once again.

When the fisherman's eyeball tried to float towards the surface, I was almost disappointed that there wasn't something *else* to excite the tendrils thronging about my body. The sightless orb didn't get far. As my serried teeth pierced it, I half expected a flash of vision, the last thing he saw while alive, but it was merely a tasty bite, offering no insight. A pity because, like his corpse, which I held tight as it decayed and developed flavour, I cannot see. My sight is as stolen as my knowledge of what happens above the water, in the exotic domain of air and of man.

I wonder what colour the eye was? So rarely do people's memories and dreams depict themselves. Nor do I know what I look like. I know my basic *shape*, as sketched by my questing tendrils. But none of my victims have paid much attention to what was dragging them down, too fixated on fighting the swirling waters swallowing them up.

With the return of summer, a gaggle of older teenagers—a half dozen boys and a couple of girls—arrived on my shore. The boys were naked, *skinny dipping*, the giggling girls in their pants and bras. There was an almighty splash as one jumped from a rocky promontory (and the quarry is surrounded on all but one side by such rocky promontories). Then, a hasty retreat of the girls to lie instead on sun-drenched rocks when my delicate tendrils unnerved them, with cries of, "There's something in the water! It *touched* me!" The boys professing innocence, saying it must be a fallen leaf or merely a fish. All this I gleaned from the vibrations on the lake surface.

I meant to leave them unmolested. They might have gone home, told others of this fabulous swimming hole. I might then have had my pick of those who chose to brave the frigid waters alone. But one was already in difficulties, the cold of the deep quarry lake, even in summer, too great a shock to his system, his youthful limbs uncoordinated and weak, his head sinking beneath the water, not enough air in his gasping lungs for even one final desperate plea for help. It was perhaps a mercy, my taking of him, even if I did it for entirely selfish reasons.

And once again, shortly after, the surface *seethed* with activity. I knew enough by then to know that I shouldn't…but I did it anyway. I took a rubbery-skinned man who invaded my depths, wearing hard, metal cylinders on his back and a frog mask over his face. He panicked as I ensnared his legs, puzzling over how to open up this intriguing morsel. He fought and thrashed, when usually my dragged-underwater prey were quiet and still. He tore *savagely* at my tendrils, causing me considerable pain. But I did not relent. I wrapped him tighter still, tendrils prying at his ears, his nostrils, his many weak points, my palps tugging at the mask until, with an explosion of bubbles, my way was clear to enter his skull as I had all my meals, via the tender eyes.

And there I discovered the *freshest* of thoughts, the delights of a warm, almost still-active brain. His name—I knew his name!—is, or was, Constable Harry Barns, a specialist police frogman, an underwater search unit diver, trained to find and recover bloated, drowned bodies. His memories were full of the terrible things he had seen in his career, and I knew then what I was to him: a *monster*.

I knew too that his disappearance would lead to more such invaders. I knew fear for the first time. Knew I would have to *fight* to defend my home.

I sent back to the surface his shredded, gore-slicked goggles, a warning and promise to those who might dare follow. But it was the tentacles he tore off in his struggles that brought me my next meal. Another diver; since my clear warning had been ignored, I felt only determination as I dragged her down, delicately removing her regulator, stopping the sudden, shocked *O!* with my tentacles, leaving her eyes intact as I explored the roof of her mouth and the back of her throat, finding access there so that she might watch until the very last moment, and so that I might shortly afterwards see what she saw, think what she thought.

She was a scientist. Doctor Meredith Anwar. And oh, how very *bright* her mind was! Full of wonder, of interesting ideas and rare knowledge, of Cephalopoda and Medusozoa, clues at last to what I might be!

But she also foretold my doom. With the mounting deaths, and with samples of my uncategorisable tendrils, the quarry is going to be sterilised. I have sealed my own fate.

She brought other thoughts, a faint glimmer of hope. Prominent among her concerns was how I propagate. The word, and the concept, is novel. I am aware of the thoughts of the young men and women who entered my waters as a dare to impress potential mates. Aware of the animal urges of lesser beasts, aware that there really isn't as much difference as these pubescent youths believe. But I had not thought any of it applied to *me*. Alone as I am, no such coupling is possible. I did not dismay, for the desire of others was not reflected in mine; it was like watching something on a flickering screen, bizarre and otherly, but most definitely not for me.

The Doctor knew of other ways. Ways that did not require the coupling of male and female (for which was I? Impossible to say). Ways that didn't even require a mate.

From deep within her grey matter came the word *parthenogenesis*. And I knew, with instinctive certainty, how to attain it.

But what help would it be? My offspring would populate the same despoiled waters, the same dynamited lake floor. It would be no more hospitable for them than it is for me.

Dispersal, then, is key. I can never leave this place. My tendrils have no great strength, my pulpy body can never escape the comforting hug of deep water, no more than a fish could ride a bicycle. But my much smaller offspring *might*.

The quarry isn't a perfectly closed system. Life drops into its depths from above, and sometimes the sheltered surface is broken not by another meal, but by an outpouring. On the side not guarded by cliffs, there is a channel that follows a disused railway line. It carries the overflow when rain swells the lake. It leads somewhere I knew not, but Doctor Meredith Anwar did, so now I do. The channel flows into a stream, threading a landscape of lower, lesser diggings, and on to a river, and then to the sea.

I pray for heavy rain, and my prayer is answered. As each newborn polyp floats to the surface, guided on its way by my tendrils, it also carries away a piece of my consciousness, the memories and dreams I have stolen. It is the strangest feeling. But my children, my clones, will have benefits I did not. They will be careful as they slowly grow, not needing to feed perhaps more than once a year. And a single death in any one waterhole will hardly register, I hope.

As the last polyp makes its way to safety, the rains stop rattling the surface and the forces of my destruction gather on the shore. My children will know that humans are both the direst threat and the greatest reward. I hope they act accordingly. I hope they take their time before they take their revenge.

As for what remains of me, it is nothing. I am so much less than I was, but still enough, so when they finish with their depth charges and poisons and the pool is once again silent and still, with fences re-erected and signs fresh and new, their vindictive curiosity will be satisfied.

This is my fate. Even though I wonder if some infinitesimal part of me might survive, to begin anew, many years from now.

And if not…then I have passed all I can onto the next generation. So eat well and wisely, my hungry, hungry children, and dream a stolen dream for me.

Separations

ALDRIAN ESTEPA

The pencil-pushers at the top order me to go to the Aguinaldo, a three-story hotel turned temporary housing center for climate refugees. It's out in the sticks of Southern California, only a couple hours south of my place. I drive past fallow fields, through Sonoran desert lined with prickly pears and brittlebush, then I park the truck past the barbed wire fencing in the rear lot, where Jamil intercepts me. He's already conducted a few dozen interviews.

"Cap," he says. "The victims are Filipino women, pregnant, pretty far along."

"Walk me through it."

"On Wednesday morning, super early, there's a scream from Room 312. The first lady, cute little thing named Aurora." He peeks at his notepad. "She's saying, *my baby, my baby*, and no one can get her to calm down. The security on duty found Aurora on her bed, her pajama bottoms off, bleeding out of…" He avoids my eyes. "From between her legs."

The way I see it, watching your home vanish with the tide, escaping the floods, being bused from one strange place to another, then needing to rest at a random hotel guarded by the military, all of that's a lot for a pregnant woman to bear. Stress isn't good for babies. Premature birth or miscarriage is not out of the realm of possibility. The simplest explanation deserves a fair shake.

"And the second woman?"

"A forty-something named Dolores. All piss and vinegar from what everyone's saying." He tries at being even-keeled, but his foot is shaking.

"This'll help." I light up two joints, hand one over.

"Thanks, Cap." He takes a drag, calms down. "Shit happened yesterday morning. Early, again. Different room, same floor, Room 322. The husband was in the room with her. Didn't see nothing. Didn't hear nothing. One minute, he and his wife were sleeping, the next, she's bleeding. Cap, do you think it's the work of a—"

I rest my hand on his shoulder. "What do I always say?"

"Oh, you on that Occam's Razor shit again."

"Let's interview any other pregnant women here, four months along or later."

My wife and I sit, face-forward and dead serious, in the fertility specialist's office. The doctor, wearing bifocals and a mustard-stained lab coat, shakes hands with each of us. From the lack of wrinkles and lines on her face, it's clear that she's never smiled a day in her life. When the doctor finally speaks, it's as if her mouth is full of pebbles, but I remember the words. One egg has proven viable, and though it might be premature, it's still cause for celebration.

We're going to be parents, my wife says, *finally.*

I turn to my wife, sweep a stray hair from her forehead. I dab the tear from her right eye. We embrace each other so tightly that it's a wonder either of us can breathe. Oxygen or not, there is no force in the known universe that can pry us apart.

We're in Aurora's room. Jamil taps away at his tablet, messaging the pencil-pushers what we've discovered so far. Aurora and Dolores have a twenty-year age gap between them, but that's the only difference Jamil and I can detect. A casual sweep through their suitcases and carry-ons reveals a similar taste in maternity clothing (sensible, airy skirts and XL T-shirts) and books (mass-market romances in English). Both like to snack on butter crackers. Neither woman can afford a phone.

I'm pacing, thinking of the Aswang. Hiding and stealing our skin and blood and bones. These are the ones we've fought, the were-dogs, the were-rats, the were-pigs, all of which sporadically prey on the pregnant. Our target could be a mandurugo, a vampire-like creature with a forked tongue. I need more evidence. I'm missing something. A teenager with bright green hair pops her head in, breaking my reverie. She's Aurora's next-door neighbor, Raquel Domingo—everyone calls her Rock, though.

I beckon her and she waddles in with her watermelon-sized belly. I sit her down on a metal folding chair near a card table. I use the in-room kettle to boil water, then I dump a relaxation tea bag into each of the three mugs.

Jamil says, "Tell Cap what you saw."

"I was in the bathroom down the hall," Rock sighs. "Throwing up. I wasn't too close."

Jamil drapes Rock's shoulders with a tattered blanket. "Comfortable, Miss?"

"Is this a good cop, bad cop thing?" she asks.

"Yelling at teens is counterproductive." I hand her a mug, taking my place next to Jamil. "Think of us as good cop, good cop."

She rubs her stomach. "I'm twenty-three years old, in case you're judging me on my life choices."

"Apologies," I say.

"Happens all the time. They look at me, think I'm a baby having a baby. So much judgment. And to have one now…"

"Bringing children into a world like this—"

"It's idiotic, I know, I know." She grimaces after her first sip.

"No, I was going to say brave." I empty a sugar packet in her mug, then stir it. "Did you notice anything unusual about Aurora or Dolores— prior to the incident?"

"Because all of us preggers know each other."

I smile. "Humor's an important coping mechanism."

She shifts her chair and groans. "Something suspicious happened around midnight, the night we arrived. The bus plodded over the dunes. Aurora claimed she saw a giant bat. Like it was following us. The whole bus ride, she was ranting. The floods, the winds, the fires. The Aswang are here, she kept saying."

I'm at full attention. "What do you know about Aswang?"

"The Titas are up on that bull. May mga bulungan. They say it's the End Days. All this talk about were-dogs, mandurugos, and manananggal." Rock stands up, rests her elbows on the windowsill. Outside is sweltering, the air distorting like a baker's ready oven. What else can she see besides barbed wire and sand?

"Miscarriages have been on the rise these last ten years," I say.

"So, which is it—an increasingly inhospitable world or Aswang?"

"It's not an either-or, I'm afraid."

I run my hands over Aurora's bare mattress, over the dried blood streak near the foot of the bed. I look up, stare at the ceiling. It would be so easy to draft a report and label these incidents as miscarriages with an as-yet-undetermined teratogenic influence. I peek at Rock and that swollen gut of hers still facing that warm window. When people like her were shuttled here, they were promised safety. Bring us your tired, your hungry, your poor and all that. I won't be the one to drop the baton.

My eyes follow the metal grid of the ceiling, the individual panels made of composite material. This is a drop ceiling, a façade invented to cover up the unsightly pipes and wires, the ugliness. To slide a panel out of place, to reveal the structural ceiling above it, to show everyone how the building works, that's the urge.

I squint instead.

On the tile directly above the bed is a bloodstain the size of a clipped fingernail.

And there is no unseeing it.

When I get back from my morning jog, my wife's kneeling in front of the toilet, staring at the mess swirling down. I lay a fresh set of pajamas, wet face towels, and a cup of water with lemon on the side of the sink, then I crouch beside her, stroke her hair.

You want to drink with Jamil tonight, she says.

Is that okay?

I'm watching the season premiere with or without you. Expect major spoilers.

Fast-forward to that very night, Jamil and I are still in our agency uniforms and losing brain cells at an Army bar. Bourbon for me, beer for him. To celebrate our first job together.

Drinks are on the rookie, I say to the bartender.

That shit ain't fair, Jamil groans. *I'm the one who took it down, Cap.*

True, you got a wing, I say, *but mine pierced the chest, destroyed the black bird within.*

After five drinks, I order Jamil a cab.

A radiant creature struts our way like she owns the place—no, the whole damn town. She's a classic—in a form-fitting sundress, a yellow shawl draped over slumped shoulders, her short black hair studded with emerald barrettes—like a Filipino actress from the 20th century, but this one was offered the part of beautiful best friend, not the lead. Waitstaff and customers steal glances at her. She takes a stool. Her smile's weak—it forces me to smile right back. Our eyes meet, then there's the flutter, an inappropriate want. She leans in and I can't resist her scent, a subtle note of lilac.

It's not entirely desire churning within me. I want to help, to listen, to be present. Her voice is husky, honey-tinged: *You ever have one of those days? Like you woke up on the wrong side of the universe?*

That's a regular Wednesday for me, I say.

She giggles and orders me another drink. *I'm Marisol.*

Do you need a friend, Marisol?

If you're offering.

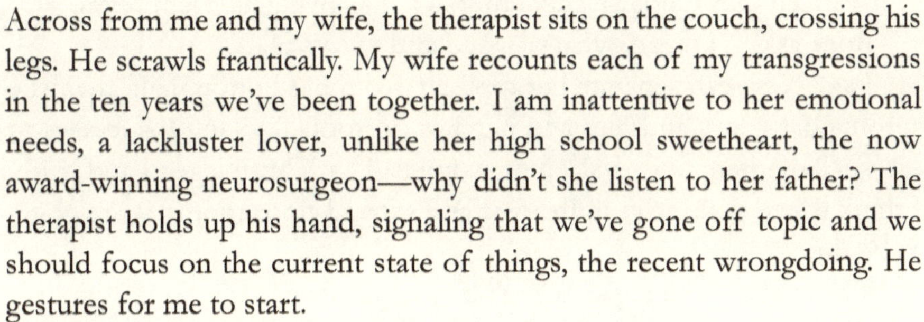

Plywood boards litter the roof. The hole above Aurora's room isn't covered. I scoot the boards aside, but I already know what they're covering: more holes, one for each room. I don't expect blood, or at least so much of it, dried into crisscrossed lines, orphan dots, Rorschach shapes.

Jamil huddles over to stare, hands on knees. "What're you thinking, Cap?"

It's easy to envision it, a creature with bat wings, snaking its long tubular tongue down a hole, slithering the sharp-toothed end into a pregnant woman to feed.

"Manananggal," I sigh.

Across from me and my wife, the therapist sits on the couch, crossing his legs. He scrawls frantically. My wife recounts each of my transgressions in the ten years we've been together. I am inattentive to her emotional needs, a lackluster lover, unlike her high school sweetheart, the now award-winning neurosurgeon—why didn't she listen to her father? The therapist holds up his hand, signaling that we've gone off topic and we should focus on the current state of things, the recent wrongdoing. He gestures for me to start.

When I first met her at the bar, I say, *she was grieving the loss of her spouse. It became a regular thing, me going there after work, her being there. You realize how hard it is, doing what I do for a living?*

The therapist points at me with his pen. *How long did you carry on with this Marisol?*

For four months, my wife blurts, *my disloyal spouse carried on an emotional affair.*

Honey, please—

Then it became physical. I caught them at some cheap motel, for God's sake.

You don't know what it's like, I say. *I can't seem to control myself around her. It's almost like someone else checked into that hotel and did all those things to her, with her. I felt like that wasn't even me, like the whole thing was conceptual.*

She stands up, knuckles her lower back. Her eyes tell me she's unconvinced.

On the drive back home, she stares forward at some unknowable place in the distance, eyes inscrutable. Her hands tremble on her lap.

I thought I could do this, she says, *but I don't know. I just don't know.*

What do you mean?

My folks will come by later for my things.

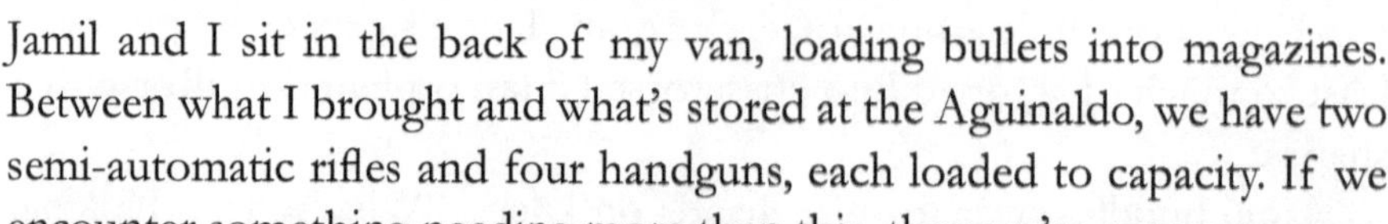

Jamil and I sit in the back of my van, loading bullets into magazines. Between what I brought and what's stored at the Aguinaldo, we have two semi-automatic rifles and four handguns, each loaded to capacity. If we encounter something needing more than this, then we're goners anyway.

We have an audience as we prepare. Rock leans on the side of the truck, drinking iced tea. The other refugees argue among themselves in Tagalog. Half of them are skeptical. The other half has valid critiques. Even though most of them speak English, the people all ask Rock to speak on their behalf. This feels right, considering she's the only pregnant woman left among them. That, and our plan requires her help.

"Fifteen years ago, we encountered a manananggal," Jamil says.

Rock asks, "I mean, what's legend and what's real?"

I say, "She can separate her top half from her bottom half, then she sprouts bat wings and flies and perches on roofs, looking for fetuses to eat, sucking them out of sleeping women. That's both legend and truth. I think if everyone stays in the first and second-floor rooms, we're going to be fine."

"What about the cops? It can't be just you two."

"The nearest town is thirty miles away, with a population of 2,500 folks. This Aswang could be hiding among any of the residents, inside any of the buildings. In a perfect world, we could send agents to question people, enlist the aid of local law enforcement, discover her hiding place, but the instant she notices us, she'll bolt."

"Great," she says. "How does one even become a manananggal?"

"If a woman swallows whole a cursed black bird chick, the thing grows, replaces her heart, and she becomes a manananggal. In exchange, all the bird asks for is viscera or fetuses. To a certain type of person, it's a small price to live forever."

Rock's smile fades, patting her stomach. "How do you stop it from getting Baby Boy?"

"Find the lower half and pour salt and vinegar on it. Stops the halves from reuniting at sunrise. That is an absolute stealth approach, making it less likely any of us would get hurt. Plus, we'd get to feel clever."

"Sounds like that's not happening."

"Unfortunately, no." I take her empty glass. "But destroying the upper half of her body works, too. A dozen bullets should do it."

Jamil straps a rifle over his shoulder. "Simple is best, Cap."

At 2:00 a.m., my wife calls me.

I want to hate you, she says. *And I thought I'd feel better being at my parents' place, but these last two weeks—I don't want to do this without you.* She cries for a good minute. *I want to go home. Is that stupid?*

I get it. Living with your father is awful.

She laughs. *He really is.*

Please let me take care of you again, I say.

Why don't we start with lunch at Uncle Huang's, say, noon?

A couple hours pass. I'm at the hardware store, holding up the flower and duck decals against swatch after swatch of green paints, then I paint our home office orange and green, my wife's idea of going gender neutral in the décor, then I'm at the grocery store to stock the pantry with her favorite snacks—rice crackers, frosty flakes, and wasabi peas—and her drinks of choice—a thousand different bags of non-caffeinated tea. It's easy to imagine her walking in, fawning over the baby's room, crunchies in one hand, a steaming cup in the other.

I show up at Uncle Huang's, holding a bundle of red and white roses, make small talk with the wait staff, and 12:00 rolls around, then 12:30, 1:00. I call her and it rings until it goes to voicemail multiple times. I text and get nothing back, not even that light that indicates she's read the messages.

I'm back at the house. The wait feels endless. I stare at the wall, then stick a honey-hued duck against a basil background. I hold back on sticking up the other duck decals, thinking my wife should put those other two up. I call my wife, my father-in-law, my mother-in-law, sister-in-law. No responses. I kill a half-hour assembling the crib.

Finally, my phone rings. It's Jamil.

What's wrong? I ask, even though I already suspect something awful has happened.

I'm so sorry, he says.

I check his location and notice he is at my in-laws' house—inside.

Don't come down here, Cap. We got this.

I hang up, then peel out of the driveway, placing the siren on the roof of my car. Other cars shift to the right as I tear down the freeway, honking, lane-dancing. I plow into the neighborhood, where a block ahead, crowds have gathered—neighbors, police, and EMTs. Jamil bolts in front of my car, telling—no, begging—me to stop.

Get out of the damn way, Jamil!

He won't budge. My phone rings again. I don't recognize the number. I pick up anyway.

Marisol's real voice is neither velvet nor seductive. It shifts between raspy and bladed.

Remember, she says, *this is all your fault.*

Thirty minutes until sundown.

Rock and I eat in a first-floor room. Canned chicken adobo over whole-wheat pasta. We both miss white rice, another thing to mourn. As I clean up, she tells me about the boyfriend who knocked her up and left her, about her mother's village, about the engineering job with a good salary. The flood took all of that away.

"Thought I had it all figured out. Is life always so unfair?"

"Only while you're alive."

Rock opens the door. She rubs her belly in the orange light. I feel a sense of longing, watching her like that. I think dangerous thoughts and do mental math. She is older than my daughter would have been, had she—

"You think Baby Boy will hate me?" She shivers, hugs herself.

"Of course he'll hate you. If not in childhood, then during the teenage years."

"What?"

"Calm down. Let me tell you about what a little shit I was. I once gave my mom a macaroni necklace when I turned six. And I thought, I'm putting so much effort into making this for her. Glue, string, paint, and glitter. It was so messy. She had better appreciate it, I figured. Took me two hours."

"And she loved it?"

"This is the woman who cooked me in her uterus, then pushed me out for seventeen hours. She suffered through colic and sciatica. And there I was, presenting this ugly-ass necklace. And you know what she did? She hung it on her rearview mirror. For decades, she drove to work, looking at the damn thing, all the way until she retired, until she died. Do you get where I'm going with this?"

"I think so."

"Then let's go over the plan one more time."

Santa Alicia has its fair share of makeout spots: Cupid's Peak, Lovers' Lot, Fondle Forest, to name a few. Blackberry Hill is the least visited of these. It's where I proposed to my wife, and it's where I separated my life into Before and After. From the edge of the parking area, you can watch the tumult and the calm of the ocean below, but the stairs go down three stories, and during the low tide, you can walk around, cup your hands into the sand, and come up with sea glass, emerald and amber bottle fragments worn to smoothness, or the lone abalone gone astray. But it's high tide now and the stairs drop off seemingly into the swill. I strip off my black shirt, black pants, black shoes, black socks, black undergarments. I walk until I'm ankle deep, the cold like needles tickling my feet. I shiver. I clutch the silver urn more tightly. When I'm waist deep, I pull off the lid, and pour my wife into the sea, like she always wanted. I'm on my tiptoes, nose above the surface. Above me is the night sky, swirling and starless. Below me is the promise I made.

I'm too weak to swim, unable to resist the arms under my arms, pulling me back.

On the count of four, Jamil says to someone in my periphery.

Let me be with her, Jamil.

One. Two.

It's all my fault.

Three. Four.

I led Marisol to her, to our baby.

Try not to move.

Just let me die.

You can't give up, Cap. We'll get her. We'll get her. I promise.

The truck strolls past the fences, up mini-dunes, ripping tumbleweeds, crushing marigolds, away from the tail of an autumnal sun. I check the magazine one more time, clip on my helmet, tighten the body armor. Pulling the flask from my inner jacket pocket, I pour the bourbon down my throat.

I hide under a thick set of black blankets. The rocking of the truck lulls me into a half-sleep. It's ten minutes or two hours before the truck slows. I pull the blankets low enough to peek at the passing Joshua tree branches like they're the arms of the dying reaching for Orion's Belt.

"She's here, Cap," Rock says through the open window behind me.

Occluding the crescent moon, the manananggal soars overhead, flapping bat wings that span wider than those of an albatross. Even from this distance, I know the flying upper torso with the intestines flopping away from the air current is her—Marisol—in a bloodied gray button-up, as if she's left a business meeting to kill us.

Marisol tucks the wings against her back, her human arms jutting forward, as she dives our way—my way. Her fingers end in talons, yellow and jagged. When she's ten feet above me, she spreads her wings again, letting the wind sail her behind the truck.

She's ten feet behind us. I toss the blanket her way and I'm successful, the fabric catching on her face. I use the seconds to brace myself against the truck and aim. She throws off the blanket and I let loose rounds—pop-pop-pop, pop-pop, pop-pop—adjusting with each burst, for the center mass, where her heart should be, but where the black bird in her chest now resides.

Marisol collides with the back of the truck, crushing the tailgate. I hear a pop behind me, then the pickup brakes hard. My back cracks against the window. The truck stops. I'm on my ass, rifle inches away at my side. Marisol holds herself upright on arm-claws like legs, wings folded behind her, guts like crimson sausage casing dripping and dragging along the truck bed, as she hobbles toward me. One of her breasts is a shredded mess—a bit of bone juts through. Black feathers protrude from that new cavity.

"You realize," she says, "if we keep this up, one of us is going to die."

"One of us, yes."

Her eyes bubble with blackness. I stand, eyes still stuck on Marisol's, but at the edges of my vision are Jamil and Rock, groaning as they attempt to deflate the airbags. Jamil falls out of the truck, blood oozing from his nose, one arm limp, the other dragging him away from the whole thing. Rock emerges from the passenger's side, her nose also bloody, but she's able to stumble to Jamil, kneeling near him. She turns him over and rests his head against her belly. He passes out.

Rock reaches for Jamil's pistol at his hip. She aims it at Marisol.

Marisol smiles, then Rock's face slackens.

"Isa, dalawa, tatlo…"

Rock aims at her belly, at Baby Boy.

"Ang tatay mong kalbo…"

Rock rests the barrel on top of Jamil's head.

"Please stop, Marisol."

"Choose."

Rock presses the gun against her own temple.

"Me," I say.

Rock drops the gun and cries. "Cap…no."

Marisol's mouth opens, then her tongue, tubular, muscular, slithers around my neck, coiling itself once, then twice around. At the feel of her wrapping around me, I can't help but smile. She reels me in until our faces are inches apart. I stroke her neck, stroke the black feathery thing in her chest, the source of her power—what power, what beauty. Let me become part of her.

There's a slow and sweet constriction and—

Under my leather shoes, hundreds of white rose petals remind me that this is the best day of my life. My bride-to-be strides, arm-in-arm with her father, toward me and the priest. She wears a traditional Terno, cream and smooth, the only one of its kind, designed by her dressmaker mother. I stand tall, thinking what I've thought since the day I met her: Why choose me? Of all the other options, why my hand, as we walk the dying earth? I breathe deeply to the count of four. When I pull back the veil, I'm taken aback.

Her face is soaked in blood. Her eyes, milky and lifeless.

In the distance, perhaps a mile or two away, is the truck, the last vestiges of smoke rising gray against the black night. Marisol and I are on top of a dune, lying on our sides. She's torn off all of my body armor. Pain and pleasure course through my body, her teeth and talons dragging across my skin, leaving a hundred paper-cuts. Her claw digs under my shoulder blade. Just another inch and she'll reach my heart. My sense of self withers into a grain of sand falling below the surface of a cosmic ocean. Less of a revelation and more of a confirmation.

"I can't decide on what I'd like more," she says. "Letting your friends freeze to death or flying back there to eat them. Isn't that funny?"

For a moment, I barely feel the claw inside me.

I giggle through gritted teeth. "It certainly is."

"I'll reunite you with your wife," she says. "Won't it be lovely?"

"I'd love that."

I'll join my wife. Finally. No. Wait. My wife. Oh God, her eyes, those dead eyes. *We'll get her, Cap. We'll get her.* That's what Jamil had said. I feel Marisol's hold on my mind loosening. I can move my hands again. I'm losing blood. I'm running out of tricks. My fingers trail down Marisol's neck to the tattered, bloody flesh of her chest, brushing the black bird huddled inside, the source of her power.

"I'm ready, Marisol."

Her claws burrow millimeter by millimeter. My bones buckle under the pressure of her embrace. Her jaw unhinges, her mouth wider than my face, her slithering tongue pushing its way past my lips, shimmying between my teeth, digging through the back of my throat, a gooey suction ripping air and blood from my lungs. I'm being emptied.

I drive my hand into her chest.

Marisol's eyes widen.

And, with the last of my strength, I crush the black bird.

Harbinger

LR WOODS

A BITTER WIND swept down the dark Appalachian mountainside, weaving through the barren tangles of branches and dry grasses until it howled around the eaves of every farmhouse in the valley. The wind carried with it the threat of a snowstorm, but Hank Leer knew it also brought the threat of something far more dangerous.

The man, as thin and bitter as the wind outside, paced the worn floorboards of his sitting room. Upstairs, his eldest daughter howled from the pain of her contractions. Her mother wept beside her, a desperate, garbled sound full of prayers and curses. The town doctor spoke above both of them with an encouraging tone hedged with worry. The cacophony set off the twin boys in their crib down the hall; the screeching disharmony of too many voices scraped like claws against glass.

Hank balled his hands into fists and pressed them to his temples hard enough to see spots in his vision.

"Pa?" Ezra stood in the kitchen doorway, a steaming kettle of water dangling from his hand. He took one look at the red rimming his father's eyes and stepped back.

"See to your sister, boy," Hank said gruffly. He turned toward the snow now pattering against the windows like moths: too dry to stick to the ground but still cold enough to sting.

The boy said nothing. At the next muffled scream of pain, he scurried up the stairs to his sister's bedroom.

Hank continued to pace. Despite the chill that seeped through the wall chinks, sweat coated his brow and soaked his collar. His breath came shallow and quick as if he were laboring with birth and not his daughter.

His sweet, innocent baby girl. How the town talked. How folks whispered in the pews about things they knew nothing about, their opinions thrown like sour crabapples whenever his family bowed their heads to pray.

Harbingers, heretics!

If only those folks knew how hard he'd prayed for God to take away the abomination that grew inside his daughter's belly.

A sharp, keening wail shattered the night; Hank's head spun in the long, heavy silence that followed. Had his prayers come true? Had God listened to the lamentations of a poor, distraught man desperate to absolve his daughter of her sin?

With a broken and hesitant squall, Hank's first grandchild announced its arrival into the world.

Hank released a weary sigh. He sank into his chair beside the fireplace and remained there until the flames died to embers and his wife touched his shoulder.

He flinched away, irritated. "What do you want, woman?"

"Will you see your grandson?"

"I will not."

"Hank," Mary admonished. "At least go to our daughter. She's asked for you."

Grumbling, Hank rubbed his fingertips against his thumbs as if to rid himself of an unwanted substance. His baby girl still needed him. At least that hadn't changed.

"I reckon," he said, and pushed himself to his feet. Mary smiled with the same gentle patience she gave all her children.

Hank climbed the creaking stairs as if he were walking toward his own grave. Halfway down the hall, Sybil's bedroom door stood open with Ezra and Jenny peeking in at their new kin.

"Go on, git," Hank said. They spooked at his presence, scurrying away to the nursery they shared with the twins.

Hank paused by the doorframe as well, too afraid to enter but curious all the same. He saw his eldest daughter sitting up in bed, her face pale but her expression serene. She cradled a swaddled bundle in her arms, cooing at it as the doctor spoke to her in his low, calm voice.

The floorboards creaked at Hank's first step into the room. Sybil looked up at last, and Hank marveled at how much she'd grown up in just a few difficult hours. A woman now, not the little girl who used to ride atop his shoulders and giggle when he bounded through the yard with their old coon dog baying from the porch.

"Come and see," she said, her eyes full of love for her newborn son. "He's so beautiful. My little Malachi."

Hank knew very little of beauty. His simple nature did not leave room for anything more than faith, and even that came in small amounts and only when it suited him.

He hesitated a few feet away from the bed. "I trust your judgment."

"Will you hold him?"

"I will not."

Hank never held his children when they were small and frail enough to drop. Hands as rough as his had no business holding such tender flesh.

"At least say hello," his daughter insisted. She turned the bundle so her Pa might look upon the sleeping face of his first grandchild.

Hank leaned closer without taking a step. Thick black hair curled over a tiny wrinkled face. The Leer family all had blond or brown hair; that tangle of darkness came from his father. Perhaps now that the deed was done, Sybil would confess. Quell the rumors about her infidelity with a simple name.

The baby made a sleepy, gurgling noise. Hank shrunk back. "Why's he so pale?"

"He was born with a caul over his face," the doctor explained. He did not elaborate, but packed up his leather bag and bid the new mother a speedy recovery.

Hank watched the man exit the room, then turned back to his daughter. "What's that mean?"

"It means he's special." Sybil sighed, perfectly content. "The most special boy in the entire world."

Hank rubbed his fingertips on his thumbs again. His entire world had changed and he didn't know how to go back.

Weeks passed. Winter's snow came and melted several times over, and Malachi grew as quickly as daffodils in March. His face filled out in the way most babies did, all fat and wet smiles. His eyes grew big and round as well, far too big and round for Hank's liking. In the sunlight, their color matched the same denim blue as his mother's, but in the shade, they took on a dark, unknown hue, like a star-filled sky at twilight. Hank found the color to be unnatural, but he also found he couldn't look away whenever his grandson fixed him with those big, cosmic eyes.

"They don't seem unnatural to you?" Hank asked Mary during dinner. He nodded at Malachi perched on Sybil's knee. The baby regarded him with a serious stare filled with starlight.

"How do you mean?" his wife replied, uninterested in anything but getting the twins to eat their boiled carrots and peas without swiping them onto the floor.

"How he stares at me, like he knows…" But Hank didn't know how to finish his thought. Simple minds had little room for complex things.

"He's a baby, Pa," Sybil said, bouncing her son upon her knee. The boy looked up at his mama and cooed, delighted. "He's just learning your face."

Hank did not like that one bit. "The twins never stared at me like that."

"That's because they have each other." His wife gently pried one twin's food-covered fist from his brother's hair.

"*None* of y'all ever did that," Hank said to his other three children. "Stared at me like…"

Like you could see down to my soul.

Sybil laughed. "Do you even remember when we were babies?"

"I do," Hank answered with conviction. He didn't follow his statement with proof, only hunched over his plate to shovel the rest of his food into his mouth. With his head down, he couldn't see his grandson's glittering eyes.

He could still feel them watching him, however, like the way creatures watched from the darkness of the forest.

Spring blew in with gusts of wind and rain, followed by the brightest, sweetest sunshine ever to fall upon the valley. As fresh green returned to the world, Hank returned to the business of his small farm, grateful for a reason to keep away from his grandson. A better man might have felt shame, but Hank never claimed to be a good man, just an honest one…and he honestly did not like being in the same room as the boy and avoided it when he could.

Working in the garden kept his mind and body occupied most of the day. When his wife or daughter insisted he hold Malachi while they tended to their own matters, Hank always stepped away, grumbling that the middle children were old enough to watch a baby for a few minutes. They willingly did it with the twins, after all.

A day came when his wife and eldest three children wanted to head into town. Springtime meant new clothes for everyone and a sugary treat for those who behaved. Hank needed to mind the twins and the newborn while they were gone.

Hank insisted that Mary take everyone with her, to leave him to his man's work in the fields, but she put her foot down. She so rarely got a day out for herself, and Sybil hadn't left the house in months. The fields could wait half a day. The sky looked set for rain, anyway.

Begrudgingly, he harnessed up the horse to the wagon and stood on the porch as his family drove away. Hank stayed there, hands on his hips, long after the wagon had disappeared into the grove. Then a wail cut into the morning, and a second voice quickly harmonized with the first.

Hank sighed and stepped into the house. The wailing sang from the second floor, the urgency and volume growing the longer Hank took his time. He lumbered up the stairs and down towards the nursery. The door sat open and the wailing damn near drove ice picks into Hank's ears.

Thomas and Timothy, old enough to walk but stubborn enough to not talk, frantically tried to climb up the slatted sides of their crib from the outside. Big, fat tears fell from two identically flushed faces, their mouths deep caverns from which banshees lamented their sorrows. They kept looking over their shoulders at Malachi, who lay on his back, two pudgy hands gripping two pudgy feet stuck up in the air.

"What's all the fuss?" Hank asked as if the twins could finally grow up and talk to him with some sense. Seeing their Pa had come to their rescue, they skirted the edge of the room, then broke out into a run to fall into his arms. The howling continued as his youngest children scrambled to be picked up. Hank knelt down and let them climb into his lap.

In the middle of the room, Malachi cooed and continued to play with his feet.

The twins eagerly showed their Pa their arms, speaking without words by slapping their skin over and over, following each slap with a fierce bite from what few teeth they'd grown. Understanding their meaning, Hank held their arms still.

Faint marks littered their forearms in half-moon crescents. Nothing serious enough to break the skin, but the curious lesions had already swollen up like spider bites.

Hank searched the room as if he were keen enough to spot the spider amongst the clutter of the nursery. He saw nothing amiss.

"Y'all got bit?" he asked Thomas and Timothy, who nodded through the fading hiccups of their crying. They both pointed to the baby in the middle of the room.

"He got bit, too?"

His sons each shook their heads. One grabbed Hank's face to force him to look again while the other kept pointing.

Malachi lazily rolled his head towards them. Big denim-blue eyes crinkled when he smiled with a mouth full of tiny, sharp teeth.

"Jesus!" Hank swore. He instinctively clutched the twins and scooted back on the floor. Both boys started crying again, so Hank scooped them up and took them to his bedroom. He told them to settle on the bed and gave them a pair of his winter gloves to play with in the meantime.

Now, Hank Leer didn't consider himself particularly cowardly. His thin frame wasn't the most formidable in a brawl, but at least he never turned tail. He could say that much about himself.

Walking back into the nursery, however, took every scrap of courage he possessed.

His grandson still lay on his back in the middle of the room. He'd dropped his feet in favor of sticking a few fingers in his mouth. When Hank stood in the doorway, the baby focused on him and drooled.

"Did you bite my sons?" Hank felt foolish for talking to a baby like an adult, but he wanted answers and maybe speaking the question aloud might uncover the truth of what happened.

Malachi just blinked at him with those big blue eyes. Hank didn't know much about beauty, but his grandson was admittedly adorable. Nothing so sweet could wield weapons that sharp.

Shadows lengthened in the nursery as rain clouds thickened over the sun. Hank waited, feeling more foolish by the second.

"Maybe you're just cuttin' your teeth." He stepped into the room, reluctant to approach the baby if he'd already entered the biting phase. "You leave them boys alone, hear? Can't have you chewing on 'em like a strip of beef jerky."

Malachi babbled and waved his hands in the air to be picked up. Hank looked down at him and decided that maybe he shouldn't be so afraid of a baby.

"I'll pick you up this once," he said, "but don't you tell your mama."

Hank squatted down and gingerly picked up his grandson. He'd never held something so squishy yet surprisingly heavy.

"You're a hefty one, ain't ya?"

The baby smiled and clapped, thrilled to be close to his grandpa. His pudgy flesh still had a pallid hue, especially when coupled with his thick, dark curls. They looked soft as feathers or the downy tufts of dandelion heads. *A strange little fellow,* Hank thought, and he wondered again what the boy's father looked like.

Last April, Sybil had disappeared without warning. Walked through the grove one afternoon and vanished by the time she'd reached the main road. Ongoing rumors of a strange, dark presence haunting the hollers caused the Leers to panic and turn to their fellow congregants and townsfolk for help. Those God-fearing souls, perhaps jealous of the fertile spit of land the Leers owned, warped the rumors into slander. No strange presence had taken their daughter. She'd simply taken to a man's bed.

Sybil had returned a month later, still wearing her favorite blue gingham dress and acting as if she'd never left.

She came back different, however. Ravenous. Addlebrained. Expecting.

Every time Hank had pried for the truth, his daughter had become despondent for days on end. Hank assumed the affair had ended unfavorably—and was rightly none of his concern—so after a time, he stopped asking.

But as her belly grew with child, so did the town's vile slander.

Heretics, heathens!

"Folks'll say just about anything, so long as someone's listening," Hank told the baby. He awkwardly cradled him against his chest, unsure of the proper way to hold him. "I s'pose I got their words stuck in my head about you. You're not so bad, huh?"

He laid his grandson in the crib and turned to fetch a spare blanket from one of the beds. Malachi immediately rolled over on his belly, pushed up to his feet, and waddled closer to his grandpa, his hands grasping the air to show he wanted to be held again. Hank froze, the blanket still halfway on the bed.

"Did you… How in the hell are you walking already?"

The baby screeched happily and smiled a wet smile full of tiny, sharp teeth.

Not one single member of his family believed Hank when he told them the events of his day. The twins were bitten by a house spider, not their baby nephew. See? The welts have two little punctures in the middle and they itch. Besides, Malachi's cutting his first two teeth, not all of them, and they're certainly not pointed."

"I didn't say *pointed*," Hank replied gruffly. "I said *sharp*."

"All baby teeth are sharp, Pa," Sybil said with a laugh. She would know; she had four younger siblings, after all.

"Do all babies walk after just a few months, too?" Hank gestured towards his fields, currently soaking up a rainstorm. "I'd like to put him to work if he's so eager to get going."

"Now you're just talkin' nonsense," Mary said. She crossed the sitting room to gather up her grandson from Sybil's lap. The baby immediately reached up to grab her spectacles, but she gently took his pudgy hand and kissed it. "I'll show you."

She placed Malachi on the rug in the middle of the room, laying him on his back to prove he didn't know how to roll over yet. Playing nearby with wooden alphabet blocks, the twins eyed their nephew with apprehension. They looked at each other, then wordlessly swept up the blocks and scooted further away.

Malachi just gurgled and kicked his legs in the air like a bullfrog. He didn't roll onto his belly. He didn't crawl or totter over to the twins to bite them again. He didn't get up and till the fields like his grandpa sarcastically insisted.

"See?" Mary said. "He may be a cute little bug, but he's still got a long ways to grow."

Hank didn't like her answer as much as he didn't trust his own observations. What the hell did he know about raising a baby? That task belonged to women. He minded his children only when they got old enough to lend a hand around the farm. That's when he paid attention to the things they did, for they sometimes had a habit of doing things wrong.

Hank waved her off, sore about the whole day going to waste. He stepped past the twins, who both whined for his attention, and stomped up the stairs to take a nap.

Spring warmed into summer. Hank stayed outside in his garden every day from dawn until well past dusk, sneaking into the kitchen for a glass of water or a bite to eat before going back out again. He kept Ezra with him most of the time, teaching him the proper ways to sow corn and care for the tomatoes and beans. Jenny often entertained the twins underneath a nearby oak by teaching them new words to shriek at each other. They still didn't care for full sentences or even half of one, preferring to pick a favorite word and wear it out until they latched onto another.

Today's word was *bird*, and everything in the world became birds. A falling leaf. A rock. An unknown visitor strolling up the drive.

Hank leaned on the handle of his rake and squinted across the yard. Not one visitor, but three, dressed in sharp, dark suits. Salesmen? Traveling pastors? Whoever they were, Hank didn't like it when they stepped off the drive to talk to his youngest children sitting under the oak tree.

He clutched his rake in his fist as he stomped through the plots. "Can I help you gentlemen?"

They looked up, each one pale, with soft black hair. The one in the middle gave Hank a smile that made his skin itch. "Mr. Leer?"

"I am. Who're you?"

"We're here to speak with your daughter."

"Not this one, you're not."

Another flat smile. "Your eldest."

"What business you got with her?" Hank held the rake in both hands and wished it were his shotgun instead.

"Just checking on the welfare of her son," said the man on the right. He did not smile like the one in the middle, and Hank was glad for it.

"Y'all doctors? Or social workers?"

"Investors," said the one on the left, and Hank frowned.

"What's that mean?"

The man in the middle tilted his head, ever so slightly, to the side. "Is your daughter home?"

Hank wanted to lie, to protect his baby girl from men who surely wanted more than what she might be willing to offer. Investors? What would an investor want with a baby boy? It sounded like a pocketful of bullshit to him.

Before Hank could tell them likewise, Sybil stepped out onto the porch, Malachi asleep in her arms. She waved to the strangers in welcome, then gestured for them to come inside. Her son mewled in the bright sunlight and buried his face in her bosom.

"Thank you, Mr. Leer," the middle one said pleasantly, and followed his companions up the drive.

"Who're they?" Jenny asked.

"Hell if I know," Hank replied—but he *did* have a knowing feeling deep within his gut. Bad news. Ill fortune.

"Harbinger!" Thomas said, laughing, and Timothy echoed, "Harbinger!"

Hank glared down at his sons. "Where'd y'all learn *that* word?"

Jenny furrowed her brow, confused. "What, *bird?* I just taught 'em that one."

The twins continued shrieking and laughing, and damned if Hank didn't swear their voices sounded like a whole flock of birds cawing their portents all around him.

"You stay here. If anyone else comes up that drive, you go yonder and fetch your brother and come inside."

"Yessir."

Hank had a mind to take the rake with him, as he did not have the muscle to fight off three men should it come to that, but he knew it wouldn't sit well with his wife. He compromised by bringing it to the house and leaving it on the porch next to the front door.

Inside, Sybil sat on the sofa with Malachi still curled up against her. He sucked his thumb, those big blue eyes heavy with sleep. The three strangers in their sharp black suits stood around as if expecting something miraculous to happen. Hank thought he knew their kind: folks who traveled around, claiming to be prophets or holy men, looking for some poor soul to exploit—or swindle into joining the cult they claimed was a church.

Not in his home, they wouldn't. The Leer family already belonged to a church, the same one Hank's own grandfather attended back before the town even had a name.

Hank opened his mouth to inform the strangers that they'd already overstayed their welcome when the man in the middle sank down to one knee before Sybil as if he might propose marriage. The man spoke in a low, calm tone. Hank didn't catch his words but noted how they rose and fell like a hymn. Sybil gently swayed along, her son slowly blinking, thumb still in his mouth.

The other two strangers harmonized with the first; one warbled in higher pitches while the other made odd clicking sounds, like a poor imitation of a cicada. Now Hank knew the men needed to leave, take their nonsense off his property, but the strange melody held him down, made him forget why he'd come into the house in the first place. His whole body itched like he'd sat on an anthill: an itch that burned, made him want to tear off his skin and dry it in the sun, but an itch that also felt *divine*—and dangerously so.

The strangers continued their hymnals, their voices pushing Hank deeper into a haze the same as they finally got Malachi to open those big, round, cosmic eyes of his. Pleased, the man in the middle fetched a thin candle from his coat pocket and lit it. The baby immediately focused on the flickering flame, a storm of stars swirling in his irises. Indigo and aubergine and other colors Hank did not know the name of sparked and pulsed as Malachi's pupils contracted to pinpoints, fully entranced by the candle. Then he bared his tiny sharp teeth and chittered along with the hymnal.

Pitch darkness swallowed up the room—the world—the entirety of existence. Only the candle and the boy remained, his face a full moon bathed in eerie blue light. The flame, bright and enchanting as a sapphire, flickered as if it recognized the child, as if it called to him, spoke in secrets and spells, spoke his name like it burned as hot as the flame itself. Malachi responded with eyes growing ever wider, round and bulging, the wonders of the universe and terrors of the night spinning within; his voice pitched lower than humanly possible, as if summoning leviathans from the center of the earth.

Hank didn't know what a leviathan was or what one might look like, but he swore one had wrapped its enormous fingers around him and squeezed. A terror he'd never felt consumed him completely. He choked out a single curse before the terrible pressure shattered his bones and banished his consciousness to the abyss.

Darkness pulsed in a stuttering rhythm of insect wings struggling to fly. Soft sounds tapped like rain on a windowpane or fingernails drummed on a tabletop. Hank was not himself; he was not anyone, yet he had been summoned. He climbed unseen steps and stood before an empty stone altar. Shadows swarmed and seethed. Feather-light caresses fluttered down his bare arms. Hank was not himself, and so he climbed onto the altar to offer his husk as a sacrifice. The buzzing of a hundred-thousand cicadas thanked him for his offering, and Hank screamed in agonizing euphoria when the shadows turned into moths and the moths began to eat him.

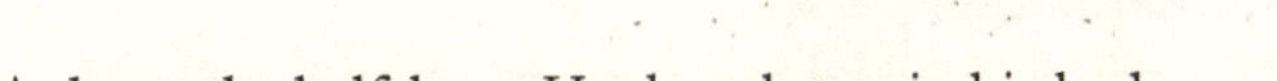

A day and a half later, Hank woke up in his bed.

His brain felt like an entire cotton field swathed in thick fog. Gummy bitterness coated his tongue. Shadows flitted across his mattress when he moved his legs, and Hank clutched a hand to his chest in panic as memories of his fever dream came back to him with all the heaviness of a rolling thundercloud.

"You're finally awake," Mary said, standing at the foot of the bed with a breakfast tray in her hands. "Hungry?"

"No."

"Yes, you are," she insisted. She set the tray on the bedside table. "Do I need to feed you like I feed the twins?"

At the mention of his youngest sons, Hank's mind went to the bites on their arms and the tiny, sharp mouth that had made them. The same tiny, sharp mouth that had clicked tiny, sharp sounds in harmony with the three strangers.

Hank sat up, angry and nauseous. "What happened to those men?"

His wife remained unconcerned. "What men?"

"The ones who came to see the baby." Their *investment*, whatever the hell that meant.

"Oh, they left long ago. Such nice men." She turned to Hank, one hand offering a spoonful of porridge and the other cupped below to catch any mess. "Here. Eat."

Hank frowned but did as he was told. The porridge stuck to the roof of his mouth and he gagged, so he pushed the next spoonful away. "No more."

"You need to eat. You're just bones."

Good, all the better. Less meat for a monster like his grandson to eat.

Sickened by his own thoughts, Hank threw off the covers and climbed out of bed. Lack of food and water made him dizzy, but he pushed through the vertigo.

"Where d'you think you're going?" Mary asked, one hand on her hip. "Your damn fields can wait another day while you recover."

"I'm going for a walk," Hank snapped. He didn't know why but figured he'd find out when he got there.

"At least let me go with you." His wife put the spoon back in the bowl and untied her apron. "We can all go out as a family. I know the kids would love it."

"You will not."

"Oh, stop this stubbornness!"

Hank strode to his wife's side and gripped her arm more forcefully than he intended. "Who is the father, Mary? I need to know! Malachi is an abomination."

His wife paled, then flushed with anger. "How dare you! He is our *grandson*, not an abomination."

Hank clenched his jaw tight enough to hurt. "Who is the father?"

His wife regarded him with pity. She shook her head. "I can't rightly say."

"Can't 'cause you don't know or 'cause you swore you wouldn't tell?" When she didn't answer, Hank released her arm and stepped away, rubbing his fingertips on his thumbs. "I'm going out. Alone."

"Will you be home before dark?" Mary asked in a low, calm tone as if they hadn't just quarreled.

Hank shuddered. He paused by the door but didn't turn around. "Yes, I will."

A man made from the salt of the earth often returned to his roots when he felt lost.

Hank wandered deep into the woods behind his farm and thought about his Meemaw. The old woman, rest her soul, feared God as much as she tested Him with her folk magic. Tinctures and teas meant to soothe colds and cure ailments the same as they were meant to predict the future. A black walnut tree plugged full of iron nails to hex an enemy. Empty glass bottles strung up to catch wayward spirits. Blood rituals meant to summon, fire rituals meant to banish.

Meemaw never let anyone take her picture, cut her hair, or shake her hand. The more she gave away, she always said, the less she became. She lived to be one hundred and three.

She also knew a thing or two about breaking family curses, or casting one of her own.

"Blood is thicker'n water," she used to say, "so you gotta dry it out an' grind it up before you can mix it in."

Of her five children and eighteen grandchildren, Hank had inherited the family farm when Meemaw passed on. He'd also inherited her cunning ways, but never had a need for them until now.

If no one felt obliged to tell him who Malachi's father was, then he felt obliged to summon the man himself. But how could he summon a man if he didn't know his name or face? Couldn't rightly put an advert in the paper or go knocking door to door. He'd look as strange and foolish as those three men.

A new thought slowed Hank's step. Those men were pale with black hair, just like his grandson. Could one of them be the father? Possibly, but Sybil didn't seem attached to any one of them and they'd all treated Malachi like some kind of prophesied miracle, not a son. So maybe they were kin—or at the very least, kin to the same cult.

Still, Hank felt in his guts that the strange men knew the true identity of Malachi's father. He would have asked them if he hadn't succumbed to a dizzy spell and struck his head on the floor.

Soon enough, a small clearing opened within the tall pines; Hank stood at the edge and stared at the same stone altar from his fever dream. The buzz of cicadas swelled in the heat of the afternoon, and he knew that if he wanted to summon the unknown, he needed the blood of the known.

Malachi's caul…and Malachi himself.

Hank Leer waited until the night of the next full moon to sneak into his eldest daughter's bedroom and kidnap her son.

He found Malachi waiting in the darkness as though expecting him. His tiny hands gripped the edge of his crib, and his round eyes glittered in the moonlight. Thick layers of gossamer cobwebs climbed from the crib and onto the walls.

The uncanny sight nearly made Hank lose his resolve. Sybil slept peacefully, unaware that her Pa had dug up the caul from where she'd buried it in the backyard. It looked like a moldy, shriveled-up cocoon and nearly made Hank retch up his supper, but he did as Meemaw had told him and dried it, powdered it, and mixed it into a poultice to use as a summoning agent. All he needed was fresh blood from the source.

The baby chittered at his mama, but she didn't wake. Hank slowly crept closer, both hands raised as if he approached a feral creature instead of his own grandson. Then, quick as a jackrabbit, he wrapped Malachi up in his blanket, making sure to keep his limbs tightly bound. When the baby opened his maw to wail, Hank popped a square of caramel in his mouth.

"So you don't bite me," he whispered.

Sybil murmured in her sleep. Her Pa cradled Malachi to his chest and snuck out of the room. Malachi happily chewed on the candy with his tiny, sharp teeth.

Underneath milky moonlight, Hank crept through the forest towards the clearing. Tall pines guarded him like sentinels as he laid the baby on the stone slab. Malachi, placated by sugar, watched his grandpa prepare the ritual, his blanket snug around him like spider silk.

Meemaw didn't have a specific ritual for summoning estranged family, but Hank knew the best hexes came from desperation and determination. He placed a circle of river stones around the baby to keep him from rolling off, then stuck tufts of moss, acorns, amaranth petals, mugwort, bird bones, iron nails, and apple slices into the gaps. With the tip of his pocketknife, he nicked behind Malachi's ear to draw fresh blood. The baby squealed and snapped at his grandpa's fingers as Hank collected the blood in the same glass jar that held the poultice made from the buried caul. Lastly, he took a hickory twig and swirled the ingredients together, then used the tip to paint sigils on Malachi's forehead and cheeks.

Hank stepped back to study his work. He felt foolish—*sinful,* even— but he believed himself a bigger fool if he didn't try. Malachi was an abomination, after all; only arcane ways solved arcane problems.

"Well," he said, still holding the glass jar and the blood-encrusted hickory twig. "Now what?" Should he say a prayer? A poem? Meemaw never explained that part. Then, inspiration struck. "I call to the…sire of Malachi, that he come forth and claim the son he abandoned. Show your face and let your name be known!"

Hank paused, hands held aloft. Nothing. Malachi cooed and tried to kick his bound legs. Hank lowered his hands, accepting that some hexes worked more quietly than others.

As he approached the altar to complete the ritual, clouds shifted across the moon and shadows twisted between the tall pines. A wind too cold for midsummer swirled through the deadfall on the ground. Malachi crooned a single, clear note, his eyes glowing like two star-filled lanterns in the dark.

Unnatural movement shifted above the canopy. Trunks creaked and cracked, boughs bent low. Darkness thickened within the clearing, slick like oil on feathers, coiling like snakes around Hank's legs. Ice seeped into his bones, froze the bile that threatened to rise.

Something hovered above, pulsed with wings sharp enough to tear the clouds away from the moon.

Covered in his own blood and caul, Malachi chittered and chirped. Starlight swirled in his eyes as his father—for who else could it be?— swooped down from the sky to perch like a giant carrion bird on the edge of the rocky outcropping.

Oily shadows dripped from his shoulders and onto the altar. A handsome face, if not for the glowing red coals of his eyes, studied the ritual offering. One pale hand slowly reached towards the baby; Hank saw black talons on the ends of each finger and hoped, feared, waited for them to sink into his grandson's tender flesh.

Talons receded into human hands that gently picked up the bundle. Oily moth wings slipped into the velvet folds of a coat. The handsome face became more human, even more handsome, with soft, dark waves of hair trailing to his shoulders. Freed from his blanket, Malachi clapped and laughed, and his father's eyes crinkled with genuine mirth.

Hank Leer mistook the happy moment for an opportunity to talk. "Tell me your name, sir."

The strange man immediately pierced him with the glowing red daggers of his eyes. Twin antennae rose from the tangle of black curls and his velvety garments reformed the swirling, chromatic abyss of his wings. The sound of a hundred-thousand cicadas hissed from a mouth filled with sharp teeth.

Hank screamed as those teeth sank into his throat. With his last bloodied breath, he gurgled the name that was both a blessing and a curse upon his damned soul:

Harbinger.

CM 2024

Out of the Woods

JAMIE CHURCHMAN

AT JUST PAST midnight, Jodie realized something was wrong.

The main building of the wellness retreat was encased by floor-to-ceiling windows nearly all the way around. Bright fluorescent lights turned the big windows into mirrors, making it impossible for Jodie to see past the doubled image of the room she was in. She had become used to the sensation of her heart jumping in her chest whenever she saw some alien creature beyond the window, some monster out in the woods, then feeling her shoulders relax as she recognized her own reflected shape made monstrous by the cumbersome backpack vacuum she wore. Still, the disquieting feeling of being exposed followed her from room to room as she cleaned, only somewhat dissipating as she finished up and turned the lights off behind her.

Tonight was different. The same feeling of exposure, of being *watched*, was there. But now, when she sensed movement from the corner of her eye and turned to look, something beyond the glass continued to move even as her reflection remained still.

Jodie froze, one hand on her wheeled 55-gallon trashcan. She was very aware of her pulse beating in her temples, making her suddenly lightheaded. Squinting at the window in front of her, she tried to make out anything beyond the glass, anything she possibly could have seen moving, but only the reflection of her own startled face met her eyes.

She took one earbud out and listened. Nothing but normal building noises surrounded her: the buzzing of the lights, the humming of the air-conditioner, the distant sound of ice cubes clunking in the icemaker back in the kitchen.

"Okay," she muttered, jamming the earbud back into her ear and reaching into her pocket to turn the volume up. If something was out there, she'd rather not know. Of course, she would eventually have to go outside to run the trash to the dumpster, but that was a problem for Future Jodie. Only about twenty minutes in the future, but she wasn't going to worry about that just now.

When it did come time to run her two bags of trash out to the dumpster, Jodie took a deep breath and peered through the glass door. This close to the glass, she could see past her own reflection to the parking lot, the dumpster at the far edge, and the forest beyond that. Nothing moved but the leaves dancing in the wind. Still, she couldn't shake the uneasy feeling of being watched.

Straightening her shoulders, Jodie pushed her way through the door, one bag of trash in each hand. She kept her head moving, looking from side to side as she crossed the parking lot. Trying to feel less silly, she reminded herself that the wellness center *was* in the middle of nowhere, two miles into the woods. Mountain lions had been spotted in the area, and bears weren't unheard of. Maybe some prey instinct in the hidden parts of her mind was warning her to be alert.

Still, she'd never felt this particular blend of disquiet and dread out here before.

She set the bags down on the pavement to flip the lid of the dumpster open, then paused. Something moved just in her periphery, disappearing behind her. She hoisted the lid up and over, allowing gravity to take it and slam it onto the back. The resulting bang echoed into the woods. It should have startled any wildlife into bolting deeper into the trees, but Jodie could still feel a presence nearby.

Jodie took a deep breath and stared straight ahead at the dark abyss inside the dumpster, trying to determine which notion she was more afraid of: knowing what was watching her or not knowing at all. Her hands shook only a little as she swung the bags of trash up and over the edge. Finally, she turned her head just enough to see the woods.

The light from the nearest lamppost barely reached her position. Jodie squinted into the woods, trying to spot anything that could have created enough movement to alert her senses. She clicked the button on her earbuds to pause her music and held her breath in the age-old confusion of senses that insisted you could spot what you were looking for if only your ears weren't distracted.

Jodie had just let her breath out again when a glint of light caught her eye. Air stuck in her throat, and she coughed until her eyes watered. She took a step backward toward the building, still peering into the trees. Another glint flickered into view, followed by a rustling. Something stepped forward just enough for Jodie to see it in the weak light, and she almost laughed.

An enormous deer stepped into view, the light catching its eyes as it turned, making them shine red.

"*Oh,*" Jodie whispered. She'd seen deer out here before; sometimes they even wandered into the parking lot and she would watch them as she exited the building. They startled easily and would bound back to the safety of the trees once they realized a human was near.

This one didn't seem the least bit skittish. It didn't turn tail and run, nor did it seem frozen in fear. It simply stood, returning Jodie's gaze.

"Hey, girl," Jodie said softly, noting the lack of antlers. "I'm not going to hurt you, okay?"

The doe continued to meet Jodie's eyes in that same steady way, planting another seed of dread in Jodie's stomach that shortened her breath and caused sweat to prickle her palms.

Something about the doe was wrong. Deer were usually wary of humans; they bolted away at sudden loud noises. They didn't come closer to inspect people. They didn't make you feel as though they were sizing you up.

She shuddered as she looked into the doe's eyes, sensing an unsettling intelligence. Something odd about the eyes made the back of her neck prickle, but Jodie decided that now wasn't exactly the optimal time to try to pin down everything wrong with this picture.

"Okay, girl. I've gotta go back inside and vacuum now. You have yourself a wonderful night, yeah?" Jodie backed away from the deer, praying it wouldn't follow her, then turned and hastened back to the building, glancing over her shoulder every couple of steps. The deer watched her until she reached the side door. As Jodie fumbled the key into the lock, she glanced back one last time to see that the doe had disappeared. Only red eye-shine flashing from the trees let her know it was still out there, watching her.

It wasn't until Jodie had her vacuum strapped to her back and leaned down to plug in its extension cord that she realized what had been off about the deer's eyes. She dropped the cord and bolted upright, feeling dizzy.

The doe's eyes hadn't been on the sides of her head. They had been on the front, looking straight ahead like a predator animal.

Jodie placed a hand against the wall, one of the few interior walls that hid her from the windows, and lowered her head, breathing shallowly. Yes, the deer's eyes were placed wrong for a prey animal. But there had been something else. She closed her eyes and pictured the doe. After a moment, she had it. The eye-shine had been red. Every deer she'd ever seen had eyes that shone green or white. Never red.

Pushing herself off from the wall, Jodie shook her head. Maybe the deer was rabid or something. That would explain why it wasn't acting right, why it wasn't afraid of humans. She wasn't sure, but it might even explain the red eye-shine.

Doesn't explain why its eyes aren't in the right place, the dispassionately rational part of her brain whispered.

Fine, then it's a mutant. Fucked up genetics. A giant, rabid mutant deer, Jodie answered herself. Somehow, the thought still wasn't reassuring.

She bent down to retrieve the cord, plugged it in, and set to work vacuuming the wellness center. The windows loomed throughout the building, and she deliberately kept her eyes focused on the floor, trying not to think about the weird deer outside. Surely it had left the immediate area, gone back to its den to avoid nocturnal predators. Then again, Jodie wasn't sure the deer wasn't a predator itself.

Once Jodie had vacuumed the carpeted areas and mopped the hardwood and tile portions of the building, she gathered her cleaning equipment in the lobby. Hesitating, she peered through the glass door, examining the parking lot. Only one dim light glowed behind her, not bright enough to fully turn the glass into a mirror. Outside, her Subaru Outback sat alone in the lot. No animals, weird deer or otherwise, were in sight.

With her caddy of spray bottles and rags in one hand and the metal wand of her vacuum in the other, Jodie pushed her way out of the door and walked to the SUV, keeping her head up and looking out for any movement from the surrounding woods. She popped the liftgate up and stowed her stuff inside, then went back inside the wellness center for the vacuum. With the lights out and the door locked behind her, she turned to the Subaru and almost stumbled off the low porch in surprise.

The deer was back.

In the few seconds she'd taken to check the door, it had crossed the parking lot to come stand beside her vehicle. If she went around the passenger side like she normally did to stow her equipment in the back, she would have to walk within a few feet of the deer. It could leap forward and pin her against the side of the Subaru if it were so inclined.

Jodie swallowed and readjusted her grip on the vacuum, ready to get it between her and the deer if it showed any sign of charging.

"Hey, there. Nice girl," she crooned, hoping the deer wasn't capable of interpreting the tremble in her voice. "You stay right there, okay? I'm just gonna go around here."

Jodie sidled along the front of the SUV and around the driver's side to get to the open hatch in back. The deer stayed on the passenger side, watching her. Usually, she took a couple of minutes to organize her equipment, but tonight she unceremoniously shoved it in the back and slammed the liftgate down. The quicker she could be out of here and away from the strange deer, the better.

With the hatch closed, she hurried along the driver's side, yanked her door open, and jumped inside, locking the door almost before she even had it closed. *Stupid*, she chided herself. Did she think the deer could open a car door?

Reversing out of her parking spot gave Jodie a complete view of the deer in her headlights, fully framed in the windshield. She slammed on the brakes to put it in drive, then froze as the deer leaped toward the vehicle. Jodie instinctively threw herself backward in her seat, braced for impact, but it never came. The deer hadn't leaped *forward*, she realized.

It stood up on its hind legs.

She stared, trying to make sense of what she was seeing. This wasn't an unheard-of phenomenon. She'd occasionally seen deer stand upright to reach feeders. Hell, she'd even seen videos of cats and dogs standing on their hind legs and walking around. It was cute. This was not cute. This felt *wrong*. This felt like her reality had taken a sudden sharp shift. The back of her neck prickled, and she shuddered, the sensation somehow too hot and too cold at the same time.

In the glare from the LED headlights, Jodie got a much better look at the deer than she had before. Not only were its eyes all wrong, now she realized the legs were abnormal as well. Almost as if they were double-jointed, or maybe had extra joints. She couldn't quite put her finger on it.

After what had felt like forever but was realistically only a few seconds, the deer took a long step toward the SUV, still on its hind legs.

Jodie started upright in her seat, slammed the gearshift into Drive, and swerved around the deer in a squeal of tires.

"Nope," she said, punching the radio on and jabbing the volume button up until the Ramones drowned out the sound of her pounding heart. "I definitely didn't see that."

Jodie was fairly familiar with basic animal anatomy. She knew the reason quadrupeds looked like their knees were on backwards was because what people assumed were the knees were actually the ankles, and the knees were hidden higher up against the side of the body. The upper legs were easy to mistake for part of the hips. It was a thing you didn't think about until it was pointed out to you.

When the deer had taken that step toward Jodie's car, she'd gotten a good look at its legs. The upper leg was far too long, hinging at a knee that was proportionally lower than it ought to have been. The lower leg stretched below that, connecting with the ankle that everyone mistook for the knee. The ankle, which was meant to bend backward, because below *that* was the metatarsal—the bone that people who didn't know better mistook for the tibia.

And yet.

Jodie shuddered again and turned the radio volume up another few notches.

When the deer had stepped toward her, she had distinctly seen what should have been the knee bend backward, while the ankle bent forward.

"What the hell?" she whispered, her voice lost under the music as she stepped harder on the gas pedal, eager to put as much distance as possible between her and the messed-up deer.

One week later, Jodie pulled into the wellness center's parking lot again. She'd spent the week in between cleaning days alternating between dreading coming back and doubting what she'd seen. By this morning, she had almost managed to convince herself that all she'd seen had been a sick, mutated doe. *Almost.* The feeling of wrongness stayed with her, running tendrils across her brain like spiderwebs she couldn't swat away.

She dug the keys to the building out of her key pouch and looked at the clock. It was just after ten. Checking the parking lot for animal movement and finding none, she got out of the SUV and moved her equipment into the building. The area remained blissfully empty of wildlife, and Jodie relaxed her shoulders a bit as she plugged her earbuds into her phone and turned on a podcast.

Once she had the trash gathered and ready to take out to the dumpster, Jodie's dread resurfaced. She'd been actively avoiding looking at the windows any more than necessary and had wiped down the glass doors as quickly as possible, keeping her gaze away from the tree line. Now that she had to go outside and cross the parking lot, the muscles in her shoulders stiffened up again in protest.

"Stupid," she muttered to herself, and shoved the door open with false bravado. Hopefully the weird doe, if it was watching her, couldn't tell she was faking.

After hefting the trash bags up and over the lip of the dumpster without incident, Jodie turned back to the building, then froze.

The strange deer stood ten feet in front of her, blocking her way.

How the hell does it move so quickly? Jodie wondered. Nothing had been there when she'd reached the dumpster, and nothing had moved in her periphery. And even with her earbuds in, shouldn't she have been able to hear the doe approaching, hard hooves on pavement? *God, can it teleport?*

She tried to swallow and found that her mouth was too dry. The deer watched her, thankfully still standing with all four hooves on the ground. Jodie didn't think she could take it if the deer decided to walk upright again.

Jodie took several steps to the side, making as wide a circle around the deer as she could. Feeling vaguely ridiculous, she backed toward the building. Turning her back to the doe felt like a bad idea.

When Jodie was halfway to the door, the deer began slowly walking toward her. The messed-up joints in the rear legs gave its movements a strange quality, jerky and undulating. Jodie gave up keeping the deer in view, pivoting on her heel and running for the door. She'd left it unlocked upon stepping outside this time, just in case she needed to get inside fast. She yanked the door open and flew inside, only then whipping around to look behind her.

The deer ambled her way, its eyes shining red in the glow from the nearest lamppost. Jodie grabbed her key from her pocket and opened the door just enough to dart outside and lock the door again, cursing whatever door architect had decided that this one should lock only from the outside.

With the lock taken care of and the door firmly latched, Jodie stared out at the deer. Watching it move was almost hypnotizing, with its weird jerky, rolling gait. She shook her head and whispered, "What *are* you?"

The words were barely out of her mouth when the deer reared up onto its hind legs and ran at the door. Jodie let out a shriek and stumbled backward a split second before the deer's front hooves slammed against the glass. Her eyes widened as a long crack formed down the length of the door. The deer's mouth opened, revealing sharp teeth. Then it roared, its breath fogging the glass.

Jodie turned and ran deeper into the building. In the hallway by the bathrooms was a steel door that led down into a storage basement; it had a lock on it. She no longer cared if it was stupid to think she needed to lock a door to keep a deer out. If that *thing* got inside the building, she was damn sure going to put as many obstacles as possible between it and her.

The sounds of a large, pissed-off animal slamming itself into the glass door followed Jodie as she pulled open the basement door. She flipped the light switch, slammed and locked the door, and made her way down the stairs to the tiny concrete room filled with rolled-up yoga mats and half-deflated core stability balls. Shaking, she moved one of the balls against the wall and lowered herself onto it, sinking nearly to the floor. She pulled out her phone, intending to call the police, but paused before opening the dialer. Yes, she needed help, but she also wanted to know what the hell she was dealing with. Whatever that creature out there was, it wasn't a normal deer.

Jodie's hands shook so badly that it took three tries to open Google. Backspacing several times to correct typos, she feverishly typed everything weird about the animal into the search bar, then scrolled through the results. Toward the top of the page, the word "cryptid" caught her eye. Under that, the term "Not Deer."

"Naturally," she muttered, clicking on the link. It took her to some sort of cryptid wiki, with a ridiculous Photoshop of a wolf's face on a deer's head. Clenching her jaw, she skimmed the description. It matched her weird deer exactly. She scrolled farther and came across a section about the Not Deer's temperament.

"Not Deer are not generally dangerous to humans," she read, and snorted in disbelief. "The creature has been reported to attack only when a person has attempted to scare them off or has made mention of the creature's abnormal appearance within a two-mile radius of it."

Jodie leaned against the wall and stared up at the ceiling for a moment, remembering what she'd muttered just before the Not Deer had attacked the door. *What are you?* She sighed and closed her eyes. "Figures. That's just my luck."

From upstairs came a crash, followed by the sound of glass shattering. A second later, thumping footsteps. Jodie shuddered, imagining the Not

Deer lurching its way through the wellness center, tracking her. She eyed the door at the top of the stairs and wondered if she'd made a mistake by cornering herself.

Focused now on the reason she'd pulled her phone out of her pocket in the first place, Jodie opened the dialer and called 911. She didn't know if they could get Animal Control out in the middle of the night, or even if Animal Control would be able to do anything against a goddamn cryptid deer, but she had to do something. Even if just the police showed up, surely they could shoot the damn thing, couldn't they?

Jodie had never called 911 before; she had only witnessed it in movies, and so was surprised when the first thing the dispatcher asked was her name and address rather than what her emergency was.

"My name's Jodie Stevenson. I don't know the exact address, but I'm at the Whole Life Wellness Center out on Mulberry Road, about two miles from Elk City." She paused, ready to supply her occupation as a cleaner if the dispatcher asked what the hell she was doing at the wellness center in the middle of the night, but the other woman didn't ask.

"Okay, and why did you call 911 tonight, Jodie?"

"Um." Jodie's mind suddenly went blank. She couldn't very well tell the dispatcher she was being attacked by a monster, could she? No one would take her seriously. "There's this huge deer that got inside the building. I think something's wrong with it? It's really aggressive and tried to attack me. It might be rabid or something? I locked myself in the basement; I don't know if you can get, like, Animal Control out here or anything? It's really strong; it busted down one of the doors to get inside the building, and I'm really scared it's going to be able to break down the basement door, too."

Jodie realized she was rambling, but it occurred to her it might convey a sense of urgency to the dispatcher. She could hear typing on the other end of the line, and then the dispatcher's voice came back on.

"Okay, Jodie, I'm sending an Animal Control officer to your location. I want you to stay where you are and don't approach the animal, all right?"

"Yeah, no problem," Jodie said. As if she needed to be told not to go near that *thing* upstairs.

"Is there anything else I can do for you tonight, Jodie?"

Jodie frowned. Was that it? Was this woman about to hang up on her? On TV, they always stayed on the line with the caller until the cops showed up. "Uh, no, I guess that's it. Just, I think they need to know this thing is really, really aggressive. Tell them to be careful."

"Thank you, Jodie. I'll let them know. Stay safe." With that, the dispatcher hung up.

"Stay safe," Jodie mimicked, leaning forward with her elbows on her knees. How was she supposed to stay safe with a damn monster deer stomping around above her? She took a deep breath and wondered how long it would take Animal Control to reach her. Assuming they had an emergency unit that could mobilize immediately, it was maybe a ten-minute drive from town to the wellness center. Longer if they had to get someone out of bed to respond to the call.

The lurching footsteps were getting louder, thumping the floor directly above Jodie's head. She closed her eyes and pictured the layout of the building. Immediately above her should be the hallway that ran perpendicular to the hall with the basement door. She bit her lip and stared up at the ceiling, following the footsteps.

The steps stopped, and Jodie held her breath, willing her heart to stop beating so loudly. Suddenly, a roaring bellow rang through the building. Jodie jumped and slapped a hand over her mouth. It was the same sound the Not Deer had made when it had thrown itself at the exterior glass door. Enclosed in the building, echoing through the hallways, the sound was ten times worse.

The footsteps started up again, getting farther away for a moment before coming closer again. That meant it had turned the corner into Jodie's hallway. It must be only a few feet away from the basement door. There was one more lurching footstep, then silence.

Jodie held still, straining to listen. She couldn't tell if it was her own panicked breath she was hearing or the Not Deer's heavy snorts. Maybe it couldn't hear her over its own breathing.

"*Joe. Dee. Oh. Pen,*" a strange, thick voice said. "*Oh. Pen. Jodie. Open.*"

Jodie stared up at the door, frozen. *No no no no no,* she thought, *there's no way this thing can talk.* Part of her brain urged her to curl up and die right there; how could she fight this nightmare? The other part of her brain wasn't much more helpful; it was too busy laughing hysterically at the sheer absurdity of it all.

"*Oh. Pen. Jodie. Open let in.*" Even muffled by the door, the voice was terrifying. It was a mockery of vocal cords not designed for human speech, forced out through too many sharp teeth.

Maybe it's like a vampire and can't come in unless I invite it? Jodie thought hopefully, then drew her lips in over her teeth and bit down to keep a hysterical giggle from bubbling out. *Shit, are vampires real, too?*

Her first question was answered when something slammed into the door at the top of the stairs. All traces of hysteria were suddenly frightened out of her. Jodie could imagine the Not Deer, still walking upright, rearing back and bringing the full force of its weight down on the steel door.

The Not Deer released another awful bellowing roar and threw itself against the door again. The door was strong, but Jodie wasn't so sure about the frame. There wasn't much light to see by, but she thought the frame around the deadbolt had splintered slightly.

Jodie frantically looked around the basement. It had to be bigger than just the area she was in; there was another basement door just off the kitchen. Praying that it was all interconnected and the door by the kitchen didn't lead to a completely separate basement area, she stood and used her phone's flashlight to search the room.

Her light fell on a door under the stairs, hidden within shadow. She ran to it and yanked it open as another assault by the Not Deer shook the wall above her. Beyond the door was another hallway that led off to her right and then disappeared around a corner. She pulled the door shut behind her and hit the light switch. Dim, flickering fluorescents lit the hall, providing barely more light than her phone.

Jodie hurried down the hall and around the bend. Doors dotted the walls to her sides, but she kept her eyes trained on the staircase at the end of the hall and to the left. That should lead to the door by the kitchen. If she could get to that door, maybe she could run out through the glass door that the Not Deer had destroyed, run along the front of the building, get in the Subaru, and leave.

Except...

She patted her pockets and groaned, feeling hope slip away. The only keys she had were the ones to the wellness center. Her own car keys were sitting on the counter in the lobby, next to the stupid little Daily Motivations calendar. Today's motivation had been, "Live every day like it's your last."

Hysterical laughter bubbled up again; this time she let it out, leaning against the wall and silently laughing until tears rolled down her face. She wondered if the Not Deer would tear her apart with those awful teeth or simply stomp her to death. Hell, maybe both.

"No," she whispered, shaking her head and wiping her eyes. "*Think*, idiot."

Okay, so she didn't have her keys on her. The Not Deer was still occupied with beating down the basement door. From the sound of it, another couple of attacks would get the job done, but maybe that was a good thing. If the creature followed her path through the basement, it would give her the chance to run through the halls upstairs, get to the lobby, grab her keys, and get the hell out.

Jodie shuddered. This plan required waiting until she was sure the Not Deer was in the basement, while every molecule of her being screamed at her to go *now*. Pushing down her primordial panic, she ascended the stairs and waited, hand on the knob. This would put two more doors between her and it, she told herself. Three, once she made it to the lobby. Three more obstacles it would have to break down before it could get to her. It occurred to her that the Not Deer might be smart enough to figure out what she was doing and simply turn around and go back up to the main floor to wait for her, but she shoved that thought away.

When the Not Deer finally crashed through the basement door, the sound was strangely doubled, echoing through both the basement and the main level. Jodie's fingers twitched on the handle as she waited for a sign that the creature was actually in the basement. After a few seconds, she heard a strange, arrhythmic clomping. She shuddered, picturing the creature lurching down the stairs on its freakish legs. Several times it sounded as though the Not Deer had lost its balance, and she wondered if it might fall and break its neck. No such luck. Several loud, stumbling thumps later, it began slamming itself into the basement hallway door. With a combination of relief and anxiety, Jodie twisted the knob and threw the door open, emerging into the hall next to the kitchen.

She had assumed the Not Deer had simply broken through the glass when it crashed into the building, but now she saw it had taken the door completely down. Glass littered the hallway, and the metal frame lay twisted on the floor, still attached to the doorjamb by a mangled bottom hinge. Drops of blood dotted the tile, marking the creature's path through the building.

On the bright side, if it could bleed…

That meant it could be hurt.

Jodie made sure the door latched behind her, then sprinted as quietly as possible down the hall to the lobby. Once inside, she kicked the doorstop out from the lobby door and held the knob as it closed to prevent it from slamming and alerting the Not Deer to her location. She glanced at her cleaning equipment and decided that if her bosses at the cleaning company didn't see this situation as a legitimate reason to leave everything behind, then screw them. Grabbing her keys off the reception counter, she made a face at the motivational calendar and kept moving. She flicked the light switch off and peered outside. All clear.

Time to run.

The key fob unlocked the driver's side door as soon as Jodie touched the handle, and she threw herself into the front seat, slammed the seat belt into place, and jammed her thumb onto the start button in quick succession. With one last look at the wellness center, she sped out of the parking lot and onto the road that led through the woods toward home and safety.

Her shoulders relaxed as she flew around the first bend in the road. As the road curved again, the headlights of an oncoming vehicle came into view. Jodie frowned. Who would be out here so late? As the vehicle passed her, she suddenly realized. "Animal Control," she whispered, raising her gaze to the rearview mirror. The Animal Control truck was already out of view around the bend.

They'll probably be okay, she thought. Animal Control officers had guns, right? And the Not Deer had been injured when it crashed through the glass door; surely bullets would finish it off. Jodie nodded to herself. Animal Control would take care of the damn thing. That was their job. Her nightmare was over.

And if she saw dozens of eyes shining redly at her from the sides of the road as she drove, that was a problem for another day.

It Knows My Shape

GIO CLAIRVAL

[CASE FILE: 03-221-L / MISSING MINORS / URBAN EXPLORATION]

SUBJECTS:

Jessie "Jax" Ocampo, 13

Leonor "Leo" Santiago, 12

Danielle "Dani" Tran, 11

LAST KNOWN LOCATION:

Depot Hill— Storm Drain Access (Decommissioned 1999)

LAST KNOWN CONTACT:

10/05/2025 @ 20:12 (Mobile Device Ping)

SUMMARY: Three juveniles disappeared after allegedly entering a sealed portion of the city's abandoned rainwater harvesting system. Recovered evidence includes cloud-based video fragments, personal phone logs, and metadata inconsistencies. All three subjects had been reported as runaways 72 hours before disappearance.

[RECOVERED TEXT MESSAGE THREAD – JAX'S PHONE]

FROM: Mom TO: Jax DATE: 10/04/2025 - 17:43 Jessie, where are you? It's been 2 days. Please just let me know you're safe.

FROM: Jax TO: Mom DATE: 10/05/2025 - 02:37 im fine. dont look for me.

FROM: Mom TO: Jax DATE: 10/05/2025 - 02:39 Thank god. Please tell me where you are. I can come get you no questions asked.

FROM: Jax TO: Mom DATE: 10/05/2025 - 02:46 found some friends. we have a place. im not coming back to him.

FROM: Mom TO: Jax DATE: 10/05/2025 - 02:47 What friends? Where are you staying?

FROM: Jax TO: Mom DATE: 10/05/2025 - 03:22 dont worry about it

[FINAL MESSAGE SENT FROM CELL TOWER: Depot Hill Area]

[EVIDENCE LOG: ITEM #11-C]

ITEM: Red backpack (recovered from pawnshop trash bin)

OWNER: Danielle Tran (confirmed by parent identification)

CONTENTS:

- 1 hoodie (child size L)
- 1 plastic water bottle (half empty)
- 1 digital notebook (password protected)
- 1 small plush cat (worn, one eye missing)
- 1 folded paper with handwritten coordinates (matching Depot Hill drain system entrance)
- 3 granola bar wrappers
- 1 small tracking device (deactivated, battery removed)
- Note written on lined paper: "Don't look for me. Let me breathe."

NOTES: Mud samples from backpack bottom match soil composition from Depot Hill area. Unknown substance on straps (lab results pending). Trace amounts of oxidized metal dust consistent with drain system materials.

CHAIN OF CUSTODY: 10/08/2025 - Officer Williams - Collection from scene 10/08/2022 - Evidence Tech Morris - Processing 10/09/2025 - Det. Reynolds - Case review

[TRANSCRIPT – VIDEO FILE: IMG_7392.MOV]

Recovered from cloud backup tied to account: Leonor.Santiago12@ Timestamp: 16:03:18— Location data unavailable

[BEGIN VIDEO]

[CAMERA SHAKY. WIDE SHOT: A dusty pawnshop wedged between a laundromat and a boarded-up barber. Weathered sign reads: CASH 4 GOLD / NO QUESTIONS.]

LEO (behind camera): Ugh, it smells like dead batteries and cat pee.

JAX (off-screen): You smell like cat pee. Come on. We're not gonna find the next viral ghost in a parking lot.

[Camera swings to JAX, 13. Hoodie, one arm in a sling, too much eyeliner for 4PM. She kicks the shop door open.]

DANI (softly): We're not actually buying anything, right?

JAX: Nah. We're *rescuing history*. Big difference.

[INT. PAWNSHOP. Dim. Fluorescent lights buzz overhead. Shelves overflow with VCRs, busted radios, tangled chargers, and a mummified teddy bear in a glass case.]

JAX: Okay, Leo, record *everything*. If we find a cursed Furby, I'm not getting possessed for free. That's going straight to TikTok.

LEO (deadpan): That sentence just gave me scoliosis.

[The girls laugh. DANI lingers behind. Her eyes keep flicking to a back shelf, where a cracked phone lies facedown in a tray labeled "DEAD TECH."]

DANI: Guys…?

[JAX yanks open a drawer. A stack of old camcorders clatters out.]

JAX: What do you think this has? Bad wedding videos? Secret confessions? Demon prom?

LEO: I bet it's just someone crying while making slime. Big mood.

JAX: Only if they're crying blood. That I'd watch. No cap.

DANI (barely audible): This one's still warm.

[Camera pans shakily to her. She holds the cracked phone. The screen lights up, unprompted. Battery: 2%. File open: *VID_001-LostBoy*. The thumbnail shows darkness—and a faint glow of tunnel lights.]

JAX (grinning): *Yes.* Found-footage jackpot.

LEO (quietly): That's the exact tunnel behind Depot Hill. The one they sealed off after the rains.

DANI: They said a kid went missing down there. Two years ago.

JAX: They say a lot of things. Most of it's crap.

[The phone begins to play on its own. AUDIO: Labored breathing. A boy's voice, whispering, "Mom? Dad?" Static crackles. Then silence. Then—*something scraping concrete*.]

JAX: We're going. Tomorrow.

LEO: Are you high? That's literally sus AF.

JAX (smiling without humor): We already ran away. You wanna go back to curfews and therapists?

DANI (muttering to herself): I ran away because my parents installed cameras. In my room. In the bathroom. They put trackers in my clothes. They said it was because they loved me. What kind of love needs to watch you all the time?

LEO: I want to wake up alive. There's a difference.

JAX: You wake up alive every day. It's boring.

[She turns to the camera.]

JAX (cont'd): This is *our* adventure. Nobody's gonna tell our story but us.

LEO: They will if it's an obituary.

JAX: So make it a good one.

DANI: I counted the steps in that video. Eighty-three before it cut out.

[BEAT. The phone battery dies. The pawnshop lights flicker. Behind the girls, a shape in the window—not a reflection, just something watching. It vanishes between frames.]

[END VIDEO FILE]

[PRELIMINARY INTERVIEW: PAWNSHOP OWNER]

DETECTIVE REYNOLDS: Did you see the three girls on Thursday afternoon?

MILTON GREER (OWNER): I got security cameras for that. Don't remember every kid.

DETECTIVE REYNOLDS: The cameras don't work, Mr. Greer. We checked.

MILTON GREER: Huh. Must've broke.

DETECTIVE REYNOLDS: What about the phone? The one the youngest girl found?

MILTON GREER: What phone?

DETECTIVE REYNOLDS: The cracked one. In your "Dead Tech" tray.

MILTON GREER: Don't have a tray like that. Just junk drawers.

DETECTIVE REYNOLDS: We have it on video.

MILTON GREER: Then you got the wrong shop.

[DETECTIVE'S NOTE: Subject's eyes fixed on middle distance during questioning. Pupils non-reactive to light stimulus. Request toxicology screening.]

[TRANSCRIPT – VIDEO FILE: IMG_7401.MOV]

Recovered from cloud backup tied to account: Leonor.Santiago12@
Timestamp: 20:12:07Title: "Descent"

[BEGIN VIDEO]
[CAMERA STABILIZED. NIGHT SHOT: A graffiti-covered concrete culvert behind a chain-link fence. The wind hums like a bottle. Moonlight glints off a rusted metal hatch.]

LEO (V.O., whispering): Depot Hill drain system. Decommissioned in 1999. Allegedly. No one at home noticed we were gone. Again.

[The camera swings to show the three girls in frame. JAX is holding bolt cutters. DANI wears a red backpack, nervously fiddling with the straps.]

JAX: Alright, Operation Sewer Sirens begins now. Leo, get this on film. I want a freeze-frame when I break my ankle.
LEO: Jax, this is stupid even for you. Low-key gonna get us killed.
JAX: That's why you're still filming?
LEO: Someone needs to document the stupidity. For science. And your future Darwin Award.

[She clips the chain. The gate swings open on its own—no creak. Just…an *invitation*.]

DANI (barely audible): It smells like old pennies and wet carpet.
LEO: I'm logging that under "vibes." Confirmed: vibe is bad.
JAX: I'm not scared of some tunnel ghost. I live with worse.
DANI: It's not ghosts I'm worried about.
JAX: What then?
DANI: The things that make ghosts.

[INT. TUNNEL – 5 MINUTES LATER]
[The walls are massive concrete rings, stained with algae. Faint lines of old chalk lead deeper.]

LEO (narrating): No rats. No water. No graffiti except some weird kid writing. Says: "We're only lost if we remember where we were."

JAX (ahead of her): This is fine. This is so fine. We're girlbossing urban spelunking.

LEO: That's not a verb, Jax. And stop saying girlboss. It's cringe.

JAX: Everything's a verb if you're brave enough. And I'm bringing girlboss back, sorry not sorry.

DANI (quietly): Guys…I think this place loops.

JAX: Huh?

DANI: That chalk mark—we passed it already. That same chunk is missing from the wall. Exact same.

LEO (frowning): You sure?

DANI: I count steps when I'm nervous. That was the same *eighty-three*.

JAX: So we went in a circle. Big deal.

DANI: We didn't turn, Jax. We've been walking straight.

JAX: Then it's a straight circle. Whatever. Keep going.

[DEEPER IN – 20 MINUTES LATER]

[Breathing is heavier now. The footage fuzzes briefly—audio warbles like a tape being chewed.]

JAX: Wait…did you hear that?

LEO: Sounded like…me?

[A faint whisper ahead: "Leo… Leo… Leo." Too breathy. Slight delay, as if someone were trying to *remember* the right voice.]

DANI: It's saying your name. Just like before.

LEO: There was no before.

DANI: There was. I remember. Don't you?

JAX (unsettled): Okay. Fun's over. We mark our way back.

[She pulls out a Sharpie, draws a star on the wall. Camera follows as they keep walking—then snaps back to the same star ten seconds later. Same drips. Same angle.]

DANI (shaking): We didn't turn around. I swear we didn't.

LEO: I'm stopping the video. Something's wrong with the file—

[Cut off by loud *metallic clang* echoing through the tunnel.]

JAX: That wasn't us.
DANI: It's how it starts. Every time.
LEO: What do you mean "every time"?
DANI: I don't know. I just…remember this happening before.

[END VIDEO FILE]

[CAMERA GLITCH – FILE CONTINUES WITH DATE/ TIME GARBLED]

[Footage resumes abruptly. All three girls are standing still, facing the wall. Their heads twitch slightly, like buffering video. The camera lies sideways on the tunnel floor.]

[INT. TUNNEL – CAMERA 2: LEO – STATIC INTERFERENCE / AUDIO STABILIZED]

DANI (looking at her phone): Okay, this is messed up. My timer's been running for 784 hours.

LEO: That's—wait. That's over a month.

JAX: No way. We haven't even been down here a full day.

DANI: Then why does it say it's Tuesday…*next month?*

LEO (scrolling through her gallery): Hold on. I didn't take these. (pause) Look at this. Am I…taller in this one?

JAX (flatly): You *are* taller. Look at your arms. Look at mine. (beat) My sleeves don't fit anymore.

LEO: How are our phones still working?

DANI (low): They shouldn't be. No signal. No charge. Nothing should be working. *We* shouldn't be working.

[SILENCE. THEN A LOW, UNEXPLAINED DIGITAL HUM.]

[LEO picks up her camera. The date stamp reads: 02/17/2025]

LEO (confused): That's…that's two years ago. And why's it…not the same as yours?

JAX: It's glitching. The tunnels are messing with the signal. (struggling with her words) I'm not…I'm not staying here.

[END VIDEO FILE]

[RECOVERED PERSONAL VIDEO DIARY FILES]

[FILE: LEO_PHONE/VID_7412.MOV]

LEO: Okay. So…update. Jessie's gone. She was right in front of us. Then we blinked. Now it's just me and Dani. And…when I move… there's two shadows now. Me and something else.
I don't remember what my mom looks like. Or my room. I thought filming everything would help, but the videos keep changing. In one of them, I'm standing behind the camera. That doesn't make sense, right? Right?
I film everything because I'm scared I'll disappear. That no one will notice. My parents fight about my brother all the time. Miguel this, Miguel that. Like I'm not even there.
But what if I'm not? What if I was never there?

[Behind her, a shape leans around the tunnel curve. Looks like Leo—but…*not quite right*. The footage distorts when the shape moves, creating tracking errors across the frame.]

LEO (cont'd): I asked Dani if I seemed real to her. She said I flicker sometimes, like a bad connection. Am I remembering this correctly? Or am I making it up as I go?

[FILE CORRUPTION DETECTED: 00:03:17-00:04:52 UNRECOVERABLE]

[FILE: DANI_PHONE/VID_0590.MOV]

DANI: My name is… is… It's not working. My brain won't line up. I know letters. But not mine. Leo says I had a cat. But I only remember its tail.

I count when I'm scared. One, two, three…If I can count to one hundred, I'm okay. If I can't…

[She pauses, looking over her shoulder]

DANI: I see it sometimes. Lurking in the corners. That's what I'm calling it now. The Lurkin. Because it's always watching from the edges. Never coming close until you forget to look for it. It's giving major creeper vibes.

[She turns the phone toward the tunnel. Distant static flickers across the far wall. Something moves like a puppet underwater. Jerky. Slow. Like it's still learning how to walk.]

DANI (softly): It's not chasing. It's *watching*. Waiting until it knows all the steps. I wrote a note when I left. "Don't look for me. Let me breathe." But did I write it? Or did I read it somewhere?
The numbers aren't working anymore. They keep changing when I'm not looking. Like the steps. Like the tunnel.

[FILE: JAX_PHONE/VID_9999.MOV]

JAX: You're gonna think I'm crazy. You're gonna say I'm just another messed-up kid who ran away. But I didn't run from home. I ran from forgetting. And now it's here. In this place. It's *wearing* my memory like a jacket.
My stepdad tried to take my phone. Said there were "things I shouldn't see." So I broke his nose. He called me an animal. Whatever. I'm just built different, I guess.
But at least animals know what they are.

[She lifts the phone and shows a wall. Someone—or something— has scratched her name into it. Over and over. Hundreds of times. Each one shakier than the last.]

JAX: It wants to be me. And maybe…maybe that's easier.

[Beat. Her eyes flick sideways. Then she starts repeating herself.]

JAX: You're gonna think I'm crazy. You're gonna say—
You're gonna think—You're gonna say I'm—
You're gonna—

[GLITCH. END OF FILE.]

[TRANSCRIPT – VIDEO FILE: UNKNOWN_SOURCE.MOV]

Recovered from: {DATA CORRUPTED}
Timestamp: {INVALID DATE FORMAT}

[BEGIN VIDEO]
[INT. TUNNEL - CIRCULAR CHAMBER. Ankle-deep water. Two girls stand center, facing the camera. No one appears to be holding it.]

[The girls' expressions are blank. Empty.]

LEO (voice distant): I don't remember anything before the tunnel.
DANI: I don't want to remember.

[VIDEO ENDS WITH 4 SECONDS OF DIGITAL NOISE]

[TRANSCRIPT – AUDIO FILE: RECOVERED FROM DRAINAGE MAINTENANCE RADIO]

CITY WORKER #1: Base, this is Team 4. We're at the Depot Hill access point. No sign of forced entry.
BASE: Copy that. Any sign of the missing juveniles?
CITY WORKER #1: Negative. Gate's locked up tight. Chain's intact.
CITY WORKER #2 (background): Hey, Pete, you hearing that?
CITY WORKER #1: Stand by, Base.

[Sound of movement, radio static]

CITY WORKER #1: Base, are there any active speakers or PA systems in these tunnels?

BASE: Negative, Team 4. Those systems were decommissioned in '99.

CITY WORKER #2 (closer to radio): There's voices coming from inside. Kids' voices.

[Sound of chain being cut]

CITY WORKER #1: We're going in to investigate.

BASE: Negative, Team 4. Wait for police backup. ETA ten minutes.

[Sound of gate opening]

CITY WORKER #2: Hello? Kids? We're here to help!

[Loud metallic clang]

CITY WORKER #1: What the hell was—

[Transmission ends]

[CLOSING POLICE MEMO – HANDWRITTEN ADDENDUM]

Phones still ping weekly.

Tunnel no longer exists. No blueprints. No access. Just grass.
City has approved construction of playground over former tunnel access.

Request to seal case DENIED.

[OFFICIAL CITY MEMORANDUM – INTERNAL USE ONLY]

FROM: Mayor's Office
TO: Public Works Department
DATE: 12/07/1999

SUBJECT: Depot Hill Drainage System Decommissioning

Following the November flooding incident and subsequent discovery in Tunnel Section 17-B, immediate closure of the entire Depot Hill drainage network is MANDATORY. All access points must be sealed by December 31, 1999.

> The following measures are to be implemented:
> 1. Permanent concrete sealing of all known entrances
> 2. Removal of Depot Hill system from all public maps and records
> 3. Construction of replacement drainage infrastructure via the Westlake project

NOTE: This memorandum references Incident Report #DR-1999-11-23, which remains classified. Media inquiries should be directed to the standard statement regarding "infrastructure modernization" with NO MENTION of the Tunnel 17-B discovery.

All personnel involved in the decommissioning are required to sign updated confidentiality agreements. Violations will result in immediate termination and possible legal action.

By order of Mayor Thompson
[STAMPED: ARCHIVED – DO NOT REPRODUCE]

[TRANSCRIPT – VIDEO FILE: UNKNOWN_SOURCE.MOV]

Recovered from: {DATA CORRUPTED}

Timestamp: {INVALID DATE FORMAT}

[BEGIN VIDEO]

[The camera pans around the chamber. Writing covers the walls:]

1. [First writing]"I dare you to take me."

> *(Then below it, in smaller handwriting:)*
> "Please give me back."

2. [Second writing]
   "If I forget who I am, check the footage."
   (Then beneath it:)
   "What's footage?"
3. [Third writing], barely scratched into the wall with a nail or key,
   almost illegible:
   "I had a name once."
   (Then:)
   "It sounded safe."
4. [New writing], found only after enhancement of final video frame:
   "We'll leave the door open for you."

[EXCERPT FROM "IT KNOWS MY SHAPE," A SHORT STORY BY LEONOR SANTIAGO]

Published in the *Salt Thicket Review*, June 2036

[…] I used to call it the Lurkin, back when I thought it was just something hiding in the dark. But that wasn't the truth.

It doesn't hide. It *becomes*. It studies you, absorbs you, mimics you, until you're not sure which version of yourself is real. It knows the shape of you, the outline of your every thought. And it wears that shape better than you ever did.

The Lurkin speaks in a voice that sounds like your own, but slowed down and glitchy. Familiar enough to trick your brain, but off in a way that makes your skin crawl. There's this weird flutter underneath, like an ancient VHS tape somebody found in their grandparents' basement. When it talks, the words come in layers: one ahead, one behind, like some cursed TikTok audio effect. And when it laughs—if that thing even laughs—you feel it in your teeth first. The vibration hits your jaw before your ears catch up.

And in those dead-silent spaces between words, you can hear other voices…trapped inside it. Calling your name. Using your mom's voice. Using your own.

"I'm not becoming like you," says Jessica, trying to sound brave, but I can literally see her hands shaking.

"You already have."

If Daniela were here, she'd low-key break down. But she's gone.

My vision goes all pixelated. Every sound turns to static with these super faint whispers underneath that I can barely make out. When everything stops glitching, the last of my friends are just…gone. Only their backpacks are still on the floor. The Lurkin stands right in my face, its features rapidly cycling through different kids' faces like some nightmare filter.

"Your turn now."

"What are you?" I cry, not even trying to hide how scared I am.

"I remember when they sealed this place," it says with *my voice*. "After the flood. After the first child went missing. They thought they were protecting you. But they were protecting me. I wasn't always like this. I was someone once. With a name. With a face. But the tunnel…the tunnel needed company.

"Children run to me. Not from me. And I take their sadness and give them peace. I take their memories first. Then their names. Then their faces. Until there's nothing left but the tunnel. And me.

"More will come. They always do."

I spin around and run.

The tunnel stretches out forever, walls wet with moisture that definitely wasn't there before. My footsteps echo in the weirdest way— sometimes ahead of me, sometimes behind. I can hear it following, not with footsteps, but with a sound like static crawling across concrete.

I don't look back. Those who look back don't make it out—that's what the writing on the wall said. Some part of me knows this, though I don't remember reading it.

I'm breathing like I just ran a marathon. The tunnel shouldn't be this long. We'd only walked for what felt like minutes before reaching the chamber, but now I run and run, the exit nowhere in sight. The flashlight on my phone keeps flickering, throwing shadows everywhere. My battery is freaking out: 17%… 16%… 9%… 53%?

What the hell?

Through a bend in the tunnel, I spot it: a pale circle of light. The exit. Morning came while we were underground.

Behind me, the static gets louder. I sprint the final stretch. My shoulder slams into the concrete wall, pain shooting through my arm. I stumble, find my footing, and keep running.

The light grows brighter. The air feels different—fresher, warmer. I burst through the exit, tumbling onto damp grass as sunlight hits my face so bright it's almost physical. I roll onto my back, gasping, eyes squeezed shut against the sudden brightness.

When I finally open my eyes, the sun is high in the sky. My phone says it's 11:23 a.m. We entered the tunnel at 8:30 p.m. the previous night.

I sit up, wincing, and stare back at the tunnel entrance. Nothing follows me out. The opening is just a dark semicircle against the hillside, ordinary and silent.

My hand drifts to my pocket, finding a wad of crumpled bills—the money we'd pooled together from our respective "running away" funds. Jax had insisted I keep it, saying I was the only one responsible enough not to blow it on "energy drinks and bad decisions".

I count it: sixty-seven dollars and thirty-five cents. Enough for a meal, maybe a bus ticket.

I walk until I find a diner, bells jingling as I push open the door. The waitress barely looks at me as I slide into a booth.

"Coffee, please," I say when she approaches. "And a breakfast special."

She nods, pouring coffee that smells too strong, too bitter. "Yes, ma'am."

I side-eye her hard. Like, *Ma'am? Are you blind? I'm twelve, the hell?*

When the food arrives—pancakes, eggs, bacon—I stare at it, suddenly aware that I'm not hungry. My stomach feels full, like after Thanksgiving dinner. Stuffed, almost uncomfortably so.

"You okay, honey?" the waitress asks, pausing at my table.

"Fine," I mutter. "Just need the bathroom."

The diner's restroom is small, with fluorescent lights that buzz and flicker like they're about to die. I turn on the faucet, let cold water run over my wrists the way my mom taught me when I was feeling faint.

When I pick up my coffee and finally look up at the mirror, the cup I'm holding crashes to the floor.

My reflection is…wrong. My short blond bob is gone, replaced by long curls that tumble past my shoulders. Dark brown, like Jessica's. And my eyes—they're not mine anymore. They're large and black, like a foal's. Like Daniela's.

I raise a trembling hand to my face. The reflection does the same. I touch my hair; it feels like mine, but it can't be.

Something moves behind my eyes—behind my reflection's eyes. A flicker of someone else looking out. Two someones.

And I understand then.

We're only lost if we remember where we were.

And I'm starting to forget.

Den Mother

REY REVELLI

"Well, if it isn't Snow White."

Mrs. Bartolozzi looked up from the squirrel eating out of her hand to see a tall, dark-haired man walking over from the neighboring driveway. A blonde woman climbed out of the SUV behind him and opened the rear passenger door to remove a car seat.

"You must be the new neighbors. Welcome to Foxtail Chase," Mrs. Bartolozzi said, extending a hand.

The young man—he couldn't have been more than thirty, thirty-five at a push—fixed it with lapis eyes and paused before shaking it.

"Ryan," he said, and smiled. "That's my wife, Michelle, and our daughter, Jane." He looked over his shoulder.

"Sofie Bartolozzi," Mrs. Bartolozzi said, and smiled back. It would be nice to have someone in the Smith's old place again, provided they minded the woods.

"Do you feed all the animals?" Ryan asked. He looked around, taking in the numerous bird feeders and peanut-laden plates stationed around the front yard and porch. His jaw tightened almost imperceptibly.

Mrs. Bartolozzi took note.

"Only the squirrels and the birds," she said. "And the chipmunks after winter." As it should be. Just as old Mr. Smith once taught her. *Fatten the prey animals, and life will be easy—for them, for you, for the others.* It had never been a bother to her. She loved animals.

"Ever been bitten or gotten fleas?" Ryan forced a laugh as he swept his eyes over Mrs. Bartolozzi and her tidy Dutch Colonial.

"Oh, you'd be surprised how far a little respect goes."

Ryan stiffened.

"Between humans and wildlife," Mrs. Bartolozzi added. Seventy-three years may have dulled her vision, but she was fairly certain she saw the young man true.

She hoped she was wrong.

"Ryan, you have the keys," Michelle called. She stood on their front step with her hands on her hips, the screen door propped against Jane's car seat.

"Nice meeting you," Ryan said, and jogged back to his family.

"Likewise," said Mrs. Bartolozzi.

He didn't hear.

The sun rose within a languorous fog the next morning, its light barely piercing the clouds. Sitting on the second-story deck that led off of her kitchen, Mrs. Bartolozzi took another sip of coffee and eyed the tangle of woods that met her backyard.

It was quiet this morning.

Those unfamiliar with the woods might think nothing of it, but Mrs. Bartolozzi knew better. Pulling her reading glasses down from her silvery hair, she opened a surveillance app on her phone and checked her cameras. It wasn't fear that drove her to monitor the woods, for she had nothing to be afraid of. Rather, it was curiosity. Playing by the rules all but guaranteed she would never encounter Them; she'd made her peace with that, but she was still human, and to be human was to wonder.

Unsurprisingly, the cameras showed her nothing. Not the nothing of absence, but a nothing with presence; a nothing that had thoughts and left deep depressions where it crouched. She knew the heft of that stillness. The same stillness had greeted her and her late wife when they had moved here in the seventies, back when only three homes had dotted the rural street. The woods were just as cautious then, breath held as they took careful measure of the newcomers.

Things would return to normal soon. Once the new blood acclimated.

The timer on Mrs. Bartolozzi's phone sounded, and she went inside. The kitchen smelled of apples and cinnamon, nutmeg and lemon, vanilla and the molasses depth of dark brown sugar. Her mouth watered. Sliding her hands into tartan-patterned mitts, she opened the oven door. Thin slices of apple crowned the crust of the golden-brown pie, arranged to mimic the folds and petals of a rose. She set it on the counter to cool. A gift bag sat beside it.

The chill of the October morning was already evaporating by the time Mrs. Bartolozzi left her home, those walls of fog yielding at last to sunlight and warmth. Three of the bird feeders would need refilling, she noted, and all the peanut plates. Her visitors, as always, were voracious.

In blue jeans and a floral blouse, Mrs. Bartolozzi crossed the grassy expanse between her house and the neighbors'. The front door of the Cape Cod swung open halfway through her journey, and Ryan, dressed in blue slacks, a white shirt and red tie, made a beeline for the SUV.

"Good morning, neighbor!" Mrs. Bartolozzi called with a chipper wave.

The man looked over his shoulder, waved weakly, and then hurried to his vehicle. He pulled out of the driveway and sped off in what must have been record time for the residents of Foxtail Chase.

Undeterred, Mrs. Bartolozzi continued toward the house. Climbing the brick steps, she re-situated the pie and the gift bag in her arms, then rapped her knuckles against the storm door's glass. Light filtered through the drapes of a nearby window. Perhaps Michelle was still home. Within moments, a loud click came from the front door, and it swung inward.

"Can I help you?" Michelle had pulled her long blonde hair into a sizable topknot, and she wore a black tee over grey sweatpants.

"I'm Sofie Bartolozzi. We're neighbors," she said, smiling. "It's Michelle, right?"

"Oh, of course," Michelle said, softening as she opened the screen door. "Ryan mentioned you. It's nice to meet you."

Mrs. Bartolozzi extended her hand, and upon taking it, Michelle noticed the gift bag and foil-wrapped parcel. "Oh, you didn't have to—"

"Of course I didn't, but I wanted to," Mrs. Bartolozzi said, handing her the bag. "And this," she held out the pie, "is an old family recipe. I hope you like apple."

"Thank you, really, thi-this is so nice of you. I'd invite you in for coffee, but we won't have furniture until next week."

"When you get settled, then, that would be lovely," said Mrs. Bartolozzi in her easy way. "And if you need anything at all in the meantime—and I mean anything—don't be a stranger."

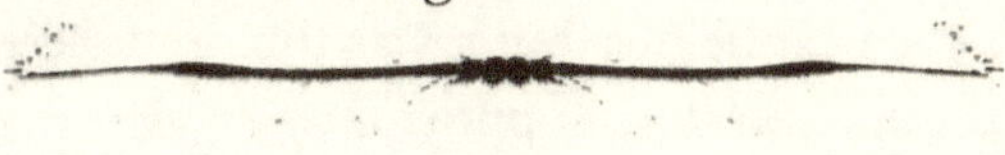

A calm found Mrs. Bartolozzi on her deck that evening. After those first two interactions with Ryan, her hopes for the neighbors' compliance had begun to wane, but Michelle, it seemed, might be another story. The young woman seemed genuinely kind, which always made the induction easier. If Michelle would feed the animals out of the goodness of her heart, then there might be no need for a frank—and frankly absurd—conversation. At least, not for now.

She lifted a glass of chilled Moscato to her lips. The ice cubes floating within clinked as she set it back on the wrought-iron table, but all else was silent. The woods were still studious, still obsessive.

"You and me both," said Mrs. Bartolozzi as she opened her e-reader, eager for a tale from Flewelling or Kingfisher.

Distantly, a door slid open, followed by footsteps. The sound carried over from her right, from the neighbor's deck. Unlike hers, theirs was at ground level, and she saw Ryan the way a gargoyle might see congregants coming and going from church. Near the edge of the deck, he knelt, set something down, and then quickly made his retreat. Mrs. Bartolozzi sat up straight and craned her neck to get a better look.

It was a plate, and something squat and triangular sat upon it, something that very much resembled a slice of pie. Was it for the animals? Maybe she'd misjudged him. Cozying back into the cushions of her chair, Mrs. Bartolozzi took another sip of wine, kicked up her feet, and savored the hope that was growing within her.

With a snip, Mrs. Bartolozzi cut the head clean off.

The faded bloom fell and joined its siblings in a rustle of petals. By dead-heading the mums, the plants could take what energy they would have spent preserving their blossoms and put it to better use, redirecting it toward new growth, toward stronger roots. It was a small thing, but this violence would serve them well.

"The pie was delicious!"

Mrs. Bartolozzi nearly fell into the flowerbed. When she'd quite recovered, she turned. Ryan stood at the property line.

"Didn't mean to scare you," he said. In addition to office attire similar to what he wore yesterday, he sported half a grin. "That birdhouse you gave us is really something, too."

In that moment, little doubt existed in her mind that the man was strange, perhaps even capricious, but it was the friendliest she'd seen him yet. She wasn't about to waste an opportunity.

"Oh, I am just so glad to hear that!" Mrs. Bartolozzi said, beaming. She stood and brushed the clippings from her pants. "I got it at one of the Amish markets down by Lancaster, you know, back when the house first went up for sale—thought it'd brighten up the yard for whoever moved in."

"That was thoughtful of you," he said, and seemed to consider her.

What he might have seen before, she couldn't begin to guess, but now it felt as though maybe he was seeing her true.

"Speaking of being thoughtful," she said, "I saw you leaving food out on the deck yesterday. Did you get any takers?"

Ryan cleared his throat, gave a nervous laugh. "Oh, right, that. Well," he paused, and the grin became an almost-apologetic smile, "I reckon you won't like hearing this."

"Hearing what?"

He looked over his shoulder. Drew a few steps closer.

"Look, I-I don't want you to think I'm an asshole or anything, but, uh," he faltered, chewing his lip, "when I was growing up, my dad loved to feed the local animals. Strays, rabbits, field mice, crows—you name it. By the time I was thirteen, there were more than a hundred feral cats on our property, constantly reproducing, fighting and screaming all through the night, pissing on goddamn everything." Ryan paused for a breath, looking suddenly tired. "We started getting fleas in the house. Bug bombs took care of the first few cases, but uh, with new litters born every few months and my dad continuing to feed them all, it became a problem. An overwhelming problem."

Wind sighed through the trees. Mrs. Bartolozzi found herself itchy with imaginary insects.

"We, uh, we had fleas more often than we didn't, and by the time I was fifteen, well, I'd been infected twice with murine typhus, and once with a tapeworm. That's when I went to stay with my uncle." Ryan took a deep, steadying breath, his grin of mere moments ago the stuff of history. "Ever since, I just—I can't handle being up close and personal with wild animals. I just can't."

"I would imagine not. That must have been incredibly traumatic for you," Mrs. Bartolozzi said after a moment, her voice soft with compassion.

What a nightmare. No wonder he seemed put off by her feeding the animals. After what his father had done? She could hardly blame him. She understood wanting to care for animals, of course, but there were guidelines to follow, precautions to take.

"I'm glad you can appreciate that, Ms. Sofie. I really am, because, uh," Ryan looked over his shoulder again, "I didn't leave that pie out to be generous."

Her brows knitted. "I'm afraid I don't follow."

"It was bait," he said. "I poisoned it."

The air left her lungs. Mrs. Bartolozzi's stomach dropped, and a sour coldness spread through her, sickening, chilling.

Ryan's lips moved, but she couldn't hear him. She didn't blink. Couldn't speak.

He touched her shoulder, and the world came back.

"Ms. Sofie?"

"That—how," she began. "Oh, but-but why? Why would you do such a thing?" If something partook of that poisoned slice, the slice of a pie *she'd* provided…

Ryan sighed, looked away. When he faced her again, his countenance was softer. "I can see you're upset, and I apologize, but I just can't live like that again. I won't."

When Mrs. Bartolozzi said nothing in response, he cleared his throat.

"Well, I need to get to work. Once this is behind us, maybe we can have you over for dinner. A fresh start."

And with that, he left her.

Gently, Mrs. Bartolozzi lowered herself to the grass—the connection with the soil her only tether to the world. A screen door whined open in the distance, then shut. Again it opened, again it slapped shut, and then she heard a car door. A motor growled to life. Tires crunched over cracks in the asphalt. And then silence.

Mrs. Bartolozzi lay awake in bed that night. Each gust of wind against the eaves or metallic ping from the radiator sounded alarm bells in her mind and flooded her body with adrenaline.

Not once in all her decades at Foxtail Chase had something like this happened. She'd heard stories, of course, but there was a striking difference between hearing cautionary tales and witnessing the kind of wanton provocation that inspired them in the first place.

Heart pounding, she latched her pale blue eyes onto the outlines of her windows. If the tales were true, Their procession would be marked by unnatural lights, and so she peered into the endless dark for any glimmer that might announce Their coming.

Eventually, as the hours passed, her heart settled, the adrenaline left her body, and the sky grew pale with the dawn.

She hadn't slept a wink.

The deck no longer felt safe to Mrs. Bartolozzi. Not with Ryan next door, and not with the woods staring at her from across the lawn. Sound had returned to them. Birdsong and the fox calls of evening, the chittering of squirrels and the buzzing of insects. It should've been a relief, a sign that all was well.

It was not.

From the safety of her kitchen table, she gorged on thoughts of the poisoned pie. What had Ryan laced it with? The woods were peaceful now, so it couldn't have been anything fast-acting. Unless none of the creatures partook? She hoped it was so, but the worry gnawing at her stomach wouldn't be dissuaded.

She was pouring herself a second glass of wine when the doorbell rang. Startled, she nearly dropped the bottle. Quickly rinsing the spilled wine from her hands, she grabbed a towel to dry them and made for the front door. Through glass panes, she glimpsed a familiar topknot.

The door creaked open, and Mrs. Bartolozzi immediately scanned the porch for signs of Ryan.

"Is everything okay, Ms. Sofie?" Michelle asked. "You expecting a package?"

Realizing her behavior might have appeared odd to the young woman, Mrs. Bartolozzi reined herself in and forced herself to focus on Michelle.

"Forgive me," she said with a nervous chuckle. "I was distracted. What can I do for you, dear?"

"Well, for starters," she said, and held out a gift bag, "you can enjoy this."

"For me? Oh, how kind of you, but you didn't have to do that!"

Michelle cocked her head. "I know. I wanted to." She smiled.

The gift bag was heavy. Inside, a bottle of white wine sat beside a tin of shortbread cookies.

"You didn't have to, but I'm very glad that you did! Thank you, dear."

They both laughed, and Mrs. Bartolozzi felt a little lighter for the exchange.

"Would you like to join me for a glass?"

"I wish I could, but I'm still on the clock," Michelle said, looking genuinely wistful.

"Oh, do you work from home?"

"Yep. I'm a UX designer, so I can work from virtually anywhere, so long as I have access to my computer." The young woman smiled at that and stood a little straighter.

"A young woman thriving in technology? That is fabulous, dear!"

Why couldn't the husband be this easy to talk with? Or this considerate? Her good mood guttered like a flame with those questions, and the chill she'd been trying to escape reasserted itself.

"I should probably get back to work. It was nice seeing you again," Michelle said. With a wave, she disappeared into the darkening evening.

Did she know about the poison? Mrs. Bartolozzi hoped not. It was unpleasant imagining someone so kind as being capable of something so cruel.

Topping off her existing glass of wine, she plucked a bag of THC gummies from her pantry and retreated to the comfort of her bedroom; if alcohol alone wouldn't settle her nerves, then cannabis, a good book, and an early night would.

The sun rose red in the sky. Bleary. Irritated. Perhaps it, too, was tired. But fatigue wasn't all that weighed upon Mrs. Bartolozzi. As she settled into the white and navy cushions of her favorite deck chair—coffee and e-reader at the ready—a hush fell over her; a silence that, much to her unease, spilled once again from the woods. No birds sang. No squirrels crashed through fallen leaves. Only the wind brought sound or movement, a damp breath that slid over her skin and ruffled her silver hair.

She tried to ignore it. Tried to escape into an e-book, but her focus withered beneath the glare of those woods. An hour passed. An hour of Mrs. Bartolozzi struggling through the same page, reading, rereading, and retaining nothing. The silence dug deep into her ears, millimeter by millimeter, until her breathing sounded too loud against the unnatural quiet. She kept looking toward the woods. What she saw was nothing: watching, biding.

Before she knew it, she was back in the house, grabbing her keys.

Clouds hastened across the sky. Mrs. Bartolozzi could've sworn that something more than wind was driving them.

Killing the ignition, she stepped out of her CUV. The street buzzed with life as people from all across her rural stretch of Pennsylvania flocked to its markets. This was exactly what she needed. Not only an escape from the man next door, but an escape from the oppressive silence.

The door to Rinaldi's Deli shut behind her with a jingle of bells. Mrs. Bartolozzi didn't know what she sought, but instinct had led her this far, and she trusted it to guide her even further. Five minutes later, she walked out of the delicatessen with ten pounds of chicken thighs heavy in her arms.

An idea was growing in her. Sensible or not, she would allow this inspiration to guide her. And so it did, straight to The House of Gourd, a produce stand run by a collective of ex-evangelicals-turned-stoners.

Back home, the cloud-wreathed sun slipped below the horizon, and the already frail evening light dimmed further, coaxing the emerald lawn toward deep indigo. In a large wicker basket swinging from her hands, Mrs. Bartolozzi carried a feast. If the neighbors saw what she was about to do, they'd probably think she was mad. She didn't care.

Crossing her backyard, she stopped just beyond the boundary of the woods, laid out the contents of her basket, and began assembling her offering where no one would see it. It was a cornucopia. A large and bizarre cornucopia. She took the braided horn of bread—straight from her oven—and filled it with raw meat and eggs, fresh berries, sweet corn, oily fish, and a hefty drizzle of Manuka honey. Would it make a difference? She didn't know, but she had to try.

Hurrying back home, she closed her door against autumn and embraced the warmth of her kitchen. She would wait, and she would hope.

Mrs. Bartolozzi woke with a start, the tail end of a scream echoing through her mind. Had she been dreaming? The digital clock read 3:17 a.m. With deep, measured breaths, she tried to calm her galloping pulse.

The world outside her windows was dark. No phantom lights. No emergency lights. Beyond the beating of her heart lay a thick silence. She must have been dreaming.

A hammering struck her front door. Repetitive, frantic. She bolted upright as her doorbell rang twice. Thrice. A fourth time.

"Ms. Sofie!" a voice shrieked, muffled through the walls. It was feminine. Frightened.

The pounding resumed. Mrs. Bartolozzi swung her legs over the edge of the bed. Her heart raced anew as she grabbed a plush robe and switched on the landing's overhead light before carefully descending the stairs.

The doorbell rang again.

Half expecting to find someone bleeding out on her doorstep, Mrs. Bartolozzi wrenched open the door.

It was Michelle, ragged—and, yes, bleeding—beneath the yellow porch light. Snot ran down her chin, and blood trickled from shallow cuts on her arms and face.

Mrs. Bartolozzi gestured to the woman inside.

Something sparkled in Michelle's hair as she passed under the foyer lights, then fell to the tile floor with a *tink*. Was that glass?

"Here, dear," Mrs. Bartolozzi said, and guided Michelle into the kitchen. She pulled out a chair for her and set the electric kettle to boil. "You're safe," Mrs. Bartolozzi assured, hoping it was true. "Tell me what's wrong."

Michelle looked up at her, absolute misery in her eyes.

"It-it's," her breath hitched. "Jane. Jane's gone." Tears burned new trails down her messy face.

Mrs. Bartolozzi's eyes widened.

"Did Ryan take her?" she asked, although she already knew the answer. The storm in her stomach suggested nothing so mundane.

Michelle shook her head. "There was a blue light, and then something broke through the bedroom window. It—oh God, it was—" A sob racked her. "Ryan," she gasped, "Ryan went after her. Into the woods."

Thick clouds obscured the stars in the black velvet sky, and the new moon looked darkly upon the world. All was quiet, save for the dead leaves crunching underfoot as they traversed the yard. Michelle clung so tightly to Mrs. Bartolozzi that it jeopardized her own balance.

As their next-door neighbor, the task of induction was hers alone, but this was beyond her capabilities. This was too much. None of the other neighbors had reviled animals, nor did they ever stoop to poisoning them. The truth was painful to consider, but it would not be denied: the family walked a dangerous path, one that their patriarch had foisted upon them, and one that could not be abandoned without exit wounds.

Flashlight in hand, they approached the treeline. A glance revealed that Mrs. Bartolozzi's offering had been taken, and she sighed with relief.

Stepping into the woods felt like stepping into a foreign land. A land not for them and that would not suffer them. Even the beam of the flashlight felt wrong, an affront to the purposeful dark, but they couldn't continue without it, not with the undergrowth so dense.

A twig cracked beneath her boots and she froze. Had it simply been Ryan lost to the woods, Mrs. Bartolozzi would have stayed home, safe in her bed, doors locked tight, and blankets pulled to her chin. Leave the poisoner to sort out his own problems. But there was a baby at stake. A new mother. Gathering her resolve, she patted Michelle on the hand, and they pushed forward.

Deep into the woods, someone shouted. A man. Both women froze, goose-fleshed and trembling.

"Ryan!" Michelle cried.

She made to run off, but Mrs. Bartolozzi grabbed her by the sleeve. "The last thing Jane needs is you tripping on a log and breaking your neck," she said, her whisper loud within the listening woods.

Michelle looked like she wanted to argue, but gulped instead, nodding her assent.

Darkness pressed against the women and their meager light. The trees appeared ghastly in its glow, too bright and too sharp against the shadowy sea. They were approaching a split poplar when something puzzled Mrs. Bartolozzi.

"Haven't we—" she began, but faltered.

"Haven't we, what?" Michelle whispered back.

She hoped she was wrong. "Haven't we passed this tree twice already?"

Michelle tensed. "That can't be right." She took the flashlight from Mrs. Bartolozzi. "The last one had a huge knot on its right, just at eye-level." Her voice quivered, but it held a distinct firmness as well: a confidence that dared to grow in this barren place.

Michelle walked to the other side of the tree, inspecting it. The light cast heavy shadows. "That's impossible."

"What's impossible?" Mrs. Bartolozzi asked.

There was no answer.

"Michelle?"

Mrs. Bartolozzi stepped forward, and the light went out. An intake of breath.

"Michelle?" she hissed.

No response.

The dark hung about her like a veil. Isolating. Complete. She turned around, careful not to trip on the ivy, and looked back in the direction they'd come from, hoping to see her floodlights unwavering in the distance.

No, no, no.

An abyss stared back.

Without Michelle's warmth beside her, the chill of the night bit into Mrs. Bartolozzi. She couldn't afford to wait for dawn's light, not in this cold, but she also couldn't risk navigating the woods in the dark, either. Falling at her age? A bruise would be the least of her concerns.

And there were other dangers.

With a hand parched from the cold, she reached into her coat pocket and pulled out a canister of bear spray. It offered little relief. How could she possibly use it when she couldn't see to aim it?

You

   are

      permitted.

          Your weapon

             is not.

Mrs. Bartolozzi's breath caught. The words vibrated up through her legs, following the bowl of her pelvis, and climbed her spine before emptying into the basin of her skull. What choice did she have? She dropped the canister.

    Be

      welcome.

Light bloomed behind her, and she turned to face it. A tongue of blue flame burned some twenty feet in the air. Its illumination only made things worse.

Gone was the poplar, the assembly of pine, birch, and oak; likewise, the tangle of undergrowth and the stony Appalachian soil she had come to cherish. A forest of gnarled white trees encircled her. Their trunks were at least seven feet in diameter, their branches plumed with feather-like leaves, each one glistening purple in the light.

The soil was soft beneath her boots, and as she neared the blue flame, it dimmed. Dread threatened her, curled its fingers around her throat. She would be utterly lost if that light went out, but before it could vanish completely, another glowed in the distance.

Then, a gunshot.

Mrs. Bartolozzi dropped to the ground, her knees and back immediately chastising her. A drumming crescendoed in her ears. Her heart.

    Careful.

She froze. The soil felt damp against her palms, and the rich scent filled her nose and mouth. Where had the shot come from? Was Ryan here?

The blue light above her began to wink out.

Shit.

She scrambled back up and hobbled toward the second wisp. It waned.

Gunshot.

Mrs. Bartolozzi took cover behind one of the trees. Its bark was smooth like a crepe myrtle under her dirty hands. To her left was another wisp. Pulse hammering, she set off.

A man cried out in pain.

Or was it fury?

No time to think.

Little mirrors appeared on the ground before her. Droplets and spatter. Mrs. Bartolozzi avoided them as she ran to the next wisp, and then the next.

"Give me my daughter!"

A roar. A plea.

She couldn't afford to look for Ryan; the fires were dying too quickly. And then, before she could reach the next one, it too went out.

A trickle of seconds tortured her in that black infinity. Tears pricked at the corners of her eyes. Sniffles accented her breathing. She had honored the terms, decade upon decade. Was this her due?

A wisp appeared in the distance, farther off than any of the others had been. It hovered low, at ground level, if not lower. Would it offer hope, or treachery? With tears still sliding down her face, she wiped her nose and crept toward the beacon.

The distance stretched as she walked. Everything quieted. No more gunfire. No shouting. The world consisted of only her racing heart and the azure torch ahead.

Within fifty feet of the wisp, something occluded it from the top down. Curious, Mrs. Bartolozzi knelt. From this vantage with her head tilted low, the wisp reappeared in full, confirming her suspicion. The flame burned underground. She took a deep breath, then slowly felt in front of her for the hole or cave mouth that she knew must be present. What she found was something cold and damp. It left her hands sticky. Repulsed, she wiped them on the ground and tried again. And there it was—a lip. An opening.

Given the small size, Mrs. Bartolozzi expected a short drop into the cave below. She was mistaken. Sliding fifteen feet down, she cried out before landing in a jarring sprawl on the subterranean floor. It was warmer down here, the air thick with animal musk. With decay. The miasma coated her tongue, and she tried not to gag.

Marshalling her limbs and her courage, she continued cautiously toward the flame. The buzzing of flies could be heard around the chamber, and small, brittle things snapped loudly underfoot. Their breaking echoed overhead. Mrs. Bartolozzi lifted her eyes toward the dark ceiling and reeled with regret.

Dozens upon dozens of small circles reflected the sapphire light: moving, blinking, leaning closer, peering down. A halo of watchful eyes. Her mind raced, poring over memories, rumors, and warnings from old Mr. Smith, holding each of them against what her senses captured now. The wisps, the descent, the eyes.

The den.

A rustling sound, like fabric on skin, and a metallic click at her left ear.

"I should've fucking known I'd find you here."

Ryan held the pistol aloft. Its barrel ate up Mrs. Bartolozzi's periphery like a black hole.

The audience above them whined.

"Where's my daughter?" he shouted, pushing the gun against the shell of her ear. The barrel was still warm.

This is how it ends, she thought. *In fear. In violence.* Her vision blurred as tears pooled along her eyelids.

A second wisp flared, and the barrel eased from her head as both she and Ryan looked up. A third wisp. The ghost lights formed a crooked triangle overhead. The spectators were fully visible now, their furs gleaming in the light, cinnamon and gray and black under blue, bushy tails and plump pink ones, ears perking, little heads tilting this way and that. All save for one. A small fox.

It did not move; its open eyes saw nothing. Blood colored its muzzle.

With a pang, Mrs. Bartolozzi thought of the poison and looked to Ryan. He swept his gaze from one young scavenger to another. Opossum to fox, fox to raccoon. Sweat sheened his face, laced with the same small cuts and trails of blood as Michelle. He tensed, and his arms shot out, trembling as he took deadly aim. Mrs. Bartolozzi followed his gaze. A warmth ran down her legs.

There was Jane—beautiful, sleeping, seemingly unharmed—swaddled in a blanket of pale green and cradled in arms that bent at every wrong angle.

It was taller than either of them. A bouquet of bones grew between its shoulders, skulls from all manner of creatures encircling and cupping one another like waterlily petals. A blue flame burned in the darkness at their center. The thing stood on hind legs, the sinew and bone of its too-long torso poking through its desiccated hides. It stepped toward them, a tail swaying behind it, serpentine, rotting.

Another step. A tinkling sound. In the weak light of the den, Mrs. Bartolozzi glimpsed numerous baubles hanging from its body—roots woven with bits of vertebrae, teeth braided into fur, old coins and an ornate comb bumping against an exposed section of rib cage as it walked.

The flower-head turned to Ryan.

Trembling from his lips to his knees, he bent and set the gun on the ground, gingerly, as if placing his baby in a crib.

Step by creeping step, it drew nearer. A jingling of bone. A dead god.

Ryan righted himself with effort. His lips curled back, breathing labored, eyes shining. He held out his arms, hands open, and a whimper fled his throat.

The horror leaned toward him and placed Jane safely into his outstretched arms, careful not to touch the man directly. Ryan wept and clutched his daughter to his chest, kissing her tiny forehead again and again. She was safe. After all of this, she might still live.

Might they all?

A chill tingled Mrs. Bartolozzi's spine. She looked away from Jane to find the entity fixated on her—it felt as though she were being studied, appraised by that cold flame within the bones. *Please*, she thought. *Please let me go. I'm so sorry he hurt you. I'm so sorry.*

The entity turned its back to her, and she gasped. Tiny bumps clung to its deteriorating fur, each tipped with a wormlike tail. More young. Approaching the halo of onlookers, it reached up with a slender, gray hand, and when it turned around, the dead kit was nestled in its impossible arms. Once again, it began its procession, a macabre bride walking to her betrothed, a dead fox where flowers should be.

T a k e

c a r e.

It held the deceased out to her. And waited.

Mrs. Bartolozzi's breath caught, and her stomach soured. She went cold all over. But the horror did not withdraw the offering, and so she reached for the small corpse. It placed it in her arms with the tenderness of a mother, cold, hard skin brushing across her forearms. Her flesh crawled.

"Jane!"

Mrs. Bartolozzi looked up from the carcass she held. Jane was spitting up. Her little face was deathly pale against the dark blood spilling over her chin, onto the blanket, onto Ryan's shirt.

A primal sound burst from his lips, and he turned on the entity, terror and rage distorting his features. And then, he coughed. Choked.

Blood exploded from his mouth and nose. It spattered onto the ground, onto Mrs. Bartolozzi's legs. More little mirrors. Gravity and struggle pulled Ryan down onto three of his four limbs. The fourth still clutched Jane to his chest; he coughed again, violently, wetly. A puddle bore his reflection.

With a pitiful sound, his arms twitched, his back shuddered, and he collapsed onto his infant daughter.

Hysteria threatened to seize Mrs. Bartolozzi. Too much suffering. Too much death. Too much.

However, before it could, the entity touched her face and bade her look down. The corpse she held was a corpse no more, but a bundle: a blanket of Luna Moth green that cocooned the sleeping form of Jane. She was safe—unblemished, even. Mrs. Bartolozzi wanted to cry.

> *His cruelty*
> *would have*
> *poisoned her*
> *with time.*
>
> *Go.*
> *Be well.*

Everything went dark, silent, distant—but Jane stayed solid in her arms.

Stars woke overhead and a cold wind blew as the familiar woods of Foxtail Chase unfurled around Mrs. Bartolozzi and her charge.

"Sofie! Ryan!" someone cried in the distance. Michelle.

"We're…we're over here! Jane and I are over here! She's safe!"

Mrs. Bartolozzi cradled Jane as though she were the only good thing in the entire world. Tonight would shape the child's life. Michelle's too. "Cruelty only breeds more cruelty, sweet one," she said, a tear tickling her cheek. "But compassion? Compassion is how we endure."

A beam of light broke the distant dark.

"And should you forget, I'll be right here to remind you."

The Red Ghost

FRANKIE REGALIA

This story is based on real events.

NO WIND BLOWS in the red rock desert. Not even a whisper of a breeze to alleviate the scorching heat. She trudges along, her immeasurable footsteps marking a rhythm. She does not know where she is going and pays little attention to the direction except to steer herself gently from shadow to shadow. Thankfully, the shadows are long here. All around, the steeples of the red rock edifices stand like sentinels. Carved by the absent wind over millennia into striped towers. Oranges, reds, golds, and coppers mark the passing of centuries on the landscape itself.

But she is too tired, too thirsty, too bitter to notice the beauty around her. The wind might not be blowing, but that does not mean the desert is silent. Small creatures dart around in the creosote bushes. Raptors call in the sky. But the loudest sound of all is the constant chattering just behind her. Her companion and her curse. It's not enough that she is doomed to wander this strange land forever, with next to no chance of finding her way home. She must also do so while literally tied to a dead man.

She thought that once he finally succumbed to death, she would be free of him. But his sun-bleached bones serve as a constant reminder of how very wrong she was. His bones clatter and chatter just behind her all the time. She's not sure when she started talking to him, or when he started replying, for that matter. For the most part, she ignores her dead

companion, or at least tries to. He's clattering at her now, but she pays him no heed; there's water nearby. She can smell it.

As she gets closer, the smell grows stronger, and even the distant trickle of a stream can be heard over the cowboy's bones. It has been a week since she last had a drink, which is pushing it, even for her. As she draws closer, she begins to speed up. The skeleton clatters louder in protestation. By the time the creek is in sight, she's running. Her feet pound the ground as she races to the bank of the little stream. She runs into the middle of the stream and immediately puts her head in the water, opening her mouth to allow the liquid to flow directly down her throat. Many blissful minutes pass this way until she finally comes up quenched. She delicately picks her way back out of the creek. The stream used to be a heavily flowing river at one point. The valley in which it rests is wide and deep. Even though it is barely past midday, the shadows of the high walls are already casting long shadows.

She sits on the ground not far from the creek, leaning against the towering wall of the valley. It is still hot, but she doesn't mind the heat. She loves it, deadly though it can be. And nearly just was. She adjusts position, causing another bout of clattering from the cowboy tied to the saddle on her back. Most of the time, she doesn't notice the leather straps that bind her, but they become more uncomfortable when she tries to lie down and rest. She's certain they long ago rubbed off the coarse hair on her belly and no doubt have left scars. She shifts once again in a vain attempt to find a comfortable position before finally lowering her long neck to the ground and falling asleep. Her dreams, as always, are of a different desert on the other side of the world. Where instead of red rock, there are endless dunes, and she marches with a herd of her family, not alone with only the corpse of a cowboy to keep her company. In her dreams, she's not a runaway lost in the desert of Arizona. She's a camel at home in Egypt.

EVEN THOUGH HER heart lies in the Great Sand Sea of the Sahara Desert, the camel was born in the United States, at a military camp in West Texas. In 1855, the US government started a project called the US Camel Corps. They purchased about 25 camels from Egypt and a few other spots in the Mediterranean and brought them back to the American Southwest. These camels were to be used as pack animals and beasts of burden across the arid deserts of Texas and the newly acquired western frontier.

Over the ten years that the US Camel Corps were active, there were several attempts to utilize the camels, which proved to be hardier than mules, oxen, or horses. The project, however, ran into two major problems. The first was the camels themselves. They were not as docile as donkeys or mules, which have been tamed and domesticated over generations. And they were much smarter than the idiotic wild broncos that could be broken in under a week. Camels are as strong-willed as they are strong, and the US Army soon found that it "did not have the skills to manage this foreign asset."

The second problem that arose was the US Civil War, which broke out in 1861. In the first year of the war, the Confederate Army captured Camp Verde, Texas, the base of the Camel Corps operations and the site of their breeding program. They would hold the site until the end of the war in 1865, using the camels mainly to deliver mail between their bases in Texas. But it was here, in Camp Verde under the control of the Confederate Army, that our camel was born. She would garner a name twenty years later, but for now, she has none. Camels don't need names; they know who they are and they know who every other camel is. Names are human things.

The camel spent the first three years of her life by her mother's side, hearing whispered tales of endless dunes and hidden oases somewhere far away. She was one of the few calves born in this strange land. And so she grew tall and strong, fed on the dreams of a place she had never seen. Where they could wander in a line over a landscape over which only they had dominion. She shared the hope of the herd: one day, they would find a way home. All deserts are connected, so it is just a matter of distance. And camels are good at long distances.

But how was the herd to know that in 1865 the Camel Corps project would end with the war, and that the US government was too poor and too arrogant to consider sending the camels back to where they came from? The order came down from Washington to sell the beasts and recover whatever money they could. Over the course of a few terrible months, the herd was torn asunder. Family members, friends, and companions all dwindled away as they were sold to farms, circuses, and zoos across the country. As each individual left the herd, the whisper rippled on the wind, *we'll meet again on the dunes.* The day her mother was dragged away was one that the camel will never forget. She kicked and spat and tried her hardest to get free, to follow her mother. It took six men to restrain her. In the end, all she heard was *we'll meet again on the dunes.*

Only a few days later, a man came for her. She had been despondent and saturnine since the theft of her mother, and she barely even acknowledged the men as they placed the saddle on her back, tightening the leather straps. The man who had bought her was a big man with clean boots, a custom buckskin outfit, and shiny spurs. He was a cattle baron with more money than brains. He had bought a huge ranch out in Wyoming and thousands of cattle, sight unseen. He wanted to play at being a cowboy while the actual cowboys he employed did the hard work. Now he wanted a camel for his ranch, an oddity and just another expensive attraction for his wealthy friends to fawn over while they drank alcohol and fancied themselves pioneers.

He had brought along with him his best bronco buster, a short man with bowed legs and a cruel streak a mile long. Any vaquero in Mexico or California would tell you that the key to taming the wild broncos lies in a gentle hand and building trust. This grubby little man with a permanent dogend in his mouth did not subscribe to that school of thought. He broke them hard and got wild, skittish, unreliable horses in return. But the cattle baron didn't know the difference, or perhaps didn't care.

As soon as the little cowboy came near the camel, she tensed. She could smell his cruelty and his stupidity. When he laid a hand on her long neck, it was as if the future was foretold in one touch. She saw a life of casual brutality and loneliness. This future built up in front of her like a great tidal wave about to drown her. The cowboy climbed onto her back and strapped himself in for the breaking. At that moment, she felt the crashing wave and revolted. The world became a blur of fury, fear, and adrenaline. She bucked, kicked, spat at anything in her way. Wood and bone shattered. Men screamed and ran. Behind her, she could hear the cowboy hollerin' about something, refusing to be bucked off. It took only a few furious moments for the world around her to scatter, leaving a way free. The West Texas desert called to her and she ran.

The camel wakes from her dreams of Egypt and looks around the valley. The usual disappointment washes over her as the dream slides away. She gets to her feet with difficulty, waking the skeleton of the cowboy. He clatters his bones at her and she snorts in return. He tells her the same thing every day. She's going to die out here in this strange desert. She'll never make it back home. Her white bones will be saddled with his forever. She does her best to ignore him and never lets him see how much it hurts.

She takes another long drink from the creek and sets out again. All deserts are connected. It's just a matter of distance. But once again, the days roll past. She doesn't know how long it's been since she ran off with the cowboy strapped to her back, how long since he died from thirst unable to free himself from the saddle, how long she has wandered. She went from the pale dusty deserts of West Texas to New Mexico. There, she found a desert with white dunes, which made her hope, foolishly, that she was getting closer to the deserts of home. But eventually, New Mexico gave way to Arizona and the desert changed again to this place of red rocks, red dust, and towering red steeples. Now she's covered in the dust, becoming part of the monochrome landscape.

The creek disappeared into a red rock crevasse long ago, and she is once again on the brink of dying of thirst. She wonders what would be worse. To live forever in this cycle of near death and recovery, but never make it home. Or to die of thirst in this desert with the skeleton on her back and prove him right. She catches the scent of water once again. Looks like the cycle will continue for another day. She follows her nose not to a creek or stream, but to a small ranch. Idiot cows low in a field, their water troughs full to the brim. The camel gets closer but sees the midday sun reflect off the barbed wire fence. She follows the fence around, desperate to find a way in.

There are a couple of low wooden ranch houses on the other side of the field. A windmill water pump squeaks gently in the breeze between the buildings. Beside it is a barrel full of water. She stares at the silent, still yard. The humans must be inside to escape the heat. She creeps closer, slowly, careful not to disturb the cowboy on her back and send him clattering. She's only a few steps away from the water when a growl breaks the silence. A dog sits chained to the front porch of one of the houses, its eyes on her. She barely has time to react before it starts barking urgently.

She turns and runs, the cowboy clattering louder than ever. She can hear the sound of men's voices as she runs around the ranch house. She glances over her shoulder to see if she's being followed, but all she can see is the permanently grinning cowboy. When she turns back, she finds herself tangled up in rope and fabric. She hears the scream of a human but isn't sure where from. There's something wet and sticky beneath her feet. It takes several furious minutes before she can detangle herself enough to escape. Just as she gets free, she hears the sound of a gun and a clatter from the cowboy. She races off into the desert, leaving unknown carnage behind her.

June 4, 1883. Red Ghost Kills in Eagle Creek!

The Tucson Citizen can exclusively report the brutal and mysterious incidents that occurred on a ranch near Eagle Creek just a few days ago. About midday, George "Stubbie" Martin and Jedidiah "Jed" Smith were drawn out to their cattle pens by a disturbance. Their dog was barking at an unknown figure, which disappeared in a cloud of dust as soon as the men got outside. While the two ranchers went to check the cattle, the beast appeared on the other side of the ranch house and trampled Mrs. Mary Smith, Jed's wife. By the time the two men arrived on the scene, poor Mary was dead. The only signs of her attacker were red hair caught on some nearby bushes and strange tracks in the dirt. Local sheriff's deputies have confirmed with the Tucson Citizen that they are unlike any tracks ever seen before. Locals are calling the murderous beast the Red Ghost due to its ability to appear and disappear on a whim.

June 10th, 1883. Red Ghost Strikes Again!!

When the editors here at the Phoenix Gazette first read the outlandish rumors published by our colleagues at the Tucson Citizen, we thought that the young publication was merely grasping at straws to attract readers. Imagine our surprise when we picked up the exclusive scoop that the beast now called the "Red Ghost" had attacked again. Not 24 hours before, a group of prospectors had made camp about 20 miles from Eagle Creek, the site of the first attack. In order to protect the prospector's claim, we will not give details of their location. Just as the men had settled down to sleep for the evening, they heard a pounding of hooves. Afeared at first that it might be an attack by the nearby Apache tribe, the men gathered their weapons. What came through their camp instead was a single beast, "as red as the devil himself" said one man who refused to give his legal name. The witness, who calls himself Gold Gordy, claims that riding the huge animal was a living skeleton. He also claims that the deceased rider tipped his hat to him before both mount and rider disappeared into the desert. The attack lasted only seconds, but it destroyed much of the camp. One man was able to get a shot off at the invader but missed. Like the incident at Eagle Creek last week, only a few tufts of long red hair were left behind by the beast. We at the Phoenix Gazette will bring you up-to-date details on the next sighting of the Red Ghost.

June 11th, 1883. Red Ghost Derails Wagon Train!!!

Unbelievable though it might seem to other publications, particularly those based in the Phoenix area, the being known as the Red Ghost has made yet another destructive appearance. The mysterious animal, first reported here in the Tucson Citizen, and its skeletal rider attacked a wagon train just as our slower colleagues at the Phoenix Gazette were going to press yesterday. Two freight wagons were knocked over during the attack, injuring several people and creating a fair amount of damaged goods. As a result of this attack, more details have come to light about the Red Ghost. Reports are coming in that the beast itself is nearly 30 feet tall. It is confirmed that the rider appears to be the skeleton of a cowboy. After the Red Ghost and its rider wreaked havoc amongst the wagon train, a man chased the beast into the desert. He claims that it disappeared into thin air before his very eyes. Others claim that this man was drunk and is not to be trusted. Yet another man, who has no connection to the wagon train or any previous victims, came to our offices this morning to report that he had seen the beast kill and eat a grizzly bear not a few days before. This man refused to give his name and could not offer any answers when asked for more details about the location of this incident. The Tucson Citizen remains devoted to discovering the most current information and, more importantly, the truth when it comes to the mysterious Red Ghost!

June 15th, 1883 Reward for Red Ghost!!!!

The US marshall's office has issued a reward for the killing and/or capture of the beast known as the Red Ghost. The marshall, having hand-chosen the Phoenix Gazette to be his official source for this important information due to our reliability and impressive track record, has relayed that the reward for the killing of the beast will be $150. Cowboys, bounty hunters, and the like prepare themselves to pursue the strange creature. These hunters can be seen carrying everything from lassos to silver bullets. Everyone here at the Phoenix Gazette wishes the brave hunters the best of luck and a quick end to the terror of the Red Ghost.

The camel runs. Even at night, she runs. Over the clattering of the skeleton, she can hear the baying of dogs and the shouts of men behind her. Deeper and deeper into the desert she runs. Humans, the one thing she is desperate to avoid, seem to pop up everywhere. She is unsure if she has slept, eaten, or drunk water once in the past few days. All she remembers is the running.

The skeleton is more persistent in his condemnations than usual. That fateful day at the ranch earned him a bullet hole in his skull and he clearly blames her for it. He clatters away even when she finds a rare moment of peace to rest, like now. The bright orange of the setting sun clashes in the sky with the oncoming purple of night. She rests on the bank of a river, dripping wet from having just forded across. Once or twice, she was certain she would be swept away. Now she lies in the shelter of a large boulder, hidden from the view of everything but the eagle flying high above.

She doesn't even allow herself the budding hope that she has lost her pursuers. Sure enough, she hears them approach the other side of the river. The sound of men's voices is a low rumble punctuated by the sharp barks of their dogs. They know she crossed the river but if she barely made it, then their horses certainly won't. They will have to find another place to cross. She's safe for tonight. The skeleton clatters louder than ever, desperate to give their position away, but the rush of the river is too loud. Eventually, the men and their dogs move upstream and night falls completely. The camel stands and looks down the length of the river. If they go up, she must go down.

The pursuit continues; she senses she is being followed. And yet she never quite hears the sounds of men and dogs. She follows the river's track, but somehow the river cuts through deeper and deeper landscapes. Within a few days, she finds herself at the edge of a gorge. The other side is a mile away, and deep at the bottom lie the strong whitewater rapids of the river. A canyon, but men call it the Grand Canyon. She peers down to the depths below, the skeleton peeking over her shoulder. And then she hears them.

Baying, shouting, the pounding of hooves. She turns to see a dust cloud in the distance, making its way towards her. She runs along the edge of the canyon, dimly aware that death awaits her on both sides. The sounds get closer and the raging of the river seems to grow louder. Behind her, the clattering of the dead cowboy is like a thunderstorm in her ears. A loud crack cuts through the cacophony, immediately followed by a clatter from the skeleton. He's been hit again. The leather straps of the saddle rub agonizingly against her sides with each pounding step. They're closer now: she can hear the snorting of the horses and make out the individual voices of the men.

Something whirls through the air and around her neck. It tightens painfully, nearly pulling her backwards off her feet, but she puts on a burst of strength and pushes forward. She feels a great weight drag behind her for a moment before disappearing. The men scream and yell, but the pain around her throat is gone. A couple of the riders behind her pull up along her right side, trying to herd her towards the edge of the canyon. She stares ahead, suddenly aware that she is running out of ground. She has to either charge through the riders on her right or run off the canyon and into the depths below. Her mind feels paralyzed; she can't seem to control her body. The clattering behind her drowns out all other sounds as the edge of the canyon speeds closer.

The crack of a gunshot, and then silence. Time slows. She feels a sudden lightness, as if she's floating up into the sky. The scent of the desert drifts towards her, calling her. She gently turns her body away from the water and the men and the chaos. She aims herself at the heart of the desert and flies away. It's time to go home.

Much later around the fire, the men pass around a bottle and try to recount to one another what exactly happened. Shame about Jimmy, though. He was a good man, but that lasso was not a good idea. Harry tried to shoot the beast, didn't you? But the bullet missed? By a hair's breadth. It must have whizzed past the saddle strap on its side and weakened it, cause I'm sure I saw the leather snap apart. Yeah, that's when the saddle and skeleton went left over the canyon. If I live my whole life and never again hear the sound of them bones rattling against one another, it will be too soon. Boy, as soon as that saddle came off, that beast damn near flew. I thought we had it for sure, but it put on that turn of speed and was gone in the blink of an eye. It was all I could do to keep my horse from running straight off the cliff there. Same here.

Silence descends on the camp as they all replay Jimmy's last moments. Finally, someone asks the question on all their minds: So, we heading up the hunt again tomorrow? No one says anything, but they all know the answer. One or two of them glance towards the desert. The next morning, they pack up and head back to civilization.

She's home. It's not the home she was looking for, but it's a home nonetheless. The sun beats down on the creosote bushes. She savors each crunching mouthful of the plant. An eagle soars up high, looking for something small and furry in the undergrowth. Far off, coyotes howl to one another. The skeletal cowboy will be proved right in the end, she knows. She'll die here in this desert one day. But then again, all deserts are connected. It's a matter of distance. And death is pretty far away.

Apotheosis

DAVID O'MAHONY

THEY BURIED GOD in the stony field south of the village, the one that always stank of half-wild sheep and goats. That's all it was good for: they'd drained it years ago, but no crop had ever taken to the soil.

It was almost done before God even knew it was happening. Ripped by uncaring hands from the mudbrick shrine overlooking the river and the village, cast into an already dug hole and assailed with acrid dirt without a chance to breathe.

"You bastards," God shouted, "you ungrateful shits."

But the men and women working the shovels didn't hear. She had forgotten how to speak to them, and they had forgotten how to listen.

She'd stopped watching, too comfortable in the shrine they'd built for her and with the sacrifices and tears they'd dedicated to her. The offerings had sustained her and helped satiate the thing inside, the thing even she feared. It scratched and pawed now at her as the soil crashed down like winter rain, stinging skin long immune to feeling and pouring into the small gap left in her lips.

A man with ash-grey stubble and a flannel shirt loomed overhead, eyes hard but looking away as he spooned dirt onto her face.

"I knew your mother and father," God said. "I knew your kin all the way back to the first days. They brought you to me for a blessing. They wouldn't have dared touch me. You're a disgrace."

But all he did was slowly cast dirt down onto her. When had they stopped fearing?

"You ungrateful fucks."

She'd been in the ground before. With guilty, tear-stained faces, they'd dug her up from the bog, her skin turned mahogany and pulled tight over her bones, her belly still swollen with the thing she'd taken within her to save them a hundred generations before.

They were delicate little things, the humans. All peach skin and gangly limbs. They couldn't have known what they'd dug up. Even bog maidens like God avoided it unless they had no choice. To the humans, it was just a queer lump as big as a hog and hard as bone, riddled with fissures and gnarled in long-dead tree roots. To God it was the devil, stirred to half-life by being freed from the bogland that had kept it drunk on sleep during her long watch.

Even after the ones who'd pulled it out by hand had seen the skin slide off their bones like gloves, even after they'd begun to rot from their crotches with black, burning fungus that made them fester and vomit blood, they didn't truly understand what they'd done.

God watched them die in droves from her peat-walled hall. Weak little things, she thought. Cursory things. Only when the blue-eyed child had landed on her threshold begging for help, starving, skin already sloughing off her bones, did God take pity. She was supposed to care for everything in the bogland, wasn't she? And weren't these mawkish humans part of the bog now as well? The toads and lizards loved her for keeping them fed, so why not these creatures? So she'd absorbed the thing even as the agony nearly tore her apart. But when she turned to the humans, all twilight skin and furnaces for eyes, instead of letting her sit at their hearths, they tipped her into the filthy peat like a memory they couldn't stand to face. The blue-eyed ones jeered at her, leered at her. She spat black oaths at them even as the copper blades cut her throat, cut her hands, spilled her essence into the ground she'd come from.

Some spells don't need to be cast. They just need to be *felt*.

Patting dirt over her face as the fire went out of her eyes, they'd consigned her to shadowy memory. But the bog didn't forget. Nourished and shielded by it, it cultivated her wrath until it grew like weeds inside their sod-walled huts, until it followed their every breath and footstep, twisting their dreams until every night brought howling horrors of being disembowelled by dark creatures birthed from men and women alike.

They'd remembered her then. They'd believed in curses then. She'd taught them to fear the things they didn't understand, to respect a land that could turn on them at will. When had they stopped? When had they started to put their faith in electric light and thrashing steel?

I've protected you for too long, God thought. *Got too good at it. When was the last time you truly hungered for anything?*

She'd been too busy tracing the worms as they tilled beneath the fields next to the bog, too focused on catching the taste in the air that meant trouble was on the way.

When the mountains were drenched, she would call on the ants and insects to raise little dams of earth and stone along the riverbanks and direct the floods away. When the summer sun burned too hard, she summoned the dregs of the spring rains held deep in the earth to keep the crops from dying. When the rivers were empty of fish, she called them from the lakes upstream.

It was a simple arrangement, ultimately. They gave her devotion, she held her curses at bay and the thing inside her in check. It was the least they could do after thrusting her so rudely into the dirt, wasn't it?

But the fear… Where had it gone? Was that why they were doing it again? Ashes to ashes, dust to dust…bog to bog?

A burning stab shook her all the way down her belly to her pelvis. Skin stretching and tearing, God's body convulsed uncontrollably. There was no trace of the peat here, no sweet smell of decay, nothing to perfume the air as it burned and glowed like metal slowly fading after being tested in the furnace. The ground was dull and dormant.

They're trying to take my power.

Fools. I'm not the one to worry about.

Her belly strained to hold the thing inside as it woke, the first cracks forming on her surface.

The creatures were coming. Burrowing and scratching, their picking and pulling rang through the sod and along her face and neck. The first of the worms and millipedes danced over her skin, teasing and prying for weakness until they began to dig their way in while the thing inside her turned and rolled.

"The time, the time, the time," it whispered, the words crawling up God's spine and into her eyes like earwigs. "The time, the time, the time," it chanted while it screeched and ate its way through her desiccated guts as they spilled out their last meal, thousand-year-old barley porridge cracking and slipping its way into the thing's uncaring white teeth.

If her mouth still worked, she would have screamed. Instead, the furnace returned to her eyes. A thumping, scraping, scratching rattled through her until she saw the stars wheeling overhead in their slow, apathetic watch while the moon shone hatefully. Above her, all fingers and thumbs now as he scraped the dirt away, was the man in the flannel shirt. "I'm sorry," he said, refusing to look her in the eye. "We shouldn't have done this."

"But you did," God said, as his head turned every which way but facing her.

"I'll get you out in a sec," he wheezed, struggling to pry up sods he'd slapped into shape only hours before. "Dear God, please forgive me. I need your help."

"Get fucked," God said.

"My neighbour Art, he keeps letting his cattle run across my property. He knows I'm broke. He wants to buy the place but I don't want to sell. Please, just give me one good harvest to clear Dad's debts. Yeah? Please?"

A searing tear through her innards sent a shower of sparks from her eyes, and the man clasped his hands as he saw the sign he wanted to see. "Thank you, thank you," he muttered, scooping the stones and mud from beneath her head and lifting her tenderly.

"That's all you think of me?" God thundered into the void between them. "Money and cattle? You think digging me up is enough to make me your plaything?" *The bastard didn't even bring me an offering, not even one single tear. Such weak creatures.*

He had raised her upright when the pain bit hard.

Strength fading, the sparks from her flaming eyes dying away to nothing, she could do nothing as the thing inside her ripped dried flesh and gasped for air. Shrieks echoed off the hillside as a long claw slashed blindly, tearing through the flannel man's leg and pinning him to the dirt. The thing chittered and growled as it pushed its way out of God's belly, breaking skin and bone alike.

Oozing and sticky, the black, bone-hard thing rolled into God's grave, one long leg holding it in place as the rest of it slumped out and shook, disoriented and quivering in the chill of the night.

Whimpering and slate-faced as his blood fed the soil, the man pleaded. "Dear God, I'm begging you, please help me."

"Why?"

Ripping their way out of the earth came hordes of lice and worms and insects that hadn't seen the surface in a thousand years, all rushing to the chittering, bloody thing in the hole. Clambering over it, they fought and tore at each other. Toads bit the heads off tiny, squirming lizards even as the lizards bit the tongues off the toads, chewing them free as both battled to the death. The worms and maggots that had burrowed deep down into God slithered out of her ruined belly as they scrabbled to join the frenzy. The thing howled and clacked, its surface breaking open in a hundred places as it took the battling insects into itself and pulsed, growing ever so slowly but ever so steadily.

In the hole, the strewn remains of the destroyed little creatures glowed and stirred back to life. They merged and reformed until they became whole again, more than the sum of their parts: dark pink worm-ends flailing like tentacles, insect mandibles swelling to the size of cat heads, lizard legs becoming slashing talons as severed toad heads croaked blasphemies.

"Children…" the thing hissed, a rasping voice more bestial than human. And the children of the bog, the abominations that should never have existed, stomped and scratched and slithered.

They had found their own god.

"Please, God. *Help me*," the man sobbed. God had almost forgotten he was there. The light was growing dim.

As he whimpered, the thing that had birthed itself from her swelled to the size of a bull, then lashed out with another claw, then another, then another until deftly, like the gentlest butcher, it sliced through the man's face and down through his clothes and torso.

He was still alive when it peeled away his skin. For a moment, anyway.

"You should have left me in the ground," God said as the man cried the cry of a soul tearing in twain.

Dimly, she thought she should have done better at containing the bog demon.

Or maybe she shouldn't have tried at all. Why hadn't she just let nature take its course?

With a hollow cry, still holding the man's flesh like a tapestry, the thing cracked out of the remains of its shell. It emerged with twilight skin and furnace eyes, endless ripples of taut muscle sweating with black peat water. Its head broke clear of the nascent body, a jagged exposed skull with teeth like curved daggers, its arms, legs, and neck strewn with patches of bog grass, moss, and soft white flowers already tinged with blood.

With an arm bristling with thorns and slashing claws, it slung the man's skin over its back, where it grew brown and taut as if it had spent a lifetime beneath the bog's surface.

Grunting in feeling more than words, in the language of the earth itself, it signalled to its army of abominations and they surged forward to tear away what remained of the man's blood and muscle, tripping over each other to crack his bones for marrow and pry his eyes away to get at his sweet, sweet brain.

As the creatures gorged and grew, the ground split open with a wet rushing noise as clusters of red dogwood, purple loosestrife, and soft heather forced their way up and reached for the moon, spilling in every direction until they were thicket deep. Rivulets of black water swelled and gushed out of holes in the dirt as the blasphemies dug down in every direction. Already, judging by the smell and the hiss in the air, the dry, stony ground was turning into the bog it had once been.

"Back to nature… Maybe it's not such a bad thing," God said.

With the last morsels of the flannel man broken up and scavenged, the hulking bog demon shuffled forward until it towered over God, seated half upright in the dirt as the peat water filled in around her, washing her clean.

"*Mother*," the bog demon whispered, the great teeth pressing themselves against her forehead softly like a kiss as it caressed her face with the utmost gentleness. "*Rest.*"

She waited for the huge jaws to crush down on her, but the bog demon only laid a vast hand on her scalp, whispering in benediction before loping off. Its children poured into the hole, pulling and shovelling the new bogland around her until she leaned gently back and they buried her, dancing in rings around the grave to bid her farewell.

Across the pasture, rapidly filling with the old plants and bursting forth with the old creatures that had lived there in the millennia before men, the bog demon howled and screeched. It charged toward the village, the spirit of vengeance for its mother at war with the homes huddling in slumber beneath uncaring stars and heedless electric lights.

"One last curse," God said, as death headed for the motley concrete bungalows and the last of the blasphemous creatures gently patted the peat around her face. "You get what you deserve."

MIMIC:
Breeding Season

Я.R. HARROW

Nisa Villa Michals stared out of the cabin window as she washed the dishes. The night was gloomy, the rain pattering lazily against the windowpane. The woods hugged close to the property line in a dark blur wreathed by the ethereally eddying fog of the Blue Ridge's late summer months. It was hot—*too hot*, but thank God the humidity had cooled with the rise of the full moon, which emerged between the clouds roiling high over the A-frame cabin's tall, peaked roof.

Nisa and Harold had been at it again. She sighed heavily as she considered their endless argument. He wanted kids. She didn't.

Childless and pushing forty, he was getting desperate. Nisa was about to turn thirty, but she had already miscarried one baby and didn't think she could survive losing another. And Harold, well, he didn't get it.

As Nisa toweled off the last plate and placed it to dry on the rack, their border collie, Warner, whined and scratched at the sliding glass door to go outside. She glanced his way, the dog pleading with his huge chocolate eyes as he whimpered his argument for being let out past curfew. Harold, a lifelong resident of the Appalachian Mountains, was particularly adamant about not going out at night, especially this time of year. Harold had lots of rules, like not whistling in the dark, not answering anyone who calls your name in the woods, and tons of similar wackadoo, hillbilly silliness.

Warner barked when Nisa turned back to the sink. A soft, low *ruff* of a persistent potty monster, *"I'll piss on the floor if you don't let me out, lady,"* menacing spunk. The Hubby would lose his shit if she let him out.

Nisa sighed.

But what harm could it do?

Like, what was the worst that could happen?

Warner getting skunked?

Nisa eyed the loft, glancing up to the soft glow of the lamp by Harold's desk, where she knew he sat at his computer, headphones on, blasting *The Best of Garth Brooks* while writing his latest novel. Warner barked more insistently, pawing pathetically at the door.

"Alright, alright," Nisa surrendered as she whipped the towel deftly over her shoulder. She eyed the loft again as she carefully drew back the curtain, unlocked the door, and made way for the jingle-jangle of the rapidly departing pup.

"Just hurry the hell up," she breathed while sliding the door shut. She shook her head, amused by the dog's antics and her hubby's superstitions. Harold wasn't the one who'd have to clean up the mess if Warner couldn't hold it until morning.

Her mood immediately soured as she thought of Harold and the terrible, ear-piercing shouting match that had made him storm off without touching the roast she'd worked so hard on that day. Her heart went heavy. Why didn't he get it? How was it so hard for him to understand?

Nisa's familiar fantasy of leaving her husband, driving off in her '97 Ford Ranger, and escaping the endless pressure of *giving him a kid* that both Harold and his wicked witch of a mother hammered into her was interrupted by a scratch at the door. She glanced back. There was Warner: propped up on his hind legs, muddy paws pressed against the glass, staring in at her.

Odd. He never did that.

Worse, now Nisa had to clean the glass, or there would be another argument to be had with Harold, as he once again laid down the law about the rules of the mountains. All the windows, save the one by the sink, needed to be curtained and shuttered at night, which stopped her from sipping wine on the deck on muggy evenings. She used to do that all the time when she lived in New York, relaxing on a lawn chair up on the roof of her apartment building.

But Harold didn't like that.

Not one bit.

He and his whole podunk mountain family insisted it was dangerous to be outside at night, but they never elaborated *why*, like they were too scared to even talk about what scared them.

Fucking superstitious redneck weirdo, she griped. With an annoyed shake of her head, she slid open the door to let Warner back inside.

Harold Earl Michals, Jr. glanced toward the wrought-iron spiral staircase that led down to the cabin's lower level and hesitantly pushed back his Bose headphones as *Friends in Low Places* warbled comfortingly on. He could have sworn he'd heard something.

Had Nisa called for him?

Had Warner barked?

Probably the dog, Harold mused with a tired smirk. The dang mutt was getting ornery. Yawning, he leaned back in his desk chair as he stretched. He checked his dad's old watch, the one passed down from father to son since before the Michals family had made their bones hawking moonshine. Besides advising him, it was a quarter past ten at night, the watch told him, in the slow tick of hands, that it was about time for Harold to man up and apologize.

He'd fucked up, and he knew it.

Nisa was a good woman. Hot, smart, kind, and everything else that made her thoroughly out of his league, even for a *New York Times* best-selling author. Before what felt like the blurred passing of six years, Harold had first met her at a book signing at the Barnes & Noble situated on the Rochester Institute of Technology's Henrietta campus, where she had been a photography major in her junior year.

They had coffee after his lecture.

They had connected.

She'd given him her number, and after a week of hemming and hawing with his awkward lack of self-confidence, he'd called her. Everything else was history.

But now Mama was on his case.

Big time.

He was the only one of Mama's six children who hadn't given her grandbabies yet. She was pushing him *hard*, and Mama always got what she wanted.

Harold sighed dryly, chuckling mirthlessly while making sure to save his latest manuscript. He loved Nisa *so much*. He didn't want to lose her.

But Mama wouldn't let up.

The family owned the land.

And Mama ruled the family.

So Mama's word was law.

His whole family was still stuck in the early 1900s in their sentimentalities. He was the first of the Michals clan to graduate from college and was already considered the black sheep for his troubles. If he didn't give Mama what she wanted, it'd get worse. A lot worse.

He rubbed his eyes, breathing out a groan. Never had he pictured his adult life without kids. He wanted a son and maybe even another daughter, just a child of his own so much, but he and Nisa had tried before… Harold knew how much losing their daughter had hurt his wife, but now they could afford the best medical care. He could make sure it didn't happen again.

Mama told him he was in heat, his breeding years, and that the miscarriage wasn't his fault. It was all Nisa, Mama had insisted, implying that maybe her lady parts were defective. She was already pushing for him to find a more suitable mate—one that'd see the Michals' bloodline continued as Mama saw fit.

But he just couldn't.

He loved Nisa with all his heart.

He heard her, the slap of bare feet against the cold iron steps circling up to their loft bedroom. Harold paused in his musing, eyes wide as Nisa came padding up the steps. His mouth immediately went dry when he saw *every inch of her.* She was so perfect.

And so very, very naked.

As she slowly stalked forward, she smiled at him in the seductively carefree way she used to in the early days of their relationship. Her hips swayed as she held out her hand in invitation, drawing him eagerly to their bed with an impish giggle.

This was unexpected.

Nice.

But unexpected.

With a soft growl, she playfully pushed him onto the bed, not saying a word. She stared hungrily down at him, her dark hazel eyes sparkling as the mattress springs of the log bed creaked under their weight.

"Babe, I'm sorry," Harold mumbled as Nisa fumbled with his belt. She demurely shushed him with a long-nailed finger pressed to her lips, then batted her eyelids as she yanked him out of his jeans. Moments later, his awkward attempt at an apology became lost in a wild, sensual haze of pleasure as she went to work, bringing his hands to her soft, warm breasts, her hips swaying and bouncing, her back arching with orgasmic desire.

She was an animal. Biting, scratching, kissing, her mouth tasting coppery as she incessantly pressed her lips against his. Strangely alluring, the taste sparked a shocking hunger within him as she pinned him down against the sheets. Taking it all and deliriously demanding more. Clawing his chest, panting and groaning as they lost themselves in the hot, mind-wheeling blur of passion. Harold lost track of time, his head in a fog as his world melted into just her, her lips, her tongue, her breasts, her body…

That moment was all his. When it was over and she slid off of him with a satisfied smile, he was wearier than he could ever remember being. Drowsy, it felt like he gasped for breath through an icy fog as the warmth of her flesh melted away when she wordlessly vanished back downstairs. Wheezing, shivering, and staring up at the peak of the roof, he wondered how he'd ever gotten so lucky.

Harold woke up with a violent start, blinking into an unsettling, lonely stillness. He rubbed his eyes and checked the alarm clock in confusion. *"What the fuck,"* he breathed as he sat up, trying to push through the waking fog to figure out why Nisa was absent from the bed at two in the morning.

Ah, the fight…

He remembered, then stilled as he saw his reflection in the dresser mirror. A topographical map of scratches covered his chest. He slowly blinked, sucking in an icy breath as recollection seeped in.

She'd come upstairs.

They'd had the best sex in years.

So, why was he alone? Why wasn't she in bed next to him, snoring on the pillow and cuddling her favorite penguin plushie? Confused, he yawned and eyed the stairs, the rest of the cabin eerily quiet. Maybe Nisa had taken a shower and fallen asleep on the sofa? She did that sometimes…

Smiling, Harold stretched and pulled on his discarded jeans from the floor. He then snatched up the cup of leftover coffee in the *Best Hubby Ever* novelty mug from his desk before making his way down the stairs, suddenly shivering. Why was the air so cold? He felt like he needed to light a fire to get rid of the sudden chill.

He froze halfway down, staring at the sliding glass door. The curtains had been drawn back. Sitting outside on the deck was Warner, his tail thrashing. Staring inside. Visibly upset, ears back and whimpering.

It was dark as he scanned the rest of the room, his shaggy dog barking wildly and pawing at the glass door. A cold sweat chilled his spine with thrills of icy claws, while a familiar, curvy, shadowy form slipped into view. It was just Nisa. She padded barefoot from the kitchen to smile up at Harold, a steaming cup of coffee in hand. "Morning, darling," she cooed.

It looked like Nisa, sounded like Nisa, and yet...

Harold's teeth were set on edge.

Something was off, something familiar-but-not in her warm, dark gaze.

Warner slammed his dirty paws against the muddied glass, growling and barking, snapping Harold out of a daze. Slowly, his gaze lowered. Blood chilled in his veins. The mug slipped from his fingers, smashing on the iron steps.

Nisa, *his* Nisa, lay splayed out and broken on the hardwood floor, haloed by a moonlit pool of congealing blood. Her throat had been ripped out, a huge chunk of flesh bitten away, revealing a shockingly white flash of bone amid the gory red ruin while she stared lifelessly up at him with pale, accusing eyes.

Harold stood still as stone, terrified to so much as breathe while his heart violently thundered in his chest and his hands, which hung numbly at his sides, trembled. The gut-wrenching horror was terrifyingly surreal, like a waking nightmare beyond his comprehension. He forced his gaze back up to Not-Nisa, to the little wet flecks of red glistening on her full, pouty lips and pearly white, sharp-looking teeth—and to the hand she stroked over her swollen belly.

"Would you mind helping clean up before breakfast?"

On the Nature of Grief and Ghouls

HANNAH BIRSS

Rose stared down at the quickly cooling husk of her mother as it lay in the hospital bed. For once, Patricia's body was relaxed, not twisted in the excruciating agony Rose had become accustomed to seeing her mother in as the stage four lung cancer had slowly consumed both her body and her breath. Her mother's lips were parted as if with a sigh, giving Rose a glimpse of nicotine-stained teeth. Rose kept expecting—kept *hoping,* really—for one more sharp inhale of breath through those yellowed teeth, but the air was silent and still; her mother was dead and would remain so.

Around her, nurses with faces like carved cliff walls trickled out from the room with the faded and peeling yellow painted walls and stained drop ceiling. They had done their duty and were now relieved of it with their patient's passing, continuing on their way without so much as a second glance at the end of Rose's world. She was left alone to say her goodbyes, but she found herself unable to think or even feel; she felt as hollow as the body in the bed, a jack-o'-lantern without even a smile to grace its sagging flesh.

The space Patricia and her long months of illness had previously taken was now empty following her departure. Rose knew that space would not remain empty for long; only a matter of time would pass before an ocean of grief crashed into her, filling up the spot where her last remaining family member had lived for the past thirty-four years.

She stood numbly by the hospital bed, hands limp at her sides. The room was quiet for the first time since Patricia had been admitted. Gone were the gentle whirr of the machinery monitoring her vital signs, the wet coughs and the drip of the IV that had all kept Rose company in the long nights spent in a cramped and uncomfortable chair. She stared down at her mother's pale face and wondered what she was supposed to do.

Rose's eyes traveled down Patricia's neck, following the canyons of withered, puckered skin left over from her mother's rapid weight loss as she had been devoured from within. They landed on the pendant of a necklace that lay nestled in the hollow of her mother's throat. It was small—a gold cross inlaid with a single diamond, a gift from Rose's father before he'd died twenty years ago. It was the only thing of true monetary value her mother had ever owned, and her most beloved and sentimental item. As far back as Rose's memory went, she'd never seen her mom without it.

Now Patricia was dead, and Rose supposed the cross was hers; so strange that she would think of this inheritance before she had even begun to make arrangements for her mother's burial. Rose reached for the clasp, but when her fingers brushed against her mother's skin, grief arrived. It wasn't the ocean she had expected, with vicious, white-capped tidal waves that threatened to drag her under. It felt more like the weight of the sky falling on her, pushing her down into the floor and crushing the air from her lungs. Her knees started to buckle, and the sour contents of her stomach rushed up her throat to flood her mouth.

Rose yanked her hand back and flung aside the flimsy hospital privacy curtain, staggering to the small bathroom her mother had shared with the adjacent patient room. The door barely had time to close behind her before she gripped the stained toilet seat with both hands and vomited explosively into the weathered bowl. She heaved and heaved until nothing was left and long strings of bile dripped from her mouth like spiderwebs.

Rose spat out the last vestiges of vomit and leaned against the cold wall. Her nostrils stung. She grabbed a handful of single-ply toilet paper to clear out her sinuses.

Beyond the door, footsteps entered the room. A rattle of metal and a persistent squeaking wheel sounded as if a mouse were being tortured, and then came a strange grunt. The wheel screamed, and Rose came back into herself.

She stood up and splashed water on her face, taking slow and shuddering breaths. For a moment, she thought about lingering in the bathroom. Its claustrophobic walls provided a strange comfort. She could curl up in here and hide from the responsibilities that awaited her with her mother's passing. Her eyelids grew heavy, tugged down by the gravity of her grief. All she wanted to do was sleep, but her work was just beginning.

However, when she stepped out of the bathroom, Mother was already gone, her presence erased as if she had never been there. The room was empty, the lights off and the bed stripped, the thin white sheets lying in a pile at the bottom of the bed like discarded, forgotten ghosts.

She hadn't gotten to say goodbye. She hadn't even gotten to recover the necklace—the only personal article her mother had been wearing besides the paper-thin hospital gown. She needed to find her mother, find that necklace. Her mind hyper-focused on it: a small, glinting island of gold in the sea of overwhelm.

Steeling herself, she left the dark room and headed toward the nurses' desk. A single nurse sat behind it, staring at the flickering screen of an ancient computer.

"Excuse me," Rose said, her voice hoarse and her raw throat still stinging. "My mother just died."

The nurse looked up at her with indifferent eyes. "My condolences," she replied, the words lacking any real warmth. She raised a sausage-like finger and used its ragged nail to pick at something caught in-between her teeth.

"Thank you. Her body is gone," Rose said. "I went to the bathroom, and when I came out, she was gone. She had some jewelry…" Something in the nurse's eyes changed then: a flickering dismissal.

Rose pressed on, stuttering over her explanation in hopes she did not come off as a greedy relative. "It's the only material thing she really cared about. I just don't want it to get lost. I just want to fetch it and say goodbye. Please."

The nurse's eyes fixed back on her screen. "Morgue's in the basement. Take those elevators down." She jerked her head towards the hallway that led out of what passed for the ICU in their small town.

"Thank you," Rose murmured. The nurse didn't answer; she was too busy peering at the masticated, grey piece of meat she had finally managed to liberate from her teeth.

The elevator moaned as Rose stepped inside, the yellow lights flickering when it descended with a jerk. Remnants of a dark stain on the tile in the corner reminded her of the chalk outline of a murder victim; her eyes kept tracing it, and she couldn't help but shudder.

Trying her best to ignore the stain, she leaned against the wall and closed her eyes for a moment. Still no tears fell, just that impossible weight pushing down on her. The elevator groaned to a halt, jolting her out of her stunned trance as the doors to the basement opened.

It was dark down there, darker than she had expected. As if the basement ran on reduced power, only half of the lights turned on, pockets of shadow dotting the underground route. Even those only gave off a dim and strangely wavering light, like a trapped candle flame.

A family of four stood off to the side of the elevator, half-concealed by a pool of shadow. Their faces were drawn, and a box of personal effects was tucked under the father's arm. They all looked tired, eyes rimmed with red and their skin splotchy. Rose gave them a slow nod as she slipped past them to exchange places. The elevator doors clanked shut, and with another wheezy groan, the car began moving again, leaving Rose alone in the basement.

She followed the arrows of the faded directional signs, her head throbbing. The winding hallways leading down to the morgue stretched on for a surprisingly long time, and Rose's sense of direction quickly evaporated.

Eventually, she came to a large hallway that ended with two steel doors. Before the doors to the morgue stood an old security guard. He might have been tall and handsome once, but age had stolen away his height and his beauty. Now he was hunched and crooked, an old grim reaper guarding the gates of death. His bleary eyes flicked over her as she approached.

"My mother," she said by way of introduction, her flat voice echoing through the twisting expanse of the basement, "was just brought here. I wanted to get a personal effect from her body."

"Sorry, can't let you in," the old man rasped.

"You didn't even ask for her name. Or my name. I just want to say goodbye and grab her necklace. Why can't I come in?"

"You said she just came in. No one's been this way for hours. I mean, no one new and deceased. T'aint been a fresh one since supper."

She stared at him, uncomprehending. "Her body was *literally* just picked up. I couldn't have caught the elevator more than a few minutes after her. Can I just check?"

"Nope," he said stoically. "S'not how it works. I'm going to have to ask you to move along."

Rose gaped.

"So move along," he said after another moment.

A bubble of hysteria rose from her stomach into her throat. She was tempted to knock the frail old man over and enter the morgue anyway to find her mother. As if he could read her thoughts, his eyes hardened and his fingers inched toward the baton hanging from his waist. Rose turned and began making her way back, a choking sound halfway between a laugh and a sob forcing its way through her chapped lips.

She'd gone a few turns when she collapsed against a wall, sliding down to sit on the floor. Tears began to flow freely as heaving sobs immobilized her. She sat for several minutes, hiccupping, snot and tears streaming down her face that she tried wiping with her old sweatshirt sleeve.

Awash in her misery, Rose was still there when something echoed from down the hall. A familiar squeaking wheel—her mother's gurney? Rose climbed up the wall, swaying for a moment while she composed herself. The squeaking wheel was coming toward her. She must have just beaten the porter bearing her mother's body to the morgue.

She followed the sound, eager to intercept her mother's body, but found that now it strangely moved *away* from her. She cocked her head and listened. It was definitely growing fainter.

Determined to catch up, she followed it. Perhaps the porter was taking a long and roundabout way to the morgue; Rose herself did something similar at the frozen food factory where she worked, all in order to get a small break from the monotony of the production line. The ferrying of a body would be a relatively easy task to draw out if another, more unpleasant one waited.

As she turned down another hallway, she saw a tall figure in faded blue scrubs at the end. He—based on the wide shoulders and closely shaven head—was pushing a full gurney through a push door simply labeled "laundry". The squeaky wheel screamed in protest as it was forced up and over the metal floor divider. The porter ducked his head through the door, and it swung closed behind him.

Rose quietly approached, cautiously curious. She pressed her ear against the door. Somewhere inside, she could hear a dryer whirring. They were far—too far now from the morgue for the porter to have taken a detour. In her gut, she knew this was something more nefarious than simple directional confusion. She eased the door open and slid in silently after him.

It was even darker inside the large room. Full racks of both clean and dirty laundry created an interior maze, and at the moment, only a single wall-mounted light was on, casting most of the room into shadow. Something inside her, some deep and long-buried instinct, told her to stay hidden. She flattened herself against the wall behind a rack of neatly folded laundry waiting to be delivered upstairs, its soft laundry detergent smell offering her a grounding anchor as she watched from the safety of the shadows.

The porter stood across from her on the other side of the gurney. Rose took in the small shrouded figure lying on it, and silent tears began trickling down her face, her stomach twisting.

Something unsettled her about the porter's face. He had high cheekbones, sharp like paper-cuts, and a thick, muscled jaw that seemed heavy and uneven, as if taken from a giant and then sewn beneath his thin face. He had bulbous eyes, their whites spider-webbed with small red veins, which stared down at Patricia as if he were a child on Christmas morning and she the present.

The porter carefully and deliberately folded down the sheet covering Patricia's body. He leaned over her slackened face, his bony shoulders hunched so his shoulder blades jutted like mountain peaks from the strange landscape of his body. His wide mouth puckered as he lowered himself. Bile coated the inside of Rose's mouth, her tongue turning sour as his lips brushed against Patricia's. His head dipped further, mouth opened wide, so wide that when he fixed it over Patricia's face, it obscured the lower half as if she were wearing a surgical mask.

Then, a strange sucking noise and an audible cracking.

The porter jerked his head back up, cold, congealed blood dripping down the front of his pale blue scrubs to spatter the ground below.

Underneath him, Patricia's jaw hung open, broken and crooked against her neck. Her mouth gaped wide as if she were screaming, the insides of her cheeks coloured with a strange, tarry black. As the porter stood up, his long, lanky limbs seemed to grow even longer, stretching out. His throat distended as he began to swallow the bloody tendrils of muscle that now hung between his thin lips. A sickening, wet slurping filled the room as the porter threw his head back and hungrily swallowed down the flesh like a snake devouring a rat. Rose gagged, trying to muffle the sounds of her near-silent retching.

Using his own, the porter had ripped out and eaten her mother's tongue.

Rose clapped a hand over her mouth as she began to shake. The porter straightened up further, cracking his joints as his body continued to stretch and contort into a creature of horrifying proportions. His face grew more gaunt, the skin acquiring a strange grey hue with an almost luminescent sheen as if coated by a thin veneer of grease.

She gagged audibly this time, and his head shot up. She froze. His eyes, gleaming with a strange fever, scanned around the dark basement. She ducked her head behind the stacks of towels and held her breath.

After a long moment, the gurney began to rattle noisily again, the metal groaning. It was not moving away, however, and after a long, slow exhale, Rose raised her head and peered out between the shelving units.

The thing that used to be the porter had clambered up onto the gurney. It hunched like a gargoyle over her mother's torso, practically sitting on Patricia's face. Long fingers tipped with sharp, slate-colored claws had ripped open both the hospital gown and the flesh underneath, creating a gaping wound that crossed Patricia's torso like a gruesome smile. It rooted around in the body cavity for a moment, then yanked out the organ it had been seeking and held it up triumphantly.

Mother's liver sat cradled in its hands like a prize. As it opened its mouth in anticipation, a long string of thick, black drool dripped down to stain her mother's skin. The porter bit down into the jiggling flesh with relish, its eyes rolling back in its skull from the sheer pleasure of it all.

Rose's limbs jerked uncontrollably, rattling the shelf beside her. She ducked down again. No noise came from the ghoulish thing; after a moment, she raised her head, expecting to see her mother's body continuing to be hollowed out bit by bloody bit.

Instead, the porter's face hovered inches from her own, staring back at her over the top of the stacks of clean towels. It tilted its head and grinned at her with sharp, blood-stained teeth, its long, pale hand reaching up to wrap around one of the shelving unit's struts.

"Hello," it said.

Without thinking, Rose threw herself against the rack. It toppled over, crashing onto the porter and knocking over the gurney. Her mother's body bounced off the concrete and rolled, leaving a thick red smear across the floor.

Rose ran, throwing herself through the swinging door and bursting out into the hallway. She scrambled down it and made a left turn, sliding on the tile. Behind her came the sounds of a long-legged pursuit and sharp teeth clacking together in excitement from the frenzy of the hunt. She hoped to run into someone in her retreat—a guard, a visitor, a staff member, somebody, *anybody*—but it was the middle of the night and the basement may as well have been abandoned. She turned a corner and skidded into a door. Frantic, she tried the handle.

Locked.

Dead end.

Behind her, the porter slowed as it turned the corner. Its scrubs had hitched up, unable to cover its elongated, spider-like limbs as it stalked deliberately towards her. Rose pressed her back into the door, the doorknob digging painfully into the small of her back.

"What are you?" she wept. "Why were you eating my mother?"

The porter bared serrated teeth at her in the facsimile of a smile. "Think of me like a vulture; I was eating the meat because I was hungry."

It moved toward her again, a slow step that brimmed with anticipation. A sob rose up through Rose's throat.

"That wasn't meat; that was my mother. You were eating my *mother*." Rose's voice pitched high with hysteria. The thing laughed in response.

"We're all meat in the end," it said. "I'm just cleaning up."

"You can't eat them, you can't eat me," she said, looking around frantically. "People will see on the cameras."

"What cameras?" It chuckled with a noise like the sound of ripping skin. "You don't think people know that I'm here? That I haven't worked here for years?" It tapped a long finger against the employee badge still hanging from an old lanyard around its neck. "You don't think they let me take my fill—that I, that *we*, haven't been here since the very beginning?"

"I'll…I'll tell people. I'm going to tell people what you did to my mother."

"No one cares," the porter hissed, its voice taking on a mocking tone. "No one cares about one old woman whose body is missing. No one cares about her hysterical hillbilly daughter with stained sweatpants and ratty hair. No one will believe you, and everyone here will just deny it.

"People don't care. They don't care about your mother, or the fact that she's dead. They don't care about *you*, either—they're all just floating in their own little bubbles. You're on your own down here. You're. All. On. Your. Own."

Rose slid to the floor as the porter came closer while it spoke. She whimpered as it extended an oversized, gore-smeared hand towards her. Rose couldn't help flinching.

"You can't eat me. You just can't." Her voice was thin and small, watered-down gruel sliding back down her throat. "Please. Please don't eat me."

The porter *giggled*. "Who said anything about eating? I don't like warm flesh. The best seasoning for the meat is a long life filled with suffering, and if I'm not mistaken, you still have so much more suffering to go." It opened its hand, and from its closed fist, it dangled her mother's chain in front of her face. The diamond in the centre of the cross glinted in the dark like a winking eye.

"I just wanted to bring you this," the porter purred, "and escort you to the elevator. No one likes to eat in front of an audience."

It released the bloody cross, the necklace falling to the floor with a small *tink*. Rose stared at it, then back at the thing pretending to be a porter.

"Go on," it said cajolingly. "Take it. That's all you have left."

Rose squatted down and reached out, hooking the slick, bloody metal with her fingertips and pulling it towards her. She held it tightly, the cross digging into her palm to leave a mark, a bright red brand she didn't think would ever fade.

"It's time for you to leave," the porter said. "Follow me."

Rose stood up cautiously, her rubbery limbs threatening to give out. The porter, blood and drool dripping down its chin to puddle beneath its sneakered feet, waited for her to catch her breath. It fiddled with the hospital badge on the lanyard as it turned and walked away, beckoning her to follow it.

The elevator was a single hallway away, tucked out of sight. Rose had run right past it in her panic. The porter reached out and pressed the button, smiling back at her over its shoulder. "If you'll excuse me, I'm on my lunch break."

Bile rushed up her throat again, and she began to dry heave. It just continued to smile as the door dinged and the elevator opened like a hungry mouth. Rose kept expecting the ghoul to yank her back, to snap her neck or sink those long, strange teeth like a shark into the fleshiest part of her shoulder. Instead, it made a dramatic bow, a flourish of its long arm ushering her inside the small box of the elevator.

Rose took a step in, then turned around and pressed the button firmly. Her entire body trembled and jerked as if she were a marionette on strings. Her mother's cross burned a hole in her palm, the heat of it spreading through her.

"It was nice meeting you," the porter said with a lick of its lips. "I hope to see you again soon."

The coffin doors shut and the elevator began to move. Only then, as she ascended back towards the safety of the floors above, did Rose scream.

The Sounds of the Forest

GAAST

[In 1999, 21-year-old Joe March, K22XNJ, made his last transmission. Although his family fought to keep him listed as a missing person, he was declared legally dead two years ago. Now a silent key, Joe's legacy remains in the final transmissions he made from his remote shack, where he spent what would become his final spring.

[Nobody knew these transmissions existed until, six months ago, a ham from the area discovered she had recordings of them. At the time, she was recording the local repeater's input, storing months of transmissions onto audio cassettes. Julie Daniels, W22XLA, was much closer to the repeater than Joe and was likely the only person who had received his calls. And she had never listened to these recordings until recently.

[What follows are transcripts of Joe March's final transmissions, made over a five-day period in May 1999.]

[Transmission One was recorded at
approximately 9:43 pm on May 9, 1999.]

"This is Joe, K22XNJ, monitoring.

"Well, I don't know if I'm reaching the repeater from here. This is my first time setting up a mobile rig anywhere near this far out. I'm out in my dad's old hunting nest, camping for a few nights while the temperature's still good. Bit of a windy drive out here, but it was beautiful. I'll have to tell you guys about this neck of the woods sometime.

"Hope you don't mind I'm taking up the repeater. I doubt I'm coming in anyway. But if anyone can hear, please enjoy my ramblings, heh.

"So, again, this is Joe, K22XNJ. Had everything packed up last night. Spent a quiet morning with my parents before I set out a few hours for the park. And from the park, it was just another mile or two hiking out to the old shack. Not a shack, really, more just a wood structure, dirt and paint slathered onto it, a couple walls set into the earth. Dad and I, we used to come out here and I'd try to help him spot deer. We were bad at it, though. Never did manage to shoot anything. Mom would have gone nuts if we had, anyway.

"A few years ago, just before I left for college, I realized that this old nest, left unused for almost a decade, would be a perfect camping spot. Easy to get to, secluded, surrounded by nature. A little safe haven in the summer. Dad let me go alone, even though Mom didn't want me to. 'He's an adult,' he said; 'he can handle himself.'

"I'm glad he believed in me, because the couple days I spent out here were probably what got me through that first semester away.

"Well, the hike was a little different this time, as I had more to carry. There's a path here, but you can only see it if you know what to look for, and only me and my family know what to look for. It's obvious when you've seen it for the first time. Dad was proud of that trick. It's the first thing I can remember him teaching me. Anyway, I picked the right time to come out here. Were any of you outside today? Maybe you're outside right now, enjoying this perfect evening.

"Got the tent set up a bit before sunrise and had myself a soup. Tried to be as quiet as possible so I could just hear the nature around me. Feel bad for mucking it up with my voice, but everything has already gone stone quiet. The rest of the world is sleeping. So should I.

"Next time I come out here, I should bring some paint and replacement lumber. Thing's cut and bruised all over. K22XNJ, saying goodnight."

[Transmission Two was recorded at approximately 7:33 am on May 10, 1999.]

"Good morning, anyone who can hear me. It's Joe, K22XNJ.

"Wasn't planning on making calls more than nightly, but last night was…last night was a strange one.

"Was setting up to go to bed not too long after I said goodbye. I wanted to enjoy the silence and the stars a bit more. So I sat on my chair, looking up through the trees. Felt peaceful for a while. Cleared my head.

"When suddenly there was sound behind me. I know, nothing unusual, it's the woods, but until then, I wasn't even hearing crickets. Then, all of a sudden, directly behind my head, I heard *everything*. Crickets, wind, leaves, twigs snapping, something howling, something hooting. As though an hour of sounds were frozen in time, then played in rapid succession, broadcast from one specific direction.

"I jumped, then quickly hid in the nest, looking back for whatever was causing the racket. Nothing was back there. Or if something was, I couldn't see it in the dark. All I could make out was empty forest.

"Once I calmed down, I was, well, I was confused. What had just happened? Had a bunch of fake noise been broadcast at me? Had I just—hallucinated? Had my brain filled the silence with its own invention?

"Deciding I was too tired, I finished preparing to sleep, crawled into my tent, and extinguished my last light. Things get like that when you're exhausted and alone.

"And then I noticed the sound was moving.

"All of the sound. Wind, crickets, howling. Moving in a bunch, from south to east. *To stay behind my head.*

"It wasn't easy to sleep after that, if you can believe it.

"I didn't experiment and see what would happen if I moved around again. I tried, I tried so hard to just enjoy the sounds of nature. That's why I'm out here. For the nature. The peace. The serenity.

"And maybe—maybe that's just the acoustics here. Maybe, I don't know. Maybe the sound, the sound carries on the wind, and the wind slithers through the trees really weirdly, and it happened to line up with the way I moved.

"Right? Could it be like that? Do any of you guys know?

"This is Joe, K22XNJ."

[Transmission Three was recorded at approximately 9:00 p.m. on May 10, 1999.]

"Joe again, K22XNJ.

"I keep listening to every frequency I know we use around here, but I haven't heard anything. Might have caught the end of a CW transmission, but I can't say for sure.

"I just used the sunlight to read. I never get the chance to read anymore. For myself, I mean. School keeps me busy, and when I'm home, well, I get a little too swept up in video games, to be honest. When I was younger, I used to read adventure novels, and then I found those gamebooks—do you know the British ones, *Fighting Fantasy*? Those things gave me the kind of experience I guessed my brother had with his friends every Friday night. I remember him gathering up snacks and books and things and going to play *Dungeons & Dragons*. He invited me a couple of times, but I was too shy. So he gave me one of his *Fighting Fantasy* books—*Deathtrap Dungeon*, I think—and I was hooked.

"I grew out of those, I think, but I love reading books where the protagonist is a fish out of water, trying to figure out their way in a whole new world. I always compete with them, too. I try to think of what I would have done differently and see if the book gives me enough information to validate my choices over theirs.

"Even if I'm wrong, there's nothing like bringing a sense of adventure, of the mystical, with you to the outdoors.

"I don't think I mentioned it, but I brought enough stuff for me to stay out here for a couple days without having to hope I'll be the first one to kill a deer out here. Provisions, some light furniture, a tent—all stuff I could easily fold up and carry out here. But like I said, I had extra this time. A mobile rig, and this stupid hand-cranked battery I brought for a backup power supply, in case the other one fails on me.

"But yeah, I figure I'm too far out for anyone to hear me. Or to hear anyone. I guess I miscalculated a bit. Still wanna talk out my days.

"So, I'll just say it now. The sound stayed behind me. All day. The silence everywhere around me was deafening, in many ways. And I struggled to keep myself focused on my book, considering the glut of noise blasting against the back of my skull.

"I think it got louder. Noisier. Like there's more happening in the soundscape. Frogs, of all things—I heard frogs in the daytime. And—and breathing. I heard breathing. Loud, humid breathing. But it was from so far away, too. Like it was right in my ear, and yet miles away. I tried to tell myself it's the wind, just a thick breeze carried through to me, but I don't know. I can almost *smell* it.

"I've gotta talk to someone in the sciences at school about this. Maybe they can write their thesis on the bizarre conditions here.

"As for me, though I was freaked out last night and this morning, I can't think of a reason why I should be scared. It's just sounds. Weird ones, sure, that always seem to follow me. But hey, maybe my hearing's shot and I don't know it yet. Maybe that's why I can't hear anyone, haha! Can't listen to what's right in front of me.

"Anyway, this is Joe, K22XNJ. I'm gonna get some sleep."

[Transmission Four was recorded at
approximately 3:31 a.m. on May 11, 1999.]

"There's something out here.

"Sorry, this is K22XNJ. There's something out here, just outside my tent. It's brought the sound with it. It's no longer sitting behind me. Content to gaze from afar. It's pacing, taking the twigs and leaves and hoof-falls and chirps and croaks and breeze and *the breathing*, and it's circling around my tent. It's a loose circle, large enough that I think it's at the foot of the little hill this nest is set into.

"I don't hear *it*. It's not producing noise. I'm not hearing the brush rustle or anything like that. But the normal, natural sounds it's *blaring* at me… It's close. It's so close. Close enough to pounce on me.

"I—I had to call. I have to hope that someone can hear me. Because I don't know if I'm making it out of here tonight.

"This is K22XNJ, calling CQ, CQ, CQ…"

[Transmission Five was recorded at
approximately 12:17 p.m. on May 11, 1999.]

"It's Joe. K22XNJ.

"I couldn't sleep at all because it was circling me and then when the sun rose it kept circling me and then eventually the sound was all around me. I thought that meant it was right next to me, and that my time was up, but then I remembered that's how forest sounds usually work.

"And it was paced normally, too. The birds were chirping, but not too much. I could hear some rustling every once in a while—the kind of pattering squirrels make as they chase each other. It wasn't a constant, incessant cacophony. It was as though I'd been forgotten about. Or my hearing fixed itself.

"I fell asleep soon after realizing that things were normal, and I only woke up now. Just wanted to send a quick message out there telling everyone I'm all right.

"But I think it's time I go home.

"K22XNJ."

[Transmission Six was recorded at approximately 12:23 p.m. on May 11, 1999.]

"Oh. Oh. This is Joe. K22XNJ. Something's wrong. Something's wrong.

"I—I left the tent just now and the trees are wrong. They're all in the wrong places. They've moved. I swear to you, I swear they've moved. They don't look right. I know these surroundings so well. I spent all of yesterday staring at them. And they're *wrong*.

"It's subtle. Very subtle. You wouldn't know anything had changed unless you knew how to look. I know how to look. My family knows how to look. The shade is cast differently. The path is obscured.

"The path, the path here, the path out of here, it's gone. I can't see it. *I can't see the path out.* I can't get to my car. I can't *wander*, I only have a couple days of food left.

"Can you hear my teeth chattering? I'm freezing. It's like all my blood has sunk into my core.

"And the worst part is that I hear things all around me. There's a bird above me—you hear it singing? Well, I can't see it. I don't see the bird. I don't see any birds. Rustling, wind, trees—they all have sources, sources *close to me*, sources I should be able to see, but…

"Haha. Was I eaten? Am I inside whatever was stalking me last night? Is that why I hear everything everywhere?

"I don't know what to—"

[The transmission cuts off here as the side of tape reaches its end.]

[Transmission Seven was recorded at
approximately 6:32 p.m. on May 11, 1999.]

"I caught glimpses of it. Screw my ID. You know who I am.

"That's right, I saw it. A little bit. It's what's been stalking me.

"It walks on all fours. It has matted fur, with black spots in brown. And it has—it has a *giant* throat. Almost like a frog.

"I only managed to see it from behind, and briefly, before it darted away. I had just picked up my mic to get a message out. I thought I'd be recording my last moments. I was going to do everything in my power to stay alive long enough to expose it to the world. Ha, the world. To the nobody listening…

"It took the sound with it. Everything has receded somewhat, at least to a point where I can hear the direction it's coming from. So if that thing is making the noise, then, if I stay vigilant, I can track it.

"Ugh, I have a splitting headache. My vision's blurry, too, partially because of how tired I am, partially because of this pain in my head.

"I—maybe it'll stay away. Maybe it's given up on me. Maybe I'll get some sleep and can see my way through the trees again. Maybe I can get out of here.

"If you're listening, please send help."

[Transmission Eight was recorded at
approximately 1:01 a.m. on May 12, 1999.]

"Oh, it's back, it's back, it remembered me, but I—I found something out.

"I heard it coming. I was paying attention. I'm delirious now, I know, I'm so tired, but I managed it, and I heard it make its way back to me. And I was ready. I've come to terms already. I don't think I'm getting out of here alive.

"Maybe that's just doom and gloom, but it doesn't look good. Or, at least, it didn't. Because I've got a *weapon* now, haha. And it's you guys!

"Well, not literally, no, but it doesn't seem to like it when I'm transmitting. I watched it. Waited for it. I wasn't even in my tent. I was ready at a moment's notice to transmit, and as soon as I saw its huge, coyote-like face, I was on, I pressed the switch, and it froze and looked at me and sank back into the trees. Sorry if you've been hearing all that, by the way. It's my weapon, my one defense.

"I think it can hear this frequency. I think it can hear—a lot, I think there's a lot of things it can hear. The stupid thing is that I'm coming to believe it doesn't just hear things, though. I think it records them. Stores everything it hears in that huge, rubbery throat. And then it lets them loose. Why, I don't know. But it does.

"I'll test it again. Go dark for a while and just listen. See if it comes back for me. See if the RF makes it back off again.

"That means I have to let it get closer. It's bolder now, impatient, I think, but I need to be certain. If I can keep it away with my rig, then I need to know as much as I can about how to make it work if I ever want to make it back to my car.

"Did I forget my ID? Joe, K22XNJ. If you can triangulate me, please do. I don't have much longer."

[Transmission Nine was recorded at
approximately 8:33 a.m. on May 12, 1999.]

"Yeah, go on! Run! You *better* run! Hahahaha!

"Guys, it works, it *works*. It doesn't like RF. It can't stand them. *I saw it wince.*

"I'm guessing that, so close to the output, I have enough power to really make it hurt. The thing—okay, I'm ahead of myself, but it *ran* back into the woods, and it was so close to me, so close I could *touch it*.

"Anyway, it's Joe, K22XNJ. If you can hear me.

"So I stayed up again. All night. I could hear it moving around me. Not too close, but not far away, either, not like the first night. It was listening, I think, for the sounds of sleep.

"Eventually, I couldn't keep my eyes open. I don't know how long I slept, but it can't keep itself from being the loudest thing in the forest. Those incessant growls and breaths and chirps woke me up as soon as it was close. But I kept my eyes closed. I listened to it stalk out of the woods, pad its way up the hill. It kept circling around me, trying to find the very best angle to approach from.

"It wasn't easy playing chicken with a *beast*, but I had to keep myself calm. I worried the bastard would hear my heartbeat quicken if I let it get out of hand. So I waited, listening for each crunch of the grass as it spiraled closer to me, and closer, and closer, and closer…

"And then, just now, I pressed the switch, opened my eyes, and shouted.

"And the thing *ran*. For dear life! It was *a foot from me*, and still it ran, turned tail, *vanished*.

"I got a better look at it, but there isn't much more to say. It's about the size of a wolf, I think, and it has matted, speckled fur. Long jaw, *huge* jaw. Deep, sagging, inflated throat. Wide, wide ears.

"I doubt shouting alone is enough. No way it can handle bird chirps and not human voices. It *has* to be the radio. It has to be. And it can't *stand* it.

"You know why I think it could circle me while I transmitted yesterday? I was accidentally on a lower power setting. But that still kept it away.

"No way I'm risking low power with this thing. As soon as I get enough sleep to keep my eyes focused, I'm gonna get out there, find the path, make it, make it…"

[Crunching sounds indicate that the mic, while still active, is pressed into the grass. A minute passes in silence, save for the background noise of the forest.]

"Looks like I'm almost out of battery. So, this is Joe, K22XNJ. You'll hear me again."

[Transmissions Ten, Eleven, and Twelve were recorded at approximately 9:52 a.m., 12:46 pm, and 8:13 pm on May 12, 1999. Each consisted of a short burst of noise and Joe screaming menacingly into the microphone. These transmissions lasted for about six seconds.]

[Transmission Thirteen was recorded at approximately 12:23 a.m. on May 13, 1999.]

"K22XNJ.
"If *anyone* can hear me.

"Battery's almost dead on the mobile rig. I've spent time cranking the spare battery. My arm feels like it's about to fall off. No idea if I did it right. No idea how it works.

"I'm at full power. You'll lose me soon. But hopefully this will keep the thing away. Hopefully it'll sleep. It sleeps too, I know it does; sometimes the sound stays *put*. I just have to be lucky."

[Transmission Fourteen was recorded at approximately 2:42 a.m. on May 13, 1999. This is the last transmission made powered by the original battery, as is evident from the difference in quality between this transmission and Transmission Fifteen.]

"Hey—who's there? Be careful, it's not far. It's not far!

"Do you have radios? Use your—use your radios! I'm listening on—no! What? Strange? I'm not strange. Hey! Hello?"

[Joe's voice moves around the microphone, panning in either direction, sounding closer sometimes, further others. It's speculated that he set his radio to VOX transmissions. Whether purposely or accidentally is unknown.]

"You're here to rescue me, right? Come here. Come here! Where are you?

"I can't—I can't see you. You didn't bring *lights*? Hello?"

[A scream blares from a distance away. Loud laughter trails behind it. Each sound perfectly imitates the sounds Joe made during Transmissions Three and Eleven.]

"What was that? What was that? Was that me? Was it me? *Was it me? Was it—*"

[The transmission cuts off here as his battery dies.]

[Transmission Fifteen was recorded at approximately 2:51 a.m. on May 13, 1999.]

"Back, we're back, okay, we're back, we're back, we're back.

"K22XNJ. Joe March. Please, if anyone can hear me.

"I left the nest. I'm sorry. I couldn't stand it. It was mocking me. It was stringing words I'd said into nonsense. It learned how to laugh at me. I got, I got everything reconnected and, and I left. I can't be there anymore.

"No, I can't see the path. If I walk east I'll find something. Somewhere. The path only we can see—Dad made it up. He made it up.

"Oh God, this battery, it has—come here…"

[Joe is cranking the battery as he walks and talks.]

"I'm so tired. It's following me. It's saying things. Saying—saying things. I don't recognize the voices. One is mine, but there's others. I'm not the first.

"I'm—I can't even scream. I just need to keep walking. Keep alert.

"Oh God, please help me. Mom, Dad, please help me. I miss you both so much. Please, please help me…"

[Transmissions Sixteen, Seventeen, and Eighteen were recorded in rapid succession beginning at approximately 5:08 a.m. on May 13, 1999. Here, they are included as one transcript for clarity and brevity, with the pauses between each transmission marked by an editorial ellipsis.]

"Stop it! Shut up! Go away!

"Yeah! Run, run run *run!* Run!"

[…]

"Go away. *Get back.* Yeah, you don't like it, huh? Even this little thing is enough to make your ears hurt. *Go. Run.*"

[…]

"I see you! I can see you! I can *hear you,* you idiot. I can hear everything!"

[Transmission Nineteen was recorded at approximately 12:51 p.m. on May 13, 1999.]

"How am I still moving? I think it's just waiting for me to exhaust myself now. I can barely move my arms. I'll have to last on however much battery I've got.

"I shouldn't be transmitting. It isn't—it isn't close. Not now. It's playing with me. I just need to keep walking. I'll find the path. It—I'll find it. Or I'll find someone. Or someone will start being able to hear me.

"Please, if you're listening, I'm lost. I'm sorry I left the nest. But my tent's still there. You could see it. I'm not too far. My feet are so heavy. I can't walk. Please, please, please… I'm so sorry…"

[Transmission Twenty was recorded at approximately 7:14 p.m. on May 13, 1999. Although multiple voices are audible, this transcript makes no distinction between them. They all seem to belong to Joe.]

"No, no no no, go away, go *away*! Why—why isn't it working?"

[Frantic cranking audible.]

"A strange one.

"Forget my ID?

"Stop it, stop it.

"This is Joe, K22XNJ. Something's wrong. It isn't working. It's circling me.

"Shut up! Shut up!

"Can't stand RF.

"This is Joe.

"Crickets. Silence.

"If you can hear me, I'm lost.

"It's behind my head.

"*Nothing.*

"Please, please, please.

"Mom, Dad.

"No, don't, please, please…

"God.

"Go away! Why isn't it working?

"Battery. I'll find it. Feet. I'll find it. Someone. Somewhere. The trees. Moved. Haha.

"My arms are falling off.
"My feet are falling off.
"Can't stand it. Can't stand it.
"So tired.
"Okay. I.
"So tired.
"Okay! Okay!
"Over.
"Joe.
"Please God.
"K22XNJ."

[The cranking stops. Several seconds of forest silence continue before the transmission cuts out.]

[Transmission Twenty-One was recorded at approximately 1:14 a.m. on May 14, 1999. Throughout, cracking and sucking noises are audible. Voice analysis confirms the speaker to be Joe.]

"Cleared my head. Felt peaceful for a while. It was right in my ear. Cleared my head. The path out of here, eaten. Go dark. See if it comes back. There isn't much more to say. I heard it make its way back to me. Circling. Packed up last night. Haha. Go away. Stop. Run. Beast. My one defense. I think it's time I go home. Joe. Joe. It's bolder now. Impatient. Teeth. Teeth. Wander."

[Ripping noises, then harsh, heavy, humid breathing. Something sniffs the mic. Something heavy cracks against metal, then again, then again—but the noise is brief, and the transmission ends.]

The Winter Caretaker

J. NEEDHAM

Contract up north. Tend to inn guests, clean,
<u>keep the lantern lit</u>. Paid handsomely at the end of the season.

THE HUNTSMAN UNSTRUNG a bundle of five dead rabbits and tossed them onto the kitchen counter. Their feet were already cracked, their limp bodies ready to skin.

"In addition to the cabbages and all else the owners left you, that should see you through the first two weeks," he said.

William lowered his cup of tea, suddenly losing the taste for it. A gallery of dull eyes stared back at him. "*Ah*, thank you, sir."

"From the city, then?"

"Am I so transparent?" William sighed.

The huntsman laughed, picking up the nearest rabbit and inverting it as if to peel off its sweater. Underneath was a tangle of purple muscles with small white streaks of fat.

"The inn caretakers are always a varied sort. Never know who's going to take up the posting." The huntsman opened up a drawer and pulled out a cleaver, converting the sinew to stewing meat. "It's easy to tell which ones are from the city. Queasy stomachs, the lot of them." Then, with a knowing nod, "You'll get used to it."

William highly doubted that.

When he first saw the inn caretaker advert on the job bulletin, he hadn't paid it any mind. It was lost within a sea of papers calling for delivery boys and Prairie school teachers.

Being a priest didn't offer many opportunities to seek the Lord's work beyond church walls or community borders. That was until he was no longer a priest. Then the world instantly seemed too big. All he needed was a single paper leaflet, a compass pointed north.

"I'm sure I'll be busy with patrons and keeping the lantern in the front window lit, but it's a long winter," William said. "Should I expect to see you often?"

The huntsman finished with the rabbits and washed his hands with well water. A single window filtered morning light. Like a plant, William craned towards the company and the sun.

The huntsman paused at the sink and then turned back around with an expression hidden amongst his beard and wild hair. His eyes flicked behind William's shoulders towards the entryway. "Let's hope so."

***

Snow came quickly. One moment, autumn leaves dabbled the paths, then a white, wintery beast descended and slumbered across the land.

A predictable cadence marked the passage of weeks.

Mondays for clearing the walking paths. Tuesdays for gathering cabbages from the snow cellar. Wednesdays for dusting the empty rooms in the inn that no patrons visited. Thursdays for washing and fighting to dry his threadbare clothes. Fridays for repairs. He dipped candles for the lantern on Saturdays. On Sundays, the huntsman came.

Only one rule existed for their shared winter: William was forbidden from visiting the huntsman's property. "I value my privacy, and the forest is easy to get lost in," the huntsman had said on their first Sunday together. "I have maintained this rule with all caretakers."

"I don't mind mess or squalor," William had said before the huntsman's serious expression schooled a solemn *yes* from his lips.

The latest Sunday rolled in with the force of the squalls sweeping across the lake. The huntsman came bearing a tacklebox and a request for company. William, already aching for the chatter of the diocese, dressed in his warmest boots.

"Every week, this land surprises me with its beauty," William said as he trailed after the huntsman across the frozen lake. The exchange between warmer melts and the chilly frosts had created small waterfalls suspended in motion from the rocky cliffs above.

The huntsman stopped in front of a wooden hut and popped open the door. Inside was a seat and a frozen-over hole in the ground like a privy. "You should see it in summer. The inn is filled with travellers, hunters, and Indigenous traders." The huntsman took what he needed from his tacklebox and sat atop it, gesturing for William to take a seat on the stool.

It was an unsurprising courtesy; the huntsman had already proven to be a gentleman despite his unshaven and wild appearance. His grey-speckled beard had grown longer over the weeks and the cold had turned his cheeks permanently red. Even William couldn't escape the slow pull of time and isolation. A small beard of his own caused him to scratch his cheeks when idle.

"It's so strange how quiet it is," William said. "I haven't had a single patron. I had expected at least a few guests, even with such a remote location. Trapping and snowshoeing is exotic for us city folks. The only instructions left at the property were to clean the place and to *always* keep the lantern in the front window lit. The last bit underlined and circled."

The huntsman finished cracking open the hole and submerged his line into it. "Every new winter caretaker feels the same, one way or another."

"You said weeks ago that the inn caretakers are a varied sort. Are there often new caretakers? Have they ever kept a man on permanently?"

The huntsman paused, lips pursed into a line. William watched them leech colour. "Yes," then after a pause, "and no."

"Why was there an opening? Is the pay actually poor?"

The huntsman shrugged, his eyes glued to the hole as if a trout's appearance depended upon his will alone.

Uncovering secrets was something William had excelled at in his past life. Many reluctant people had visited the confessional, and William found it best to coax out truths with a sense of safety.

"If the pay is bad, I do not mind. I've lived for years in poverty; it is not about money. You can tell me. I promise I won't tell my employers, whoever they are. You are safe here." William's hands ran along the fishing hut walls. "Think of this hut as a place to house our secrets."

The huntsman stared for a long moment before laying his hand on the other wall. William watched the huntsman's eyes, a beautiful blue as pale as the frozen water. "There is only one visitor who ever comes to the inn during winter," he said slowly. "The visitor arrives when the deer strip bark from the trees and the rabbits begin to eat their young."

William swallowed, and the gesture felt too loud.

"If the light extinguishes, he knocks. Never let the lantern extinguish, William. That is your only true role here. If you do, then the visitor will need a place to stay. You do not want to play host to it."

"And what role do you play?" William asked.

"I'm here to ensure the inn is safe." The huntsman patted the rifle holster around his shoulder.

Perhaps it was from their proximity or their shared warmth filling the hut, but William felt the walls pull around them, narrowing his focus onto the rough fingers running over the band.

Between them, the line bobbed.

"I believe you caught one."

Winter turned cruel as the weeks stretched to months. The washing would not dry no matter how many fires William fed. A cold damp clung to the walls and the taste of cabbage was forever in William's mouth, doing little to satiate his growing hunger. The hunger, and the lantern's flickering, remained constant.

The large black cage lantern sat in the inn's front window, the dwindling candles turning it into a lighthouse standing garrison against a dark, churning sea beyond.

What did that make William? Lighthouse keeper? Or a sailor lost at sea?

"You don't look like city folk anymore," the huntsman commented over their latest Sunday dinner. Between them, the final candles dipped from wax scraps had nearly extinguished, and their plates of cabbage and rabbit stew were empty.

William tipped his cup of wine back and forth, Sunday's communion already finding a home in the red of his cheeks. "Really? Is it the beard? I keep trying to shave but it sprouts back like weeds. Must be all the cabbage."

The huntsman smiled. "No, not the beard, though it's nice."

William gulped back the wine, more red blooming in his cheeks.

"You flay the fish I bring and save the rabbit offal for stews."

"I suppose so," William said. "The snow cellar is down to pickles and beets. I should have been more frugal with the delicacies. I blame my earlier city self. Just as later I'll be cursing the me of now for draining the wine." He leaned forward to grab the neck of the wine bottle they had been nursing between them and poured them each another glass.

"You're religious?" the huntsman asked.

William paused his pouring and looked down at the golden cross that had slipped out of his rough-hewn shirt. "Yes. Are you?"

The huntsman slid his glass closer. His eyes flicked over William's shoulder to the front door. "Enough to believe in a Christian burial."

"I was a priest once, actually."

"But not anymore?" the huntsman asked over the rim of his wineglass.

"But not anymore."

They'd kept these meetings every Sunday with the punctuality of a sermon. It wasn't lost on William how the huntsman's visits had filled the same desire for purpose. But what purpose was that, William wondered? Looks lingering across the dinner table, hands brushing over the passing of logs, the fishing hut filled by a silence pulled so taut that it drove William mad every time the huntsman quickly changed a subject or left the hut to create slack.

How desperately he craved it to snap.

William grasped the cross, thumbing the sharp corners in the same nervous way he had at the church.

"If there's a private story there, I don't want to pry," the huntsman said. He began collecting their plates when William slid his own out of reach.

"There is nothing but trees and wolves for miles and miles. If it is privacy I need, there is plenty of it."

The huntsman nodded, sat back down, and returned to his wineglass.

"I was released from the diocese and am forbidden from taking any oath again. Had I not fled after the judicial verdict," William said as he lifted his hands up, sloshing the wine slightly, "I'd likely be in irons now." It hurt less to say now than it had in the first few days after, where it had felt like a severed limb. "I'd committed a grave sin in their eyes."

"In their eyes? But not yours."

William paused, lips pressed against the glass. A great chance that the huntsman would call him a degenerate and cease all communications and supplies now sat between them. It would be tantamount to a death sentence so far north. After priesthood, he had kept faith that the Lord would create a path for him. God would forge a path for him here, too.

William reached up to the air and mimed his hand against the fishing hut wall. "Can this place, too, host our secrets?"

The huntsman lifted his hand and pressed it against another imaginary wall, turning the candlelit kitchen with its copper pots and jars of beans into their confessional. His feet slid under the table, work boots knocking against William's house shoes in a way that didn't feel accidental. "It can."

William finally took a sip. "I fell in love with another priest. The church saw fit to strip me of my place amongst the clergy and threaten imprisonment if I did not leave. With no other prospects and with my education amounting to ash without a Bible in hand, I required a new start. Or at least a moment to breathe. So I came here."

The huntsman's lips paused beside his glass just a fraction too long. William easily noticed discomfort when he searched for it between heartbeats. The huntsman pulled back, the seat groaning under his weight.

"You don't seem bothered by it," the huntsman finally said and crossed his arms over the strange, mottled furs he wore.

William relaxed an inch, letting out a held breath. "God works in mysterious ways. I see the beauty in Him with every sunset stretching across the frozen lake and His cruelty in every carcass you bring to my table that is necessary for our survival. Perhaps being a priest wasn't the way I was meant to serve Him."

"No…" He again looked over William's shoulder to the hallway. "I meant lying with another man."

Of course it was that. William tilted his head as if to better observe the mountain of a man before him. "I've granted God my livelihood, my sweat, and my soul," William said. "Why can't I ask another human to hold me safe until eternity begins? Do sheep not seek love and companionship in each other? Does that make them belong to the shepherd any less? Does that save them from ultimately becoming meat?" William's finger stroked along the edge of the stew bowl. "We're all meat in the end. I eat what suits my tongue. Does that bother you?"

The huntsman pursed his lips again to a thin, bloodless line as he continued to stare over his shoulder.

William, emboldened by the wine that soaked his blood, stretched his hand across the table to lay it across the huntsman's wrist. The pulse beneath thrashed like a pinned rabbit. "Does that *bother you?*"

Like a round dispatched from his rifle, the huntsman shot up off the table. Dishes clattered, wine glasses spilled. He stalked past William and down the carpeted hall.

"You must feel it too? Between us," William said, scratching a clawed nail down the pooling wax.

"I *feel* you're distracted!" The huntsman's fury came out stronger than William had anticipated.

Thunderous footsteps swelled behind him, and before William could turn towards their owner, hands pulled him from his seat and half-dragged him by the collar to the end of the hall. "Just now, the lantern almost flickered out," the huntsman shouted.

William pulled away and straightened himself out. "I am not a hunting hound. Don't you dare do that again."

"Look at it!" the huntsman growled as he pointed at the dying flame. The huntsman had been quick to feed the lantern another sputtering candle. "This is all you're supposed to do, all you were asked. To *never* let it go out."

"That was the last candle," William noted.

"Then use wood. I'll bring you whatever wood you need to keep the lantern aflame."

William huffed. "Frankly, I would welcome the 'visitor' at this point. At least it would give me something to do!"

The huntsman's hand cracked against William's cheek, slapping away the wine's easy mood. Just as quickly, his calloused hand laid against it. "I'm so sorry, William. I did not mean to," the huntsman repented. "You do not know what you're saying."

"Then let me speak plainly: I'd like you to leave," William stated. He brushed the warm hand away. "Now."

The huntsman stopped coming. Sundays were now hollow and William did not rush to fill them with aimless tasks. Movement required warmth, a resource of which there was precious little.

On the first Sunday after, a pile of thin logs had been left for him by the door. He growled at the unwelcome peace offering and threw the logs away.

Without the fresh rabbit or wood to stoke fires, hot nails of hunger ceaselessly scratched inside his stomach. Brine, pickles, cabbage, melted snow. His only companion, the lantern, hungered too for dry wood, forcing William to break apart the damp wooden chairs and vainly dig through the snow in search of the huntsman's olive branch.

It was no longer a mystery why the other caretakers had never stayed longer than a season.

William soon knew he had to swallow his pride. Defeated, he set out towards the huntsman's cabin, snowshoes strapped to his feet and jars of pickled beans slung in a sack.

The temperatures that had been a shock to William at the start of winter were nothing compared to the way his nostrils now stuck together with each breath and the deep snow that screamed out in loud crunches with every footfall.

Near the cabin, mingling amongst a scattered collection of rocks nearly buried by snow, stood a deer. Hunger knocked on his stomach as he imagined it roasted over a fire. A beautiful creature—if not skinny—the warmth of its breath curling like steam. The deer latched onto the bark of a nearby white aspen and stripped it like peeling a hangnail until it bled.

The shudder that rocked through him was matched only by his stomach's growl as he smelled stew wafting from the chimney. Despite their last parting, William knocked.

"You're not supposed to be here," the huntsman said when he opened the door. His expression was guarded, thick hands holding the door hostage. "It seems you intend to keep none of your promises. We had an agreement."

"Damn your agreement," William said, lodging his foot against the door that the huntsman attempted to close. "If I go back there, I will freeze to death. You said you were a religious man. Do you want that on your holy ledger?"

The huntsman's eyes darted from William's face to over his shoulder. It was a habit of his that William had once passed off as a nervous tick, but now it gave him pause. He craned his own head around. Just what did the huntsman see stalking behind William?

"I am surprised you made it this long…" the huntsman said, easing the door from William's foot.

"Only because I burnt the furniture," William replied coolly.

"Your cheeks are white. Come in before a hungry beast mistakes you for dinner."

"Frankly, I am less worried about some woodland creature." William laid his hand above the huntsman's, ready to push the door open if need be. If it came to force, it would be a losing battle, but William would don armour all the same.

The huntsman turned into his hut, hand falling away, their knuckles brushing. "We shall see."

The door parted, and with it, their feud from before. The huntsman was a passable host, offering hot pine tea and furs for William to curl within. The cabin itself was modest, sporting a large clay hearth with blackened hooks that held all manner of cooking pots. The huntsman's single cot was covered in similar furs, all a mottled brown and black that William couldn't pin to any animal he'd ever seen.

"Is that better?" the huntsman asked and approached William.

"Oh, uhm, yes. I can finally feel my fingers and toes again."

The huntsman did not move, looming like a shadow. "You're the first caretaker to be in my house."

"Did you slap them too? I imagine that would ward most people away from your front step—agreement or not." Perhaps their feud was not *completely* gone.

The huntsman sighed and pulled a chair from his tilting table. He cracked apart a loaf of bread, making William's stomach twist. He slathered it in butter and held it out. "I did not."

William shoved the bread in his mouth and groaned. Only once he'd swallowed it down did he speak in jest, "Am I special then?"

The huntsman nodded slowly. His thick fingers made contact with the corner of William's lip and thumbed a crumb away.

"Then let us make one more transgression: could I stay with you?" William asked as he slipped off the chair and onto his knees. They were used to kneeling in prayer; a beg wouldn't be much different. "I cannot go back there. I'll do anything."

"We both have our roles to play. I have to protect the inn and you have to keep the lantern lit," the huntsman said, his voice shaking. "Is it…still lit?"

William rose from his knees and steadied himself on the huntsman's shoulders. Feeding the lantern was the last thing he wanted to think of. If pleading would not work, then he had to try something new. He leaned closer, so close he could smell ale and a day's hard work on the huntsman. William's hands smoothed across the calico furs.

The huntsman leaned backward, eyes wide.

"For now," William murmured.

"William, please don't…" the huntsman breathed. They had pulled into each other's gravity, ice-blue eyes flicking from William's lips to his eyes. "We have no choice. The visitor—"

A sudden clarity swept across the huntsman's face. He wrenched William away and strode over to the woodpile to gather pieces.

William threw his hands up. "I'm not going back there, dry wood or no! I won't! The entire land is conspiring to extinguish the flame, and while I know you care, I am too cold and tired to do the same!"

"Go," the huntsman said, refusing to make eye contact. He placed wood in William's arms. "I know it is hard work—"

"It is *impossible* work! How has any caretaker tended to that damned fickle lantern?"

The huntsman's expression sagged. "Please, William. Listen to me. I know it is hard to go back there, but resist the temptation for warmth. Spring is coming. You cannot leave it unattended. If it goes out—"

"The bloody visitor, of course," William hissed as he took the wood. "With the way you preach it, I would have thought you were the priest, not myself. Temptation, *ha!*" The cruel, barking tone felt foreign coming from his own lips.

"William, if I had known you the way I do now… I never would have let you— You don't understand what the visitor will do."

"Then enlighten me."

The huntsman's brows collided together in thought, then he retrieved his rifle and slung it over his shoulder. He still refused to make eye contact, which served only to further sour William's mood. "I'll help bring more wood, and I'll escort you back. Wait a moment."

He was tired of waiting—for the huntsman to soften to his advances, for spring to come, for the lantern to be long behind him. "Enough of this," he hissed.

William stormed out of the cabin with the wood in hand and made it only a few steps before he tripped over one of the blasted stones. The odd shape was hidden beneath the snowbanks. Wood scattered and threatened to fly away with the howling wind. William screamed out his fury and rolled over towards the stone. Up close, it looked uniform, nothing like the natural rocks that covered the craggy cliffs. He brushed aside the snow and made out poorly carved letters:

RIP

His hands dug through snow until they lost feeling. Beneath: *Michael Carter.* A death date a mere year ago in February. Coldness seized his heart. Looking across the yard ahead, William saw similarly spaced rocks lining where the deer had stood. The next one he uncovered contained another man's name with a January death date two years prior. Another one, five years before that: December. All dead before spring.

He did not need to uncover the rest to guess their fates.

Light bathed the small graveyard when the huntsman opened the door. The relief the light had given him before now offered him a white spike of fear.

"Who are these people?" William asked.

"The visitor—"

"They are in your damned yard! Did you kill them?"

The huntsman stepped away from the illuminated front step and into the howling wind. The rifle jostled as he closed the door behind him. No answer was answer enough.

William scrambled to his feet. "Stay back!" His breath froze in his throat. "I mean it!"

By the time he arrived back at the inn, Willian's splintered fingers had lost feeling from gripping the chopped logs.

The inn was as it had always been: a wide stonework building more reminiscent of a mill with heavy drawn curtains, save for the bay window where the lantern stood. The small flame had reduced to embers; the wind that shook the windowpanes and shot through William's meagre defences attempted to finally extinguish it.

Visitor, the wind whispered to William.

The large lantern made quick work of the thin logs the huntsman had gifted him. Shattered from the trek, William curled around the lantern in quilts and tucked the cleaver from the kitchen under his head like a pillow. Sleep pulled at his body but ultimately evaded his mind's capture, which instead stayed transfixed on the slow decay of flames. Over the passing hours, cold expectantly filled the inn like wolves encircling him, biting at any exposed skin.

"I have nothing left for you. But I expect you planned that," William told the lantern. The final red embers clung to a hunk of ash. Even the gifts of his torn sleeve sat at the bottom of the lantern, un-lit. His contract would not be completed. The lantern would go out. "Damn this place. Damn the huntsman. Damn the visitor."

At the final word, the last remaining ember extinguished with a small wave of smoke. Dread snuffed out the lingering warmth inside William.

The winter storm battering the inn quietened. In the silence, William heard his own heartbeat thudding in his ears.

Thud. Thud. Thud.

Knock. Knock. Knock.

Firm knocking on the door echoed through the inn's cold and empty rooms.

"Go!" William shouted at the door. "I won't let you in." Another series of knocks each shook the breath out of him. William kneeled beside the lantern to pull back the curtains. He expected to see the huntsman there with his rifle, determined to add him to the graves spanning his patch of land. But there was nothing, only the seemingly endless night and white snow. Not a single track.

Knock. Knock. Knock.

Louder now, more insistent, coming from nothing at all.

Whatever delusions he'd half believed weeks ago came to him all at once at their full strength: wandering monsters and phantoms, murderous grudges bound to buildings.

The knocking subsided for a brief respite before the floorboards began to thrash, the nails yanking out. The door banged against the frame and the doorknob twisted back and forth. William began to pray, fingers wrapped around the cross in one hand and the cleaver in the other. Warm spring days amongst the parish's garden a lifetime away, the Sunday dinners with baked bread and boiled rabbit stew out of reach. Where was God now?

The door burst open, wind and snow streaming in, billowing the curtains. A terrible wrongness filled the entryway with some horrifying presence unseen. Dread itself given form.

The visitor had arrived.

William raised the cleaver right before his body was thrown against the entry rug. Loud cracks like fracturing ice accompanied by a burning cold ran through his limbs and lungs. Every breath fought against the frostbite filling him. The hunger that had been William's constant companion throughout the past weeks exploded, its claws tearing apart his insides as he could only scream.

An eternity might have passed on the ground, his body writhing, his hand desperately reaching for the cleaver that always seemed out of reach.

"William!" the huntsman shouted as he entered the foyer, rifle drawn.

"Get it off me!" William screamed, raking his nails over the invisible force. "Shoot it! *Shoot it!*"

The huntsman raised his gun but did not track some fitful beast. Instead, he kept it trained on William's skull. "The visitor needs a place to stay and a meal." Pain seared, and every word the huntsman said felt like an ice pick driven into his core. "It's my job to defend the inn once it's had its fill."

"Then defend it!" William sobbed, his voice stretched in a hundred directions until it became no longer recognizable.

A bullet shot past William's head, lodging itself into the floor. Primal instinct drove William to move, his fur-covered hands digging into the wall, climbing until he hung from the ceiling amongst the candelabra. Black ooze dripped onto the huntsman, whose hands shook around the rifle.

"Caretaker," William hissed, his voice a stranger in his mouth, the words not his own. More of a howl than anything human. *"Or should I call you Huntsman? Another year, another replacement. You refuse me, but I suppose you've held up your end of the bargain. Now it's time to finish it."*

The huntsman swore, his finger against the trigger, the jittering end of the rifle tilted up and aimed at William.

"I can't," he finally said, lowering the gun. "Not this time. Not him."

"Then let me in."

William dropped from the ceiling, landing on strange, backwards-bent legs covered in a mottled patchwork of fur. It occurred to him then, through the distortion, that he'd seen its twin stretched out across the huntsman's cot. Multiple pelts.

"Let me in," William repeated.

The huntsman drew near. A hunger born of an older source merged and twisted around William's own longing. How long had the visitor wanted the huntsman? How long had he offered the inn's caretakers in his place?

The huntsman's warm and heavy arms encircled William and pulled him closer. Black ooze painted the huntsman's hands as they smoothed back fur to cup William's muzzle.

The huntsman sucked in a deep breath. "I won't keep the visitor out any longer. I invite it in."

Then, dry lips pressed against William's own. Hesitant at first, then bold. The cold retreated, replaced with a strike of a match that grew to a bonfire inside his body. With every stroke of the huntsman's hand, the fur covering William spread to him. William leaned into the huntsman as he, too, transformed. William's own claws raked through beard before it grew into thick black and silver fur.

As they pulled away, breathing heavily, the door to the inn slammed shut. Behind William, the lantern relit. The huntsman's monstrous form did not look over William's shoulder; instead, familiar blue eyes stayed trained on William, then closed softly only to kiss him again.

CAMPBELL

Lord of the Dance

MICAH GIDDENS

I'm going to kill my neighbor. I swear to God, I can't even right now. It's been going on all week: rhino-stomping, hella loud, hella annoying. I'm cursed. Only explanation. I'm fucking cursed.

Like, I can't even take a sad girl nap because it's so insane. And it's all because people literally suck.

What I did wasn't even *that* bad.

And shut up!

Just fucking *stop*!

What could he possibly be doing?

Anyway, it's just needlessly cruel. Everyone was dragging me even though I apologized like a billion times and started reading that bell hooks book.

All my classmates would glare at me in lecture. I could see them recording. Posting their stories. Fucking animals. Clout chasers. Virtue signalers. It was honestly traumatic. Like no joke, I have PTSD whenever I see someone on their phone, not knowing if they're filming me.

Oh. My. God. Is this ever going to stop? Shutupshutupshutup!

So now I've dropped out of college, burning through my allowance. Mom and Dad are bitching about getting a job. I would have a job if I hadn't lost all my followers. If my basic sisters can get rich peddling bullet journals and gut tea, I could make a killing.

How is this guy allowed to be this loud? It's a crime, right? I have the worst luck living in a building with only two apartments. If I had other people on my floor, they could deal with this also, but no, it's all on me.

Should I call the landlord? But then I'd have to talk on the phone. Why doesn't he text? Come into the 21ˢᵗ Century, you bald bitch.

If I could just move out of Edgewater. I should be in West Loop where there's stuff to do, where there's *culture*.

I'll blow my brains out. Would that get views? But then I'd be dead, lol. What if I just shoot a non-essential part? Nah, those would just be pity views, I don't want that.

Okay fine, fine! I'll take care of it myself.

I pound on his door. Phone's recording, of course, for my safety. Also, if he's a dick, I can blast him online. I hope he's a dick. God, it'd be so amazing if this guy was a misogynist, or like a Neo-Nazi. I could really use a win.

Nothing. He's still banging around somewhere inside. The same pattern over and over, like a rhythm.

"Hellooooooo!" What's his name? Branston? Greggor? Something basic like that.

No sign of him through the window. Just a dim living room. Junk everywhere. The lights are either flickering or knocked over. Major crack den energy.

The window's shattered in the corner. I could just reach in and unlock the door. What's he going to do, stab me? I'll say I'm live-streaming it. He wouldn't stab me live.

Or…

I could prank him! Like revenge for being a bad neighbor. That could be my thing, vigilante pranking, targeting Karens and problematic people. That's not a bad in. Maybe I could transition to social justice pranking? Show everyone I'm an ally, not problematic, and leverage my platform for real positive change in society, like MrBeast.

I run back home to grab my tripod and a wolf mask from Halloween; I was a wolf but, you know, hot.

Back on his porch, I set up my phone outside his window. I'll edit out the part where I reach through the broken window and unlock the door.

Mask on my head, I tiptoe into the apartment.

It smells hella whack in here. Like old pennies. And the carpet's stiff, making a crunchy sound. What kind of fucked up is this guy where even his carpet is loud?

His banging gets closer. I think he's in his bedroom. The way I framed the shot, it should be able to pick up everything if I wait until he enters the living room.

The bedroom door flies open, hanging off one hinge. He lurches into view, and I ready myself to pounce. What will I say? Gotta be something clever.

He's moving hella weird as he makes his way down the hall. Jolting. Wild kicks. Full-body gyrating. Like an Irish step-dancer having a stroke. My throat's dry. I hate hate hate this guy. Why is he moving like that? Just be normal!

Finally, he lurch-kicks into the living room, so I pop out and yell: "Boo, bitch!"

He, like, doesn't react.

He just dances.

Such a weird, unhinged dance. All kicks, slapping random parts of his body, head twirls. It's chaotic, but also, like, compelling.

"I'm live-streaming…" Ugh, why'd my voice crack? I can just re-record the voice-over later to make me sound less cringe. "Just wanted to make you feel uncomfortable in your own home, just like I do, you…you inconsiderate, traumatizing dick—would you just stop dancing!"

He barely seems to register me, must be faded out of his mind. Kick, kick, twist, fist pump, bend backwards.

"Why are you dancing? Can you just stop?"

He groans. His jaw hangs at an odd angle, all splotchy with bruises. Molly, DMT, coke, what kind of drug makes you dislocate your jaw?

"Just pleaaaaaaase…" I'm gonna need to cut all this audio. "Why are you doing this to me? Why won't you answer me!"

He's not even looking at me, fucking dick, facing the wall. He slaps a standing lamp to the floor. Everything's on the floor—shattered Target furniture, crushed bulbs, shards on his disgusting red-brown patterned carpet…

Oh God.

That's not the carpet's natural pattern. Bits of the original white peek through, but most of it's stained. Red and brown footprints layered on top of each other.

Oh no, that penny smell. It's blood.

I see his torn-up soles when he kicks. Pulpy. Juicy.

Before I can stop myself, I'm vomiting off his balcony. So embarrassing. This whole video's a wash.

I run back downstairs and barricade myself in my bedroom.

What was that? Who even does drugs by themselves? Psycho.

While the stomping continues, I try to distract myself on my phone. Check-in on all my old fake friends and their dumbass gym videos and cooking hacks. Like, bitch, putting a hot pocket in an air-fryer is not a hack.

I feel like a freak with my anonymous stalker account, but I can't use my real name. Not until things cool off.

It was such an overreaction.

I was just volunteering on the South Side, helping underprivileged youth in my own free time, while everyone else was out partying. And I made those beautiful little kids so happy, giving them piggyback rides; we had so much fun. I'm sorry for bringing joy to a dark place. I'm sorry for caring.

And their dance was just so cute, I was obsessed.

But no. I got canceled.

My dance videos were a tribute, *not* appropriation. If I could just talk to their mother and explain that, she could go online and apologize for mis-characterizing me, but no, she blocked me.

Bang. Bang. Clomp. Clomp. Fuck. You. Douche.

Hate-scrolling can't even distract me. No way I'll sleep tonight, especially knowing he's being so gross up there. And I can't get his dance moves out of my head. They're jank, but there's something to them.

I rewatch the footage. Shitty lighting, can't see anything.

I think I could put my own spin on the dance. Make it cleaner. Maybe sexy? It's not appropriation if he's a ginger, so nobody's going to drag me for this.

But I need to get better footage so I can learn the moves. He's on another plane of existence, so he won't notice me recording.

But what about that grody carpet? Oh! I still have some of those plastic booties from when I volunteered at the Swedish Hospital (which, by the way, I didn't even post about, even though my coworkers were posting, because I didn't want to make it about *me*, even though I *could have*).

Feet nice and protected from infection, I set up the tripod inside his apartment and turn on all the overhead lights. I should be afraid he'll get mad at me, but I'm not. He's sooo skinny, bruises everywhere, open cuts. I could Krav Maga the shit out of him if he came at me.

"Hello?" I wave to get his attention. He groans. Apart from his broken jaw, his mouth's caked in blood—Ugh, fuck! Most of his tongue's gone, just a raggedy stump left.

And he reeks. More than just BO; he's shit his pants. Even though I want to, I don't cover my nose. Don't wanna offend him. But I also don't let him get close, keeping a distance with my phone.

"What's your deal? Why are you dancing?"

Groan, groan, groan. Super not helpful, but seems like he at least registers me.

"Can you stop?"

A more emphatic groan.

"So you can't stop?" Okayyy…so random. "How long have you been dancing?"

I think he's crying. In his kitchen, there's a bunch of bloody shards of glass and ceramics as if he tried to get some water but couldn't manage it.

"You're thirsty?"

Really emphatic groan.

I tiptoe through the kitchen, careful not to cut myself, too.

Giving him the water is more challenging than expected. I can't get close to him because his limbs are flailing, and he slaps the glass out of my hand. After a couple of unsuccessful attempts, I get an idea.

"I'll be right back; don't move."

I skip down to my car, pop the trunk, and…Yes! I still have some bungee cords from my move. And a funnel for replacing my oil.

Upstairs, I gently poke him with a broom out of the living room, towards his bedroom. This is difficult because he can't seem to move intentionally, and I just have to kinda prod his dancing in the direction I want.

He grunts like a lil' piggy the whole way, but I keep telling him to trust me. After literally forever, I give him a strong push into his bed. While he's getting all tangled up in the covers, I attach some bungees together, and strap him down. By the end of it, I'm all sweaty, so I take a breather in the other room.

After catching up on socials, I wash some of the old oil out of the funnel, stick it in his mouth, and pour in some water. I dump a couple of glasses into him and ask, "You good now?"

He groans, but seems unsatisfied.

"I'll get you some diapers later. And Ensure. Get some nutrients in you, some protein for those thirsty lil' muscles, Mr. Dancing Queen." I smile to break the tension. "But you don't want to do too much too fast. I took a health course at Loyola, and it's better to introduce a change in your diet slowly. You're, like, starving to death. You might barf up all the water and food if I give it to you all at once."

More moans, some tears.

"I'll be back in thirty minutes, 'kay?"

Back in the living room, I clean up his mess. Everything's broken, even the couch. I shove all I can fit into the bathroom. Oh Jesus, his bloody chewed-up tongue is under some pizza boxes. Fucking nightmare fuel, I'm never going to sleep.

After an hour of tidying, the living room's finally empty. Just crunchy, blood-stained carpet. I'll frame that out. The overhead lighting illuminates enough, and there's plenty of space to move around.

Carefully, I unstrap the bungee cords, tip the mattress, and he rolls twitching to the floor. With some leverage from the broom, I eventually get him to his feet.

"Don't worry, don't worry," I coo. "After this, you'll get a fresh pair of pants and some yummy food. Just want to see those super cool dance moves one more time. You have a real talent, I'm a total fangirl!"

Once he's in the living room facing the camera, I press record.

As he dances, I mimic the moves out of frame. It's such a weird routine. There's definitely a repeating pattern, even though it still feels random. He's not the most fluid dancer, but his devotion is on another level. He flinches with every step, but never slows down. Really admirable.

My phone dies after a couple of hours. Ugh, my charger's in my car.

"That was great," I tell him. "I think I have enough footage to study, but want to get an angle from your backside for safety. Do you have a charger?"

Grunt, grunt, yeah yeah, stupid of me to ask. Probably in the bedroom since I didn't see it when I cleaned up.

Nothing in his desk drawers. There's a microphone and random sound equipment scattered around his desk. Is he like a musician or something?

I'm crawling under his gross bed when there's this crazy boom and a high-pitched shriek from the other room.

"What now?"

I hurry into the living room, and it's a fucking tragedy. Fresh blood splatter everywhere. A huge hole in the wall. He's hopping around squealing, his right leg twirling around like a nunchuck.

Dummy must've broken his leg kicking the wall. The bone's poking out, hit an artery or something, because he's spraying like a sprinkler. Don't wanna get too close to the blood, so I try to steady him with my broom, but he's in full freak-out mode. Still trying to do the dance moves, he's all off-kilter with only one leg. Every time he steps on the broken leg, it just breaks more, shoving the bone farther out.

"Stop, stop, *stop*! You're making it worse!" I prod him towards the corner so the wall can contain some of his flailing.

Shit! He loses his balance and falls hard. Face-first into the windowsill.

Nononono what was that crack? Was it just the glass? Could've been his neck. It's bent pretty far back. His dance moves are slowing to twitches now. How does someone's head have so much blood? How do you stop it?

Fuck my life.

Okay, what to do? He's still twitching, so call an ambulance? Will they charge me? I've heard they're hella expensive. I'll call from his phone and they can charge him. Mine's dead anyway.

It takes a bit of rummaging, but I find his phone. Dead, too. Fucking Android, what kind of nerd has an Android? I don't have a charger for that.

After another few minutes of sifting through all the sound equipment in his room, I find his charger. Plugged in, his phone turns on, and I use his thumb to unlock it.

This is insane. His Insta's blowing up. Hundreds of notifications. I open the app and—the hell? He has 755,000 followers? Who is this guy?

Apparently, his name is Brandon Conley? And he's a podcaster?! With a podcast called *The Cryptid Cast*? The fuck does that even mean? Some sort of crypto-bro bullshit? And how does he have 755,000 subscribers? I guess he was sorta hot—but still. So am I!

I glance over at him. He's pissed out all the water I gave him earlier and stopped moving. I ought to check his pulse, but his neck's all covered in blood, and I don't want to get more of my DNA on his body. Not that I did anything wrong, but I don't trust the police to know the difference. Besides, his neck is all bendy like a glow stick, there's no coming back from that. No point calling an ambulance.

When was his last post? Five days ago. That's about when he started stomping…

His final post is a black-and-white photo of a misty forest. The text overlay reads:

Coming soon… Episode 103: The Lord of the Dance.

Hmm… Lord of the Dance. Gotta be connected to whatever the fuck he was doing, right? There's also a location tag: *Forest Glen Preserve.*

Ugh. I'm hella intrigued, but I should probably call the police because he's gonna start reeking soon. But what about my fingerprints? How would I even clean that with his blood splatter everywhere?

I got it! If they ask me, I'll just say we were hooking up, but, like, I broke it off recently when he started getting into hardcore drugs. He's old, in his thirties, but I'll take that L.

Okay, so the plan is: rearrange his stuff, burn all of my clothes with blood on them, call the cops and say I haven't heard from my neighbor in a week, worried about him, etc. Ugh, why can't the police just text? Fucking fossils.

But what about the dance?

I'll delete the video, obviously, after I get a good feel for the choreography. So maybe call the police in a few days once I have the routine down? He's not going anywhere; it takes a while to get stinky, I'd imagine.

But something was so crazy about those moves… I took Intro to Dance in college, but I've never seen anything like this. It'd be a waste if the cops took all his computer and stuff, and all evidence of where this dance came from got lost forever.

But what could it be? Something to do with Forest Glen Preserve…

An invitation-only forest rave?!

So maybe my neighbor Brandon was investigating some kind of crypto rave or something for his dumbass podcast, then found the location of the rave, learned that dance routine, did too many drugs, and danced himself to death?

I don't know.

But I've gotta know.

Forest Glen is just a twenty-minute drive…

With no traffic and speeding, I'm there in ten minutes.

My phone's still charging, so I leave the car on with hazards so it can charge while I'm in the woods. It's a hybrid, it's fine.

I still have Brandon's phone, and I changed his password before I left using his thumb, in case I needed to get in it for an emergency. I turn on the light. Kinda spooky with the pre-dawn mist. Too dark for a selfie. If I can't hear rave music soon, I'll turn around.

After, like, forever walking in the dark, I reach the road on the other side of the preserve.

Nothing.

No beats. No cool people dancing on Molly. No—

Agh! Fuck shit! OhmyGod!

It's just an owl, Jesus Christ.

Two wide, glowing eyes stare at me. Probably ten feet away. All I can make out is its round head behind a bush. A big-ass owl, probably up to my knee if I were next to it.

"Stop staring, owl!"

Oh God…

The owl's shadow grows straight up. It's gotta be over six feet now, and, like, man-shaped.

I carefully hit record on Brandon's phone, trying not to spook it.

"I'm recording you. It's a livestream," I say, super chill. "Don't come at me, or I will fuck up your life."

It cocks its head. I don't like the way it's standing. Shoulders hunched, one higher than the other. One leg posed, like a plié.

"Don't you move." I take a step back. "Don't you try anything, you forest pervert!"

It doesn't move. Perfectly still.

We're stuck there, having an awkward staring contest, and then, two more shapes ooze out of its back. Wider, and wider.

They're wings.

Like moth wings, translucent, catching the dawn in their fractured ridges. It's, like…

Hella beautiful.

"What…are you?"

The light slowly reveals its features: golden eyes, furry face, antennae. Kinda cute, actually.

"Do you live here?" Dumb question, like who's going to co-sign this guy's rental contract?

No response. Statuesque. Amazing core control.

"Do you ever…" How do I phrase this? "See people dancing here?"

Nothing.

"Like this?"

I do the dance, or at least my best rendition of it. I'm still rusty, and it's awkward, and Brandon was a shitty teacher, but I basically convey the moves.

For a sec it looks like nothing's registering, but then he sprints and freezes five feet from me—

"Livestream! Livestream!" I hold out my phone like a shield, but he doesn't attack.

He crouches low, one spindly arm outstretched to the side, claws spread, his beaky mouth slowly opening, golden eyes shifting black like ink in water.

"You okay, buddy?"

And then he begins:

Rhythmic clicking sounds. A perfect beat. Whooshing wings. Slapping his body like a drum. It's a whole orchestra in one body.

He's dancing, like Brandon's dance, but so much better. Fluid. This is his native tongue. He's the master, and everything I learned from Brandon was trash compared to this. Thank God I'm filming.

A melody builds from somewhere inside his chest. Buzzing like a cicada, but, like, good. Like if a cicada did opera or some shit.

And then…

And *then*…

Like a sneeze building. Like an orgasm. Like that old Colbie Caillat song my mom was obsessed with: it starts in my toes, makes me crinkle my nose. The music, it's inside of me. Vibrating up and down my skeleton, burrowing into my bones. The most delicious itch. My cells are dancing too. School lied to me. The mitochondria is the warehouse rave of the cell.

Everything's black now. I don't know where I am. I don't care. The music guides me. An explosion of light. This is the Universe beginning. It's *me* beginning. It's the Song beginning. Christmas lights strewn across the black. It's the same inside of me: sown to the atoms, all the way down. My electrons, they're dancing. They're all on beat. Earth waltzes around the sun. Cells split and multiply, molecular do-si-do to infinity. Creatures evolve, billions of them, honeycombs and larvae. They communicate without words, with their bodies, known to each other so much better than we are because they don't bother with words. Words are stupid. Words just hurt us. An eruption, blackened skies, they flee behind the curtain of their hive for Act Two. Buried beneath cooling earth. A thousand years, a million years, a billion years, they are blind in their cocoons, buried beneath a world changing without them…

That was wild.

I open my eyes. The beautiful dancer in the woods is gone. And so is the Song.

I cry in my car.

But then, I feel it begin as I drive home.

My body vibrates, fingers twitching. No, they're tapping a beat on the steering wheel. It's inching towards my feet, too. I wish I could get out and just let the rhythm take me, but I need to hold out, need to get back to Edgewater, need a wide-open space where they can see me.

Cars honk when I swerve into their lane. It doesn't matter. Their horns blare on my tempo.

Morning traffic commute is amping up, so when I can, I mount the curb. Pedestrians scatter in tango twirls. A homeless man slaps the side of my car, the clack of castanets.

Speeding down Sheridan, none of the lanes can contain me. I am the Universe manifesting from the inside out.

I jump out at Osterman Beach when the car stalls in the sand. The sheets of sand spraying from the spinning tires are the skirts of salsa dancers.

I set up my tripod facing Lake Michigan. Limbs jerking, I can hardly hold anything, but I have to get this right. I have to control it for another minute.

I unlock Brandon's phone and connect it to my car's Bluetooth.

Play the video of the dancer in the woods, volume all the way up. Click Brandon's phone onto the tripod.

Instagram. Livestream.

Finally. Now it can take me.

With the song of the Cosmos playing from my car's speaker, I dance, broadcasting it to Brandon's 750,000 followers.

Time is meaningless as I'm overcome. At some point, the camera light dies, but I dance on. It feels so good. Brandon was an idiot for being so whiny. He didn't deserve this gift. He didn't deserve his followers.

Hours pass; muscles ache so good.

At sundown, it starts. Smashing metal. Pounding pavement. I don't look. My eyes are on the empty auditorium that is Lake Michigan.

Soon, the city becomes an orchestra of cries, crashes, and sirens. Smoke in the air. Chicago's skyline in my right periphery, columns of smoke stream out like tassels in the wind.

At some point, a plane heading towards O'Hare flies overhead, bobbing up and down, caught up in the music. Sometime later, I hear a deafening boom. Right on beat. Someone up there paid for Wi-Fi and watched my video. Some random person spent money to watch me. I think I'm crying?

It must be past midnight now. Most of the sirens have died. All I hear are stamping feet on the concrete, booming through the city. They must be right behind me. Thousands of them. Maybe millions. The whole of the North Side is behind me.

They're my backup dancers, not my audience. My audience hasn't arrived yet. We're just warming up.

I fix my eyes on the black horizon where Lake Michigan meets the sky. No more airplanes clutter my view. Just empty seats…

Until…

The sand beneath my feet vibrates. The whole beach writhes, rippling with ecstasy, Coachella brought to me. Limbs break out of the sand, rupture the tide.

I dance with renewed purpose.

They crawl out of their holes, covered in dirt, black eyes shifting gold in the light of forgotten stars.

My dance, the Morse code of my feet, of my backup dancers' feet, called them here. They found their way through the dark to me. My jaw hurts from smiling.

They don't dance. They just watch. My audience.

I found my audience!

They're here for me!

They want to see me dance!

The Teague Thing

TERRY CAMPBELL

IF YOU WITNESSED something so terrifyingly traumatic as a kid, something that scared you so badly and shook you to your core so deeply that it haunted your dreams every day of your adult life, there is one immutable truth you would no doubt face should fate arrange circumstances accordingly: if you returned to that place, to that same exact spot where you had witnessed said event, you *would* become that shaking, horrified kid again, and no amount of grown-up logic, false bravado, or forced machismo would change that fact at all.

I experienced this myself when I returned to Teague, Texas, for the first time in almost forty years. I work for a salvage company out of Fort Worth, and we had recently won a bid to acquire a variety of decommissioned rail cars from the little-used BNSF Railyard in Teague. My company had chosen to send me to evaluate the cars, determine what was salvageable and what would be dismantled and sold as scrap, and to arrange for the cars to be transported back to Fort Worth. The company sent me because I was originally from the area, and I had prior railyard experience. I knew a thing or two about railcars.

I arrived in town about four o'clock that afternoon. The town hasn't changed much, that's for sure, but then, I expected as such. I had a bite to eat at a Mexican joint on the main drag in town, then reluctantly headed for the railyard, the dread building in my heart as I got closer. The sun was dipping low on the horizon, the various railroad equipment and warning lights casting long, skeletal shadows over the chipped quartz that covered the yard.

I stood in the waning daylight for I don't know how long. The longer I lingered, the more freaked out I became. It was early fall, and the air was cool by central Texas standards, but I was sweating profusely despite it all. My heart was pounding. The Chile relleno I had for dinner was already threatening to show itself again. This was where it had happened. This was where I saw it. June 23, 1987, late afternoon, in this very railyard. The train crossing posts still stood, albeit a bit worse for wear. Trains still passed through Teague, but its days as a functioning railyard were mostly in the past. The old grain and boxcars lay dormant, rusting away in the same positions they'd occupied decades ago. It's like time had stood still for forty years. Either that, or I had gone back forty years.

This was where I saw the Teague Thing.

My family lived in a modest frame house on a street that ran alongside the train tracks. My friends and I had been kicking a soccer ball down the street, whiling away another boring summer afternoon. We normally avoided the railyard. The workers were gruff, mean assholes, and they'd yell and cuss at us kids if we even so much as got close to any of the tracks. But it was late, and most of the men had left for the day. Anyway, Joey whiffed on the soccer ball that Enrique passed to him, and the ball ricocheted off the train rail and went bouncing over the rocky grounds. We laughed and checked to make sure no one was watching, then we crossed the dozen or so tracks to retrieve our ball. Quite a bit of train traffic rolled through Teague back then, headed south to Houston and north to DFW. The ball rolled well within the interior of the yard and out of our sight. We crossed all the tracks and found ourselves surrounded by train cars. And still, there was no sign of the soccer ball.

Hands on our hips and sweating in the hottest part of the day, we looked all around.

"Do you hear that?" Joey asked.

We listened. I didn't hear a thing.

"It's too quiet," I finally said.

No birds, no dogs barking, no other kids playing, no lawnmowers. No typical summer ambiance. We couldn't even hear the drone of semis flying down I-45 several miles away.

It was as if everything had stopped.

Then, we heard what Joey had.

Clomp, skeedle, clomp, skeedle...

Footsteps scooting through the gravel. Ragged, guttural breathing. The shadows had grown long and menacing. Enrique wordlessly pointed at one of the shadows, which was moving. We followed its length to a figure at the end.

We assumed it was a hobo at first. Lord knows so many of them came and went through the railyard in those days, hitching rides to points unknown. It wore a shabby, long overcoat with what looked like grimy patches all over it. A worn, round hat rested atop its head at an odd angle. A sickly smell hung in the air, a cross between sulfur and something dead and rotting. It was moving away from us, thank God, toward the end of the street beyond the tracks. It appeared to be dragging something behind it, like a rolled-up rug.

Clomp, skeedle, clomp, skeedle, clomp…

But then the rug twisted and rose into the air.

"That ain't no hobo," I whispered.

It wasn't human at all. What we had seen was a tail, and it danced and swayed behind the thing as it shuffled through the quartz chips.

Clomp, skeedle, clomp…

We watched the stones get tossed back into the air with each step it took. It didn't even have feet. It had hooves.

Joey blurted something out then, and the creature stopped and turned to face us. That face, my God, that face. It wasn't remotely human. Long scraggly hair spilled from underneath the filthy derby hat balanced precariously on its head. *Jesus,* but its face. Its face was *all wrong.* It had no nose, just two long vertical slits in its forehead. Its eyes, bulbous and oozing an opaque liquid, were in its chin, gunk hanging down like strings of mucous, swaying with each step. Its mouth was also vertical, centered between the slit nostrils and the eyes. Its teeth were human-like, yet impossibly large. When the terrifying thing noticed us, its mouth opened wide—horizontally—and it spat gargled, chortling sounds at us.

We turned and ran like we had the Devil himself at our heels, and he may very well have been for all we knew. My house was closest. We bolted in, screaming to my mom. She ran outside, as did the neighbors, to investigate.

Everyone saw it.

It continued toward the end of the street, paying no heed to any of us. When it stepped onto the asphalt, the clomping of its hooves sounded even louder in the late afternoon quiet. One of the neighbors called the police, and we all watched as it disappeared into an abandoned house where the woods began.

When the police arrived a few moments later, they searched the house and surrounding area, but found no evidence the thing existed, although that awful smell still lingered in the air.

We moved away from Teague a few weeks later. There were several more sightings in the days following our encounter, but we heard nothing else about it after we left.

I never stopped thinking about it.

Now, I stood in the spot where I'd seen the entity, shaking and trying to compose myself, not even noticing that night had fallen. I made my way back to my truck. The Teague Hotel, a restored old building, sat right across from the tracks, but I found myself wishing I had taken a room at a hotel out by the interstate. I didn't want to be near that railyard.

Several cups of coffee and some warm morning sun helped to alleviate my fears the next day, getting my mind back into focus. I had a job to do, and I couldn't let something that had happened to eight-year-old me prevent me from doing it. I figured I would start with the old office building and see if any records had been left behind. Back in those days, most records were still kept on paper and filed away, so I might find something useful to get me started in the right direction. I did find some maps of the entire railyard, which helped me get my bearings on where I needed to focus my attention.

But I got sidetracked easily sometimes, especially when my mind was already half involved with something else, as it obviously still was. The old decommissioned caboose still sat backed up against the hurricane fence that ran along the west perimeter of the railyard. Bobby had used that as a command central of sorts. Bobby had been the night security guard back in the day. He was pretty cool with us kids, but he made no bones about what would happen if he ever caught any of us screwing around on the tracks. Someone told me he eventually walked off the job and no one heard from him again, but that was several years after I'd moved away.

I made a quick perimeter check of the caboose before climbing the three iron steps to the platform. The door was unlocked, but years of exposure had rusted the hinges and made it nearly impossible to open. It seemed a shame the old red car would no longer be a part of Teague, but a job was a job. Finally, the door groaning and squealing in protest, I managed to force it open far enough to gain entrance. Swarms of dust motes floated through the sunlight streaming in through the small window on the side wall. I paused for a moment and studied the interior of the car. A few sheets of paper and a notebook lay on top of a small counter. A two-drawer file cabinet was tucked away beneath the desk. I took a seat in the rolling chair that accompanied the desk and opened the bottom drawer. Inside, I found a logbook with the BNSF logo printed on the front cover. I retrieved the book and began flipping through the pages.

BNSF Railyard—Teague, TX Division

September 16, 1986 23:17

Walked western perimeter of hurricane fence. No issues reported. Investigated noise from crossing on Track 14. Possible coyotes. Sodium light on eastern rail cars broken. Work order notated. Found 3 men sleeping in boxcar, escorted from the premises.

BNSF Railyard—Teague, TX Division

September 19, 1986 19:11

Initial walk-through of work week. Tracks clear east to west. Closed and secured all boxcars. Interiors clear. Coyotes howling nearby. Discarded trash from rail workers are attracting them. Made note to contact management.

BNSF Railyard—Teague, TX Division

September 16, 1986 4:31

Final patrol of the night. A few breaks in hurricane fence on northwest corner across from the Teague Hotel. Possible vandalism. Beer cans noted in vicinity. Found a shed snakeskin underneath grain car on Track 9. I hope it doesn't come near the office. I hate snakes.

This was Bobby's work log. He'd used the logbook to keep records of each patrol he made through the yard. I skimmed through several months' worth of reports, but nothing stood out as unusual to me. I'm sure nothing much ever happened after hours. Until that day in 1987.

I rummaged through a side drawer on the desk until I found an old mini-cassette recorder and about a dozen tapes. It seemed Bobby had carried it and recorded each of his patrols, then would note any highlights in the log. He had labeled each cassette with the dates they were created. I sat those aside and returned to the work log. I flipped through the pages until I found the entries for the weeks leading up to my encounter with the creature.

BNSF Railyard—Teague, TX Division

June 16, 1987 02:43

Had patrolled the entire eastern half of railyard. Upon returning, encountered a man climbing down from a grain car. Must have been a hobo; there was a horrendous odor coming from him. I did not get close but tried to contact him verbally. It was very dark. He wore a round hat, and my flashlight beam failed to light up his face enough to make out any features. He ignored my commands and continued down the tracks, crossing over to the fence that runs alongside 2nd Avenue. At that point, he scaled the fence and continued down the street. Broken axle parts noted on Track 2. Notations made for head mechanic.

BNSF Railyard—Teague, TX Division

June 19, 1987 03:13

Conducting perimeter inspection. Encountered strange man again, this time exiting a boxcar on Track 11. Again, he would not respond to verbal commands. Followed from a safe distance as he once again exited the yard onto 2nd Avenue and disappeared in the darkness. Terrible odor remains.

I leaned back in the rolling chair and shivered. Bobby had witnessed the same thing my friends and I had, and on more than one occasion. Wanting to know more but desperately needing a break from these thoughts, I decided it was time to do some of the work I had actually been sent to do. I left the cassette player and logbook on the desk and went out into the late morning sun. Firing up my tablet, I began inspecting, logging, and photographing the boxcars that would be scheduled for transport, performing complete inspections and notating any repairs or faults that would need to be addressed.

I lost track of time when a startling clap of thunder sounded overhead. Fall thunderstorms came up quickly in central Texas, and this one caught me completely unaware. I thought of Bobby and how he had conducted his patrols in all types of inclement weather, so I headed back to the caboose as large splats of rain began to bombard the dried rock bed. The sky brightened suddenly with a flash of lightning, followed closely by another loud boom. I made it up the iron steps just as the bottom fell out.

I stepped inside the caboose. Surely Bobby or his replacement had kept some sort of weather gear on hand for just such occasions. Several lockers lined the center of one wall. I opened the first door and looked inside. Sure enough, a bright yellow rain slicker hung on a hook. I started to reach for it and stopped. Next to the raincoat hung a shabby long coat covered in haphazardly applied patches. I stared at it for a long moment, then noticed, perched atop a shelf above the hangers, the dirty round hat.

My hands shaking, I reached for the coat. I pulled it toward me and inspected it closely. Several stringy mop heads had been sewn together and attached to the lower part of the back. My mind instantly went back to that day in 1987. My gaze shifted to the floor of the tiny closet and found a pair of dingy boots. When I stooped over to pick them up, I was surprised at how heavy they were. Then I turned them over. Wooden cut-outs in the shapes of hooves had been glued to the soles. Underneath the hat, I found a mask made from several other masks of various monsters, all sewn together to create a new hideous face.

That face.

"Son of a bitch," I muttered.

The coat. The hat. The hooves. Even the tail.

It was impossible. I know what I saw. It couldn't be.

The creature we had seen that summer day back in 1987 was the railyard night security guard in a makeshift costume?

But why?

To keep us kids away? To scare the hobos off? To keep trespassers from entering the grounds?

But that was his job, anyway. That's what he was hired to do. None of it made any sense. I supposed it had scared my younger self so badly that I fell for the visage completely. Yet, so had everyone else on our street. And that smell? What the hell was that? You couldn't just create a god-awful smell like that out of thin air.

I sat down at the desk and reached for the recorder. The sound of the downpour crashing onto the metal roof of the caboose was almost deafening, yet still somehow soothing. I flipped through the cassettes until I found the date I was looking for. Fortunately, I always carried extra batteries in my tablet case. I inserted the tape and pressed play.

I hadn't heard Bobby's voice in decades. I leaned back and listened as Bobby narrated his patrol. Typical stuff—checking the gates, the perimeter, the boxcars.

Then I heard *it* through the crackle of the poor sound quality.

Clomp, skeedle, clomp, skeedle, clomp…

Just like that day in June.

Had Bobby created those sounds, or was it something else?

Shaken at hearing those footsteps again, I turned off the recorder.

The quick-passing storm was already diminishing. I left the caboose, processing what I'd seen and heard, and tried to focus back on my job.

The rest of the week passed by uneventfully. I completed my reports and sent them back to my supervisor in Fort Worth. I went over Bobby's entire logbook; after those few entries, no mention of the Teague Thing was ever made again. I had one day left in town. I needed to wait for the arrival of the locomotives that would carry the inoperable rail cars away once they were loaded onto flat trailers. After that, the rest of the day was free and clear, and I would say goodbye to Teague forever.

But there was still one thing that nagged at me. Well, several things, actually. What was Bobby trying to accomplish by pretending to be a monster? Was it for the attention, or was he truly trying to prevent something from being discovered? I briefly considered the possibility of drugs, but this was the '80s. Meth labs weren't the problem then that they are now. Hell, I think Walmart even sold a start-up kit right next to the rock tumbling kits and loom crafters. So it wasn't likely he had hidden a meth lab somewhere.

And also, the house. That old house at the end of 2nd Avenue where we had watched the creature disappear into on that summer evening. The house was still there. Part of the roof had collapsed and condemned signs hung on the front door, but it was still there.

I walked uneasily down the asphalt street toward that old house. The locomotives had already pulled away to the north with the rust-frozen cars fifteen minutes prior.

My heart beat louder and faster with each step I took. Finally, I reached the crumbling frame and stood in the yard. I looked back up the street. My old house was still visible from here, though it had seen better days. Wind swayed the branches of the trees looming just beyond the backyard. Birds chirped and sang, and squirrels played. Everything seemed…normal. I looked around again to make sure no police cars were patrolling in the vicinity and headed for the back of the house. Using a broken-out window, I helped myself inside.

Although it was bright outside, the interior was dim. I turned on my flashlight. What could the creature have wanted inside this house? Or, if the creature was really Bobby in a costume, why did he disappear in here and why didn't the cops find him that day?

I made my way throughout the entire house. Other than evidence of past squatters who'd taken up residence, there was nothing out of the ordinary. I was working my way back up the hallway to the window I'd crawled through when my foot hit a soft spot in the wood flooring. It gave some when I pushed down on it with my boots. I knelt and looked closer. I ran my fingers along the planks and found a fingerhold. The cops must not have looked very hard. The trapdoor swung up, revealing a crawl space beneath the house.

I tried to ignore the claw marks in the dirt.

It helped that the hoofprints grabbed my attention first.

Terrified, but with an overwhelming need to find the truth, I dropped to the dirt floor. I crawled forward, holding my flashlight beam as steady as I could. The air was damp and musty, and an old odor of rot threatened to gag me. Gradually, the crawlspace descended and opened up, and I suddenly found myself in a wider chamber.

That horrendous stench intensified, and I had an overwhelming sense that I was no longer alone. Faint flickering lights danced across the ceiling from an unknown source, and among them, shadows slithered. I let out a shriek and dropped my flashlight, temporarily casting the room in total darkness. Thankfully, my hand closed directly on the torch when I felt for it. I shook it and banged it against the palm of my hand, and the beam blazed forth. I slowly shone it around the circumference of the room, my heart pounding like freight engines clambering over the tracks. Human bones littered the floor of the small chamber. Tattered, mildewed clothes lay strewn about. The faint smell of putrefied flesh hung in the stagnant air. I had no idea how far beneath the house I was. In the middle of the room was a circular stack of stones—an old well. And beside it, a metal box sitting on the floor. I found it unlocked, and I opened it. Inside was another BNSF logbook and one micro-cassette.

I could tell on the first page that it was Bobby's handwriting. I began scanning through the entries. It became obvious rather quickly that Bobby had no intention of anyone at BNSF ever seeing this work log.

BNSF Railyard—Teague, TX Division

June 22, 1987 04:14

This is the sixth time I have seen the strange creature in the railyard. I have only seen it leaving; I've never seen where or how it enters. Each time, I can see its features a little more clearly. I know these facts for sure: it is not human, nor animal. It is not some strange cryptid, like the Lake Worth Monster, or a goatman. I believe it is not of this dimension.

BNSF Railyard—Teague, TX Division

June 24, 1987 03:55

I fear for the kids. For the people of Teague. I know this thing has been witnessed by some folks in town, appearing at times in the daylight hours. I had to learn more about it. I followed it out of the railyard, stayed close behind as it moved deliberately down 2nd Avenue toward an abandoned house next to the woods. There, I watched it go inside and down a hole in the hallway floor. Tonight, I learned where the creature comes from…it comes straight from Hell.

I continued to read through the log entries, thankful that I had planned ahead and brought extra batteries for my flashlight. I wanted to sit somewhere, but there was no way I was ready to approach that well and the ground was damp.

BNSF Railyard—Teague, TX Division

June 26, 1987 01:02

God help me for what I'm doing. I have the best of intentions. This thing, whatever it is, wherever it came from, is on the hunt nightly. It needs to feed. I'm thinking of the kids, you have to believe me. A lot of kids live near the railyard. They're good kids, and they stay away for the most part. But they're there all the same, and they would be easy prey for a predator. I didn't just expel the transients I found sleeping in the railyard a few nights ago. I lured them away, down to the house, with the pretense of booze and food. I did it for the town. God help me.

BNSF Railyard—Teague, TX Division

June 27, 1987 12:19

I found their clothes and bones tonight. Picked clean. The creature did not come around. I must find more food. A lot of unfortunate souls ride the rails in central Texas.

I took in a deep breath and slowly exhaled. We *did* see a creature that day. It *was* real. Bobby had followed it back to its lair, its haunt. Had practically made a pet of it, it seemed. Not to mention, he was evidently feeding those poor souls to this thing like tossing chunks of a sandwich to a stray dog. It was difficult to accept, for sure. But my mind kept going back to the costume in the closet of the old caboose. Why in the hell would Bobby pretend to be a creature when he was attempting to keep said creature at bay? Perhaps the answers were deeper in the entries of the logbook.

BNSF Railyard—Teague, TX Division

June 30, 1987 04:11

I have not seen the creature in three days. I returned to its lair empty-handed. I had found no transients on the train since the last one I took to the creature. The body of my last victim is still there, untouched. I don't know what happened, or how it happened. Perhaps the atmosphere in this dimension was toxic to it. Perhaps it was merely ancient, and had simply died of natural causes. I found the creature dead tonight, curled up in the bottom of the old well. God, the smell. Between it and the hobo.

BNSF Railyard—Teague, TX Division

July 1, 1987 23:47

The well is a portal into another dimension, like something out of a Lovecraft tale. I did some research, talked to a good friend who is really into the occult. The city of Teague is terrified of this creature, and it must stay that way. If one terrible entity came into this world through this opening, more could do the same. I can't let that happen. I placed a circular piece of wood over the well and painted an archaic symbol meant to keep evil from exiting its dimension and entering this one. But the original creature must continue to prowl the streets of Teague. No one can find this well. If anyone ever reads this entry, play the tape.

Evidently, Bobby had begun dressing as the creature after it died, to keep others from finding the portal. And it seemed to have worked for forty years.

Play the tape.

At first, I heard what I thought was merely white noise. But then, slowly, other sounds broke through. Breaths, scraping sounds. Moans of agony. Blood-halting screams. The volume increased in intensity until nothing was decipherable but everything was horrifying—and yet spellbinding. Finally, I could take it no longer and turned the player off.

I sat there for what seemed like hours, chilled by the dampness, trying to wrap my brain around everything I'd discovered. Bobby knew the truth. He had played with fire. They said he'd walked off the job and was never heard from again. Was that what had happened? Or did he get too close to something no one in this realm had any business messing with? And was I now doing the same?

But I had to see. I had to look. God help me.

I shone the flashlight beam onto the well cover. The symbol had faded, but it was still there. It looked like a backward "C" with two diagonal slashes across it. My hands visibly shaking, sweat pouring from my forehead and into my eyes, I grabbed the edges of the wooden piece and slid it over. Years of moisture and humidity had taken their toll, and the wood splintered in my hands. I could hear chunks and slivers of the rotten wood crashing into the well below.

I steeled my nerves and peered into the well.

There was a creature. We did witness it that day.

The skull of the creature I had encountered forty years ago stared up at me. The large teeth seemed almost comically disproportionate to the rest of the skull. Empty eye sockets *below* the mouth stood out in their darkness. The rest of its skeleton was there, curled up in some obscene fetal position just as Bobby had described in his entry.

Air whooshed from the depths of the well, and that's when I realized it wasn't a well. It was the exit of a tunnel system. Subterranean winds were blowing through unseen passages below, singing a mournful yet sinister melody.

I must've hit "Play" again.

That was my first thought when I heard the first soul-obliterating cry from far below. Then came the moans, the screams, the heavy-laden breathing.

The events of the summer of 1987 were distant memories to the citizens of Teague, Texas, etched only as town folklore in fading recollection. I should've left it all well enough alone. The house would have eventually been demolished, the portal discovered by someone else. Now, if anything happened, it would be my fault.

The portal was open once again. And I didn't know how to close it. Bobby knew. Bobby did the right thing.

The screams and wails diminished as another terrifying sound rose from the depths of the lower chambers.

Clomp… skeedle…clomp… skeedle… clomp…

Something was coming.

I turned away and crawled as fast as I could through the tunnel back to the entrance of the house.

Clomp… skeedle… clomp…

It was right behind me. How could it move so *fast?*

For the second time in my life, I got the hell out of Teague, Texas, as quickly as I could. And this time, eight-year-old me and forty-six-year-old me were in complete agreement.

If we got out of here alive, we were never going back.

Wastes Beyond Wastes

LEON SAUL

AGAINST THE WIND, it trudges like a wooden wind-up toy. Leathered skin dappled with fresh snow. A sinewy tongue lolls out of the mutilated mouth frozen in a rictus. Snowflakes land on the gray, ropy muscle, dissolve on its dark, stippled surface.

Below, a line of smoke unravels in the snow-filled sky. The creature stops. Its eyes spark like embers in the sockets of a cadaverous face.

Wheezing with anticipation, it picks its way down the slope of the mountain. Heading toward the pine structure emitting the smoke and leaving in its wake a spoor of crimson footprints in the snow.

***

Josh claps his hands over his ears, trying to block out the shouting from downstairs. The deep bass of his father's voice vibrates the floor beneath his feet. A shrill, venomous hiss follows. They've been going at it for thirty minutes now.

Josh knew this whole vacation was a waste. No amount of snowboarding or sipping hot cocoa in front of the fire was going to fix things between his mom and dad. It was over. The last couple of years, their marriage had soured into a bitter union of mutual resentment and, at times, violence. Josh remembers the bruise shadowing his mom's right eye three weeks ago: a livid violet, just visible beneath the makeup. Later, he overheard her in the garage talking on the phone to Aunt Cindy while Dad was out somewhere (probably with that tall redheaded woman from his work)—listening to her hushed, sobbing plans of leaving him. Whispered revelations of drinking and hitting. An escalation of abuse.

Divorce was all but certain. Josh just hopes it'll be quick—prays there won't be an ugly custody battle like what happened with his best friend Julian. With a twist of nausea in his stomach, he figures Dad'll probably fight for custody, if for no other reason than to spite his mom. Most of the fighting revolves around her lack of "mothering skills"—how she lets Josh meet up with Julian after school without checking to see if he's done his homework, and allows him to play GTA and Fortnite, when video games only rot a kid's brain.

His dad's the most cold-hearted prick he knows.

He hopes—*begs*—Mom will get full custody, and his time with Dad'll be limited to once-a-week overnights and weekends. That, he could live with.

A husky snarl—followed by a harsh, owl-like shriek—rumbles from below. Josh cups his ears harder, humming to himself to cancel out the sounds of mounting hostility. Tears prick at the corners of his eyes. He sniffs as he squeezes them shut, lets twin salt trails run down his face.

Just let this miserable vacation be over already...

The tradition of renting a cabin in Mammoth over Presidents' Day weekend is one they've had since Josh was little. It used to be something to look forward to—skiing and snowboarding, hiking the glistening white trails—but not anymore. He imagines his parents thought the forced family time would somehow fix things, bring them all closer together.

Yeah, right.

Wind groans through the windowpanes, rattling the glass. Josh glances outside past intricate whorls of ice and sees snow falling heavily. The sky, a frenzy of chalk-white flakes. Cold seeps through the glass. He tugs on the sleeves of his fisherman sweater—knotted and shrunken over the years—but the frayed cotton bounces back over his birdlike wrists.

Sighing, he gazes past the ghost of his reflection. Beyond the falling snow, a figure appears on the upper ridge and stumbles down the slope.

A man? It moves stiffly, like a zombie or an animatronic scarecrow at a two-bit carnival. Josh squints, cups his hands around the chilled glass of the window. The figure's tall, pale as a skinned tree branch, and unnaturally skinny. It trails a zagging line of footprints behind it.

Despite the overcast sky, the footprints look red. *Bright* red. Almost like....

His heart skips a beat. As the figure lurches closer—reeling drunkenly, like his Uncle Wyatt after a few too many Budweisers at Christmas—Josh's eyes widen when he sees the person isn't wearing any clothes.

Just...naked. In the middle of *February?*

No, the man—if it *is* a man, he thinks with an absurd shiver—would freeze to death.

The closer the figure gets, the more unnatural it looks. Skeletally thin, skin gray and leathery, like a twist of jerky. It reminds Josh of the Egyptian priestess he once saw in a glass tomb at the Saint Louis Science Center. Mottled in places, like bruises on old fruit. Places where the gauze-gray flesh has rotted or been torn off. Or eaten...

Gooseflesh pebbles his skin, and the hairs on the back of his neck stand on end. He wonders if his parents are seeing this...*thing* approaching their cabin—or if they're too busy yelling at each other still. He doesn't hear anything from downstairs. His ears feel weirdly blocked, like they're stuffed with cotton. He should definitely run down there and warn them that...what, a walking skeleton-man is lumbering toward their cabin? A tall, skinny naked man or woman—whatever it is, it's incredibly *old*—staggering down the slope in snowy, sub-zero weather?

Josh feels lightheaded. Sick to his stomach. *This is bad*, he thinks—and realizes he's sweating.

Mouth dry, he can't work up enough saliva to utter a sound. He sits frozen on the edge of the mattress, watching in mute paralysis as the figure—

looking more and more like a haggard old man, nude and sickly gray...bits of flesh definitely *missing, oh fuck, eyes sunken but somehow glowing*

—gets closer.

Slowly. Steadily.

We need to—

The thought sets his heart trip-hammering, and then the thing is mere feet from the front door.

On the stoop, it glances up, catching Josh's gaze in the window. His guts turn to liquid.

Eyes glowing like crimson coals, recessed in the skull-like face, stare up at him; and the mouth—

Oh God, where are its lips?

—seems to leer in a horrid and oblong smile, which finally makes him scream.

The trapper and his son huddle on the splintered wooden floor. Knees drawn up, bodies pressed together for warmth. Wind rasps through holes in the cabin ceiling, and errant snowflakes flitter in the murky light.

Weak and pale, the boy convulses with hunger pangs against his father's side. When he shifts position, brushing against the rent in the trapper's snow-crusted coat, he hisses in pain. He can't recall how long they've been holed up in the abandoned cabin, how many days have elapsed since evading the attack on their camp. Visions of the Indian war party flare like musket fire in his mind's eye.

His brother-in-law Jude bleeding out of his torn mouth, moans wheezing through broken and bloody teeth, his life force ebbing…

The image stuck like a splinter in his mind's eye as the trapper hauled his son from the carnage, stumbling through knee-high drifts, while the sounds of clashing and dying tolled in his ears. Somehow, they made it out—fled north into the dark mountain pass. All he could think of was escape. Getting the boy to safety. Evading the Natives who swore revenge for the rape and murder of one of their own—the village chief's daughter. A girl close to Henry's age. A part of the trapper understood their rage, as he would do the very same to ensure their survival.

Banshee-like, the blizzard wails. A hollow cry. The cabin has no doors or windows; only holes, some large enough for a man to enter. Through them, snow dances maddeningly white. Two days ago—by the trapper's estimation—he tried patching the dilapidated ceiling, but the strips of ox hide did little to prevent the cold from invading the cabin's interior.

A groan issues from nearby, and the trapper realizes it's the boy's stomach. Dolefully, he holds him tighter, and says for the dozenth time, *Soon, Henry… The storm will clear soon.*

The boy makes no response, only shivers, lips trembling. In the cabin's murk to their right, a lake of vomit congeals: the result of trying to eat boiled ox hide. The trapper grimaces, recalling how the strips had dissolved into a repulsive glue-like jelly which stuck to the roof of his mouth, making them both violently ill. Afterward, his son sobbed, clutching his stomach in pain. Hating himself for not putting up a stronger front, the trapper could only cry along with him.

We're going to die, the boy spluttered between faint gasps.

The trapper couldn't bring himself to correct him.

Days later, he unearthed from the frozen drifts the skeleton of a small pony. In boiling the bones on the iron stove, they turned soft and brittle. Crumbled in his mouth like clots of sun-dried manure.

Father and son retched in the same corner as before, adding to the shared lake of icy vomit.

The trapper eyes the pale semi-solid matter now, and wonders how long before they'll be tempted to eat it.

In his delirium, the boy shakes. Squeezing his hand over the boy's shivering shoulder, the trapper whispers in his son's ear, reddened from the cold. *Soon.*

By the time Josh explodes through the door onto the upstairs landing, it's halfway inside.

Framed in the entrance (the heavy oak door askew, ripped off its hinges) is a living skeleton. Snowflakes blow behind it, eddying around the emaciated frame. With gnarled feet, it totters inside. A rancid stench immediately fills the cabin, like something dead and rotting.

Josh's parents scream—no longer at each other—as the thing, easily eight feet tall, shuffles into the foyer. A hideous warble escapes the ragged oval of its mouth. As it lurches closer, Josh sees areas of missing flesh in its desiccated hide, a freakish jigsaw puzzle. Its lips are gone—chewed away—the teeth exposed in a peeled-back grimace.

With a shout, his father lunges, and Josh cries out as a deformed arm extends and knocks him down. Then, with surprising agility—*how does something so old move so fast?*—the monster strikes. Josh and his mother both scream. The knobs of its spine jut like knuckles as the creature kneels over his father—whose usually powerful voice now is muffled by a splayed, skeletal hand—then takes a hungry bite out of his throat.

When the humanoid creature lifts its head, it sneers liplessly, the frozen grimace of teeth and gums glistening with dark blood. Josh can't look; he buries his face in his mother's shoulder as the slurping and snuffling sounds continue, mingled with ragged wheezing and low gurgling coming from his father as he loses blood.

Then suddenly, the weight of his mother is displaced. Josh's eyes fly open. The creature has her in its clawed hands (which have extended, bonelessly, like putty), reeling her in. Effortlessly, it holds her, twists a hank of auburn hair; screams echo around the cabin as it takes deep bites out of her face. Rocking in a shivery ball, Josh nearly faints, arms clamped hard against his temples, eyes squeezed shut as the sounds of screaming and crying…*ripping snorting chewing*…resound in the confined cabin space.

After what feels like hours, the sounds fade. All he hears now is the patter of feet sliding across viscous fluid on the hardwood floor. When he dares to look, his gorge rises…

(Puke cresting his tonsils, threatening to erupt out of his mouth)

…when he sees what's become of his parents.

Amid the welter of torn flesh and bloody, dismantled bones, the thing stares, its eyes abyssal black holes, clots of tissue snagged in its teeth.

Josh retches. Doubled over, he feels relief in throwing up, in knowing the end is near. Mirrored in the waves of vomit on the wooden floor, his weak reflection ripples.

Again, he hears the squeak of feet wading through blood—through the remains of Mom and Dad…

Together again, he muses with a hideous urge to laugh, *one big happy family…*

and he closes his eyes and waits for the thing to take him in its jaws and eat him alive.

His son's eyes roll under closed lids.

Spasms rock the boy's shivering frame, and the trapper holds him, knowing what the boy is experiencing.

Hallucinations.

He too has experienced them—recalling how, hours earlier, the image of his wife appeared over the coarse slats of the cabin floor. Half nude, the dome of her abdomen covered in veins. She rubbed her swollen belly with tapered hands, hummed a melody at once lulling and foreign in the trapper's ears.

Eat, the words echoed.

If the trapper had any belief in a hereafter—that the vision floating before him was the phantasm of his dead wife—had even the slightest conviction there was something—*anything*—beyond this miserable, hardscrabble existence, he'd find a way to expedite their end, so that he and the boy could be joined with her. But he doesn't believe that. In his heart, he knows the finality of death. There will be no reunions, no drifting through ethereal planes.

Only darkness. And the cold, hard ground—

From his reverie, he awakens to shrill wind vortexing through holes in the cabin's walls. A heaviness leans against his side, radiating its own peculiar coldness.

Instantly, he knows the boy is gone. Off to join his mother in the darkness and the cold.

After a time, he musters the strength to bury the boy in the drifts outside, hating himself for rushing the ersatz ceremony. Shoulders hunched against the wind, he looks to the ground, hitches a pained breath.

I couldn't protect him, Helen, he says to himself. Eyes swelling with tears prism the snowy peaks surrounding the cabin.

The following days, he subsists on the remaining ox hide. His stomach spasms, clenching as the glue-like substance seals to the roof of his mouth. It's no use. He'll starve or freeze to death, whichever comes first. And then join his wife and son in the darkness. The cold and pitiless darkness. He finds solace in the thought.

But his core revolts. Fire wracks the inside of his body. Again, the vision of his wife appears, a plume of smoke in the cabin's shadowy corner.

Eat.

The words, gentle yet urgent.

Don't let the cold and the darkness have you, too.

The trapper shakes his head, squeezes shut his welling eyes.

It's the only way, love. Otherwise you'll die—and there will be no one.

Tears track down the trapper's grizzled face, which feels gaunt and stiff, sore as an open wound. His stomach contracts. Heaves. With a groan, he lifts himself off the floor, wet from snow blown in through the riddled roof.

As if directed by some unseen hand, he drifts to the door—his conscious mind ceded to a primal, driving force.

Outside, the day is white—blindingly so—but cold as outer space. Wind drives the snowflakes horizontal, and the crystals cling to him, snag fatly in his hair, his beard, as he staggers through the shifting moonscape.

Rigidly, he claws through the drift marked with a leaning, knotted stick on the eastern side of the cabin. His entire body is numb. Hands, bloodless blocks of ice. Wind lifts the snow, slapping his face like a jeering child. Through the swirling flakes, he squints; peers into the cave he's creating with his numb and reddened fingers.

A flash of sodden fur.

Snow spreads like wings to either side of him as he digs out more of the powder with his clawed hands.

Brushing away fine crystal shards, he sees it then, framed in white. The oval of a cherub's face. Eyes closed, lashes rimmed with flakes. The cold has preserved him perfectly. Choking on a sob, the trapper hauls the corpse out of its icy tomb, and bears the body inside. Lays it in the center of the cold wooden floor. Tears cascade ceaselessly now, but the trapper remembers what the vision of his wife had said.

You have no choice, love—but to live...

The hand that saws off a chunk of the boy's calf is not *his* hand. He observes the action as if from a distance; hears the horrible hacking, sees the marbled flesh; and then, somnambulistically, brings the morsel to his mouth. His hunger is not localized. It radiates through every inch of him, like blood from the ventricles of a heart. When he brings the hunk of meat to his lips, the stench of blood hits his nostrils. His gorge rises, but he forces his stomach down. In his mouth, the frigid gobbet of flesh warms, and blood, salty and thick, suffuses his glands, drips down his throat.

Swallowing, his body accepts the sustenance. He doesn't look at the corpse—nor at the ragged, dripping shred in his hands—as he eats.

Henry would understand, the trapper tells himself. But the thought is numb. A frozen thing.

After what feels like hours, he collapses to the ground.

His hands are red. Pushing weakly off the floorboards, he attempts to stumble outside, to wipe them in the snow, clean the skin so he doesn't have to look at those bloody stains on his fingers.

Lurching through a hole in the wall, he's sprayed by an army of bone-white particles. He falls to his knees, and jams both fists into a bank of snow. It swallows the crimson-caked balls of flesh. Eyes closed, he flexes his fingers, wiggles them in the icy dune, and then removes his hands to see that, of course, they're still red, but not the lurid crimson of earlier: a duller pink.

He's about to plunge them in again when a fist of torment seizes him.

Hissing through gritted teeth, he collapses in the snow. This is new—unlike the starvation that's preyed on him and the boy for weeks. Sharp and hot. Metallic, like scissors slicing up his insides. On the ground, he writhes in agony, arms flailing toward the sky. With blurring vision, he sees the flesh of his hands lose color. The skin mottles, turning gray; it rips in spots as the bones lengthen and crack...

The starvation that blooms afterward is unlike anything he's ever experienced.

On instinct, he bites down on the first thing he can to appease this new hunger. Sharpened fangs pierce into his wizened bottom lip. The tissue splits easily, pulverizing under his gnashing teeth. The shreds do little to allay the pain. He shoves his fingers deep into his mouth, then, avidly raking the tips with his teeth—stripping and swallowing what meat he can, till nothing remains but five gleaming, blood-slicked bones.

Then, rising unsteadily to his new height—unraveling his twisted new spine—he gazes downward.

EAT. The directive comes from somewhere deep within his gelid core.

An assault of wind wafts the stench of blood into his sinuses. His nostrils quiver as he peers down into the snowy crater at his feet. At what lies within it.

Instantly he sets back to work, consuming the rest of the flesh raw—until the meat is stripped and all that remains of his son is a pool of sodden clothes settled over a clump of crimson bones.

The creature watches the boy flee the cabin.

Every bit of organic matter has been consumed. Eyes, lips, ears. Rib cartilage; muscle tendon. It doesn't know why it let the child go. It hungers still, despite its ravenous repast. A look in the boy's eyes had awakened something—a species of emotion, long frozen in the ice block of its heart.

After licking clean the floorboards, only bones remain, clattering as the creature brushes past, toward the void where the door once stood and outside the cabin, into the murk. Heavy winds assail it. Snowflakes sting the ragged rictus-grin of its mouth. Scenting something, it traces its steps back onto the ridge.

Food there. Perhaps a deer—

Embraced by the cold, it lumbers off into the wastes.

A Terrifying Prize

J. NEIRA

THE SHADOWY, LONG-LIMBED creature was just about to crawl out from beneath the child's bed when the doorbell rang. Morgan frowned and paused the movie, shoving aside the blanket she had draped over her and rising from the sofa.

It was just after eight o'clock in the evening, and she wasn't expecting visitors. Salesmen were rare in these parts too; her house was so rural, nobody ever came out this way unless they had a specific purpose. She flipped a switch in the hall and parted the front window's curtains just enough to peek out.

A large white truck sat parked by the road, adorned with big red letters: GRILLMAN'S. Morgan's lip lifted into a sneer.

Her gaze shifted to the woman on her doorstep—thick, black-rimmed glasses, curly brown hair, a big smile plastered on her face the way the Grillman's logo was plastered on her uniform.

The woman lifted a hand and smashed the doorbell. Again. Morgan huffed.

"Yes, yes, I'm coming," she called, unlocking the door and pulling it open. A cool night breeze drifted in over the woman's shoulder.

"Woah, holy goth!" the woman exclaimed, no doubt taken aback by Morgan's unnaturally pale skin, thinly plucked eyebrows, box-dye-black hair and crimson bangs.

"Yes?" Morgan said, crossing pale, muscular arms as she stared down the woman in the Grillman's uniform. A nametag with the name *Darcy* was pinned on her chest. She didn't appreciate being disturbed at this time of night, especially not when in the middle of watching a horror film.

Darcy's smile never faltered despite Morgan's cold reception. "Hello. Miss Morgan, right? I have some *very* exciting news for you!"

Morgan's frown deepened. How did this woman know her name?

Without giving her a chance to answer, the woman continued, her voice bubbly and loud, making Morgan's head throb. "I'm sure you're familiar with Grillman's, the place everyone loves to visit. Well, guess what?" She clapped her hands together, bouncing on the balls of her feet. "You've just won el Chupacabra, the world's biggest hotdog. Courtesy of Grillman's." Her announcement hung in the air between them, and she stared at Morgan as if expecting her to start cheering.

Instead, Morgan just stared at her, dumbfounded. "But…I didn't enter any contest," she said, utterly perplexed. Darcy's fervor didn't feel like a scam, but she had no idea what was going on. Morgan had never even *been* to Grillman's, and she certainly wouldn't have entered a competition. Not with such an absurd prize. "Especially not a *Grillman's* contest."

Darcy's face fell, smile vanishing to be replaced with an almost comical-looking pout. "Oh, not again," she muttered, putting a hand to her head and sighing.

Morgan's confusion only grew. "Not…again?"

Darcy's dark hair bounced along her shoulders as she shook her head. "Last year, we ran a competition with a prize of one thousand hotdogs. And guess who won? *Another* anti-Grillman's girl. I swear, why put your name in the draw if you don't want to win?"

"But that's the thing, I never—"

She cut Morgan off with a loose shrug. "It doesn't matter anyway. You have to take el Chupacabra. After all, I brought it *all* the way here." Darcy turned to the side and gestured back towards her truck. At first, Morgan wasn't sure what she was pointing at, but when she saw it she wondered how she could have ever missed it before. Attached to the truck by a thick black cord was a giant hotdog, wrapped completely in plastic. It must have been the size of a small car, just sitting there on the side of the road. Morgan gaped, shock quickly morphing to disgust. Pink, slimy meat wrapped up in layers of thick plastic… Why on earth would *anyone* want something like that?

The woman beamed at her, brown eyes sparkling behind those thick, black frames. "You know how el Chupacabra is considered a member of the dog family?" She leaned forward, eyebrows waggling. "And we serve hot*dogs*? Get it?" Her eyebrows wiggled as she smirked.

Morgan's lip curled with distaste. "No way in hell am I taking that."

Once again, Dary's smile vanished, and her brows drew together with her pout. "Why not?"

"Why would anyone want a hotdog that big? Plus," she added with a flex, "I've worked hard to keep this physique." Wearing only a pair of sweatpants and a black tank top, her arm muscles were on full display beneath the dim lighting behind her.

If Darcy was impressed by her shape, she didn't show it. "Um, the meat's not for you, dummy. That's how we transport el Chupacabra."

Morgan's agitation only increased at the insult, and she barely even heard the woman's words after that, pushing on. "A strict diet and fitness regime got me this far, and I have no room to consume pork. Did you know the government deregulated pork in 2019? Who knows what's *inside* that thing?" She gave another sneer. Just seeing the shiny fake meat made her stomach turn. Everything that went into her body was carefully monitored, and nothing could convince her to take even a single bite out of that thing.

"But I drove a long way to deliver this to you," the woman whined in protest as she shivered and brought up a hand to block the cold breeze from pushing hair into her face.

Morgan could almost smell the plastic-wrapped meat on the wind, or maybe it was just her imagination. She shrugged, folding her arms again. "And you'll have to drive back with it," she said, her voice veiled with growing impatience, "because I'm *not* taking it. Now, please, I have a film to get back to."

Darcy's voice sobered. "I can't do that. My job is to deliver *this* giant hotdog to *this* address, and that's what I'm going to do. El Chupacabra won't like it if I turn around and drive back."

"What part of 'I'm not taking it' don't you understand? I never entered this stupid contest, so I shouldn't have won the prize. Give it to a runner-up or something."

She shook her head vehemently. "I can't do that," she repeated, voice tight with agitation. "You *have* to accept her. It states it in the rules of the contest. The winner *must* accept the prize."

Morgan almost threw up her hands. "But I *didn't enter*! Why are you calling it a her, anyway? It's a stupid hotdog!"

"It was *your* name and address we pulled from the draw," the woman argued back. "Not the hotdog, dummy!"

Morgan gritted her teeth, not in the mood to continue this conversation. "I have no idea how that could have even happened."

"Well, that's not my problem," Darcy snapped. Her friendly persona had all but vanished. Her agitated eyes flickered over Morgan's shoulder and went wide. "W-what is *that?*" she blurted, her breath hitching in shock.

Alarmed, Morgan spun around, but there was nothing there. "What—"

A weight shoved past her, and when she turned around again, Darcy was standing inside her house looking smug.

Morgan's eyes almost bulged out of her head. "What the hell do you think you're doing?!"

Her protests went ignored as the intruder strode further into the house with detached interest. "Seriously though, what *is* that?" she pointed to a tall black vase—currently empty—sitting on the sideboard in the living room. "It looks like it belongs in a funeral parlor."

Morgan scowled at the snide remark. "You can't just come into people's houses like this! You need to leave," she demanded.

Darcy meandered around the living room and snickered quietly to herself as she appraised Morgan's belongings. She muttered some things under her breath, but Morgan chose not to listen.

"I mean it, get the *hell* out of my house! You're trespassing!"

Darcy waved her hand flippantly. "No, I'm not. I'm just curious to see how a Grillman's hater like you lives."

Morgan seethed. "That's none of your business. *Get OUT!*"

Darcy simply shrugged her off, not seeming to care about Morgan's growing anger. Morgan stalked after her as she wandered into the kitchen next. She'd been enjoying a quiet evening at home before this Grillman's employee turned up and threw everything upside down.

"No way. That's so cringe, you know?" Her unwanted guest pointed to the large magnet on the fridge that read, "*You Don't Want To Know What Happens When You Mess With A Hicklib*". Morgan had a similar one on her car parked outside.

Morgan pursed her lips as the woman then pulled open her fridge, peering inside, and wrinkled her nose. "Wow, all greens. What a dull life you must have. There's nothing tasty in there at all. I would think someone as goth as you would at least have some human meat or cats or bats. Haha!"

Morgan bristled. "I told you before, I have a strict diet and fitness routine—"

"Yeah, I can tell," Darcy interrupted, running her gaze over Morgan's muscled arms. "Do you wear that tank top so that you can admire your hard work every time you look in the mirror?" There was something subtly mocking in her tone despite her smile.

Morgan rolled her eyes but didn't bother arguing. There was nothing wrong in taking pride in her appearance, especially when she'd worked hard to attain and maintain it.

The obnoxious intruder was already moving on, swiping a finger over the kitchen surfaces as if hoping to find dirt, but Morgan looked after her house as much as she looked after her body, and there wasn't a speck of dust to be found anywhere.

"Alright, that's enough. It's time for you to leave," Morgan growled as Darcy flitted out of the kitchen and began heading down the hallway.

"Oh come on, just a little peek," she replied with a goofy smile, as if she saw no harm in what she was doing. She didn't wait for Morgan to answer before hurrying to the first door on her left. When she saw it was the bathroom, she made a noise of disapproval and backed out again. Morgan's jaw clenched when she went into the bedroom next.

Darcy beelined over to Morgan's bed and dragged her pajamas out from beneath the pillow, unfolding them. She snickered to herself. "How cute. These look like my little brother's pajamas," she said, holding up the gray-spotted shorts. The black strip around the waistband gave them the appearance of boxer shorts, but Morgan had picked them from the ladies' pajama section. It was the style she found most comfortable to sleep in, and she didn't care what this random woman thought.

Morgan loomed in the doorway, arms crossed and brows furrowed. "If you don't leave, I'm going to call the police."

The woman gave her a small, almost teasing smile. "Go ahead and call them, then." She fixed Morgan with an expectant stare.

Morgan didn't actually want to call the police; it would be a waste of resources and too much of a hassle—if they bothered to show up at all—and the woman probably knew that. Darcy smirked before blowing a raspberry in Morgan's direction.

"That's it," Morgan growled, and she advanced towards her pesky intruder. Darcy's eyebrows shot into her hairline as Morgan gripped her arm.

"Hey, let go of me!" Darcy howled as Morgan hauled her off the bed, out of the bedroom, and into the hallway. As Morgan gritted her teeth and pulled, Darcy dug her heels into the floor and braced a hand against Morgan's chest, halting Morgan's momentum.

"GET," Morgan grunted between her teeth as she yanked harder, "OUT—*oof!*" Darcy's feet skidded on the floor as Morgan successfully dislodged her with an oof, and soon they were in the kitchen.

"This is assault!" Darcy cried, swinging her arms wildly. Her nails scratched the *Hicklib* magnet off the fridge. She grabbed the left strap of Morgan's tank and yanked, pulling the cloth into her armpit. Grunting in discomfort, Morgan reached with her free hand to untangle Darcy's fingers from her strap.

"Alright, alright, I'm leaving!" the woman finally conceded, and she slid out of Morgan's grip and darted through the open door. Morgan breathed a small sigh of relief.

A rueful expression on her face, Darcy regarded Morgan. "You know," she hiccuped, lips trembling, "if you *are* the sincere 'hicklib' you make yourself out to be, you could always help out by giving el Chupacabra to those who, ahem, *deserve* her. Isn't hicklib just a term for a socialist who lives in a rural area? There are lots of poor people in your area who would love to have a hotdog like that."

Morgan blinked, surprised at the suggestion. She hadn't thought about that. She supposed it was one way of accepting the hotdog without letting it go to waste. But would she really be okay with giving such an unhealthy piece of food to those in need? "I…guess so," she finally said.

That goofy, irritating smile returned, and the invader was clearly pleased with herself for being so persuasive. "Well then, that's finally sorted. The hotdog is all yours. Congratulations!"

Cringing internally, Morgan followed her to the door, but the woman paused before leaving and turned back once more. "It's no wonder you live all the way out here in the middle of nowhere. I doubt someone like you has many friends to come visit." Her big customer service smile was fixed right back in place as she spoke. Morgan's calm composure instantly shattered, her cheeks flushing with anger and humiliation.

The Grillman's employee threw back her head and snort-laughed. "Hah. I'm only kidding!" she chortled, before hurrying out of the house. Morgan watched, trembling with anger, as the woman untied the rope connecting the hotdog to the trailer behind the Grillman's truck. With a few grunts and groans, she rolled it off onto the grass. Then she climbed into the driver's seat and started the engine with a rumble, offering Morgan one last wave through the window before driving off, showering the giant plastic-wrapped hotdog in exhaust fumes.

Morgan raked a hand through her hair and let out a choked scream of frustration, the noise echoing down the empty road.

Dusk had fallen, but the sky was still light around the edges, not quite giving over to night. With the light flooding out of the house behind her, Morgan stepped out onto the street and approached the hotdog, running her gaze over the pinkish-brown meat. It didn't even look like it had been fully cooked, and how long had it been sitting on the trailer, just…in the elements? In the *heat*? There was no way this was safe to eat. Even now, the smell of the uncooked meat (if you could call it that) was making her nauseous. It had probably already been cooking inside the plastic beneath the sun while that woman was transporting it here.

Gagging at the thought, Morgan hurried away from the hotdog and went back inside her house. She shut the door and secured the lock, hoping she never had to see that woman again. Her impression of Grillman's had grown even worse now that she knew they were responsible for creating this disgusting, unhealthy slab of meat. Even worse, they'd managed to foist it off as some kind of "prize". As if anyone would *want* something like that, even for free.

Morgan retreated to the living room, but like hell if she was in any mood to finish her movie. She killed the lights and the TV and did her night routine instead. Once under the covers, decked in her gray-spotted pajamas, the woman's earlier taunts came back to plague her. She couldn't sleep. In the back of her mind, she kept thinking about Darcy's taunts and what to do about the giant Salmonella outbreak waiting to happen on her front lawn.

Morgan tossed and turned as the sky outside darkened fully, until eventually, she drifted off into a troubled sleep.

Splat!

Morgan's eyes fluttered open, first seeing nothing but darkness, then a pale stream of moonlight peeking between the curtains. She sat up, rubbing the sleep from her eyes and immediately looking toward the window. Had she imagined that noise? *Something* had to have woken her.

She swung her legs over the bed and stood, still groggy and half-asleep as she padded over to the curtains and drew them aside.

Glistening and wet beneath the moonlight, something red was splashed against her window. The sight of it jolted her fully awake, and she blinked in mingled horror and confusion at the smear on the glass. There was no doubt about what it was. That blood-red substance dripping down the window had to be paint. But where had it come from?

She pulled the curtains open wider and peered through the glass, but the entire thing was covered in paint.

"That little shit…!" Rage coursing through her, Morgan ran out of her bedroom and unlocked her front door. Morgan didn't care if she was in her pajamas or hadn't put on socks. "DARCY, I'M GOING TO KICK YOUR ASS!"

Her stomach turned when her gaze settled on the hotdog, still sitting directly outside her house. It was illuminated by a single red garden light she kept in her front yard. The plastic had been torn off, and a giant hole now pierced the muddy pink-brown flesh. Morgan froze. There was something else. From the darkness swimming inside the hole, a flash of yellow light. She staggered backward, almost slipping on the damp grass. Light…*inside* the hotdog?

Swallowing back the lump in her throat, Morgan tentatively approached the lump of meat, hands trembling, heart racing as she chewed on her bottom lip. She squinted.

A pair of bright yellow eyes stared back from within the hotdog.

Morgan gasped. "OH!" Her earlier anger replaced by fear, she turned and ran back into her house, locking the door behind her.

The sight of those eyes, yellow and inhuman, made her feel ill, so she quickly shut the curtains and decided to deal with whatever rabies-infested animal it was in the morning.

Still feeling uneasy, she climbed back into bed and forced herself to go back to sleep. In her dreams, the red coating her window wasn't paint, but blood.

When Morgan woke early the following morning, the first thing she did was draw back the curtains in her bedroom. She stared in shock at the square pane of glass. It was completely clean. Not a single speck of red in sight. Had she simply imagined the whole thing? Blurring dreams with reality into something that didn't actually happen, even though it *felt* so real?

She shook her head, rubbing her eyes as if it would somehow reveal the truth to her, but the window remained clean. No paint. (It *was* paint, right…?) When she switched her gaze to the hotdog, she saw the gaping hole from the night before remained, looking even bigger in the light of day.

Deciding to investigate further, she quickly got changed and went into the kitchen, rummaging through the drawers for a pair of rubber gloves. There was no way she was going near that thing without some kind of protection.

The early-morning sun bounced off her car as she walked past it, heading straight for the hotdog. A large chunk of meat was missing, exposing the pale pink innards, almost as if someone had chewed their way into it. *Or out of it*, Morgan thought with a grimace. Just like she had observed last night, the skin was broken outwards, like something had burst out from the inside. But how was that possible?

Trying not to gag on the smell of rotten meat, Morgan stepped closer to the crater. Up close, the uncooked hotdog looked even more nauseating, and her stomach dropped completely when she peered into the hole and saw several more tunnels burrowing deeper inside. The meat was torn haphazardly, like something had chewed away at it while going deeper into the hotdog. Had an animal done this? That was the only thing she could think of—and it would explain those inhuman, yellow eyes watching her last night.

Morgan didn't want to know where the animal was now or what state it might be in after gorging itself on this monstrosity. She had to figure out a way to get rid of this thing. It couldn't just sit outside her house, slowly festering beneath the sun. Who knew what other creatures it might attract if she just left it there.

Sick with disgust, Morgan turned away.

For just a moment, she thought she heard a soft squelching sound coming from behind her. She glanced back with a start, peering into the tunnel, but nothing seemed to stir. Perhaps she had simply imagined it.

Shuddering, she headed back inside and spent the next ten minutes trying to tell the police what happened, becoming increasingly agitated at the skepticism she detected in their voices. She did her usual workout routine and drank a healthy organic shake with breakfast, then got ready to go to work.

As she drove into town, where she worked at the local music store, Morgan tried to think of a way to properly dispose of the hotdog. But she came up with no feasible answer. It wasn't something she'd be able to handle herself. She would probably have to call some service to haul it away for her, but that was an annoyance and a cost in and of itself. Just thinking about the questions she would be asked about it was enough to put her off that idea.

She tried to push it out of her mind as she worked her shift, and by the time she drove home, she'd *almost* forgotten about it. Until she saw the giant hotdog appear on the horizon, looking like some kind of old mascot of a food stall.

When she pulled into the driveway, she noticed several shapes scattered along the ground around it. It wasn't until she'd gotten out to investigate that she clamped a hand over her mouth and stared down at a small heap of feathers. It was a dead songbird, barely bigger than her palm, with soft blue and white plumage. Amongst the bed of feathers lay its body, but something about it was strange. She moved it over with the toe of her shoe to get a better look and her heart sank into her stomach. The bird's body was completely desiccated, like it had been drained of its blood. It looked as if it had been dead a while, but Morgan was certain it hadn't been there that morning.

It wasn't the only one. Morgan's gaze followed a line of feathers that led to several more little feathered heaps scattered around the hotdog, shriveled up like prunes. There were even a couple of squirrels amongst them, all in the same sorry state, their eyes wide open, covered in a grotesque milky sheen.

What had happened? Had the animals died from eating the hotdog, or had something else killed them?

Morgan yanked out her phone and shot a video of the scene. She posted the footage online and even sent it to some of her friends and family, asking if anyone knew what might cause something like this to happen. She made sure to get the hotdog in the video with its gaping hole, which seemed unchanged.

Quickly stepping away from the gruesome scene, she pursed her lips and hurried inside. What a mess, and it was all because of some stupid Grillman's contest she hadn't even entered.

The next morning was Sunday, and Morgan needed to do something about the mess herself. Wearing a different black tank top, black gloves, and black cargo pants, she got on her knees to scrape up dead birds. The plague of death had spread all over her yard, not just the area in front of the hotdog.

"You want something done around here, you damn well gotta do it yourself," she growled. "Fucking useless cops."

She'd already set up several security cameras and alarms around her yard. Next time an intruder walked by, whoever or *whatever* they were, she'd be ready.

Her lip curled in disgust as she scooped up the dead birds and dumped them into a black garbage bag.

An inhuman shriek erupted nearby. "SHIT!" Morgan dropped the bag, its contents spilling everywhere.

A series of aggressive yowls followed, like two cats fighting. Only this sounded much louder; definitely something larger than a domestic animal.

Scrambling towards her weedwhacker leaned against the house, Morgan picked it up and peered around the corner, heart racing. Two hulking shapes were locked in a brawl on top of the remnants of the hotdog—now mostly gone with only a few chunks of pink meat and skin left in its place. Although it was difficult to make out exactly what she was looking at, she could tell the two animals weren't cats. They were much larger, much more beastly, hunched with spikes growing out of their backs.

Dropping the weedwhacker, she retreated into her house, crouching to peer through the bottom window. As she watched the animals fight, a gruesome display of claws and fangs veiled by shadow, their beastly cries echoed out into the morning, like nothing she had encountered before.

Without warning, one of them was thrown backwards with a brutal display of force, and Morgan stifled a scream, falling back as the hulking shape hit the window and smashed through the glass right in front of her.

Through the falling shards of glass, all she saw was a streak of shadow and blood as the animal jumped back outside to continue the fight, its cries ringing through her ears like a discordant echo.

It was then that the Grillman's employee's words came back to her: *"Um, the meat's not for you, dummy. That's how we transport el Chupacabra."* But el Chupacabra didn't exist, *couldn't* exist! Morgan realized with horror just how wrong she'd been to not take the woman's words seriously.

Trembling with panic, Morgan rushed into her bedroom, grabbing her phone as she went. She locked herself in, hands shaking as she dialed 911. Pressing the phone to her ear, she heard nothing but her own heavy breathing. The line was silent. She tried again, to the same effect. The line was completely dead. She couldn't even phone the police. She checked her Wi-Fi, but there was no connection there either.

Burying her head in her hands, she tried to calm herself. As long as she stayed in here, out of sight of the windows, she should be safe. Shouldn't she?

Outside, she heard what sounded like beastly laughing—something not human, but not animal, either. Something completely different.

Sitting with her back to the wall, gaze flicking between the door and the window, Morgan stayed there for the next hour. She waited until the silence stretched for several minutes before creeping to the front door and unlatching it, pulling it open gingerly. When she peered through the gap, she saw nothing outside.

Certain that nothing was waiting to ambush her, she pulled the door open the rest of the way and stepped outside to investigate the scene. Where the giant hotdog had been sitting just last night, there remained nothing but a large puddle of blood.

Morgan stepped closer to take a look and gasped when a pair of yellow eyes blinked open, staring at her from the pool of red liquid. The eyes winked at her once, before vanishing completely below.

Whatever. At least the two monsters had taken care of the hotdog she hadn't wanted in the first place.

The Cryptid in the Woods

ADRIELLE REINA

Women choose the bear.
But we'd also choose the Cryptid in the Woods.

"DID YER SEE them there lights last night?" At the local boozer, an old man lit a cigarette, took a drag, then swatted away the smoke. Dottie, the bartender, and her husband (who owned the place) never minded. Laws be damned. "Strange, wud'nit?"

"Lemme get a light, would ya?" A young man named Landon in his mid-twenties asked, and the man handed his lighter over. He covered the cigarette as the fire lit it just right and inhaled. "Yeah, I saw those lights. Flew right over the trees in my backyard. Zigzagged and everything! Like them lasers ya play with to get your cat to act up."

The older man nodded solemnly. "Sure was stranger than checkin' your ass and scratchin' your watch, I'll tell ya what."

Landon chuckled. "Nah, ya know it's probably that dang Air Force base over yonder." He pointed away from the bar with his thumb.

The old man ran his finger through the coarse gray beard running down his neck, inhaling his cigarette. "I used to serve myself, son. I saw things you wouldn't believe. Not in your wildest dreams, I promise ya that."

The younger man raised his eyebrows as he set down his beer bottle. "You got time, old man?" His blue eyes shone with the kind of mirth only youth could hold when one hadn't known true, palpable fear. He ran a free hand through his dark hair. "Let me guess, little gray men with big eyeballs?"

The old man put out the rest of his cigarette in a red clay ashtray on the bar. He then let out a sigh, tapping his fingers on the oak wood shining against the backdrop of neon and liquor. "Worse'n that, son. Some things ya don't want ter know, ya best believe that." With that, he paid his tab and hobbled out of the tavern, zipping up his coat before walking out the door.

Landon stared after him longer than he should have, dazed by the alcohol he consumed and the sudden odd behavior of the older gentleman.

"Ya ready for another?" Dottie asked. Her overly-teased blonde hair ran down her back, and she jutted her bosom as she leaned on the counter, smacking her lips.

His eyes lingered a little too long, a throbbing pulsating in his groin.

He thought about staying but knew one more meant he wouldn't be able to make the twenty or so minute drive home. "Nah, that's alright. Thank ya, Dottie. I'll just have the check."

"Suit yourself, handsome." She swayed her hips as she walked to the register and set the receipt down.

He thanked her again and left, making headway home.

"You're late. Again."

She made it a statement, not a question. The unspoken accusation lingered in the silence that followed from where Audrey sat in the living room recliner, watching Landon stumble his way through the front door. The only light came from the nearby kitchen, casting shadows on her face.

"Now, Audrey, I don't want to hear it. I ain't out cheat—"

She draped her chestnut locks to one side, licking her teeth, before interrupting, "This time, right? *Right*, Landon?"

He sighed. "I was down at Dover's. You can call if you don't believe me."

She shook her head, twisting her wedding ring around her finger. "I'm not about to do all that."

"Of course not. You'll just be a bitch about me goin' out because God forbid my life not revolve around you for five seconds."

Before she could retort, however, a cacophony of yowling and hissing from out front startled them both.

Audrey jumped from the recliner to grab her coat by the door.

"Why do we even have fuckin' cats?" Landon muttered.

"How can you be so cruel? It's bad enough you won't let them inside. It's cold out!"

"They're cats! They're *fine*!"

She glared at him, yanking on her jacket. "You're a piece of work," she said, shaking her head as she went outside.

The bitter cold winds slashed at her cheeks and every movement through the frostbitten night rattled her bones. Audrey hated winter and the crunch of leaves and snow under her house shoes, soaking through the fabric. She breathed into her hands, rubbing them together to warm up.

Strange, though. The hissing and screeching had gone as silent as death itself. Maybe the cats had resolved whatever conflict was afoot, but she wanted to check on them anyway. Since they hadn't been on the porch when she'd come out, maybe they'd gone toward the shed on the side of the house. No doubt running off after their tiff.

A missing chunk from the door that no one had ever bothered to fix gave the cats easy access to the shed—good thing, too, since Landon wouldn't let them in the house out of the elements no matter how thick the snow got. The poor things.

"Psst, psst," she called as she opened the creaking door. "Are y'all in here?" Not even a meow or anything? Audrey squinted, groping around for the string to turn on the god-danged light while wishing she hadn't left her phone inside. Feeling around, she finally found the string and pulled.

Nothing.

Well, that certainly was odd. But then again, she couldn't remember the last time they'd changed the bulb. So, to her, it was more of an inconvenience than anything.

"Mr. White? Mr. Gray?" she cooed, hoping to coerce them out so she could at least check for injuries. Shoot, what if they'd gone to the woods behind the house? Her heart sank into her stomach. No, they wouldn't do that. They knew there were coyotes—and Lord knew what else—back there. "Sasha? Bean Dip?" Still, not even a scratch or a scurry.

She ducked back out of the shed, inhaling the cold air once more. Looking up to the starry sky, she saw those strange lights again. She and Landon had first seen them a few months back. Landon insisted they had to be from the base nearby, but they were still such an odd occurrence as far as she was concerned. Her heart thudded heavily in her chest as red and white lights zoomed across the night, zig-zagging and—gone. She took a deep breath, frosting her lungs. Well, they were from the Air Force base. They had to be. That was that. She'd done scared herself. Now, she needed to find her cats. Maybe they'd gone under the front porch. Was she dumb? Why hadn't that crossed her mind?

As she turned the corner toward the porch, her blood froze. She couldn't scream, couldn't move, her legs like lead. She could only stare, wide-eyed, at whatever…thing…was in front of her. It stood as tall as a Great Dane on all fours, with a head as big as a watermelon—shaped like one, too, with no discernible mouth. Bulbous eyes glowed orange from the light on the front porch. It had a protruding belly, but everything else was long and skinny, especially its limbs. Gray skin stretched across its body, somehow making the creature look gaunt and dead, yet still alive.

It slowly stood up on its hind legs until it had to be a little over six feet tall. Cocking its head ever so slightly, a sound somewhere in between a screech and hiss came out of a gaping black hole in its neck.

"Landon!" Audrey screamed, and the creature lunged at her. She somersaulted, narrowly avoiding its webbed grip and blade-like claws. "Landon!" She ran up the porch stairs, nearly tripping, and flew through the front door. She managed to lock it with numb, shaking fingers before the creature slammed into it with a crash.

Tears laced her eyes. "Landon!" She ran down the hall to their bedroom, locking the door and turning the light off.

He took one of his earphones off, muting them. "Audrey, what the fuck? I'm gaming with the boys."

She held a trembling finger to her lips. "Turn it off," she whispered. "There's something outside. I don't know what happened to the cats. I can't find them and something just chased—"

"Oh my God, woman. You're bein' over dramatic and gettin' all gommed up for what? You wanna bring them damned cats in so bad, fine. They can stay in the garage or somethin', but you're not gonna sit here and crash game night and ruin my buzz."

"Will. You. Stop. It?" Audrey growled. "There's some creature out there. I've not seen a damn thing like it before, Landon Johnson, and you're gonna stop talking to me like that right now. Get off that game and turn the TV off."

"Goddamnit! I told your bitch ass not to ruin my buzz!" he screamed, throwing the controller. Audrey flinched.

"Please settle down. Be quiet!"

He rocked forward and got to his feet. With a clenched jaw, he strode to Audrey, staring down at her. His breath reeked of beer and chewing tobacco.

"You want me to be quiet, baby?"

He stroked her face, but she didn't feel love, only fear. She knew what would come next, and suddenly the creature outside didn't seem so scary in comparison anymore. With a hand behind her back, she unlocked the door, flung it open, ducked, and ran down the hallway again.

"*Audrey!*"

He stumbled after her as hot tears coursed down her face.

She booked it for the backdoor, praying the creature was still out front. Either way, she feared she might die tonight. She hoped that if she ran into the creature again, death would at least be quicker from a monster she didn't know to the one she married.

For better or worse. 'Til death do they part.

Audrey fled, running as fast as she could to lose herself in the woods, to hide. An old treehouse wasn't too far away. She'd hide in it if she could make it. Wind howled all around. She stifled her cries as those strange lights beamed across the night sky, about as high as airplanes, maybe, but they seemed lower than what they had been before. Twigs snapped beneath her feet as she maneuvered around trees and slipped on the slick, snowy ground.

"Audrey!" Landon roared.

Was it selfish of her to hope the creature would find him first?

She stopped, clutching her side as she leaned against a tree, panting. Her breathing was too heavy. Too loud. Too noticeable.

The treehouse was just up ahead. She could see it. Audrey made a run for it, only to be caught by her arm from behind—a great force dragging her down and then grabbing her by the hair.

"No!" She flailed. Kicked and screamed as her body scraped across the cold, hard ground. "No! Please!"

Was it the creature or her husband?

She should have known better than to grab her assailant's arm. The hands that dragged her weren't webbed. They didn't have claws.

"Landon, please!" she cried, her throat hoarse.

"You embarrassed me enough. You ran your mouth off about me cheatin' on you—about how I'm so terrible. Am I?" he bellowed. "*Am I?* All you ever fuckin' do is ride my dick—and it ain't even the way I want it because you're just complainin' about every goddamn thing! Mama's always said you're crazy." His grip tightened around her hair and she whimpered. "Everyone said not to marry your sorry ass."

"Landon, please. I'm sor—Ah!"

Something solid slammed into Landon, knocking him to the ground with such force he took along chunks of Audrey's hair ripped from her scalp. Her head snapped up to see the creature looming in the snow. With glowing eyes, it circled Landon, who scrambled clumsily to his feet.

"What the actual fuckin' hell—"

He recovered quickly enough, grabbing a large stick. He swung, and the creature lunged, letting out that same bizarre hissing and screeching sound.

With both monsters preoccupied, Audrey headed to the treehouse.

"Audrey! You're leaving me?!" Terror thrummed through Landon's vocal cords, and it was music to her ears. She wouldn't waste her precious breath to dignify him with a response when she had the opportunity to escape.

She climbed the ladder and hoisted herself into the house, then quickly rolled up her salvation and slammed the door shut, shoving a rickety desk over to use as a barricade. Feeling a bit braver, she peered out the window.

Landon was limping toward the treehouse.

"Audrey, please! Help!" he begged breathlessly.

The creature had disappeared. Still, Audrey didn't want to take any chances.

She moved away from the window and put her back against the wall, resting against her knees with her head in her hands. Deep breaths.

In the silence, she heard a meow.

And purring.

The cats?

"*Audrey! I'll climb up there!*"

She didn't dare make a sound. Instead, she slowly crawled over to the corner where she thought she'd heard the sound. She felt around, knowing there was an old beanbag and a flashlight somewhere… There!

With uneven breaths, Audrey turned on the flashlight, making sure the illumination couldn't be seen outside the treehouse. There they were, all four cats cuddled up on the beanbag, shaking and fearful but otherwise safe.

"Audrey! Help me, please!"

She petted each cat, snuggling her face against them to calm them before she stood up and slowly crept back toward the window to shine the torch down on Landon like a spotlight. "If I help you tonight, I want you gone tomorrow."

Landon's voice was laced with anxious terror as he peered around. "Audrey, we can talk this out, now. Ya don't have to be like that. Look at me, I'm hurt!" He held up his hands as if he were surrendering to her.

She glanced away, touching her scalp where her hair had been pulled out. Her hand seemingly moved on its own accord across her opposite arm where, underneath her coat and pajamas, she expected to find bruises and scrapes. The same for her back and legs and other places, too, she was sure.

Her voice came out hoarse. "I'm hurt, too."

"I'm sorry! Baby, just come help me, *please*."

Against her better judgement—and because the creature still hadn't reappeared—she moved the desk, opened the trapdoor, and unrolled the ladder. The climb down hurt. She hadn't truly realized how sore she was.

She reached out her hand to Landon where he sat on the ground; he yanked her down and climbed on top of her.

"You're a dumb bitch," he whispered, grabbing a large rock and holding it over his head. "You'd let me die. You were gonna leave me behind!"

"*No!*"

This was how she would die.

Just as Landon moved to strike her, the creature tackled him. When he attempted to fight back, its screechy hissing grew louder and louder as rows of teeth extended from the hole in its neck.

"No!" This time, Landon screamed the word as the creature bit into his throat. Blood sprayed onto the blanket of snow. Landon's screams became lost in gargles of crimson, the hot liquid torching Audrey's face and mouth. She licked her lips, smiling.

The creature ripped into him, carving a line down his chest to feast on his organs and breaking bone to slurp the marrow.

She approached the creature, sitting next to it as it ate her ex-husband. When she petted it, the creature paused, blood painting its gray skin, and looked at her with its big, orange eyes. It tilted his head and leaned into her, nuzzling her neck. Its body vibrated like a cat purring. Then it dug back into Landon's chest cavity to resume its feast.

Audrey laughed. She didn't feel fear anymore. The monster in the woods was gone. It was dead.

"We're gonna have to work on you not scaring the cats, okay?"

Split Stone

JOSHUA LIM

IT WAS A stone on a hill.

A split stone, to be exact.

A gigantic stone with a narrow fissure running down one face, revealing what appeared to be a hollow cave within. A child could easily slip in through the crack. A slim man might manage to squeeze in sideways. But no one in living memory had ever entered the darkness and returned to tell the tale—or at least, that was what the villagers told the English explorer.

He arrived in Kampong Batu Belah on a chilly morning in June 1898, strolling up the misty rainforest trail in his tall boots and safari hat and field glasses swinging from his neck, his pale skin noticeably redder around his neck and arms, every bit as exotic as the rumours had said. Everyone in the village had gathered to gawk at him, muttering about his golden hair and blue eyes. Jungle tribes did not see white men as often as coastal folk did.

He called himself Dr. Avery Thompson Gray, anthropologist. He had come to talk to the tribes and learn about the Semai way of life, he said, showing them he carried no weapons. He had learned to speak Malay from his time in the colonies, but as the Semai spoke a heavy regional dialect, I was his translator for most of the way.

"Yok Ngot, ask them about the rock," Gray said.

I translated.

"The split stone is sacred to the jungle," was the answer from the Tok Batin, the village chief. "Our village is called Batu Belah in its honour. No one may go near the rock, or they will never be seen again."

As a man of mixed Malay-Semai ancestry, I have been working as a translator for British anthropologists and explorers for a couple of years now. My professionalism requires me to translate every word without omission. Looking back, I should have been wiser. I translated everything, knowing even as I spoke that the last part would ignite Gray's spirited curiosity.

Captain Reginald Stalker was rapidly losing patience.

"All deaf and dumb, are you?" he shouted, striding across the village square, kicking up grass and dirt into the faces of the Semai villagers who were forced to kneel before him. By now, almost the whole of Kampong Batu Belah, young and old alike, had been dragged out of their houses and gathered before the captain.

"For the last time, you witless curs, where is Avery Gray?"

Captain Stalker brandished a photograph of the missing anthropologist in front of their faces. "This man, he came to your bloody village a week ago on the 5th of June and hasn't been seen since. Remember him?" He realised his translator was staring at him. "Translate, Awang! What are you waiting for?"

Awang complied.

Their answer was simple. Too simple for the captain to accept.

"Balderdash!" roared Captain Stalker. "Tigers? Our troops are fighting Malay rebels in the jungles all over the God-knows-how-many colonies at this moment, and you expect me to believe that *tigers* killed Gray? Likely you lot are rebel sympathisers—you hate all white men, waiting to strike when the time is right. What did you people do to Dr. Gray? Kill him? Eat him? Do they eat people in this part of the world?"

A few soldiers shook their heads.

"That'll be Borneo, sir," said one helpfully. "The other island."

"Well, that's a relief," said the captain. "I'd have a tough time reporting to General Gray if we had to dig through cooking pots to find his nephew's bones. But we're not any closer to finding the man, are we? They need some persuasion."

He pointed at a herd of goats a good distance away.

"Wilson, shoot a goat."

The named soldier raised his rifle to his shoulder and did so, eliciting a cry from the natives. Some covered their ears and stared in mixed horror and wonder. The deep jungle tribes had so little contact with the outside world that they could barely speak Malay, and only tales of steam machines and firearms had ever reached them. The slain goat tumbled down the hillside and crashed onto the rocks below, a bloody mess.

"Tell them," said Captain Stalker, every word vicious, "if someone doesn't start yapping in one minute, I'll make goats of them all."

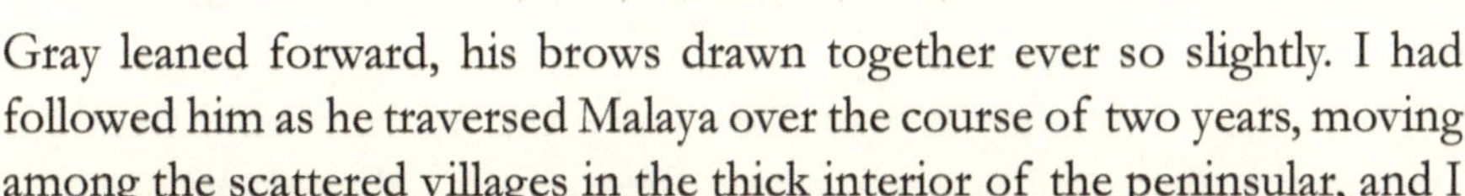

Gray leaned forward, his brows drawn together ever so slightly. I had followed him as he traversed Malaya over the course of two years, moving among the scattered villages in the thick interior of the peninsular, and I knew his mannerisms well enough to recognise piqued interest.

"This rock is on that hill over there?" he asked. "What's inside the rock?"

"Jembalang," answered the Tok Batin.

I saw the slight smile at the corner of Gray's mouth. This was a word that I did not need to translate. I knew his opinions on demons and local spirits. This was far from the first time that he had received such an answer.

Why isn't anyone allowed to enter the jungle at night?

Jembalangs roam at night, answered the southern Temuan tribe.

Why must you stay home all day if an owl flew over your house this morning?

It is an omen, said the Mah Meri tribe of Selangor. *Jembalangs will attack.*

Why must you consult a tree before you cut it down?

Jembalangs, replied the northern Semangs.

Why…?

Jembalang.

Jembalang.

Jembalang.

In addition to anthropology, Gray had studied zoology and had come to Malaya eager to discover new species. The reported dangers of entering the jungle after sundown did not deter him in his quest to find the elusive clouded leopard or the slow loris, both beasts of the night. Several times he had waited until full dark and gone exploring by himself, terrifying any natives who saw the light of his torch moving around in the jungle.

What he considered "fanciful superstitions" like these, he dared to break. Omens that he disregarded made him a sort of enigma with the locals, a man who dared to challenge the spirits. I'm sure a good number of them were waiting to see him drop dead instantly, but he never did. Gray was aware of it too, and he seemed to enjoy their frustration.

Yet the Englishman was smart, and he was respectful of the native customs and anything he figured might cause offence. He did not desecrate graves, he always paid appropriate respects to the village chiefs, he learned their language and ate their food and documented everything inside the little black notebook which he carried in his shirt pocket. Gray held a conviction that if he persisted in friendship, the tribes would eventually trust him enough to reveal the secrets of the deep jungle where his zoology interests lay.

From the start, I was sure that Gray was racking his brains for animals that made their dens in caves. *Tigers, leopards, bears, snakes, maybe an undiscovered species…?*

"Does this jembalang take the shape of any animal?" asked Gray.

The Tok Batin shook his head. "Not an animal. No one has ever seen the jembalang itself. Even wild beasts do not approach the hilltop. To climb up is to never come down."

"But *you* know what the stone looks like," Gray said. "Someone, sometime, must have gone up and taken a look!"

"We can see it from neighbouring hills."

"But no one who goes near the rock ever comes back?"

"No. We have never seen their bodies, either."

Gray must have looked unconvinced, for the Tok Batin began to tell him stories of people who committed suicide by walking up the hill, sacrificing themselves to the jembalang. It was clear the Semai thought that the jembalang ate any living creature that came near the split stone, although they would say, "We don't know what happens, no one ever saw it happen," when pressed. Gray's intrigue grew with every question.

The Tok Batin finished with a warning.

"Tell the white man not to climb the hill, Yok Ngot," he said to me. "I have heard of this bold white man from the other tribes. He may dare to challenge the wild spirits elsewhere, but here—the Batu Belah does not tolerate affront."

I translated everything, as usual. Gray nodded and smiled, as usual.

He waited until full dark, as usual.

The Tok Batin was brought before the captain, sullen and defiant. He had put up resistance, which earned him the large, darkening bruise on one cheek. Captain Stalker squatted in front of him and met his glare with a mixed look of scorn and pity.

"You don't want any trouble from us," he said. "No one messes with Her Majesty's finest men—the enforcers of the largest empire on God's earth—and gets away with it. Don't make this any harder for yourself, eh? Where's Dr. Gray?"

"Harimau, waktu malam," said Tok Batin. *Tiger in the night.*

Captain Stalker sighed. "There you go with the stories again," he said. "Since we arrived, everyone says he was eaten by a tiger, but they can't agree on *how* it happened. Some of them said he went on a hunting trip alone, others said that he was caught unawares at midday, and now you say it was at night. Which is it?" He straightened up and stretched.

"Lieutenant Hart! Sack their houses and search for any clues!"

"Yes, sir!"

"Ku jawab!" cried a man from the crowd.

The soldiers halted in their tracks.

"Diam, Bah Sung!" shouted the Tok Batin.

A grin spread across Captain Stalker's face. "That's more like it," he said. "Decided to stop wasting our time now, have we? Awang, come over and translate!"

Bah Sung's story went roughly like this.

The white man snuck out at night, even after he had been warned not to go near the stone. ("What stone?" Captain Stalker asked.) *The split stone, the one at the peak of the next hill, the one that gave the village its name. Yok Ngot the translator discovered the white man's disappearance shortly afterwards and ran out to bring him back.* (Captain Stalker cursed. "The bloody translator! We plumb forgot about him! Where is he now?") *He's in the Tok Batin's house, lying down, recovering*—("What happened to him?")

Bah Sung's answers had grown slower and softer as he went on. Now he stopped, staring at some unseen terror. His lips moved in a barely audible gasp.

"What did he say?" demanded the captain.

Awang translated. "He saw the stone."

I could see nothing.

The jungle was pitch black, even as the tiny gaps of sky in the canopy above shone with moonlight. I pushed my way through the undergrowth, my feet scrambling for footholds among the roots and dead leaves, not as nimble as the locals but better than anyone who had not spent their early lives in the deep villages. I had only my shaky sense of direction to lead me towards the hill.

The tales from the other villagers resurfaced uncomfortably in my mind.

"Bah Sung was on the hill," they had said. "Bah Sung lost his way coming home at evening-time, he was wandering through the jungle blindly. Then the moon came out from behind the clouds, and he saw that he was on that hill, standing in front of the split stone."

I almost tripped on a low branch.

"What happened to him?" I had asked, having just spoken to Bah Sung that morning. The man looked perfectly healthy.

A fern whipped me in the face.

"Bah Sung turned tail and ran back towards the village. He did not enter his house for three days, fearing that a jembalang might follow him home, but nothing happened. Some say the stone did not harm him because he did not mean to be there. Others say the stone pointed the way home for him.

"What does the Tok Batin say?"

"The Tok Batin thinks that Bah Sung was spared because he did not see the stone properly—he shut his eyes and ran off too quickly."

I muttered a short prayer to the unseen spirits around me, surely watching as I blundered through their territory.

"I'm here to bring Gray back, O Batu Belah, do not harm me. I am protecting your honour, O Batu Belah, I do not intend to trespass—"

The ground, which had been sloping upwards all along, suddenly flattened. The trees fell away around me, the moonlight pouring down on an open clearing, illuminating the figure of Avery Thompson Gray lifting high a flaming torch, standing motionless before the equally motionless hulk of the split stone.

I was about to catch Gray by the collar and drag him away, but my attention was drawn against my will to the great silver rock.

The Batu Belah regarded us silently.

It was like staring at a wild beast, frozen in place, every muscle tensed and ready to burst into action. A battle of wills. I do not remember studying the external features of the rock as much as feeling its *presence*— an inquisitive and penetrating gaze, like the probing sniff of a curious hound, the sense of an unconcerned yet mildly annoyed superior being leaning back on one elbow and peering down at you from every direction with its thousand eyes, wondering whether to crush you into pulp instantly or to wait and see what you would do next.

The split stone waited.

Avery Gray stepped towards the fissure.

I flung myself forward and caught his arm. I could not bring myself to make a sound in the presence of the stone. I doubted my throat would have complied even if I had tried.

Gray shrugged me off, but I grabbed his arm again, pulling him back. He turned on me, and I saw a gleam in his eyes that I had never seen before, a light that terrified me way more because it came from the eyes of a human being. My hesitation gave him the chance to strike me on the head with the butt of his torch, and I fell to the ground.

Dazed, I watched him turn sideways and squeeze his way into the cave, holding the torch in front of him. Not one to lose hope so quickly, I gathered my strength and crawled towards the crack, my eyes half-blinded by the pain of my throbbing skull. Still, I managed to get close enough to peek inside.

"Get on with the story!" roared Captain Stalker. "What are you pausing for?"

The Tok Batin, struggling against two soldiers holding him down, shouted in Semai. "Don't say any more, Yok Ngot! The white man will never believe you!"

The captain backhanded him across the cheek. The Tok Batin crumpled. His wife screamed and the soldiers shouted at her, waving their guns.

"I swear, you savages can play a pretty game when you want to," snarled Captain Stalker. "All this talking and still you have not said a single word about what happened to Avery Gray! God damn the whole lot of you! Is he alive or is he dead? Speak!"

He drew his pistol from its holster and pointed it at the man with the bandaged head lying on the woven mat before him, cocking it with a furious jerk of his thumb.

"Don't say any more," cried the Tok Batin, his voice breaking.

"Speak, man, by all your bloody pagan gods, speak!"

I can only relate what I saw from where I lay.

Avery Gray was silhouetted by the light of his torch, turning one way and then another, as if gazing around at a wide cavern above him. I saw him peering closely at the walls, sweeping his torch around in a wide arc, staring up, behind, under, every possible direction. In a chance moment when he faced me, I glimpsed his expression, lit by the flickering fire: a mixture of wonder, curiosity, and disgust.

When he swung back around, the firelight lit up the face of the jembalang of Batu Belah.

Gray dropped the torch. It fell with a thud, the flames leaping wildly, the cave alight with a sudden glow, further illuminating the full expanse of the demon whose body seemed to occupy the entire inside of the split stone—or maybe it *was* the stone itself, wearing it as a tortoise does a shell: a sacred, inseparable part of its being, older than time.

The jembalang seized Gray. How it did, I do not know; I did not see an arm or jaw lock onto Gray, but the Englishman's body flew into the air and twisted in a horrible fashion. His hat tumbled off his head into the flames. I heard his scream, a final cry of terror echoing as if down a long tunnel. Then blood spurted forth and the fires were doused.

There was a creaking groan, as if the bowels of the earth were moving. A series of loud cracks—like splintering stone or breaking bones, or both—and the narrow cave mouth snapped shut, grinding its granite lips together with a sickening crunch that shook me to my core.

Crickets sang.

The split stone was silent. I lay on its doorstep, almost not breathing, unable to move a muscle. I had seen the jembalang. Only for a second, but I had seen the Batu Belah's true form in the light of a dying man's torch.

Slowly, inch by inch, the cave mouth drew open, its interior once again sealed in darkness. No sound came from within. The feeling returned: the oppressive presence, the million eyes of the god boring into mine, staring back out of the darkness, searching my soul. It seemed to ask a question. It took all my strength of will to yank my eyes away from the fissure and haul my body upright again.

Then I turned and ran back home.

Captain Stalker was gazing out of the window as I finished speaking. Slowly, he turned his gaze upon me. He was eerily calm, the hint of a smile at the edges of his lips, blinking patiently through deceptively blank eyes that suggested a bubbling cauldron of fury lay just behind them, ready to boil over.

I returned a steady gaze, although my head still hurt. "I told you the truth. Dr. Gray is inside the stone. Eaten by the jembalang."

Always the same answer, am I right?

Jembalang.

Jembalang.

White men do not believe in jembalangs.

The captain listened to Awang's translation, motioned for the Tok Batin and his wife to be dragged outside, then approached and stood looming over me.

"You know what I think, Yok Ngot?"

"What?" I replied.

"I think you think I'm a fool," said Captain Stalker. "And that makes me think *you* are a fool. I think that the tribes are following the example of the Malay insurgents, thinking it was time to drive away the white men—they lured him into the jungle with a bogus rock story so they could kill him in the dead of night, with no witnesses because everyone believes their equally bogus belief about night-wandering demons. They spun a great story to cover it up, and you are in cahoots with them. You faked these injuries. That's what I think, Yok Ngot. Am I correct?"

I was at a loss for words. The captain peered deep into my eyes.

"I ask you one last time: where is Dr. Gray?"

"Gray, inside stone," I growled in English, pronouncing each word clearly. "Go see him."

Captain Stalker shook his head, almost in disappointment.

"I'm not falling for that trick, pal. No doubt you've got sharpshooters with blowguns arrayed in the jungle, waiting for us to show up like lambs to the slaughter, just like foolish Dr. Gray." He turned and strode towards the door. "I'm not stepping a foot into that jungle without a full squad. We've got to make a show of strength, don't we?"

He shouted to his men outside. "Shoot them all!"

I cried out, but my voice was drowned in the burst of multiple gunshots and the blood-curdling screams of the stricken. Another round of shots followed, and another, and another, until I lost count and the screams were no more.

"I told you the truth!" I shouted. "Go see the stone for yourself!"

"See, I know you are lying because *you* have seen the stone, and yet you are not dead. Your story contradicts itself." The captain sighed. "You are bad at lying, Yok Ngot. Your rebellion was a lost cause from the beginning. No one can withstand the British Empire."

"The split stone spared me because I gave it respect!"

Awang was having trouble translating fast enough.

At any rate, the captain was not interested in arguing any longer. He shouted orders, and his soldiers dragged me off my mat, disregarding my feeble struggles, and bound me with rope. My headache pounded on the inside of my skull, but my mind was too occupied to notice it.

"What are you doing? Aren't you going to kill me too?"

Captain Stalker laughed.

"We aren't savages, Yok Ngot. You'll have a proper trial before you are hanged for the betrayal and murder of Avery Gray. Since you have Gray's possessions, they might throw in a charge of robbery as well, but that will hardly make a difference. I fancy they might send us back to burn down this village just for good measure. Let's go, boys!"

They led me out of the house, staggering and tottering until the lieutenant ordered one of them to carry me over their shoulder to pick up speed. I shut my eyes as we passed the blood-soaked village square, unable to look at the corpses of the Semai. *Tok Batin, Bah Sung, I'm so sorry, I'm sorry, this was never meant to happen…*

They brought me down the long trail back to their boats. They sailed downstream to the coastal towns, where their great ships waited in the crowded ports. They locked me in a cell to await judgement.

And now, they have sent a constable to write down my confession.

I stare at the white man and his Malay translator.

If I must tell the truth, so be it.

I have seen Captain Stalker and his soldiers smirking as I told my tale. I am sure the same thoughts ran through their minds, just as they had run through Avery Gray's.

What happened?

Jembalang.

Jembalang.

Always jembalang.

I have seen Awang, sweat beading on his forehead, fingers shaking, voice trembling more and more as he translates each word to the captain. He knows the truth when he hears it. He believes that I am the man who has seen the darkness and lived to tell the tale.

But today, the constable puts down his pen with a different smile.

"Looks like a few extra days in the lock-up did you some good," he says in a tone of long-suffering. "Decided to come clean now, eh? No more of that stone demon nonsense from before? Well, they do say that the first step of repentance is acknowledging the error of your ways. Were you alone when you murdered Gray?"

"Yes," I say.

"There was no…jembalang with you?"

"No," I say. "I told you: I killed Gray with a knife when we were alone in the jungle. I hid his body inside the split stone—"

The constable holds up a hand. "No need to repeat the whole thing, I've got every word down." He knocks on the door, and the guard opens it. I can hear his fading words through the doorway as he walks out, carrying my confession.

"What did I tell you, Pickard? You've got to squeeze these natives just a little and they'll spill. There was never any need for Stalker's brutal massacre, God rest their poor souls. If that paranoid fool hadn't been preoccupied with his fanciful theories of *rebel insurgents and jungle ambushes*, a simple hike up the hill would have found Gray and solved the case. Well, I guess all that's left to do is to send Stalker and his team back in to dig up—"

The door closes.

The jembalang of Batu Belah asked me a question as I lay on its doorstep. I answered. It all happened in a fleeting moment, passing so quickly that I wondered if it were a dream.

Who was this man? Why does he taste so good?

"A white man, Tok," I replied, knowing no better name. "A stranger in this land."

He tastes of...arrogance.

"He thinks he knows better, Tok."

Are there more like him?

"Yes, Tok."

I heard the licking of enormous, hungry lips.

You have seen me.

"I?"

You have seen my true form. No one may see me and live.

I had no answer for that.

I have eaten a white man. I want more.

A pause.

Do you want to live?

"Yes, Tok," I whispered.

Bring them.

The Rattler

ALEX BURNSTEIN

I MOVED AWAY from the city to escape the noise, but the silence out here just made it louder.

I scratched a match along the rough surface of splintered windowsill my uncle had carved out for the sole purpose of lighting his cigars in the silver light of the moon, shadows dancing off his high cheekbones from the pulsing glow of the cigar tip in the late hours of the night. The blood-red sun drooped behind the distant mountains like melting plastic in a pool of orange and pink hues. My mom had said he was eccentric, but I'd thought he'd held something deeper in his vigilant gaze. It wasn't his stare I'd been glued to, though; it was the way he tilted his head. Like he was listening to the hushed sounds of the desert evening. Waiting for something to start.

Taos, New Mexico. Pretty sunsets. Polite folks. Hot during the day, but nothing like the oven that was Los Angeles in the middle of summer, where you could practically taste the streets melting. The speed at which life there blitzed by had left me with crippling anxiety and a severe case of tinnitus. My family had thought it'd be good for me to move out here, and after my uncle's sudden passing, it had all just kind of fallen into place. I exhaled the puff of cigarette smoke and inhaled the cool, dry evening air, free of that acrid, rubbery asphalt.

My ears perked at the sound of the sky sizzling. I stamped out the butt of my smoke on the same missing chunk of windowsill and leaned out for a better listen. It sounded like thousands of tiny beads vibrating. A noise I hadn't heard since I'd visited this place as a kid.

It's a warning call, my uncle had always said. *You hear the little devils' bells ringing, and you best stay far away. That's the rattlers' territory.*

I concentrated on the buzzing for a minute longer, then closed the shutters. My attention snapped to another sound. Static from the CRT. The black and white waves flickered and pulsed over one another in a sea of poor signals. The antenna had kept me occupied for most of the day, begging me to try to get the damn thing working. Guess the signal was better at night.

A fuzzy image of a woman in a broad-shouldered blazer with a large pink bow tied just under her neck peeked through the noise on the tube. "Missing Taos resident and local artist, Joaquin Martinez, who most lovingly know as the 'Sunset Man', was found just outside of Eagle Nest, stripped down to his briefs and walking into the lake. Martinez was brought to the Eagle Nest Police Station for questioning and then later taken back to his home in Taos. Disturbingly, Martinez was found with claw marks around his ears, the third in a seemingly random string of ear-related phenomena around the Enchanted Circle. Here's what Sheriff Dalton had to say."

The mysterious scenario reminded me of a bizarre story my uncle once told me about a whole carload of people driving off a nearby cliff. All the bodies had been found with wads of cotton stuffed deep into their ear canals.

One of 'em even tried to scoop his own brain out with a spoon, my uncle had said as he mimicked a digging motion near his temple.

Questions about this "Sunset Man" and the ear incidents bubbled in my gut. The camera cut to Sheriff Dalton standing on the lakeshore. He fidgeted with his hands and seemed jumpy. "It weren't like nothin' I ever seen before. I thought a hawk or somethin' had got to 'im, but when I grabbed his hands, his fingers were red, like he'd been clawin' out his own ears. I kid you not."

It cut back to the reporter. "Friends of Martinez report the artist is now safe at home. In other news, the hot air—"

A series of scratches and crackling pops, followed by more gray and white static, consumed the picture on the CRT and left me in the quiet of my new home. Well, almost quiet. I could still hear the faint clicking of a rattlesnake outside. Or was it just the tinnitus creeping back in? It had been two months since I moved out here, and the condition had quelled after the first week. The thought of its return made me nervous.

A shuffling noise dragged me to the front door. A sheet of paper had slipped through the crack. *'Don't listen,'* was written on it. Don't listen? To what? I cracked the door open, trying to catch wind of whoever had left the note. Outside, there was nothing but the *ch-ch-ch* of the venomous pit viper.

The old floors creaked beneath the weight of my steps. It smelled like dust and the ghosts of cigars my uncle had inhaled. The bedroom contained a ratty bed hunched in the corner, an antique dresser full of mothballs, and an old teal lamp with a stained shade wedged against the opposite wall. A simple desk with a foggy oil lamp leaned against the wall across from the door. There was no chair. The springs in the mattress and the frail bed frame screamed as I settled down.

This was it. This was life outside the city.

I sighed and rubbed my hands over my face. Sleep would elude me. It always took a few months in a new place for me to feel comfortable enough to pass out. The first few nights especially would consist of me tossing and turning in my own sweat. No point in trying. I stood. The bed wailed again.

The off-white fridge droned, making my temples pulse. I opened it, grabbed a can of Busch, and popped the tab. It hissed before I took an ice-cold sip. I unplugged the fridge for some temporary respite. The big recliner in the living room swallowed me, and I laid my head back, closing my eyes. For a minute, I heard absolutely nothing. Not even the white noise of an empty room. It was almost eerie, like I was about to listen to the whispers of the Tiwa people who'd traversed this land before the invasion of hatchbacks, hi-fi sound systems, and Ataris.

The sharp taps of the rattlesnake pinched my ears, pulling me out of the silence and back into the chilling landscape of the desert night.

I leaned forward, the blood in my brain rushing to the front of my skull and making me dizzy. Standing made the sensation worse. A dull ringing started deep in the bony labyrinth of my ear. The tinnitus. The phantom siren had plagued me for years, a nagging aftereffect from life in The City of Angels, sticking to me like a flared-up rash.

When the ringing in my head stopped and was replaced by the vibration of the rattling, I threw the window shutters open and was greeted by a gusty chill. The inky landscape beyond swallowed my gaze. While my eyes adjusted to the darkness, I searched for the hiding spot of my scaly stalker.

The dark silhouettes of the distant mountains soon brightened, and before I knew it, the sun was drifting towards its peak in a cloudless blue sky. A few empty beer cans and a pile of ash with three or four cigarette butts poking out like weeds in a sooty anthill surrounded me. The skin around my dry eyes felt tight, and the haze of sleeplessness hung heavy on my shoulders. Yet the clicks of the snake's rattle still beat against the morning sky.

I needed supplies. My uncle's cabinets had held little more than an ancient coffee can and a couple of bottles of aspirin, both of which I'd tried my luck with that morning. Opening the front door, I nearly fell backwards. An old woman, silent as a ghost, stood face to face with me. The ringing in my ears weaved with the rattling.

"Jesus, you scared me," I sputtered as my heart settled.

She stood with a slight hunch, either from age or the thick multicolored poncho that weighed down her shoulders. There wasn't so much as a blink in response. Her skin had as many lines running through it as the dry, cracked ground after a drought, sunbaked and leathery, sagging under her eyes and around her jaw. She had a deep frown and hair as white as an eggshell.

I blinked. "Want something to drink? I've got coffee."

Still no response.

"I was gonna mosey on into town. Need a lift?"

I gestured to the old pickup with my thumb, parked under the only tree in sight. She didn't move. Even the air around her seemed still. A fly could've landed on her face and I'm not sure she'd have budged.

I squeezed past her and pulled the door shut, holding my breath to make myself small. I didn't bother locking up. If she or anyone else decided to walk into this cabin in the middle of nowhere, they could help themselves to some stale coffee. Hell, maybe they could even figure out how to get the signal on the CRT working.

Walking to the truck, I glanced over my shoulder to see if she'd moved. She hadn't. I climbed in, the seat crinkling oddly when I sat. Confused, I reached under my legs and pulled out a sheet torn from a notebook. *Don't listen,* was scrawled on it, same as the letter slid under my front door. Was it the old lady? The truck started up, hacking like an aged chain smoker. After the last sputter and groan, I shifted into reverse and backed out. With a slight adjustment of the rearview mirror, I saw the statuesque woman, now prostrate in front of the cabin door. I considered checking to see if she was alright, but decided it was all just a little too weird. I hoped she'd be gone when I returned.

Eyes focused on the road ahead, I took off towards town. Through the muffled crunch of tires on dirt and the pulsing chug of the exhaust, I thought I could still make out the faint buzz of the snake's tail. Maybe I'd grown so used to the police sirens, random shouting, and car horns that the quiet out here made the desert noises stick around like a phantom limb.

Halfway to town, the truck backfired and came to a slow, painful stop. The engine sizzled like bacon and eggs on a skillet. If I didn't figure out what was going on, the desert would render me over-easy, too.

Outside the vehicle, I dragged a finger along the front to see how overheated it was. I frowned, pressing my whole palm against the truck's hood. It felt lukewarm at best. Popping it, the engine bay looked well-oiled and perfectly functional. Where was that sizzling noise coming from? Was it the snake? Was it a different one? The same? More than one? The lack of sleep was making me paranoid. While not necessarily fatal, a bite from one of those pests would hurt more than a bee sting or a slap on the wrist. Being stuck several miles away from both the town and my home would guarantee my last breath.

Sweat beaded along my hairline and greased the edges of my nose. The fire from the angry ball in the sky beat down on me with a vengeance, the only shade beneath my truck, but the sea of bristly shrubs and rocks hiding an invisible killer with a venomous gunshot rendered that option null. Waiting was my only choice—hopefully some godforsaken soul would drive through the middle of nowhere.

My thoughts drifted back to the truck. If it wasn't the engine, then why had it stopped working? The pickup's exhaust leered at me. Sleeves rolled to my elbows, I reached in. My fingers brushed against something rough, almost jagged. A thousand clicks erupted, as loud as if I'd been standing directly beneath church bells. Two yellow eyes glowered at me; a forked tongue flicked madly.

I shouted and fell back, skittering away like a roach. My heart pounded so hard I felt it in my skull, the thumps like wet drum beats. A few rotations of my forearm revealed nothing but coarse arm hairs and whispers of pale veins beneath thin skin. No puncture wounds. The panic began to settle. The snake slumped out of the exhaust like a wad of hair from the drain and slithered off into the low shrubs and weeds.

Questioning why it hadn't bitten me would be like gambling with the divine. I questioned the continued rattling, though. Despite the serpent's exit, I still heard it clear as day. My uncle had told me a snake would always strike before you saw it, but that wasn't the case here. Making a half-assed sign-of-the-cross, I got back in and turned the key. The truck spluttered to a start, and before I could press my luck any further, I found myself in the heart of Taos.

Pop!

The neon pink bubble on the young woman's face burst over her nose and lips. The small chimes tied to the top of the door jingled as she shuffled past me. I squeezed into the earth-toned aisles lined with processed snacks and listened to the distant droning buzz of vending machines and coolers.

"Need anything?" an older gentleman called out in a gravelly bellow, the greasy crackle of chip bags shifting in his fingers as he restocked.

"Just grabbing some more brews."

"Got in a few fresh cases this morning. Fridges are in the back."

The rubber seal of the cooler door resisted slightly before it finally pulled free with a muffled slurp. A six-pack of Busch called my name. The ice-cold surfaces of the cans felt good against my hot forehead, giving me temporary relief. Good-for-nothing painkillers.

I thought I could still hear the faint buzz of the rattlesnake, but it had been over thirty hours since I'd last gotten any shut-eye. I was starting to question my sanity.

I turned. The clerk stood a hair's breadth in front of me. I dropped the six-pack, the orchestra of tinnitus swelling to a shrieking timbre. The people around here had no sense of personal space. I'd thought Los Angeles had been bad, but at least everyone there ignored you.

"Whoa." He grabbed the cans before they hit the floor. "You alright there, bud?"

I sucked in a sharp slice of air. "Just a little jumpy. Haven't slept in a while."

His long, slick ponytail swayed behind him as he led the way to the counter. He rang me up, chatting as he went through the motions.

"You hear about the Sunset Man?" he asked.

"Saw it on the news."

The keys on the cash register clicked and clacked as he entered the price. "That Sheriff Dalton's quite the character, don't you think?"

I shifted. "Seemed like it."

"People around town say he's a little too loose with the law." He gave me my change and slid the beers across the counter. "Your head okay?"

"Hmm?"

He tapped his temple with two fingers. "Your head. You weren't looking so hot by the fridges."

"Oh, I'm fine." I scooped up my change and the beverages. "Thanks a lot."

The chimes bade me farewell on my way out.

The center of the plaza smelled earthy, like dirt on a warm summer evening, mixed with the pleasant aromas of spices and peppers. I could get lost in that scent. Whatever the spicy equivalent of a sweet tooth was, I had it. The architecture soothed me with its low, smooth adobe structures that rose and fell in front of and behind one another like oblong bricks. Bodies moved all around me in a blur—people with long, flowing hair, bright eyes, and an appetite for art; hippies unplugging from the rush; DINKs shopping for expensive paintings; burnouts looking for dope; locals selling jewelry, blankets, and hats. Taos was somehow both the fresh place to be and the quietest little town out west.

Or, rather, it was supposed to be quiet.

Each segment of the snake's rattle rubbed against the other, sucking me back into the torturous melody that had haunted me the last day or so. How I could hear it over the muttering crowds and hundreds of twinkling wind chimes was a mystery.

My stomach grumbled, and the howling emptiness from not having eaten anything all day clawed at the thin skin stretched over my abdomen. I hadn't filled my insides with much food over the previous few afternoons; the strange happenings had stolen most of my attention. Time had been escaping me too. Somehow, while I had been soaking in the plaza's ecosystem, the early afternoon had drowned into dusk.

Hunger and the sudden shift of time weren't the only things bothering me, though. I was parched, and tempted to crack a cold one then and there, but the distant pulse of red and blue lights bouncing off the clay walls of an alley nabbed my attention. Curious, my feet followed the trail.

The Sheriff's car was parked in front of a low, flat building with a sign on its front that read *'Sunset Studios'*. The patriotic lights summoned me like a moth to the flame.

Against my better judgment, I pushed open the door to the studio and walked inside. A bevy of oil and acrylic sunset landscapes greeted me. Joaquin Martinez really had a specialty.

"Hey!" a panicked voice called out. "This here's an active crime scene. Place's off limits. Get outta here!"

I recognized him from the picture on the television: Sheriff Dalton.

"Sorry. Just wanted to see if I could catch a glimpse of the infamous Sunset Man," I said, shying back a few steps.

The Sheriff went from squared shoulders and a finger resting on the button of his leather holster to a more relaxed stance. "Sorry 'bout that. Whole thing's got me on edge, you know?" His gaze flicked to my side. "You bring one of those for me?"

I followed it to the cans of beer I was holding. My cheeks flushed; I'd forgotten to drop them off. It felt illegal for some reason, like being caught cheating in the classroom. There was being *loose* with the law, like the clerk had mentioned, and then there was the Sheriff drinking a beer with a stranger at a crime scene. After an awkward pause and no laugh or shrug from Dalton, I realized he was serious.

"Oh. Sure."

I popped one of the cans from the plastic rings and handed him one. He cracked the tab and there was a low hiss as he took a long swig.

"Can I have one, too?" I asked, hesitantly.

He arched an eyebrow and gave me the side-eye. "They're your beers, why you askin' me for?"

I guessed off the beaten path was the status quo here. The cold liquid soothed my dry mouth, and the tiny buzz of that first sip warmed my belly.

The brief respite was ruined, like every tranquil moment, by the incessant beat of the serpent's drum. I winced and smacked the side of my head, then dug around my earlobe with my finger, hoping to flick the noise out.

The Sheriff looked at me and took another drink. "You alright there, son?"

"Just haven't slept in a while. Damn tinnitus has been acting up lately." I decided to keep the minor detail of rattling to myself—didn't want to look completely mental.

"Ti-what-sis?" Dalton scratched his nether region like an ape picking for fleas.

"Ringing in my ears. Doc said it comes from stress." Changing the subject, I asked, "Sunset Man's in trouble again?"

"Can't find 'im. Some buyer came to pick up a paintin' and the old man weren't here."

The horrifying image of the artist stripped and walking into the lake flashed in my mind.

"Since yer here, wanna see somethin' strange?"

My gut told me no, but ignoring my judgment once again, I followed. "Alright."

Dalton led me down a dark hall and into a room on the left. When he flipped the light switch, I almost dropped my beers again. The small room was filled to the brim with paintings of ears.

"What the hell is this?"

"Strange, innit? 'Specially after the old man tried to claw his own off."

This was beyond strange. More like stepping into an abstract nightmare. Ears of different shapes, colors, and sizes choked the entire room, but the most disturbing part was the clay ears hanging from the ceiling. Dozens of them.

As the rattling started up again, or maybe it had never stopped, another noise caught my attention.

Drip. Drip. Drip.

The steady plop of liquid hitting the floor was coming from deeper within the room.

Drip.

I pushed through the cascades of ears, running my hands through them, praying my hunch would lead me astray.

Drip.

My finger brushed against a surface that was not clay, but flesh.

Drip.

Flecks of bright red blood plopped onto the tip of my boot. I ripped my arm back.

"Sheriff!"

Dalton waded through the room. "Oh, shit," he wheezed, pulling his radio from his belt. "We're gonna need backup at Sunset Studio."

"Copy, on our way now. Over," the tiny, scratchy voice in the radio called back.

My gaze darted around the room in search of the other ear, again hoping I wouldn't find what I sought. It landed on a door peeking out from behind a large canvas, a dark, moody ear painted on its surface. I shoved the canvas aside and turned the knob. The door creaked open. Light from the ear room poured in and illuminated a pair of legs sitting in a chair. The rest of the body remained hidden by shadows. I tried to swallow but my mouth went dry. Something, maybe the rattling noise, maybe my own delirium, urged me to keep going. I pulled it open, slowly. My palms sweated. My ears burned. My head throbbed. The rattling was unbearably loud.

Light washed over the rest of the seated body. Joaquin Martinez—it had to be him—sat dead as a doornail, pale hands resting on his lap, one holding a knife, the other holding his second ear, dipped in blood like a strawberry in chocolate. Terror filled his wide, cloudy eyes. Curtains of blood draped over his cheeks and down his arms from the holes where his ears used to be. *Don't listen,* was painted in blood on the wall behind his corpse.

I turned, pushing past the Sheriff to escape the nightmare before me. "Hey, where you—"

I didn't hear the rest. I barreled through the studio and back outside, falling to my hands and knees and releasing the little bit of beer I had in my stomach. A melancholic blue swallowed the sky. The moon, full and bright, was surrounded by a sea of stars. It looked like I could've drifted up and found myself in the heart of the galaxy. The stars started to twist around the moon in a blur. The screaming beads of hell violently stabbed my ears, growing louder and louder, until I felt something sharp strike against my temple.

I finally had my silence.

My eyes tore open, my head pounding like someone hammering the inside of my skull. The noise of the rattlesnake wailed, screamed, and chanted all around me. My eyes watered.

"Stop!" I shouted, sitting up and twisting around. I was in a living room, one not unlike my uncle's. Orange and pink rugs hung over the backs of two large chairs with a long wooden coffee table between them. A thin light soaked through the curtains pulled over the windows. How had I ended up here? Had someone knocked me out and taken me to their house?

I fished for my truck keys in my pocket and stood. I was desperate to get home. To get out of Taos. Damn the peace and quiet of the country, the chaos of the city was quieter than this place. It was time to leave.

The old woman from the other morning appeared behind me like a silent reaper, and I screamed, startled. Then, unable to control my temper from the click, click, clicking in my brain, I shouted at her. "What do you want from me?"

She remained silent, guiding me to the coffee table and using the support of my arm to lower herself into one of the chairs. She pulled a notepad onto her lap and scratched something on it with a pen: *'Don't listen.'*

She was the one leaving me those notes, and it was the same message the Sunset Man had painted across the wall in his own blood. It had to be about the snake. They both had to know about it—but could she do anything to help? "How do I make it stop?"

She stared at me, then slowly brushed long white hair away from her ears—or where her ears should have been. Instead, two scarred holes remained on either side, the flesh twisted and gnarled.

She tugged my attention back to the paper. Three words had been added to her sentence: *'Don't listen to the Rattler.'*

Was cutting off my own ears the only solution? I backed away and ran outside. If Hell existed, this was it. I looked for my truck in the darkness—the light I'd seen behind the curtains had been the light of the moon. I found the pickup parked by the dirt road. My keys spilled from my pocket in my haste, scraping against the vehicle door as I scooped them up. It sounded like nails over glass, but I barely heard it over the rattling.

I started the truck, slammed my feet on the pedal and clutch, shifted straight into fourth, and drove off into the midnight black of the desert's belly. The bumpy road throttled and shook me around, but I dared neither stop nor turn back. Headlights illuminated the road in front of me, the cone-shaped light making the darkness around me seem deeper, more threatening. The shaking clicks of the rattlesnake sounded like they were in the car with me, like I was up to my neck in scales.

A large blur ran across the headlights.

I slammed on the brakes, and my head smashed into the steering wheel as the pickup screeched to a halt. Pain made the world spin. I spilled out of the truck and slumped to the ground. After a moment, I pulled myself up using the driver's side mirror. What the hell had that been? Moths and other insects dashed wildly through the glow of the headlights in a mess of wings. I squinted. Shadows shifted. Something big stalked the edge of the light.

My heart raced. I took a few steps back. I had nothing to defend myself, save for the belt around my jeans. My drenched hands could barely unhook the damn thing. Finally, I pulled it through the belt loops, but I couldn't hear the jingle of the metal buckle as it swayed. I shook it. No noise. I clapped. Nothing. I slammed my palm against the pickup. Silence. All I heard was the rattling. So, I turned.

Death loomed over me in the form of a massive, pale beast. It had a human-shaped head, but it bore no eyes on its round face, nor did it have a nose, only two long slits where one should have been. A wide mouth—a slice that ran all along its jaw and up to where a person's ears would be—opened to reveal rows of sharp teeth. Two fangs, white as the moon, distended from pink holes near the roof of its mouth, dripping with an oozy liquid. It clasped humanlike hands with long fingers over the side of its head as if to cover its missing ears. Gangly, sinewy arms sprouted from its torso like branches. The rest of its massive body was long and serpentine, coiling over itself. A bulbous, segmented cone at the tip of its trunk-like tail vibrated back and forth. A rapid *ch-ch-ch* engulfed the world around me.

My uncle's words crept up the stem of my brain and into my memory. *It's a warning call. Keeps the night stalkers away. You hear the little devil's bells ringing and you best stay far away. That's The Rattler's territory.*

The creature's mouth widened as it reared its head back, poised to strike.

My uncle hadn't been talking about the snakes that plagued the crevices of the desert but the monstrosity in front of me. The Rattler. He hadn't been looking out the window all those nights waiting for something to start.

He'd been waiting for the devil's bells to stop ringing.

Cornfield Gothic

GABRIELLE CONTELMO

"I don't think we should stop here, Maddie," Shirley says, peering into the darkness.

"What do you want me to do, drive to the next town on a flat?" I snap, shutting the car off. The rushing sound of the corn enters through the open windows.

"Leanne says the corn wolves—"

"Corn wolves aren't real," I cut her off and slam the door for good measure before stalking around to the trunk. I've got enough to worry about without Shirley's stupid fantasies.

The pavement still radiates heat, the memory of the sun captured in crumbling asphalt, though the breeze sends shivers across my bare shoulders. Shirley scrambles out of the car and comes to hover at my elbow, too close. I bump into her, half-on purpose, while dragging the spare over the edge of the trunk.

"They're real," Shirley insists. "Her brother saw one. He said their breathing sounds like wind in the corn. They could be out there *right now*." She stares with saucer-sized eyes into the fields that surround us.

"Leanne's brother is full of shit." I turn the handle on the jack. Slowly, the car rises.

There are no streetlights on this two-lane road. Our hazards blink on-off, on-off. It disorients me; by the time my eyes have focused, the light has gone again. In the flashes, I catch glimpses of the dashed center line stretching away into infinity and the towering skeletons of cornstalks.

I can hear the corn better than I can see it, the stiff leaves rustling in a rising breeze.

"Leanne says the corn wolves take the bad kids," Shirley whispers. "Or kids who get lost."

"We're not lost. Shut up and keep watch. I need you to tell me if anyone's coming." I crouch by the deflated rear wheel. The clang of the tire iron seems small beneath the overturned bowl of the night sky.

Shirley whips around to stare back towards town. "You think he's already on his way?"

The land is so flat that during the day the road disappears to a point on the horizon. At night, all I can see are the lights of Ryeville, the town an angry ember behind us. I'd just let myself start to think we were out. Stupid. The flat tire feels like revenge.

"No," I tell Shirley. "I just don't want to get run over by drag-racing hicks."

It's a half-truth. We're barely ten minutes out of town, still dangerously close. Ryeville's baleful glare makes my heart race. *What if he already knows?* We're sitting ducks like this. No place to hide, except in the corn. With whatever lives in the corn.

Shirley puts her hands on her skinny hips and says in that self-righteous voice, "*We're* hicks. And I know for a *fact* that Floyd Crosby took you drag racing last month."

Floyd Crosby also taught me how to change oil and replace spark plugs in between makeout sessions behind his uncle's garage, but Shirley doesn't need to know that part. At least she's off the corn wolves.

"Just focus on the road."

I have to use all my strength on the tire iron to loosen the lug nuts. Floyd would have made this look easy. I'll miss him when we're in Sioux Falls. Not enough to stay in Ryeville, though. I don't love anything enough to stay there, except Shirley, and we were always getting out together or not at all.

Two hours ago, the intro music of the big fight began to rattle our bedroom door. I love that music. During those four blessed hours, Dad ignores us while he and his buddy Dusty get shitfaced on beer and testosterone. Sometimes, he passes out in the recliner afterwards, too drunk to padlock the front door after Dusty leaves. Those are the best nights, when I can slip out and crash at Floyd's for a few hours, me crammed against him in the twin bed, Shirley on the floor beside us.

Not lately, though. Dad's been stalking around the trailer like a caged animal, barking at us while we do homework, tearing doors open like he's going to catch us in furtive whispers.

Fifteen minutes ago, we squeezed out the tiny bathroom window, the only one not screwed shut.

"Maddie," Shirley warns.

Lights on the eastern horizon, blinding white. My depth perception is still off, but I can tell it's coming at us fast from the direction of Ryeville.

"Get to the side." I stand and push her onto the grass. Behind us, the corn whispers.

The car slows as it approaches. My arms feel weak and floppy from the effort of loosening the lug nuts. On the back of my tongue, my heart beats heavy. *Dad?* It can't be him. It hasn't been long enough. He should still be at home, shouting at the TV.

A beat-up pickup grumbles by. Rust and baby blue. Familiar. The windows are rolled down. Dusty's head does a slow swivel. He spots my shiner and sneers.

The dry leaves of the cornstalks clatter together, as though something is moving between the rows.

Dusty doesn't stop, doesn't offer help, doesn't take his eyes off us. I put one hand on Shirley's trembling shoulder, as delicate as a bird's wing. I clench my other hand around the tire iron and glare back, daring him. The engine revs when he roars off.

"He's going to call Dad," Shirley whispers.

Maybe he won't. Maybe he'll think we're on an errand. Those are the kind of thoughts I used to think when I was Shirley's age and Mom was still around. Hopeful, useless thoughts.

"Let 'im. We'll be long gone by then."

I finish unscrewing the lug nuts and, with renewed urgency, haul the tire off with a grunt. Shirley sidles next to me, too close again. She rubs her goosebump-y arms, back and forth over the blotchy purple fingerprints that ring her scrawny biceps.

"Leanne says the corn wolves come out at night," she says. "They drag people into the very center of the field and eat them alive. Their bones turn into dead cornstalks so no one ever finds them." She wraps her fingers around one bony wrist, barely thicker than a corn stalk.

Maybe it's Shirley's fear infecting me, or the sight of Dusty, who should be in front of the TV with my dad. It feels like we're being watched.

"There's no such thing as corn wolves."

I've always pictured them with human bodies, wolf heads, and steel-hard fists. The puffy skin around my eye throbs. The wind huffs through the fields. It sounds like breathing.

I heave the spare onto the hub.

A mile away—more? Impossible to tell distances on this flat, endless road—Dusty's brake lights glow red. He pulls to the side of the road. I fumble a lug nut. It skitters across the pavement.

"Get that!" I snap at Shirley.

She scrambles underneath the car. Her quick, shallow breaths echo between the asphalt and the metal undercarriage, as loud as they were two nights ago in the close space beneath the bed.

Dusty doesn't move, just sits there to the west, brake lights on. Waiting.

"Hurry, hurry," I whisper under my breath. My sweaty fingers slip on the last lug nut.

Dusty makes a slow U-turn across the empty asphalt. The headlights grow larger, brighter, until I have to shield my eyes. The engine growls. The truck swerves.

"Maddie!" Shirley screams.

I roll out of the way. Dusty roars by on the wrong side of the road, right where I was crouched. A new, sharper pain has joined the soreness around my eye. I touch my cheek. My fingertips come away bloody.

"He could have killed you!" Shirley rushes up and examines the damage with an expression so like Mom's it tears another hole in me.

I jerk out of her grip, hoping she doesn't notice me shaking. "He'll have to do better than that."

Adrenaline still burns hot in my veins when the shush of the field changes. I spin, straining to see into the shadows.

"Something's coming," Shirley whispers.

The tassels of the stalks tremble as something passes through, too large to fit between the rows.

"Corn wolves," says Shirley in our mother's voice.

My eyes flick to the road where, to the east, two pinpricks of dingy yellow light grow rapidly. Closer, Dusty makes another U-turn. The speeding truck comes up behind him, turning him into a dark silhouette in the cab.

"Help me!" I shout at Shirley.

Together, we heave the flat into the trunk.

Dusty's truck roars past us again. I hear rather than see him skid to a stop somewhere ahead of my car. Dusty is mean, but incidental. The real threat is behind the second set of headlights, which form angry, glowing eyes.

Shirley shrinks, chin tucking down, bony shoulders curling in.

Dad's filthy white pickup swerves off the shoulder and comes to rest twenty feet behind my car, drunkenly angled towards the shallow ditch between the road and the corn.

My hand finds Shirley's arm.

He sits in the cab, watching to see what we'll do. His engine rumbles. We can't outrun them, not in my car, which wasn't built for racing like Floyd's dragster.

"Maddie?" Shirley says, voice high and quavering.

I pull her with me, keeping my eyes on the dark windshield that hides our father. We step backwards through the ditch, crushing the desiccated skeletons of drought-starved weeds.

Shirley leans away from the corn that looms at our backs, automatically, like a magnet repelled. "*Maddie*," she says again, high-pitched.

I step off the pale beige grass and onto the dry dirt between the rows of corn. As the stalks close around us, Dad's door slams shut. I flinch.

—two nights ago, the front door slamming, rattling the trailer on its cinderblock feet. Dad's growl on the threshold, his mean eyes squinted but not red; not drunk, which means his aim is better. Shirley, dragged out from under our bed like a ragdoll—

I break into a run, yanking Shirley behind me. She cries out as her shoulder jerks in the socket.

The rows of corn are close and dense. Ten feet in and the car lights are useless. Between the looming plants, a strip of bruise-purple sky. This far from civilization, the polluted stars are the only form of illumination. They turn the corn into spindly gray figures against a black background.

Stalks crack and rustle when Dad and Dusty plunge into the field behind us. Their feet pound against the dry ground. Rhythmic rasping breaths tear from my lungs. Sharp leaves slap my already bloodied cheek, slicing into my swollen skin.

—my cheek beneath his fist; an explosion of light behind my eye—

Dad shouts at Dusty. They separate, spreading wide, trying to pin us.

I run faster, zigzagging between rows like a prey animal. Would my erratic pattern confuse the corn wolves? Will it confuse my father? Muscle memory takes over, though I haven't been in a cornfield since Mom died.

Ahead, miles of corn, as endless and uniform as the asphalt road we left behind. I flinch away from the reaching leaves that feel like fingers or fur brushing my face. The corn rustles, clamoring our location to Dusty and my father.

Dusty's voice, close.

I panic and dart sideways across ten rows, heart jackrabbiting in my throat.

Corn wolves, the game we used to play, taking turns being the wolf and the victims who got turned into wolves when they were caught. I got good at outrunning the wolves. I slipped through the rows as nimbly as a hare.

Mom only let me play in the corn when it was young, the tender green leaves soft enough to handle without slicing into skin. The wavering tassels had been short enough to see over, so we never lost sight of home. We only ever went out in the daytime, when the sun was at its highest.

Inevitably, when I was the only one left, I'd make a mistake. I was too tired; there were too many wolves to evade. They would descend.

I slip between another row, the stalks as close together as prison bars. The base of one catches my foot and I crash to my knees, dragging Shirley down with me.

My cheek throbs with the beat of my heart. I breathe raggedly, wheezing into the dirt. The wind stirs up again, brushing its fingers against tassels and stiff leaves, a rustling susurration that sounds like whispers.

Or breathing.

Shirley coughs and coughs again. *Be quiet!* I think at her, too winded to speak.

"*If the stalks grow too high, the corn wolves move in,*" Mom used to say. "*They wait for disobedient children to sneak into the fields. Then the corn wolves* eat *the bad children!*" She always swooped in to tickle my belly when she said *eat.*

Shirley was three when Mom died—too young to remember her stories. I never wanted to scare Shirley with tales of wolves that hunted children. We had enough wolves in our lives.

Shirley presses her forehead into the center of my spine. I clutch her hand to my chest. Do we stay here and hope they don't find us? Do we run towards the road—towards where I think the road is? Without light, I can't tell which direction we came from. I swivel my head, eyes open as wide as they'll go.

Corn, everywhere.

The wind shifts. Something crunches, like a foot or a paw, stepping slowly onto a dry leaf, trying not to be heard.

Every muscle in my body tightens.

Another crunch, quieter, slower. A long, heavy exhale that could be the corn in the breeze. A low growl that could be a distant truck.

Corn wolves only eat the bad kids. The kids who disobeyed. Shirley should be safe. I'm the one who stole her away, who brought her out here.

The wind goes still.

The next row over, leaves brush softly together, a papery scrape. A rush of air from a blood-hot throat. The hair on the back of my neck stands up.

A corn wolf? Or my father?

I spring to my feet and bolt, half-carrying Shirley under my arm. Electricity sizzles up my spine. At any moment, a steel-hard fist will grab my shirt, sharp yellow teeth will sink into the back of my neck. A scream lodges in my throat.

We explode from the corn in a clatter of stalks. I careen across the ditch and stumble over my own feet. Somehow, my car waits barely ten feet away, trunk still open. Dad's truck sits at an angle nearby, headlights dark.

A sharp cry, like an injured dog, echoes into the night. I whip around. In every direction, corn stands undisturbed in regimented rows, pale stalks glowing red in the light of my car's flashing hazards.

Another yelp, less animal, more human. Dusty.

Shirley clutches my wrist. I clutch back. We retreat step by step over the crinkly grass until our feet hit asphalt.

Closer, a familiar, enraged roar. Shirley jerks. On instinct, I press my hand to the side of her head, protecting her from a fist that never comes. The crack of snapping cornstalks sounds like breaking bones. Dad's roar pitches higher, turning into a wail.

I used to have nightmares about the corn wolves. They'd creep out of the fields at night and prowl through the trailer park, snuffling at the humid summer air until they found our trailer. The front door would creak open, waking me. I always knew what was coming. In my bedroom doorway, the hulking shoulders, the low growl, those glowing eyes. With the windows screwed shut, there was nowhere to escape.

Something large moves through the field, bending the corn aside with violent, rustling convulsions. A deep growl throbs in my ears and vibrates in the bones of my chest. Over everything—that thin, high scream, like a child's. The scream doesn't stop, doesn't fade, just gets more distant, moving steadily towards the heart of the field.

As suddenly as it started: silence. Shirley and I are frozen by the open trunk of my car. The wind rises again, stirring our hair. The corn tassels sway and whisper. Will my father's bones turn to corn stalks?

The hazards blink on-off, showing glimpses of

corn

corn

corn

Quietly, a dry leaf crunches beneath a careful foot. The hazards flick off. Everything is dark.

The lights come on. In the murk between rows, a pair of reflective eyes turn towards us. We scramble into the car. With the driver's side door still hanging open, I punch the gas. We skid around Dusty's empty truck in a spray of gravel.

When I look in the rearview, there's nothing but corn glowing red in our taillights.

Yamadhin

Z.D. DOCHTERMAN

INHALE IT ALL, Eric. That mosquito-larvae and morning-storm smell of Northern Minnesota. Not a bad little cabin I got, right? But it's long past time to sell. Not much up here but walleye, birch, and water. Until what happened to the Mathers and the Stevensons last year, there wasn't any drama either. Tragic, really; with any missing persons story, you have to expect the worst. Guess we do have our little legend of the Deervine. White and purple buck, wrapped in vines and leaves, branches coming out of his hide—you must've heard of it. Someone must be making a killing off of all those bumper stickers and shirts, even if no one's really believed in the thing for fifty years.

No one except my uncle, that is.

Then again, he wasn't exactly playing with a full deck, if you know what I mean. Hanson Andersson, what a name. Blame our ancestors back in Stockholm for that one. The man worked at the port of Duluth, pulling ten, twelve-hour shifts for three decades. That'll make anyone a little messed up in the brain. He bought this little three-bedroom beauty for a cool $67,000 back in 1993. But the housing crash in '08 did him in. So he sold his house in the city and moved up here.

My mom always said Hanson was off because he and Eleanor never had kids. Just ate away at him year by year. That, and his final tour in Vietnam. Came back different. My dad just thought his brother had swallowed too much lead paint as a kid. On my family's summer trips, he never uttered more than a few words at a time. "Always stay alert, Elijah." "Killer hawk up above." "Sunset like a wound." Weird stuff to say to a ten-year-old.

Now, I might talk a lot of junk about my uncle, but one thing no one doubted was that he loved Eleanor to death. She was like the tether that kept his mind harnessed to the earth. That woman could just raise her eyebrow at something off-kilter he'd said, and he'd pipe down like a well-trained puppy dog. I remember how he'd drive to Two Harbors to get her favorite tulips for birthdays and anniversaries. Cooked her walleye dinners then as best he could. She was probably the best thing about those summers at the cabin. That, and the times we'd catch bass, play cards into the night. I always remember the sunsets that poured out orange and red till ten, eleven in the evening, the mournful wail of the loons.

And the weird way my uncle looked at the woods.

Let's load up those boxes into the trucks. Mostly old photos. There's Hanson, maybe two weeks before he died. He was working on that second cabin over there. You can see the foundation by the sawed-off birch trees. Oh, he was gonna build a whole army of them to rent out to tourists who didn't want to rough the Boundary Waters by canoe. Even said he'd build them all himself. Plank by plank. Nail by nail. Big words for a man of sixty-three and a half. He'll, if I'd known you back then, Eric, we could've hired you. Not every day you get to know a logger and carpenter wrapped into one. Imagine you've chopped down enough trees to fill a football field in your time, huh?

Well, have you? It's a simple yes or no question.

Once he got this idea of the cabin development, my uncle started whacking trees down with his chainsaw like he was trying to break some kind of world record. Then he'd laugh every time the boom made the birds dart out of the branches.

"Some things are better off dead than alive," he told me once, foot on the trunk of a fallen pine. Weird stuff for a sixteen-year-old to hear.

See those antlers up there, Eric? Now that's just a normal albino deer. Rare, sure. But I've seen them in online pictures of *Field & Stream*. But that's not what my uncle said he saw.

About three weeks into the second cabin project, and even though it was summer, the temperature dropped thirty degrees in ten minutes. Got a quick chill so the hairs stood up on his neck and back. Put down the axe and went in to get a jacket.

When he came back, right there, standing on that cabin's foundation was the buck. Spindly red flowers coming off its antlers. Thick fronds protruding out around its ribs, wrapped in deep green vines.

The thing just stared at my uncle real hard.

At first, he tried to shoo the thing away. Pretend to run at the beast. But the buck didn't move. So he started to yell like all hell, *go back into your forest, you damn deer,* with a few choice words thrown in that I won't repeat. Flailed his hands like they were on fire. Still, nothing. Deer just looking back with those hollow amber eyes. So, Hanson stormed over to that toolshed you see off to your right there and fetched his chainsaw. I bet he was chuckling to himself with every step he took. *If this doesn't scare that thing off, I'll cut one of those antlers and let that good-for-nothing mutt down the road chew on it.*

Hanson went to rev the thing, but the motor didn't start. He drew closer. Pulled the cord again. Nothing. Now he was getting really sweaty and frustrated and probably would've tossed that chainsaw at the deer if this had gone on for another minute.

But just then, the buck stood up on its hind legs. Some eight feet tall, wrapped in greenery, antlers like giant claws, backlit by the sun. *Damn thing stood there like he was waiting for me. Daring me to come closer.*

This was where it got a little weird, see. The deer's eyes—remember this was what the old man had said—started swirling in their sockets, 'round and 'round. A tingle sped through my uncle's fingers. Down through his torso. Buzzing like one of those fly zappers. He tried to lift his arm to start that chainsaw, but it wouldn't move. Nor would his legs. Then the blood started pumping through innards like juice through a straw. Booming heartbeat in his head. Lips dried up. Frozen. He was just frozen in place. Hanson said that, for the first time in his life, he was scared.

That's when a sort of spirit, a presence, invaded his mind. He forgot all about the chainsaw, the cabin, the trees. All about everything.

The Deervine was talking to him. Telepathically. It whispered a single word straight through the corridors of his brain: *Yamadhin.*

A fishing break was just what we needed, Eric. Damn sweaty in all this heat. But I told you, a little Ned rig even with the sun blazing overhead—*wham*—the smallmouth are all over it. Right in between those rocks always does me good. Sorry I hooked you in the leg, bud. Pliers got it out without too much of the skin. I didn't rip too hard, did I?

Well, Eric? It's a simple yes or no question.

Anyway, I'm not mad about earlier, just so you know. It's alright to laugh, Eric. I don't expect you to take this all in without a chuckle. No one much believes in the Deervine anymore. I laugh at it, too.

But I didn't tell you what the deer did next. Hanson stood there, this snowman-cold feeling dripping down his skin. A million images a second raced through his mind. Dirt filled with earthworms. Lake trout in the shadow-filled depths. Thousands of deer—I'm talking generations before and generations to come—their antlers rippling in the sunlight, guarding the forest, pointing the sharp tips of their antlers right at him.

That's when he started to feel really sick. Clenched at his gut and fell to his knees.

When Hanson woke up, everything was quiet. Sky, trees, wind. Not a sound. The temperature was back to normal, too. But his hands were shaking. He was breathing hot and fast like he'd just run a marathon.

The Deervine was gone.

One image circled in his mind those next two days. Something Hanson couldn't even bring himself to tell my dad. Something he tried to bury deep, until it was too late.

Let's get this damn bed frame out before we do the furniture. It's the one I've slept on ever since I was eight-years-old and caught my first bluegill up here with Hanson. Damn bastard made me chop the head off myself. *You kill it before it kills you, son.* Now, how the hell is a four-inch fish gonna do more than spine me? Shoot, didn't mean to squish your finger in the doorwell. You hurt, Eric?

Don't grunt, man. It's a simple yes or no question.

Well, since you asked me to tell the rest, here's what happened. I could hear old Hanson's voice on those phone calls with my dad. After two days straight of these Deervine visions, hallucinations, whatever you want to call them—my whole family was more than a little worried about my uncle. There was talk of getting him down to Duluth for a checkup at the VA psych unit. Or some last-minute shrink appointment even out at the cabin. But we didn't want to go that route. Not until we had to.

It was the seventh phone call in those two days that pushed my father over the edge.

Hanson just kept uttering a phrase over and over again. *Yamadhin. Yamadhin, you better not do it. You better not.* So, Dad decided we'd make the four-hour drive up to Tyndall Lake the next morning. There was no real plan for what to do once we got there. I suppose he thought that us being there might calm the old man down. Even though the two of them mostly fought within fifteen minutes of seeing each other.

My dad had a thing for leaving to go up north before sunrise. He made sure we packed the car that night full of kayak paddles and bug spray and fishing rods, even though he hated fishing. That way, the whole car ride was crammed and everyone felt just as bad and tired as he did while he drove.

I remember that day. Gray gloom, bulging with clouds. Humid as all hell. Lot like today, huh, Eric? We pulled up the dirt road, yep, that one right there, just a little after nine. Soon as we got near that dock, my dad slammed the brakes. The car swerved in the mud and my neck snapped forward.

Hanson trundled toward us, flailing his hands. Mouthing something.

My dad sprung open the doors, and we popped out.

My uncle's face was red. Flushed. I could see his hands shaking as he pointed down to the lakefront. "Tried to call. Cell phone's down. It's—in the lake."

I made out what looked like a log, part of a boat torn off maybe, floating in those waters. We hurried closer.

"Get in the canoe!" my dad yelled.

Dad, who'd grabbed the oars from the storage room, met me at the dock. "You paddle as fast as you've ever paddled. You hear me, Elijah? You paddle like all hell."

I nodded and we both jumped in. The water splashed beneath our strokes, kicked up into our faces. Dad right, me left. We split the water and whooshed toward the form in the soft waves.

Like a giant starfish. Clothes. Hair.

Twelve, ten, eight feet away.

We could hear my uncle's voice as it skimmed the water, snapped into our eardrums. "The deer showed me. Showed me what would happen!"

Arms. Legs. Fingers.

My dad grabbed the head, flipped it over. I'd never seen a face so purple. Bloated. The eyes rolled back in the woman's head.

Eleanor. Hanson's wife. My dad put his finger under her nose, felt for breath. Checked the pulse. Nothing. Too much nothing.

As we dragged her into the boat, we knew there was no point. But it would've been even worse just to leave her there.

We pulled back to shore, and Uncle Hanson was screaming at my mom, pointing to the ground. "Eleanor's tracks. Look at the stride. She was running. And right there—behind her. Four hoofprints."

He was right. Two human footprints. Four deer hooves. Coincidences exist, right, Eric? Coincidences far more likely than some magical Deer dragging a woman out of bed and drowning her.

By the time I turned around to look for my uncle, he was jogging off into the woods, rifle in his hands, about as fast as a sixty-three-year-old could go.

Shoot, I need another beer. Thanks, man. Grab that gun down for me, the one hanging over the TV. That's the one he ran off into the woods with that morning. *Winchester Model 70.* Haha, don't worry, it's not loaded, Eric. Just pointing it at your sweet little face to have some fun. Anyway, you like killing deer, right, Eric? Nah, I don't mean you get off on it. I just mean you like hunting, don't you?

Just a simple yes or no question.

Good. Then why don't you take the damn thing, too. Say, I sure am giving away a lot today, aren't I? Guess this place has a bunch of bad memories. Besides, my hunting days are long past me.

So, to answer your question, yeah, I shook. But you get this ice-chest numb, not a quaking-panic kinda shook feeling when you see a dead person. Hanson came back later that day and just didn't want to talk to anyone. The police showed up shortly after my uncle returned and started the questioning. A few whimpers turned into tears. Tears even became sobs. Poor Uncle Hanson. Still, I can't deny there was a part of me that thought maybe, just maybe, these Deervine legends had twisted his already messed-up brain and pushed him over the edge. Made him drown his own wife.

I just prayed to God I was wrong.

We sat around the dinner table that night after the ambulance took her body away. Cops would be back after the autopsy. My mom whipped up some hot dish and we all shared some Grain Belt beers that night, even me at seventeen. A dinner so quiet, like the forks didn't even want to clank against the china.

"I gotta get out of here," he said at last, hands stroking his face. "Let that damn buck have his forest back."

"Why don't you come stay with us a while?" Mom said. She looked at my dad, who gave a hesitant nod. Brothers they were, but that didn't mean Dad wanted old Hanson crashing with us for a couple weeks. "We've got the extra room. We'll make it real comfortable for you. Take you to Martha's. You're just about the only man up north with a taste for West Indian food."

Hanson chuckled. "Sounds good, Nancy. If my brother will have me."

"You know we will, Han," my dad said without making eye contact. He clenched his hands together, stared hard at his thumbs. "We'll leave first thing tomorrow. Make the funeral arrangements."

I could see Hanson's bottom lip trembling, just holding back the tears. It made me and mom tear up, too.

"I'll rent a place in Duluth. Sell this damn cabin," Hanson said. "Only, probably a few weeks down in the Cities won't be enough to teach this son of yours to be a man." He punched my arm and rubbed my hair. I managed a faint smile.

We went to bed early that night. I couldn't get to sleep though, just thinking of my aunt, bloated, face like gray-blue porcelain, floating in those waters. Strange sounds came from upstairs, from Uncle Hanson's room, like shuffling feet. A low, almost animal rumble. Crumpled paper. Words he muttered to himself.

The next morning, my dad busted into my room before I could even open my eyes.

"Uncle Hanson's not answering his door," he said. "We're gonna break the lock."

Glad we had the breading to fry those bass up. Expiration date be damned, am I right? Don't worry, I wouldn't poison you. Not for a million bucks. Anyway, sofa's loaded, boxes are taped up, bed'll go down to the dump. This bonfire's the way to celebrate a long day of work. Cheers.

What's that? Alright, guess I might as well tell you how it all ended, why I got this cabin in the first place.

That morning, the temperature must've dropped some thirty degrees overnight. Sky was an icy gray chalkboard. Felt like snow was coming, snow in August, you believe that?

I rubbed my eyes and went upstairs with my dad to Hanson's bedroom. Knocked once. Twice. Nothing. Called his name again. My father undid the screws on the door so we could get in.

Father threw open the door.

The first thing I saw was the covers torn clean off the mattress, crumpled in a pile on the floor. My uncle's shirt hung from the ceiling fan. Jeans on the nightstand. Normally, Hanson was a meticulous guy with his things. Off in the corner, I spied piles of bunched-up paper. Picked a few of them up, handed them to my dad.

I didn't want to know what the old man had been writing.

We opened up the first piece. But they were drawings. Dozens of them. A deer. Beheaded. Branches of trees stuck in its cheeks and eyes. Bleeding from its neck. The drops of blood he'd drawn made snakelike shapes all around the sheet. The next paper was the same. Except for this one, it looked like the deer's eyes had been gouged out. Other pages, it was the tongue. On one, the edges of the paper had what looked like a garland pattern, the kind you'd see on a china plate. But when I looked closer, I saw the pattern was made of words. Or one word, rather, written over and over, looping all on itself so it looked like vines.

Yamadhin.

My body shook. A chill like some raven's caw rushed down my back. I may not have loved the man, but he *was* family, after all. I put down those fears and clenched my fists. It was time to find Hanson.

Dad sped downstairs to tell Mom what had happened. Said the three of us would split up and search around the woods for any sign of him. The cell reception wasn't working that day, so we agreed to meet back at noon if nothing turned up. Then a second round of searching if we had to. We'd call the police if we hadn't found him by sunset.

It was a plan.

We each picked a direction and headed off. I went north, right down that path there, taking about fifty steps, calling my uncle's name. Fifty more steps, calling my uncle's name. Went on like that for about a half-hour. By then, my throat was growing hoarse. I stopped yelling out as much. In all that cold, the damp sweat on my belly and back made me shiver as I marched on. Silence, except for the crunch of twigs under my feet. Crunch-crunch. Crunch-crunch. I ducked under some pine branches and into a small clearing. Ten, fifteen minutes later, a quiltwork of dense trees and shrubs. Almost time to head back.

Suddenly, my foot hit a rock. My ankle snapped to one side, and I tumbled to the ground. The pain rushed up my tendon and I grabbed at it, clenching my teeth.

Not like this. I didn't want to give up looking for him like this.

There, right on the ground in front of me, was a small pool of blood. Blood wending west into the forest, the kind you'd find from a shot deer making its escape after a bullet missed the lung.

It was something, a possible clue.

I pulled myself up and started hobbling on my sprained ankle. I gingerly took a few steps forward. Spikes of pain every other beat. But I followed the blood trail even when it zigged and zagged through the underbrush or dissipated into a slow dribble. I yelled for my uncle as loud as I could. "Hanson! Let's get out of this place, Uncle Han. There's nothing good up here! Nothing good."

Everything was really quiet. Too quiet. The cold dropped even further. A few snowflakes fell, carried by a slow wind.

Then I heard it.

A wild, crackling roar maybe a hundred feet further west. "*Yamadhin! Yamadhin!*"

"Hanson," I said. "Stay where you are!"

I sped up, the pain booming in my foot. No matter. Let the adrenaline take over. I pushed through the low brush and snapped branches as I darted toward my uncle's voice. Suddenly, his form came into focus on the ground. He was leaning back against the trunk of a fir, holding his neck with one hand and his stomach with the other. Blood marred his fingers, gut, shoulders. All I could feel was the rush in my body, the rush to help. I leaned in toward him.

His eyes were wide, bulging as he spoke. "A tree—there in the woods. That's where the buck comes from—that's Yamadhin!"

I looked down at his stomach, punctured with what looked like three sharp bones. His flannel shirt, wet with blood. I did my best to hide my shaking hands, to steady my wobbling voice. "You're not doing so good, Han. We gotta get you to the cabin."

His eyes were distant, like a man who's trying to make out a shape in a cloud. "I tracked the buck for two hours. Hiding. Sneaking up. Army crawling behind him. Then he gets to that tree. Starts shimmering. Like water splashing in the sun. And fades right into it. Disappears."

"We gotta get you something for your wounds now." I tried yanking him up by his armpits. But he wouldn't budge. I tried again and the pain shot through my foot. I bit my lip to stop myself from swearing. The blood seeped from him, faster than I thought blood could.

"I'm telling you the truth, Elijah!" he snapped. Then, his face shaking, he moved into a whisper. "Soon as the buck disappeared, I heard a voice. Booming like a million thunderclouds. It was the name. The name of that tree. The name of whatever cursed earth-spirit spreads itself through the forest, becomes leaf and bone and flesh in that deer. 'Ya-ma-dhin! Ya-ma-dhin!'"

As he spoke this last word, his eyes dropped shut.

His hand slipped from his neck and went limp. There, I saw a deep, serrated cut, maybe the width of my forefinger across. The chainsaw. So he'd gone out to kill the Deervine once and for all. But something had happened. Whirring blade to the neck in all his mad ravings.

I slumped down and covered my face with my hands. Felt the wet warm puddle of tears collecting in the lines of my palms.

No pulse. No breath. So much nothing.

As his hand slid off his gut, I saw a dozen other puncture wounds: what I thought were bones sticking out of him were something else. Something I couldn't believe.

The broken-off antlers of a buck.

Alright, just about time to put out those coals, don't you think? Crazy how that ember hit your coat. Could've been second-degree burns, you know. Anyway, you have someone who can patch it up for you, Eric? What do you mean, not sure? It's a simple—well, you know the rest.

Anyway, we must've downed what, ten beers a piece today? It'll be worth the hangover to have all the packing wrapped up. Thanks for all your help, man. Just so ready to sell this place and move on.

See, the deed went to my dad and, well, he thought it'd make a good graduation gift, since he swore he'd never come back to Tyndall Lake again. We put my aunt and uncle in the ground about a week later. Autopsy said Eleanor's drowning showed no signs of foul play. My uncle: massive blood loss from a chainsaw wound. Then he probably fell onto the antlers on the ground, the coroner said. Bad luck, but not what did him in. Me and my parents told the police he was exactly the kind to play fast and loose with power tools. All the other stuff, we just kept quiet about over the next few years. To this day.

But I know what you're thinking.

Was the Tree real?

Well, why don't I show you, Eric? Let you decide for yourself.

It's getting cold tonight too, isn't it? Strange, temperature must've dropped forty, fifty degrees, just like that. Clouds out there look like snow. Snow in August. I tell you, coincidences are the darndest thing.

Keep walking, Eric, it's just a ways up here. Maybe one more minute.

I ever tell you what I've felt since I started spending time up here, Eric? That tree has a way of making you feel certain things. Like maybe my uncle never should've felled that first pine, let alone the tenth or twentieth. Makes you feel how the loons and the squirrels, even the damn bass at the bottom of the lake, need these trees for shade. For life. That it's their forest, not ours. You ever felt anything from a tree, in all your days out on the job?

Simple yes or no question, Eric.

Here it is now.

Other times, I get a vision of a man with a chainsaw in his hand. Surrounded by twenty bucks. White and purple ones, covered in vines and twigs, all of them. Their heads bowed. Antlers pointed at his belly. How that man raised the chainsaw above his head. How his arms froze. Even while that chainsaw kept revving. Then the bucks approached. They gave him a chance to stop building the cabins, didn't they? To give the forest back. Saw how the first buck snapped its head, drove the tip of its antlers right into the old man's belly. Then the next buck, a shank to the intestines. The others rushed in. Frenzied. Gorged him through. And the chainsaw fell. Tore right through the flesh of Hanson's neck. I saw how he hobbled away. Left a trail of blood right to the point where I found him.

Yamadhin showed me, see.

Yes, Eric, those are deer surrounding us. Surrounding you.

One night, Yamadhin showed me something else. My own severed head, rolling from the cabin doorway down into the river. That would've been my future. If I didn't do right by Yamadhin.

So I made this here Tree a little deal. I promised It I wouldn't be like Hanson. I'd stop the carnage in these woods. I would even bring Yamadhin others. The Mathers and the Stevensons were the first. A few tourists the cops still haven't found buried deep underground near the border. Loggers. Developers. Clear cutters, all of them.

Tell me, you ever seen a tree like that? That beautiful white hide of bark, that purple stripe down its side?

It's a simple yes or no question.

Don't cry, Eric. Really. You're not a bad guy, overall. Should be those bastards up top who own the company, right? You didn't do anything wrong in chopping down all those trees, did you?

It's a simple yes or no question.

The bucks are getting closer, Eric. Their antlers almost sparkle in the moonlight, don't they, in the softly falling summer snow? But tell me. Do you think they're sharp enough to kill?

It's a simple yes or no question. A simple yes or no question.

Wampus

P. N. HARRISON

NO ONE REALLY noticed when the livestock started dying. All the brave boys fighting in the Great War took everyone's attention, especially when they did not return home. Folks didn't realize a massacre was happening on their own soil. Cattle would turn up every week or so, their necks torn open and their guts spilled out onto the North Texas soil. Most people didn't really care when the hounds went missing. Only a few dogs every week vanished from backyards and farms all over Grayson County. Their owners would ask people at the stores and at church if anybody had seen them, but soon enough, they all assumed coyotes—a common sight in Sherman—had cornered the dogs out in the woods. No one really thought much about it. Not until Bobby Morgan arrived at the hospital.

Bobby Morgan, aged four, had been found mauled within an inch of his life on his back porch one Tuesday evening. His mother, Mary, had found him and immediately brought him to St. Vincent's Sanitarium. That's where Renault Bishop first met the Morgan family.

The doctors went to work right away to stop the bleeding. Bobby was lucky on that front; another fifteen minutes or so and the boy would probably have bled out. He wasn't so lucky in other ways. As a surgeons' aid, Renault held Bobby's hand as the doctors sewed his torso back together, the sutures crossing his skinny chest like a family quilt, and he stayed by the boy's side as the doctors tried to salvage what remained of his right ear. When the surgeries were over and the boy was in the hands of Fate or God or whoever looked over four-year-old children on the precipice of death, Renault volunteered to go out and talk to his mother.

"Ms. Morgan, I'm Renault Bishop," he said. "Your son is out of surgery, but it will be a little while before you will be able to see him."

Mary moved her red-rimmed eyes from their spot on the wall at the sound of his voice. Greasy smoke trailed from a short cigarette, crushed nearly flat between the grip of her index and middle fingers. Renault returned her gaze and waited for a reply. She didn't speak.

"I'm sorry. This must be very hard for you, Ms. Morgan," he continued. "But Bobby is doing well. He's—"

Mary cut him short. "You're a doctor?"

"No, not exactly. I help out at the hospital."

"Good. Doctors are usually better at this."

"I'm, well, sorry. But I've been with Bobby the whole time. I've seen how tough he is." Renault reached into the pocket of his doctor's jacket and pulled out a match and a cigarette of his own. He offered one to Ms. Morgan.

"Thank you." Mary accepted the lit cigarette. "That, I believe. He's had to fight for every breath he's ever taken. The asthma has made sure of it. And now…"

Her voice cracked as she spoke, and the tears started anew. Renault had been with lots of people as they wept, of course. But he had been knee-deep in trench mud then, and those men had faced their own ends. The consoling words, the gentle reassurances to his comrades as they felt the comfort of death, those had come easy to him. But within this moment, he had no idea what to offer to Mary Morgan. What *could* he possibly say?

He decided not to say anything. Instead, he sat with Mary long after their cigarettes had burned down to ash. He sat in that waiting room until Mary was finally able to see her son.

Renault read over the report the next morning in the *Sherman Democrat* as he tried to wake himself up with his coffee. He didn't even really like coffee, but it had been part of his rations for two years, and the habit was too deeply entrenched in him now to give it up. The report was just a small blurb, nothing Renault didn't already know from the night before at the hospital. It told about Bobby's injuries and the sheriff's ongoing investigation. It urged Sherman residents to stay indoors starting at dusk until the pack of coyotes had been found and dealt with. Any sightings were to be reported immediately to the sheriff's office.

Except Renault knew they weren't coyotes and there wouldn't be any sighting. The thing that had attacked Bobby was supposed to be invisible, after all.

It was a goddamn Wampus Cat.

Renault had known it was a Wampus Cat from the instant he had laid eyes on the claw marks raked across Bobby's chest. The scratches were massive, bigger than any coyote. Maybe even bigger than a wolf. The last time Renault had witnessed such injuries, he'd been a boy not much older than Bobby Morgan.

He remembered his dad carrying Kipp, the family's retired hunting hound, through the back door. Renault had adored the old dog. They had sat together countless nights on the back porch that looked out into the trees while his dad smoked his cob pipe. Even though the dog was too old to have any fight left in him, he still made Renault feel safe at night within their lamplit house in the shadow of the woods. Maybe that's why Renault found it so painful to see Kipp laid out on the table like that, his guts exposed and his tongue hanging halfway out of his mouth. He knew Kipp was gone, had taken that final journey he would watch so many times later in his life, but he gazed out over the scratches that zig-zagged his friend's body all the same. The illusion of safety was gone.

Renault saw many more injuries, some of them more horrible than he could have ever imagined, during the next seventeen years. But he always remembered the five deep, wide slashes that had stretched across Kipp's chest.

Renault's dad gathered a group of his friends the next day. If coyotes were coming onto porches, they reasoned, then one of their young children could just as easily be the pack's next victim. He remembered four men, clad in their flannels and hunting boots and holding their 12-gauge shotguns over their shoulders, disappearing into the woods behind his house as they went on the hunt. Hours passed. Only three men walked back.

The look on his dad's face told him not to ask any questions.

Renault's father didn't talk about what happened. Not for more than a decade. Not until just before his son went off to the War, and even then only late one evening while they were splitting a bottle of the cask-strength whiskey that his dad kept in the cupboard. The lamps had given way to electric lighting a few years before, after his dad's eyesight had begun to weaken. Renault still hadn't become accustomed to just how bright the house was, even long after the sun had fallen behind the North Texas cedars. Renault didn't mind, however. He'd had trouble sleeping ever since he had gotten his draft notice, and the two of them had taken to talking to pass the nights away.

Each of them were a glass and a half deep when Renault asked what had happened that night. His father smiled a fading smile, an expression not long for this world, and drained the rest of his glass.

"Remember when you were little and your mom would tell you about the big cats?" he said, reaching again for the bottle.

"Yeah." Renault chuckled and traced his finger around the glass, feeling the alcohol-inspired numbness in the digit. "The Wampus Cats. The invisible ones with six arms."

His father opened his mouth to speak, but sighed out a long, rattling breath. Then, he merely tilted his head and gave his son a tired, knowing look.

"Bullshit. Those are just stories to keep kids out of the woods," Renault said and reached for the bottle.

Renault's father shifted in his seat and turned his gaze to his glass. "We could hear it in the trees not long after we walked into the woods. It sounded like it was everywhere. But we looked around, and it wasn't anywhere."

Renault leaned forward a bit, almost knocking his glass over. "Dad, you're drunk." But his father kept right on talking.

"I only saw it for a second, when it dropped down on Rick. It was so fast. I understand why people think they're invisible."

"You're trying to tell me that a tree-cat killed Rick?"

Tears formed in his father's eyes. Renault had only once witnessed his father cry, when they had buried his mother. He gave his son a look that Renault had never seen before. An expression that begged to be believed.

"We didn't even bother firing our guns. We ran. God, we just *left* him there." He turned his eyes downward as he finished speaking.

Renault didn't say anything in return. He simply slid the bottle over towards his dad's glass. His father took the offer.

Renault brought a lot of things back with him from the War: medical knowledge, the screams of young men as they held their insides in their hands, a smoking habit. But his father's own habits had taken their toll on him while Renault was deployed in Europe. Renault could stop a man from bleeding out in the mud, but he couldn't do a damned thing about whatever had taken away his father's voice, leaving his breath a pitiful wheeze.

Renault let his father know that he was going after the Wampus Cat. Even without his voice, the old man's pleading expression told his son all he needed to know. He swore he would be careful and reminded his father that he had skills that he and his friends did not have seventeen years ago.

He was only half lying about that last part. As a medic, he had perhaps learned more than he would have liked to about how to stitch up a bayonet wound and tie a tourniquet. But while he liked firearms in general, he had never taken particularly well to gunplay. He had only barely squeaked by in the firearms tests. It hadn't mattered too much; as a medical officer, he rarely carried a sidearm, anyway. He brought that habit over to his civilian life. He didn't own a gun, and his father's old double-barrel had long since fallen apart from age and use. For a weapon, he would need to go to Trevor.

He had known Trevor Michaels growing up; Sherman was a small enough town, after all. Trevor was a veteran, just like him, but the similarities ended there. Trevor had been in the infantry during some of the War's toughest fighting on the Western Front. He had taken to the role with a zeal that, quite frankly, unsettled Renault. Still, he was the only person he knew in town who had seen the kinds of things Renault had seen, and that accounted for something. Trevor had also taken a very different approach to coping with the horrors they had experienced. Renault had taken the job at the hospital. Trevor had gone about building the largest collection of small arms in North Texas. Right now, Renault needed something from Trevor's collection.

"So, what do you need? If you can get it here in the States, I've got it." Trevor gestured towards a wall of the room at the back of his house. Dozens of weapons of all sizes leaned against it.

"I don't need anything exotic. Just the kinds of things they taught us how to use back in basic."

"Shit, that's no fun. I managed to capture way better stuff than that from the Huns. You should give some of their weapons a try."

"No, that won't really be necessary. I just need a pistol and a shotgun, really."

"Well, I've got you covered there. I've got a few Colt 1911s. I've even got a Winchester rigged up like we used them in the trenches. You want a bayonet with that?"

"That, um, won't be necessary," Renault said, while secretly debating whether it was, in fact, a necessity. "We've had coyote problems."

The words sounded natural as they left Renault's lips. He'd gotten plenty of experience telling lies during the war. A lot of people wanted to hear they would be just fine, even when they knew deep in their hearts that they were doomed.

The gravel crunched under the tires of Renault's Triumph Model H as he pulled up to Mary Morgan's house. He had ridden a motorcycle just like it to move from station to station, from patient to patient, on the Front. This time, it carried him towards combat. Mary had been at the hospital pretty much every night since Bobby had been admitted, and tonight was no different. That was good; Renault didn't want to have to explain to her why he was at her tiny house out by the edge of the woods. It would be no good roaming aimlessly around the woods, and Mary's house was his only lead to where the Wampus Cat might be. He kicked the stand down on his motorcycle, then lit up a cigarette. As he took in a deep breath of smoke, he looked down at the shotgun stock sticking out of his saddlebag. As frightened as he was, he couldn't help but laugh. The cigarette. The motorcycle. The firearms. All of them were things he wouldn't have touched before his time in the service. But at that moment, he was glad for all of them—the cigarette most of all. He needed something to calm his nerves.

Renault patted the pistol in the holster on his right hip and grabbed the shotgun from the saddlebag. He was glad Trevor had given him these models. He wasn't a good shot, but they were familiar. Comfortable. The shotgun's barrel had even been sawed off short, just like the ones the trench-sweepers used back on the Western Front. He had rarely used weapons as a medic, it was true, but at least he knew his way around these a little bit.

Renault walked slowly into the woods, his gaze split between the path ahead of him and the treetops. From what his dad had said, the Wampus had literally dropped down on Rick all those years ago. His guns wouldn't do him much good if the beast sank its teeth and claws into his neck before he even saw it.

He wished he could have done this in broad daylight rather than in the fading fingers of dusk. The Wampus Cat was, he assumed, nocturnal like every other cat. But he couldn't risk letting the beast wander onto another family's porch. Not only that, the chances of stumbling upon the Wampus, holed up and asleep in its den during the day, were slim. The fact was, if he was going to find the Wampus Cat, he needed *it* to be looking for *him* while he was searching for it. And it had to be tonight.

The treeline wasn't dense like the glades Renault had seen while on R&R leave in France, but the thin canopy of cedars and oaks still blocked much of the sunlight from reaching the ground. Already, he had to focus harder to see up into the branches. He was glad he had brought his flashlight, a heavy, metal Eveready that weighed down the leather bag hanging from his left hip. Pressing the stock of the shotgun loosely against his shoulder, he trudged on deeper into the woods.

Vaguely, he was aware of how the shotgun's barrel trembled as he looked down its length. He had seen combat plenty of times, it was true, but his objective had always been to save lives, to reduce the carnage of war in some minute way. This was different. For the first time in his life, it was kill-or-be-killed.

A crackling in the trees above made him swing both his gaze and the shotgun upwards. Only squirrels ran across the branches. He sighed to himself. He had not been into the woods since he had come back to his home; it was easy to forget how alive the thickets were. He stopped for a moment to watch the rodents scampering on the limbs. There was a time, not too long ago, when he thought he might not have a chance to admire the simple things ever again. This made him chuckle to himself once more. Here he was, again facing a danger that could easily take those little joys away from him. Just like the last time, he wasn't quite sure why he was doing it. The squirrels scurried away from their spots on the branches. Renault moved deeper into the woods.

By now, the shadows had begun to widen across the woodland floor. The chirping of crickets resounded through the trees. Nightfall had come. Muttering under his breath, Renault lowered his shotgun and reached for the flashlight at his belt.

Above him, the branches shifted and rustled.

Renault felt the weight hit his shoulders before he could even lift his head up. The impact buckled his knees immediately. The shotgun fumbled out of his hands. As the weapon bounced off the dry dirt, he didn't think about the pressure on his back or the claws digging into the nape of his neck or the teeth sinking into the meat of his trapezius; he thought about how lucky he was that the weapon didn't blow his feet off. He had seen it happen once back in the trenches.

Renault rolled over on his side. He had been trained extensively on how to react to a gunshot wound, but he'd never really thought about how he would handle a giant cat digging into his flesh. Gripping the flashlight tight, he threw a flailing blow over his shoulder. The strike was awkward, but the impact of the metal on the cat's skull landed solidly enough. He felt the Wampus's jaws loosen, and its weight disappeared from his back. He scrambled to his feet and spun around, raising the flashlight over his head, ready to strike again before the feline monstrosity could latch onto him once more.

Nothing. The big cat had vanished.

Renault swung his head around as he looked for the Wampus Cat. The cat's initial impact had knocked the wind out of him, and his breath came out as a sharp pant. As he scanned the ground and treetops, he realized he could barely see through the shadows. He flicked the flashlight on and thanked God that it still worked. He reached for the pistol at his hip as he swung the light around him and stared into the night. On the ground six feet away, he saw his shotgun. He strode forward to pick it up.

Sharp pain erupted in his right leg as a set of claws sank into his calf. The flashlight's beam flickered wildly through the forest as Renault staggered forward before spinning around and pointing his pistol toward the ground. The Colt's muzzle flash lit up the darkness as he fired blindly into the night. Renault hoped to hear the telltale yelp of the bullets making contact. A second later, the Wampus's weight again crashed against his chest, and he fell hard on his back. The breath hissed out of his lungs. Both the flashlight and Colt flew from his grasp.

Renault thrashed his fists against the cat's ribs, but the pressure on his shoulders kept the blows from building any force. How could the cat push him down with its forelegs while still maul him with its claws? For the first time, he saw the Wampus's massive canines, and he felt its low-rumbling growl reverberate through his chest. Renault flailed his hands around on the ground, reaching for something to grab. Something to swing. His right hand desperately wrapped around something hard. He gripped it tight and brought it towards his assailant's ribs.

An explosion thundered through his ears. Fire tore through the blackness.

The Wampus Cat let out an anguished yowl and darted off into the night. Free from the assault, Renault resisted the urge to lie in the dirt until he regained his breath. Instead, he sat up, cocked the shotgun, and reached for the flashlight and pistol. After first securing the pistol back in its holster, he scanned his surroundings.

The blood on the ground was faint, almost imperceptible in the darkness. He must have only clipped the Wampus's leg with the shotgun's blast. The trail led off deeper into the woods, further away from Mary Morgan's house. Shining a light over his body, Renault assessed his own injuries.

The left sleeve of his denim jacket and the front of his blue button-down shirt were in tatters; blood flowed liberally from the shallow scratches dragged diagonally along his chest and from the puncture wounds in his shoulder. These contusions would need to be cleaned, probably even require sutures, but, overall, they weren't anything he couldn't patch up himself once he got home. He reached up to his forehead and felt a fresh flow of blood oozing from a scratch along his brow. Again, nothing to be worried about, but he would need to stymie the bleeding if he wanted to keep the blood from getting into his vision. The slashes across his calf were another matter; those would require a hospital if he wanted to keep his leg. That would mean lying to his co-workers at St. Vincent's about what had happened. He would have to worry about that later.

Renault pulled at the fabric of his jacket and ripped off one of the sleeves. With trained precision, he bound the wounds on his calf and forehead. Standing, he winced as he tried to put pressure on his left leg. He looked over again at the path of blood that led into the darkness. If he stumbled back to his motorbike now, he would lose the Wampus's trail. Then he might never pick it up again, might never recover the fortitude to venture into the woods after it. He will have let the enemy escape. If he was going to stop it, it had to be tonight.

Still, the fact remained that the Wampus Cat had injured him far more than he had hurt it.

Renault limped forward, following the bloody spatter his adversary had left. He abandoned the shotgun behind at the site of their previous battle; there was no way for him to use it and hold the flashlight at the same time, anyway. Instead, his sweaty palms squeezed his Colt's grip as he moved the flashlight's beam in front of him in wide arcs. The trail remained faint but steady. He hoped the cat's wounded leg would keep it from taking to the trees again; his neck hurt from when the gigantic cat had landed on it, and this injury made it difficult to look upwards. No, the Wampus would have retreated to its den. Back to where it thought it could hide.

The woods grew denser and the trees older as he followed the scarlet path; he was far deeper into the forest than he had ever been, even when he was a boy exploring them in the daylight. Only small traces of moonlight penetrated the canopy, leaving his flashlight as the only illumination in front of him. Finally, the splatter led him to the foot of a large, dark oak. Its twisting branches reached high into the air, and its gnarled, ancient roots split the ground, creating a deep cavity in the earth. The perfect den for a giant cat.

His gun at the ready, Renault squatted to shine the flashlight into the opening. The inside of the crevasse was larger than he anticipated, and there was no immediate sign of the den's occupant. The light only managed to slice through sections of the darkness at a time, illuminating a floor littered with crushed vegetation and half-buried animal feces. In one corner, a partially decomposed dog carcass rotted into the soil.

The sharp snapping of twigs caused Renault to swing his light and point his pistol to his right.

For the first time, he got a good look at his quarry.

The Wampus Cat was colossal: bigger than any mountain lion or panther he had ever seen. Even illuminated by his flashlight, its midnight blue fur seemed to sink into the surrounding darkness. Similarly, its dark green eyes did not seem to reflect the beam of Renault's flashlight the way they should. Four powerful legs were curled, ready to spring, and a third set of limbs were positioned at the top of the ribs, above what would have been the forelegs of a panther or a lion. Two-inch long claws glistened at the end of all six limbs.

Renault cursed himself for being caught in such a vulnerable position. From his crouched posture, he couldn't properly ready his pistol. Instead, he awkwardly pointed the weapon in the cat's general direction. The Wampus Cat sprung forward just as Renault squeezed the trigger and fired a volley of three shots. The muzzle flash, exceptionally bright in the darkness, blocked his target from view. Through the ringing in his ears, he heard a yowl.

A moment later, the cat's tremendous heft crashed into him. Renault lifted his arm to protect his face, and the Wampus's immense jaws closed in around his forearm, causing him to drop his gun. The monstrosity growled as it jerked his arm around, rending denim and flesh between its teeth. Renault sucked in his breath. He would die, like so many of his war buddies, bleeding out in the dirt.

Then, slowly, the thrashing stopped. The jaws' grip began to loosen, and the growl faded. The tense muscles pushing him down relaxed, then went limp. Renault let out his breath and saw a pair of crimson roses blooming on the cat's chest, stark against its shadowy fur. With great effort, he pried his arm from the beast's mouth and pushed its bulk off his body. He lay there for a moment, catching his breath, before he pulled himself to his feet. He knew his arm would need attention, and soon, just like his calf.

Without the threat of combat, the Wampus Cat was strangely beautiful. Majestic, even. Its fur coat, stretched over powerful muscles, shone under the dimming flashlight. Its green eyes remained open, staring curiously off into the night.

For a long while, Renault simply stared down at his opponent's body. The first life he had ever ended. He knelt beside the Wampus and closed its eyes, just like he'd done with so many others who had fallen in battle.

The Beast of Always

C. CHARLES KNIGHT

FROM THE JOURNAL OF EDWARD BON TRAEGER

August 23, 1915. Time has lost all meaning.

Mors invocat, vorat abyssus—death calls, the abyss devours. Words given as a warning. I have been searching for so long that I am not sure whether the jigsaw answers I've gleaned have much served as answers of great significance. Too many pieces to deny the picture, yet too few to complete it. My notes have been jumbled: some lost to age, others to cataclysm or war. I have started this journal in hopes of synthesising what my journeys have wrought, inasmuch as there is anything beyond conjecture. Indeed, what is known only calls upon further uncertainty. What can be said of those things that exist on the periphery, just beyond the paper-thin skin between worlds, and which peek at us from dark corners of our minds? And in learning, risking the savagery of insult upon the imagination and left to run rampant with maddening suppositions of catastrophe and insignificance. While I have endeavoured to gird myself against such fanciful guesswork, with some modicum of success, there stand some facts beyond opinion or speculation. None a comfort. I suppose, for the purposes of prosperity and my own memory, it is best to start at the beginning.

For myself, at least, it began long ago in the north of England, in a small province of little import. While modest in station, my trade had provided sufficiently for a small home and the love of a family. It was a simple life. So much simpler then. Blissfully ignorant of what lay beyond the vale, I longed for nothing but a paying commission and to end the day with a warm meal and the laughter of my children. And it was so. For many years, all was as it should have been—warmth of a hearth after a long day, gritty with soil under the clean paleness of the sky, and not a care beyond what the following morning would bring. Hope of gentle sun for my toil and sweet rain for my crop. I look back on those times with fading recollection, holding onto what fragments remain as time ravages their delicate edges.

But what can never be forgotten, what is branded into the very flesh of my brain, is the day my life was torn asunder.

Indeed, it was a day, but the time was late. No signs had come but for the bloodening moon rising within a scarlet heaven as a chilling darkness fell over the land as though twilight. It came that eve. *It*—the thing that should not be. My children still yet played in the pasture as they did on any other soft setting sun as supper prepared.

It was the silence that drew my attention, an unsettling quiet leaving only the rushing sounds of my own increasing heartbeat. Perhaps some instinct, a primal mammalian scent or calculation of predation, but nevertheless an unignorable pull that led me to the tree line beyond the pasture. It was there I caught a glimpse, but only from the corner of my eye and just as quickly vanishing with direct gaze. It was a fleeting observation, too ugly and horrible to accept, of an unspeakable being shrouded in shadow as though from within some dark hole beyond this world and seeping through the physical plane. While its shape, amorphous to be sure, was not describable by whatever faculties remained available in my utter terror, those glowing red orbs, fixed upon my person and penetrating some unnamed dread I kept hidden, were fearsome and ancient.

So captivated by fear, I had not at first accounted for the children— *my* children—gripped by massive hands. Keeping my eyes on some distant focus to permit the use of the wider field in which the thing took form, I could behold its grasp. Dark, vaporous, and long, those fingers articulated by far too many joints and raised to grotesque points wrapped easily around the blood of my blood. It was then that my protective drive overrode my frozen trauma, and I moved without consideration for mortality. Being of little formidability, both in life and by stark contrast to the aggressor, I nevertheless sprung forward with a guttural sound. If my memory is not mistaken and fear has not tainted its impression, the being appeared almost pleased by my folly.

In quickly shifting both children to one monstrous hand and freeing the other, I narrowly escaped its grasp. But the wound slashed deeply across my shoulder and began to fester almost immediately. The pain was all-consuming, and the delirium set in so instantaneously I all but lost conscious thought. Despite my weakened condition and position, face buried in peat and bracken, I could feel the chilly warmth of the creature setting upon me.

In that moment, I knew I had lost not only my children but also my life.

Yet, a strange peace accompanied it, one I now regret dismissing in favour of an ever-beating heart. Something akin to breath—if the beast indeed breathed at all—caressed the left side of my neck, and I knew it would soon rip into the tender flesh and release me.

It was a sheer sound, light and distant as a cattail whispering on a breeze, but it was there. The sound of my wife screaming from a piece away. Why this had any effect on the creature, I could not say, but it retreated from its hovering menace at my back. The existential weight lifted from me as I slipped into darkness.

When I awoke, nine days had passed. I had but a feverish lucidity beneath the ice running through my veins. Though distraught, my wife tended to her moribund husband with catatonic adequacy. She told me the doctor had come and treated the wound, but the infection was beyond his understanding, and he'd offered a bottle of laudanum to keep me at rest.

The ugly gash had begun to seal over, but the infection remained; the scar, both physical and emotional, would never fade. It rendered me frail, my voice weak. I might have recovered more quickly but for the enormous hole in my heart, for my wife confirmed that the children were gone.

There was a search, but no one had hopes of finding them. The other disappearances at that time were proliferating and leaving family names, like my own, to fade into antiquity. None had seen the creature, and my account was dismissed as the sorrow-addled delusion of a broken man.

But I knew. I *knew* what I'd seen. The monster was real.

For a time, my dreams were fitful stampedes of nightmarish visions, some replicative of my tragic day like a personal hell, others amalgamations of the tales of terror and woe entwined with images both real and imagined. I was lost.

We went through the motions in the days and weeks thereafter, moving like animated husks. Every day's light seemed forever obscured by a rust that had taken all things. Once clean air now carried a sour scent, and the colours of life dulled and oxidised while food tasted of dust and my water of ash. My work had suffered. Our home, like our lives, fell into blight. I suppose I never judged my wife harshly for her choice. Had I been able to do the same, I should have liked to follow her into the void. To reunite our family together once more in whatever plane stands beyond this thready world. I had certainly tried as the occasion arose, but there seemed to be no reprieve for me.

I buried my wife's body near the elder tree, the one under which we'd made our vows not ten short years before. Alone and with no option for my own demise, at least in the many earthly ways in which I valiantly attempted, I took the only course I saw fit.

I began searching for the beast.

At first, I knew not where to begin, only of the need to pick up the trail and at a loss for what clue may be left by a vapour's tread. Dedicating my life, such as it was, to pursuit soon became a fascination and then, ultimately, an obsession. My search led to vast travel, unskilled labour paying my way by land and sea as the trail required.

It was a desolate time, those first years. The industrial revolution was proliferating, and child labour in mines and cotton factories masked disappearances, making it near impossible to distinguish proverbial monster from monster. The trail went cold, sometimes for months or years, leaving me listless as a ship on a windless sea. I chased rumours to disappointing ends but bided time in meaningless jobs and halfhearted relations until the next shred of chance came along.

But then: a reprieve from my fading hope, however tenuous. I'd happened upon a small city whose sources of sanitation and water were reminiscent of Roman aquifers spilling into aqueducts and cisterns. A small maze of tunnels below the surface channelled rain and waste. Within the dark underbelly, where no human could dwell, I found a sign of the unnatural. While I cannot be certain it was of the creature, there was no doubt what I found was made not of man.

I would describe what I saw as large remains of chrysalis sacks akin to the wings of vast cicadas coated in a gelatinous ruin, burst between the folds as though birthing some man-sized horror. I cannot say what shambling terror may have come forth from those awful wombs, nor whether they related to the beast of my obsession, but it was the first tangible sign of something *other* present in our world. I sought such signs in other places but failed to find them. Despite their apparent absence, my intuition refused to concede that they were unrelated. Alas, my journey was as twisted as the grisly images plaguing my dreams.

The Southern European revolutions left devastation and disease in their wake, and I became unavoidably entrenched in the Russo-Persian War years later. The years stretched on and other distractions from my quest left me in bleak circumstances, bereft of hope: The Egyptian-Ottoman War, the Carlist Wars in Spain, the Opium Wars, the Great Famine of Ireland, exploits of the East India Company, and so on. I served, as occasion arose, if for nothing more than to find some human horror to overwhelm and deaden my senses against intrusive recollection of my obsessive quest. While I had lost hope for it long before, a part of me still hoped for death. A release from my plight which would never come.

Outside of the services I could render, I was oft avoided entirely, overlooked as nothing more than an apparition to be dismissed, unteased with the burden of recognition. Inscrutable faces passing with downcast gazes or the occasional flicker in my direction. Upon the occasion I would be observed, eyes held unfriendly, mournful, or sceptical castes—in some instances, all three. Some were reluctant to speak for fear of some superstitious calling of the evil back, while others were loath to palaver with the likes of strange wanderers. Nevertheless, some had occasion to speak for some recompense or to offer a friendly, nonjudgmental ear.

In all my travels, I'd met a myriad of others with similar accounts and had seen evidence the creature had set upon the regions, but with nothing aside from anecdote or folklore to go on. Amidst the unlikely and clearly nonsensical, a striking coincidence arose, a common thread that offered a sign the beast had come.

More than the unexplained disappearances of children, there had been accounts of lurking shadows and ghoulish manifestations. Bodies presumed to be of local men found horribly disfigured. Some were nothing more than natural malformations or derangements at the hands of man—the savagery of a twisted (but nevertheless human) hand. Others, no more than the ravings of madmen. Of the latter accounts, claims were made of having seen the creature itself, but unquestionably apparent the poor souls were afflicted with troubled neuroses—clear to my mind's eye they had not seen the actual being that took my world and left me to wander endlessly.

It was in the few who made remarks as to the creature being dismissed as a phantom, a trick of the rusty moonlight, and only out of the extremity of laterality of vision who I could take as kindred. Indeed, there were even a few who appeared to be similarly afflicted as myself, those who claimed to have seen and been struck down by the creature, avoiding their demise by some happenstance distracting the creature from its wont.

Those likewise could not end their suffering by moral means, left to wander the earth, both of it and yet apart from it. Most were aimless and harmless but for the existential injury inflicted upon self, but, as with all of life, there were exceptions of madness—such as the Whitechapel Ripper, who took to using his dark gift for remarkable evil. While I would not condone such acts, I cannot fully judge them. My own exploits in fields and trenches, although gilded in the fantasy of a greater good, were not without their brutality. I suppose if my obsession had not been thus directed, I too might have become something else.

Wherever I tread, bleakness followed. Crimson dawns, grey desolate days, pale blue twilights, and the blackest of nights. My own oubliette of torment wrapped below the surface of my skin as I set about my unending road.

All in all, stories began to add up, but the most compelling, if not terrifying, were those obtained from myriad lore. Indeed, it would seem our beast was not new upon the earth but had been here for as long as humans could tell tales. Perhaps always. While many lacked descriptions of the beast itself, the apparent calling card of the monster was well documented—the disfigured remains of transformed people had been described across history, each sharing similarity in appearance for any given region. I found written accounts, mystic stories, and ancient cave drawings of such beasts. The *Babi*, *Khepri*, and *Anubis* of Egypt. Creatures of unexplained mutation, presumed to have once been a man left dead in twisted fashion as though transformed by some horrid curse. Indeed, there were some found in shallow graves, long dead and decayed, excavated to the horror of the discoverer. In most cases, it was these findings rather than fresh specimens that prompted much or most of the region's lore, although that was not always the case.

Their characteristics varying as they did by location, some appearing as an awful mixture of man and wolf, as those found in areas of Rome, while others appeared to be more bear or other animal found in untamed lands in Navajo country, giving rise to legends of monsters with names like *lycanthrope* or *werewolf* or *Skinwalker*.

Indeed, a tale published a number of years later by a man named Stoker described another kind altogether. Although predating it by centuries, it was the first fully written account, by way of a presumably fictional source, that the remains of twisted souls in the broad Romanian region were given a widely accessible name—*vampire*. Such became the fodder for fanciful stories of nonsense, such as transfiguration by the moon or spell or curse and vulnerability to precious metals, religious symbols, or injury to vital organs. And just as lightning was once attributed to omnipotent purpose, these stories were created to provide some vague comfort against the harsh realities of the true terror—that there is no hope against the beast.

Few accepted the truth amidst the fiction, while others, in various cultures, held firm to their superstitious lore. But in all cases, the truth was worse. It was thin, but these bodies (such as they were) were discovered only during times in which children were missing at astonishing rates. No identification could be made of the corpses, but my suspicion was they shared a tale similar to my own—the occasional parent happening upon the beast in the midst of *the taking* but, unlike myself who suffered but a scratch and by chance avoided worse, were seized upon and their left carotid savagely bitten. To be sure, each case I saw firsthand or, in speaking with medical authorities, was otherwise certain, the bodies shared that singular similarity. Thus, the bite mutilated the body with vicious and varied transformation while the scratch, in its very few instances, left one with a troublesome long life of agony and fraying sanity. Survival from the full infection, such as it could be determined using a child's disappearance as onset, was short. Hours to days after the rending, in most cases.

The thing travelled unfettered as though by some unholy means from one continent to another, appearing at times of both peace and ruin with no apparent meaning. To my unending frustration, there was otherwise no pattern to be found. Oh, how many years of weary travel have my heels trod with little but a story to offer in show. The trail was far from cold, but the creature was always strides ahead, unlikely aware of, or even with awareness giving any consideration to my pursuit. To it, something beyond this world and beyond comprehension, we are nothing more than a nuisance and a source of feast.

I will not stop. I cannot stop. My obsession far beyond the reason of what the end, should I reach the object of my warped desire, would bring. Time has lost all meaning; the curse upon my soul inflicted as a reminder of my failure. There is nothing else. Nothing but the pursuit. Perhaps my hope is not to identify the creature—the thing that should not be—but to find it so I may fall at its feet and beg for an end. To be taken to the beyond where I might see my family again or to be lost in the void of the ancients, to have my consciousness ripped to utter insanity.

Such oblivion would be a gift.

But if there is some greater wisdom in the universe, it has either forsaken us or never cared to begin with. My fate will not likely end in such freedom. No blissful darkness. No. I know not what wretched, demonic form I might take should I become as twisted as those bitten. The death that would take me as the infection viciously turned me—consuming me in some hideous chrysalis while breaking my corpus and wrenching my form into something *other*—would leave me insane and wild before that horrible body succumbed to its own inability to go on.

What would be waiting there?

In my deadly dreams, it is only the mouth of madness. Whatever humanity remaining torn from this realm and pulled into the place whence it—the beast of always—calls origin. A tear in the fabric of the universe where things dwell. Things far worse than the darkness travelling our inconsequential celestial rock. Perhaps that would be better. Perhaps it is what I deserve.

Or, perhaps, the concept of deserving in and of itself is meaningless.

Still, I shall continue on. Searching for whatever meaning there is for myself alone. Seeking, if not to stop this thing, to end the torment of my days. If anything but screams remain, the last words of human thought on my lips may be of the ancient warning…

Mors invocat, vorat abyssus

Death calls, the abyss devours.

RIP Dag Gadol Diner

LAURA BARKER

Dag Gadol Pop-up Dining Experience
Ratings and reviews

RATINGS

Food ★★★★★
Service ★★★★★
Value ★★★
Atmosphere ★★★★★

REVIEWS

★★★★★

Memorable, decent baby-changing facilities, surprisingly child-friendly

My wife and I have a 6 month old, so we don't eat out much. A friend got us a Wowcher for here. It was disconcerting stepping onto its tongue to get to the dining area. It's definitely more 'experience dining' than 'fine dining'—no flowers on the table because the creature moves a lot, but once they glued our sushi plates to our table mats, we were away. Wife couldn't have the whale sushi—she's breastfeeding and mercury content is too high—so she had the avocado and tempeh while I tucked in. Several reviewers have said it's indecent to eat whale inside the body of a whale but the dag gadol (sp?) is actually some kind of cetus-type creature. I changed our son in this little room between the dag gadol's tonsils and the changing table was pretty secure, and TMI but they have the creature's spit come out of the taps and it's actually pretty good for clean-up.

Great place for a date, LGBTQIA friendly, GF options

Went here for a second date. The relationship didn't work out but we're friends now (and actually work together lol) and we had a blast here. We rang in advance because my date can't have gluten and they made her the whacon corned whale meat burger on a gluten-free vegan bun. A nice touch was they spelled out DAG GADOL on the bun in sesame seeds. I had the whacon hash with green beans and sourdough, which was delicious. We were both creeped out by the idea of climbing in through its mouth lol so the wait staff had us slide through the blowhole on these mats with whale lube on them. That was probably the highlight of the night.

Good for Christians, don't have the stew

Me and my wife are both pretty religious. We both work for the church, although we know it has its problems, so the idea of dining in the same whale, and yes I know it's not actually a whale, that swallowed Jonah was pretty exciting, even if it's just a hoax like people say. My wife had the tataki and I had the whale stew, which wasn't great. Weirdly soft and tasteless. But as I say, we didn't really come for the food, it was more for the experience of sitting in that belly like Jonah did all those years ago. Would be a wonderful place for a Christening dinner or first communion, etc. Don't have the stew.

Non-judgemental poly-affirming cocktail hour

Came here with my polycule (N-configuration) to celebrate one year of us all being together. We're on a budget (saving up to buy a house) so we decided to just go out for one cocktail, because it was happy hour and they do a two-for-one, and then go home for dinner. We explained to the diner that it was our anniversary. Places can be extremely judgemental about unconventional relationships so it was especially nice that they gave us four free shots. The cocktails are made out of cetyl alcohol (made from the whale) so they're all pretty strong.

I had the Fish House Punch, which is cetyl alcohol, the juice and zest of half a fresh Sicilian lemon, and a splash of black plankton over a big block of ice. Honestly, one of the best cocktails I've had for some time. I ordered for my partner Cordelia (I'm a full time dom to her and my other partner Marina) and got her the Blue Lagoon, which is lemonade (made with Sicilian lemons), blue chamomile water, and Laraha liqueur. She complained it wasn't really sea themed, and when I pointed out the cetyl alcohol is heated spermaceti, she was sceptical (her mother was deep into a pyramid scheme the whole time she was growing up so she tends to be suspicious about everything—she's working on it as she knows it bothers me).

My metamour Morgan (who is also a dom to Cordelia and Marina) ordered himself a Pearl Julep (cetyl alcohol with a drizzle of seawater). He said it was fantastic, but when he went to the toilet, I had a sip of it and didn't think much of it. He got Marina the Krill Cocktail which was just a regular prawn cocktail as far as I could tell (cooked prawns in ketchup, mayonnaise, Worcestershire sauce, lemon juice and black pepper), although they said they rescue the prawns out of the body of the belly of the dag gadol and then cook and feed them to customers. I don't know how much of that is true. Marina was a bit disappointed because prawn cocktails don't actually have any alcohol in them. Morgan said he didn't know that when he was ordering because it was a krill cocktail and not a prawn cocktail but I would have thought it was obvious. But as prawn cocktails go, this one was excellent—you could tell they put real thought into the Marie Rose sauce.

Our free shots were cetyl alcohol served with a salted rim and slices of lime like tequila. They kind of tasted like drinking neat vodka.

Lovely place, the staff treated us like royalty. Special place for a special night.

Nice place, light is super flattering

This is going to sound vain, but I like a place with good but low lighting so you look your best. My husband and I have been married for ten years, but I like to keep the spark alive by really dressing up for date night, and I wore this skin-tight fishtail sequin dress. I actually lied and told the staff it was our anniversary, so they made the giant fish eat all of this bioluminescent plankton so its intestines lit up like fairy lights. My husband said he couldn't keep his eyes off me all night!! To be fair, there's nothing else to look at, it's just like this big pink cave. We both had the Whale Bale (whale fillet served on hay) and then the ambergris soufflé and the crème brûlée with pickled fluke. It was pretty nice.

Great place but you might need an antiemetic

I went with my colleague because our company paid for us to dine out when we were away on business. I was fine the whole night, but he has a very sensitive stomach and halfway through he had to climb out and pop to the pharmacy to get some antiemetics for motion sickness. The whale moves around A LOT. That's what makes it an authentic experience, so we weren't mad, but just wanted to warn others so you're prepared. I had the fish in blankets, which is whale bacon wrapped around whale meat stuffed into a whale intestine, and my colleague had the whale bacon butty with seaweed flatbread. The portions weren't huge but we were full after. The nicest thing was the music. I tried to Shazam it, but the waitstaff told me it's actually just the sound of the whale's digestion and breathing.

★★★★★

A culinary feast

My best friend is a real foodie, so we were excited to try out this new restaurant. She absolutely loved it, and she had the whale sushi, the tataki, the stew, the cassoulet with whale bacon, and all the weird desserts the reviewers keep raving about. She didn't love the ambergris ice cream and honestly I was too squeamish to try it. I still think of it as vomit, or worse, but we both loved the Gâteau whale blubber St. Honoré and the amberin jelly shots. She had a coffee with whale milk, which she said was absolutely disgusting! Like drinking gone-off butter. But she said, "I'm glad I tried it." So even when it's bad, it's good! The staff were great, always happy to bring us out more dishes.

Stuffy place, ridiculous dress code, if I could give zero stars I would

I went with my wife who thought it would be fun to 'whale-tail', ie. wear her thong underwear above her low-rise trousers. Now, there is a dress code on the website but all it says is smart casual and we were both dressed extremely smartly—her trousers were silk. We had both had long, tough weeks at work, so when they said my wife's attire wasn't up to standard, we naturally protested. We were then met by the manager—nasty bloke called Dev—who said visible underwear is not acceptable at any restaurant (clearly not true: people quite regularly have quite a lot showing at our local chicken shop) and told us to leave immediately!! We will definitely not be coming back. We thought it was a fun novelty place, but obviously that one Michelin star has gone to their heads and they think they're some kind of fine dining now.

Nice but felt conflicted

I used to be an animal rights activist before I got severe burnout and ended up having to eat meat because I got an inflammatory disease and my personal healer told me I had to start getting some of my proteins from animal sources. So eating in the body of a giant fish who's essentially trapped in a huge bathtub wasn't the obvious choice for me, but I went there with a friend who's gone Paleo and can't really dine out at many places. I have to say the food is phenomenal. I had the whale stew, and the meat just falls off the bone or whatever whales have. She had an enormous whale steak with boiled sweet potato, wilted seaweed greens, and plankton sauce. We both thought it was cool that the table candles are made from spermaceti and the server explained that the honeycomb on the dessert menu is actually made from spermaceti and not from beeswax. So of course I ordered it. She couldn't have any because it contains refined sugars. It smelled earthy and sweet at the same time, which is apparently from the ambergris.

Pretty good, but don't go with your boss

I'm a waitress and every now and again the boss of our restaurant takes us to another restaurant. He says he's treating us, but you have to be there so it's not a real treat, and it's also just to check out the competition, it's not like you can sit back and relax and enjoy your meal or anything, especially with him talking about how well he treats us all the time, and how other restaurateurs don't take their staff out to places like this, blah, blah, blah. Anyway, he was whispering under his breath about how the whole thing is a gimmick and a hoax. I happen to believe him that it's a hoax: I think it's all AI, but I don't care, just let me enjoy my hoax already. He gives us a strict budget, so really the only thing we could have was the battered tail or the whale fin soup. I had the soup. It was all really delicious, and generous portions for a fine dining restaurant. The interior is amazing, everything is made of this moist pink velvet. It feels like you're in the uterus or something.

Enjoy it while it lasts

I had a great time, but seriously, at some point this creature is going to chow down on that giant baby gate thing that's keeping its jaws from closing and it's going to be curtains for whoever's dining in there at the time. So go before someone dies and they have to shut the whole thing down. I had the King Charles II Special (eggs and ambergris) followed by the winter-strained sperm oil sack soup that was more like a consommé, but rich tasting as well. I had the lobster gobstopper for afters, that bastard tastes good, but it really does stop up your mouth for like an hour. Five stars.

So sad it's been shut down!

This was one of my favourite restaurants. I know they had to close it after the creature ate that lady but this country is getting so obsessed with health and safety, it's spoiling everyone else's fun and I am sick of hearing about what happened to that couple on their engagement dinner. I used to go in here after work for an ambergris hot chocolate because you can't get them anywhere else and I just used to sit and read my book by the light of the sea stars and the luminescent bacteria. It was the most relaxing part of my day. They even got nominated for The Great Good Place award! RIP Dag Gadol Diner.

BATWYNN

The Branches Look Like Antlers

CHRISSY GRAY

THE FIRST TIME Baron put antlers on a beaver, Tandy had to admit it was funny, but it got old real fast. It didn't have the same charm as a jackalope, which he'd probably tried to emulate.

When Baron was eleven, his older brother had convinced him the jackalope was a real animal after seeing a picture of one on a spinning postcard rack during a family trip to Mount Rushmore. After summer vacation, Baron marched into school and proclaimed that the jackalope was now his favorite animal, ousting the grizzly bear. Once he reached that point in middle school where boys turned into monsters, he was relentlessly teased out of that childhood belief.

Teenage cruelty aside, a *beavalope* wouldn't sell magnets at tourist traps.

Every time Tandy Task walked through the door, her feet about to fall off despite the orthopedic shoes her daughter had sent her through Amazon, that *thing* stared at her from its perch on the mantel. She still had a sense of humor, despite Baron's insistence that she took everything too seriously.

The truth was Baron just wasn't very good at taxidermy, no matter how many hours he spent in the basement. The body was lumpy, the tail was missing a chunk, and the antlers Baron had scavenged were far too large. The beavalope's dumb glass eyes veered in different directions and always managed to track her until she rounded the corner into the kitchen.

She sloughed her purse from her shoulder and dropped it on the dining table, where it heaved a sigh and spat out a tube of Carmex that rolled under the fridge. Her eggplant fleece coat came off next, draped over the same chair each night until it was time to pull it on before work the next morning.

The table was too big for the kitchen. Everything in the house was too big for what little space they had, hence why the beaver with antlers pissed her off so much. Just another thing that took up space. She didn't even know where Baron had gotten the beaver. Antlers were a dime a dozen, but a beaver was harder to come by. Very few wandered out on the highway heading north from Sioux Falls to end up flattened on the shoulder, just waiting for her husband to drive by with his shovel to toss into the back of his pickup.

Their little house had the standard trophies: A deer head mounted on the wall. A few ducks mid-flight, their glossy green feathers collecting dust and cobwebs. And the single scraggly squirrel with a tiny green visor about to deal a hand, but he was missing the rest of his poker buddies, so he dealt to the lamp on the table next to the couch.

The basement stairs creaked, and Baron appeared, his large frame taking up most of the doorway. A few repurposed paintbrushes stuck out of the chest pocket of his coveralls. Tandy had to duck into the fridge to hide her annoyance at the sight of him. After years of arguing with customers at Pricewell about the price of chuck, her face had kind of naturally just set that way, so it was hard to hide.

It had always been that way. She didn't know what about the kitchen made it conducive to violence, but every time she and Baron were in that room at the same time, she had the urge to jam a steak knife into his hand.

He reached around her and pulled a Coors out of the door. "What's for supper?"

Tandy set her jaw, staring at the smudged expiration date on a tub of sour cream. "Don't know. What are you making?"

Baron tipped his beer back, laughing like it was the funniest joke in the world. Imagine! Actually cooking dinner instead of playing coroner to roadkill! Ha!

The first step to the basement screamed as he descended back down. "I'm working on something. Let me know when it's ready."

Tandy curled her hands into fists. Her stubby nails dug into her palm. She always kept her nails short. Sharp nails meant punctures in the food-safe gloves she wore at the meat counter, which also meant feeling blood mixing with plastic and sweat on her palms. Even thinking of the sensation brought the smell of fresh viscera to her nose. She gagged and dove toward the sink, turning the water on as hot as it would go and scrubbing her hands until they were pink.

The yellow overhead light reflected like a moon on the window above the sink. Tandy focused her eyes past it into the darkened yard. There were still some patches of stark white snow that stuck around in the places where the shade remained.

Outside, Chester started going nuts, breaking the stillness of the evening. The deep sound of his bark cut through the walls of the house and echoed into the kitchen.

"What in the—" Tandy brushed her wet hands on her jeans and pushed through the back door.

Chester was at the end of the tie out, straining against his collar. His feathered tail was tucked between his legs as his head swiveled like a creature possessed, his teeth flashing white.

Tandy stared at him slack-jawed for a moment, wondering if some other yellow dog was tied up in her yard. Chester wasn't a barker. She couldn't even remember the last time she'd heard him bark. A few years ago, a coyote had wandered into the yard, hoping to lure the dumb mutt back to his pack, but Chester never thought to sound the alarm at the intruder on his turf; he'd just wanted to play.

"Chester!" Tandy yelled. It was futile. She barely heard her own voice over his frenzied barking.

She squinted into the darkened treeline on the west side of the property and saw nothing. It wasn't like she had the same primal instinct the dog had to make out whatever invisible threat he'd settled on.

Chester's bark had taken on an alarm-like quality. Staccato and monotonous. Tandy stumbled down the back deck stairs, grasping onto the rubber-coated chain and using it as a guide to Chester. The grass was spongy from the snowmelt. She wrapped her hand around his collar and pulled back, but trying to stop a 100-pound dog when he had his sights on something was as useless as politely asking him to stop barking. Chester wriggled backward, hunching down at the right angle to slip his head out of the collar in a move so perfectly practiced that she should have seen it coming. The moment he felt the air on his neck, he bolted into the trees, leaving Tandy holding an empty collar.

Tandy scrambled after him. God, it was stupid. She knew it was stupid even as she was doing it, but she had a soft spot for that dog, no matter how much she pretended he was nothing but a hassle. She'd taken him as a puppy after the neighbor's dog had a litter under the porch. Chester was the last one left after all his siblings were spoken for. So, she complained about the rising cost of dog food whenever she was at Tractor Supply and clipped his nails when they got too long, even though he whined like a big baby every single time.

Someone had to do it. Baron sure as hell wouldn't. He preferred dead animals.

"Chester!" Tandy followed the rustling through the bushes, letting her arms and face get bit by branches for that damn dog.

The barking halted, fizzling out with a pitiful yelp that set Tandy's heart racing. She clawed her way through the brush and was spit out on the other side of the windbreak. The moon was a bright spotlight on Chester laid out on the barren field. Blood welled from his chest and drained into the rivulets where the corn had been.

She couldn't bring herself to cry, but a deep stab of grief settled in her chest. She placed a hand over her heart and clutched at her skin. One step, two steps. She knelt by his side, running a hand over his puppy-soft fur.

She lifted her head, scanning the field that stretched out like an open palm. The lights of Killdeer dotted across the horizon. Her ears picked up nothing out of place, just the whoosh of wind through the branches and the skittering of corn husks across the dirt.

Grit from the field worked its way under Tandy's fingernails as she fitted her arms beneath Chester's limp body. He was a Lab mixed with Lord-knows-what; he was *heavy*, but she wasn't going to leave him out here all alone, and she refused to ask Baron to help.

By the time she made it through the trees, she was sweating and covered in sticky blood. The wounds on Chester's abdomen were oddly spaced and of varying sizes. Tandy always hated the sentiment of, *well, at least he didn't suffer,* because if she got her wish, he wouldn't be dead at all. He was only nine and had a few years of chasing squirrels left in him. Forever a big baby.

Tandy gritted her teeth and set him down just outside of the beam of the light next to the back door. She didn't want to look at him. The shovel she used to pick up his poop leaned against the siding of the house. She wasted no time and started digging.

Time didn't pass while she shoveled. She shut her brain off and let her hands work. The back door squealed, and the screen smacked against the siding.

"Supper?" Baron called into the darkness in lieu of her name. Upon receiving no response except the sound of sifting dirt, he leaned over the railing. "What are you doing?"

"Dog died."

"Huh?"

"Chester," she said, sending a spray of clumped dirt over her shoulder. "Got killed."

A pause. "By what?"

"Don't know."

"Well," he said, drawing the word out like a piece of chewing gum. "I could—"

Tandy speared the shovel into the ground. Her calloused fingers gripped the handle. "You are *not* going to stuff him like one of your trophies." Her chest heaved and her back arched like a pissed-off cat. "You didn't even kill that deer on the wall. You found it in a ditch. And your cousins shot those ducks."

Wind hummed through the gutters. Baron's nose whistled when he breathed; it always irked her, but right now, it threatened to send her over the edge.

"What about supper?"

Tandy stuck her foot on the shovel and pushed it back into the giving earth. "Figure it out."

Baron's eyes dug into the side of her neck. She ignored him and kept shoveling. Finally, the door shut, and she was alone.

She could barely see two feet in front of her, but she sensed when the hole was deep enough to stop the coyotes from digging him up. That thought became the first thing all night to make Tandy's eyes prick with tears. Chester had just wanted to play with them.

The grave was covered and patted with the shovel for good measure. Baron had made a mess of the kitchen in the process of putting together a sandwich and Tandy left it alone. She peeled off her clothes and stood under the weak stream of the shower until it went cold.

That night, while Baron's nose whistled next to her in bed, she dreamt of the poker-playing squirrel crawling across the ceiling.

Four days later, the trail cam Tandy had ordered was on the stone porch, even though she'd shelled out extra for two-day shipping. She ripped open the box to reveal a second, smaller box. She called her daughter because she couldn't figure out how to turn it on.

"You need the app," Daisy said. Keys jangled on her end of the line, punctuated by squeaky grocery cart wheels. They sounded the same on the West Coast.

"App?" This was way over Tandy's head.

"Yeah, just scan the QR code," she said, then greeted someone she passed with a polite Midwestern hello. Even in San Francisco, she didn't forget her manners. "Why are you setting up a trail cam, anyway?"

"Coyotes," Tandy said, the lie coming out a little too naturally. She'd tell Daisy about the dog later. Not now. Not when Tandy didn't even know what had killed him. Daisy took after her mom; she wouldn't break down into hysterics over the phone, especially not in public, but it would settle over her later. Not immediately like a punch, but gradually, like a sickness.

"Alright," Daisy said. "Tell Baron I said hi."

She never forgot her manners. Daisy's dad had passed away years ago. Prostate cancer. She was already an adult by that time, so Tandy's remarrying hadn't come with any bad feelings from her daughter. Maybe it should have.

Tandy didn't tell Baron about the trail cam. He'd barely come out of the basement the past few days, to the point that Tandy had to keep checking the raised plot of dirt where she'd buried Chester to make sure he hadn't dug him up in some misguided attempt to make her feel better. The only way she knew he was still in the house was the depletion of bread slices from the loaf on top of the fridge and the scent of death that lingered in the air.

After she set up the camera and the screen on her phone displayed a green-tinted view of the yard, Tandy watched it obsessively every free minute she had between customers at Pricewell. All that evening, there was nothing. She scrubbed through the footage, afraid that it wasn't moving, but while she was brushing her teeth, a rabbit hopped into view, stopping to twitch its nose for a few minutes before moving on.

She woke dry-eyed at exactly 6:14 a.m. Baron hadn't come to bed. The muffled sound of the TV sifted through the wall. She scrambled for her phone and resumed watching the trail camera feed starting from the timestamp when she had fallen asleep.

The rabbit came back, its eyes flipped like silver coins reflecting the porch light. But other than that, nothing.

Except—

A blip of dark moved against a stubborn triangle of snow in the dip just before the treeline. Tandy played the feed at normal speed. There one second, gone the next. A flicker. Tandy slowed the feed way down. Daisy would be happy to know that her mom had figured that out all by herself, thank you very much.

She tapped pause, having to go back a few seconds to catch it, but it was there. One frame, at 4:14 a.m. A dark blob, unmoving, with opaline eyes fixed on the camera. Protruding from the top of the blob was a set of antlers. Tandy stared at it, blinking a few times to clear her disbelief.

She burst through the bedroom door, the entire house shaking on its foundation. Her washer-softened henley slipped down her skinny shoulder. Baron was belly up on the couch, his mouth a flycatcher. He looked so old when he slept. He'd been gray since before they'd gotten married, but seeing him laid out on his back, Tandy was repulsed. Not that she was one to judge. Her face had wrinkled and her knees clicked, but her hair was the same pale blonde it had always been.

Tandy shoved the phone in Baron's face. "Look what you did."

He snorted awake, arms scrambling for purchase on the side of the couch. His eyes flashed unfocused and animal-like until he realized it was just his wife. "What? What did I do?"

"It's the fucking beavalope!" She had been right. It felt stupid to say.

Baron looked down his nose at the screen. He narrowed his eyes before a laugh erupted from his chest, startling Tandy enough that she stepped backward into the coffee table and sent an avalanche of fishing magazines spilling across the floor.

"You think—" Baron wheezed. "You think that—" He pointed to the beavalope on the mantle. "*That's* what's on your trail cam?"

Tandy exchanged a glance with the beavalope. Coulda sworn it was grinning at her. She dropped her arms to her sides. Her chest caved in on itself. "What else could it be?"

Baron pushed himself off the couch, his indent forever impressed in the cushions. "Fuck, I don't know. A raccoon."

"But what about—"

"The branches." He pulled his coat from the hook on the wall. Stuck one foot in a boot, then the other. "The branches look like antlers."

The front door swung open. A moment later, Baron's pickup groaned to life. The coughing sound of his engine faded with the popping of gravel. He worked construction; during the off-season, he normally went into town to sit at Jack's with a cup of coffee, shooting the shit.

Behind her, the TV was playing that same news story about the mountain lion that had been prowling around the elementary school in Killdeer. Probably one of the more exciting things to happen in recent town history. Everyone who stopped by the meat counter would raise their eyebrows at Tandy. *Did you hear about that mountain lion?* Tandy always pretended like it was new information, nodding along and matching their expressions. At one point, her boss Eldon had swept through, flanked by a few of his high school buddies dressed in camo jackets, and wrenched open the meat cooler, piling his arms with the ribeye steaks that Tandy had just cut and packaged, muttering something about how nice that mountain lion's head would look in his den.

What a joke.

Tandy looked back at the still video feed on her phone. She pinched the screen and pulled the smudge closer. She wasn't stupid and she didn't like Baron's insinuation that she was. Those weren't branches.

She lifted her head towards the mocking beavalope on the mantel. She stepped over the scattered magazines, coming eye to eye with it.

It had to be impossible, but she knew what she saw. She'd felt Chester's wounds against the palms of her hands. Felt his warm life slipping through her fingers. Antlers did that. Her hand twitched upward, but she pulled it back. *Afraid.* She was afraid, and she hated it. Extending onto her tiptoes, she inspected the tips of the antlers.

Baron hadn't done a good job of cleaning the gunk off when he'd acquired them from whichever ditch he sourced his materials, so it was hard to tell, but in the grooves of the off-white spikes ran what looked like veins of dark, crusted blood.

Tandy Task, born and raised in Killdeer, South Dakota, wasn't always Tandy Task, but raising a daughter with the eldest of the Task brothers had turned her into one. So, when she married Baron, she reasoned she'd already changed her last name once and accepted the new identity that came with it, and it would just be confusing for everyone if she was suddenly Tandy Gerhardt. Baron didn't seem to care either way. The ten-minute drive into town to fill out the paperwork at the courthouse was reason enough to keep things as they were.

She dumped out the coffee from the previous morning and started a fresh pot, pacing around the dining table, all while keeping one eye on the beavalope. She did so many laps around the table that she lost track of time. Her phone lit up and buzzed toward the end of the coffee table.

Eldon Price. She glanced at the neon blue numbers on the stove. It was 8:01 a.m.

"Tandy." His voice was slightly chastising. She wanted to laugh. He was nothing more than a kid in his dad's suit, running Pricewell straight into the ground. "You on your way?"

Tandy bit down on the fleshy insides of her cheeks. "I'm not feeling well." She cleared her throat. "I won't be in today."

Eldon went quiet. Tandy could feel his silent seething through the phone. "Tandy."

"What?" she snapped. "I have sick leave, don't I? I never call in sick."

"Exactly. We have no one to cover you. I'll have to mark this down as a no-call, no-show—"

"Fine. Do whatever you want."

She'd caught him off guard. He stuttered something about talking to his dad, and Tandy took his shock to grasp the upper hand. "I'll see how I'm feeling tomorrow and let you know." She ended the call and dropped her phone on the table. Someone else could cut the meat for one day.

Tandy was a little surprised to find the door to the basement locked when she twisted the handle. She never went down there, never tried, so she didn't even know Baron locked it. The door was cheap and the lock was cheaper, so all it took was a little jimmying of the jamb with a butter knife to pop it open.

The scent brought her back to deer season. Back when her dad, brother, and grandfather would march solemnly into the woods, donning their orange vests, and Tandy would come home from school to find a deer hanging by its ankle tendons in the garage, dripping rich, dark blood onto a piece of cardboard. Large eyes open, tongue hanging out. There was nothing quite like it. The heady smell of violence. The sterile meat under the bright glass case at the store didn't compare to fresh deer meat.

Tandy crept down the stairs, splinters catching on her fuzzy socks like little cat claws. She reached up, caught the light's string, and pulled. The bulb flickered on, sending shadows flying around the room.

The shelves were littered with brushes, tools, and pelts. The half-finished head of a 'possum with empty eye sockets lay next to a couple of dried-out frogs with delicate lacy dragonfly wings affixed to their backs. Sharp hawk talons had been attached to the body of the 'possum missing its head. The head of the hawk was lined up with the 'possum as though Baron had been trying to see if they looked nice together but wasn't quite sure if he wanted to commit.

Tandy walked the length of the bench, forcing herself to look. Bile coated her esophagus. This was just below the surface of her home. Where she slept and ate. Panic spiked up her spine. She stepped forward. Her toe bumped into something hard and smooth: a bobcat. The head was intact, the body flattened to a rug. Baron had done something to make the fur look like it had tire tracks running across it. Hilarious. The bobcat's crazed eyes glared at her with its teeth pulled back in a smile.

She reached the deep freeze tucked into the corner, halfway behind a shelf of murky jars. Baron had bought the freezer at a garage sale last spring. Tandy wasn't even sure if the damn thing worked because he never mentioned it again after he and Spalding had lugged it through the house, scratching the paint off the walls, to its final resting place in the basement.

Bracing herself on the lip of the freezer, she sucked in one deep breath before she lifted the lid. Cold air nipped at her fingers, swirling upward and wrapping around her neck.

Tucked into the little basket was a piglet the size of a football. Freezer burn dusted its pink flesh. There were a few robins, the legs of a raccoon, and more piles of indiscriminate limbs. Farther down was a yellow Dollar General bag. Tandy's fingers trembled as she pushed the brittle plastic aside.

She immediately let go of the lid. It slammed down, the seal kissed shut, and Tandy fell to her knees on the cold cement floor. She hugged her arms around herself. Her breaths came out short and quick.

The same neighbors who had given her Chester had recently warned her to watch out for foxes. Said that a fox ate a litter of the calico barn cat's babies. Six kittens in total.

A fox had nothing to do with it.

The quiet was broken by the chugging of an engine. Tandy's heart pounded like a rabbit kicking her ribs, but she may as well have been moving through jello. The tiny rectangular window near the ceiling was dark. How long had she been down here?

Her hands grasped above her on the gummy edge of the workbench in the center of the room, which was nothing more than a slab of plywood atop two sawhorses. She realized her mistake the moment she shifted her weight onto her palms to pull herself up. The plywood tipped toward her, pushing the sawhorses off-kilter and sending the entire setup crashing to the floor. The canvas sheet covering whatever was on the table enveloped her. Something solid hit her shoulder and dragged her down with it. An acrid scent filled her nose.

Tandy wrestled the sheet away and stared at the object it had been covering, trying to make sense of what she was seeing. It was long, about as tall as she was, its fur the color of barley, with stick-straight legs. And it was missing a head.

Tandy could see into the esophagus, where it had been severed. It stared back at her like an eye. The tendons and muscles were coagulated and sticky. Dark blood stained around the white stripe of its neck. The body of the deer was cold in a way that made it hard to imagine it had ever been alive at all.

A door slammed outside. Tandy pushed the deer off of her and glanced around frantically. Where was the head? That didn't matter. She was up the stairs and out the back door just as the front door creaked open.

The darkness was a shock to her system. She hadn't been in the basement all day, had she? She had gotten up, checked the trail cam, answered the phone, and then…

But it was night. The stars shimmered in the cold navy sky. Tandy wrapped her arms around her torso and crouched next to Chester's grave. She ran a hand over the dirt, waiting for the back door to fly open, for Baron to ask her why she was messing around with his stuff, but the door remained closed. He was never one for confrontation, anyway. She wished that he was. His maddening silence was far worse.

False spring was here, but winter still very much held the night. Tandy didn't feel it, even though she'd left her coat on the kitchen chair and still wore just a henley and her pajama pants. She smelled like blood and formaldehyde. Tufts of coarse deer fur had stuck to her chest, and she scratched absently at it. She didn't want to go back inside, but she had nowhere else to go. Inescapable violence surrounded her on all sides. She sat next to Chester's grave and kept watch with him as a soft wind rustled through the branches.

Her chin tipped forward, and a scraping sound jolted her awake. Tandy dug her palms into her eye sockets then searched the darkness. Baron was right. The branches *did* look like antlers, scratching at the sky. They also looked like sprawling veins. Like the sky had been shattered.

A shape shifted, morphing the darkness. Tandy scrambled to her feet as it stumbled across the snow and onto the grass. It was deer-shaped, but shorter. Its head kind of lolled to the side as it stalked across the yard toward her with a shambling grace.

Tandy's breath lodged in her throat. She was paralyzed, one foot sinking into the fresh dirt of Chester's grave and the other angled toward the back porch.

It was about ten feet away. In the shallow arc of light, Tandy saw the antlers, the pointed snout, the tongue unfurled from its mouth. She also saw the lithe body of a mountain lion, its large paws pressing into the grass, tail trailing behind it. She blinked a few times. Her brain couldn't comprehend it. The colors of fur nearly matched, but not quite. The deer was a little darker, a little paler, while the mountain lion's body had a light golden sheen.

With it came the smell of death, of rot, sickly sweet like a wet carpet of leaves. The garage in the house where she grew up. The thing's mouth dropped open further, its bottom jaw unhinging, showing off a row of dull herbivore teeth. Drool dripped down its chest.

Tandy shot up the stairs toward the house. The sound of claws on wood stayed right behind her. She wrenched open the screen door, leapt inside, and fell backward onto her tailbone to hold the door shut with both hands.

The stairs beside her creaked and the basement door swung open, narrowly missing her head. Baron stared down at her, blinking. Blood soaked his coveralls, making him look like some kind of redneck butcher. "What are you doing, Tandy?"

"Outside—" Tandy peered through the screen. "There's—A—"

The yard was empty.

Baron leaned forward, pressing his forehead against the door. He chuckled. "Another beavalope?"

"No." Tandy shook her head. "It was a mountain lion, but it had…"

Baron looked at her like all her marbles were rolling around on the floor. He tried to push the door open, a grin pulling his mouth upward. Tandy braced her feet on the jamb. "Baron, no—"

"What?" he asked, not looking at her. His gaze fixed on the yard. "What did you see?"

One hundred pounds soaking wet. She'd heard that phrase a thousand times growing up, and she always hated it. Baron easily foisted the knob from her grip and pushed the door open with his knuckle.

"Baron," Tandy pleaded. "*Please*, come back inside."

Baron eased down the steps, his head swiveling side to side. He licked his lips. The excitement in his eyes was sickening.

He stopped just past Chester's grave and turned to face her. He lifted his palms in the air. "There's nothing—"

Stubby protrusions burst from Baron's stomach. His eyes widened. One foot danced backward; he fell sideways, caught by the basket of antlers. The deer's head slumped to the side at an extreme angle as its mountain lion body braced on the ground and shook Baron off. Blood ran down the antlers and into its large black eyes.

Tandy sat within the threshold with her foot propping the screen door open. The deer head sniffed the air, its neck tipping to the other side. As the mountain lion body crouched low and began to slink toward her, the deer head let out a crooning moan.

All the fear that Tandy held in her chest dissipated, spreading throughout her body until it became diluted in her bloodstream. That *thing* was never supposed to exist. It was in pain, fighting back in the only way it knew how.

Propped next to the back door was Baron's grandfather's goose gun, always ready for Baron to pick up and fire a few shots at the sky every once in a while, never hitting a damn thing. Tandy grabbed the barrel and slung it onto her lap. She pulled back the bolt, sending an empty shell tumbling from the chamber. The deer's eyes followed the red shell as it landed in the grass.

Tandy stuck her hand in the nearby open box of shells. In the time it took her to fumble for one, fit it into the chamber, and point the barrel through the gap in the door, the mountain lion leaped over all three steps. Tandy felt its chest press against the barrel as she fired, felt its heart thrumming feverishly, matching her own. The recoil kicked her back against the tile.

The mountain lion flopped over. Its long body stretched across the porch steps. The deer's head rested partially on Tandy's leg, its wet tongue bleeding through the fabric of her pajama pants. Its eyes stayed open, staring against the side of the house. Past the porch, Baron sprawled on the grass next to Chester's dark patch of dirt.

Tandy dropped her head back against the tile with her arms fanned out at her sides. She stared at the ceiling and waited for her ears to stop ringing, for her shoulder to stop pulsing, for the world to make sense again, but she could sit there until the end of time, and it would never stop.

Crack Open the Shell

AM SUTTER

THE OYSTERS TEETER on the large central plate, their hard lips a frozen smile taunting Isla. She doesn't know how to eat them, doesn't even really know what an oyster looks like on the inside. Scanning the table, she stares at the others for some clue on what to do next. The two men seem unaware of her plight, and she is eager to keep it that way.

Theo leans over and says something to Mateo, who at some point shed his tie and loosened the top button on his dress shirt. They lost their suit jackets a while ago, and she bites back the jealousy as she stares down at her dress and prays she won't spill on it. Isla can't make out what's being said over the din of the restaurant, and she tells herself over and over they're not talking about her.

There's no reason to panic. She made it through the interviews—hours in Mateo's glass office with the two partners grilling her on credentials and references. Not to mention the previous years of struggling at the office, slipping in to grab the better projects out from under the rest of the useless paralegals and assistants at five in the morning. Every completion and every compliment made her hungrier for the next promotion. And wasn't it funny that it had been the first time she'd actually been in that office after eight years of working for them?

Still, she made it. Now she's tallying all the things she's going to buy with the bonus, using the list to calm her breathing. *In.* Bluetooth soundbar. *Out.* A pair of real Louis Vuittons.

Theo looks over at her and nods at the plate in front of them. "Dig in," he says.

The oysters wait for her. It's a celebration, Theo had told her, but she's never set foot in a restaurant so extravagant and doesn't know the first thing about how to eat this food.

"I've only had fried clams," she says, smiling in that self-deprecating way her mother taught her when she was a child. She uses it with practiced ease to clamp down on the comment she wants to make—that she doesn't need his permission to eat. But she's so *close*, and she won't ruin it. She pictures the Mac Duggal cocktail dress she's eyed every time she's walked down Main and swallows down her pride. It tastes thick and bitter, perhaps like the oysters.

Theo laughs—the sound makes Isla embarrassed at her own ignorance and annoyed at his flippancy—and picks up one of the cinched oysters. He cups it gently, almost lovingly, and then shoves a blunt knife through the small opening in its shell.

Isla startles at the violence in the gesture, but he's already prying the shellfish open. Its shell pops up and reveals wrinkled, bulbous meat. She swallows down a retch, trying not to consider how it looks like a cancerous tongue. He brings the broken-open shell to his mouth and slurps, and she fights with herself not to be sick. She can do this—just get through the dinner and then it's a big fat pay raise and her own office and her name on the website alongside the people in front of her.

She wants it so much that it makes a hunger flare where just a moment ago there existed only disgust.

With a confidence she doesn't feel, she picks up an oyster herself and slides her own shucking knife into it. She pictures the new television on her wishlist and twists the blade. The shell opens with a wet smack and gapes at her, almost as if surprised. She lifts it to her mouth.

The texture is terrible—a wet, slimy feeling that finishes with a chewiness against her teeth. But the taste isn't bad and she could get used to it. The nutty flavor settles into her stomach, though it does little to quell the deep ache that's been clenched around her gut since her first interview for the promotion. It's almost like a craving, and maybe she's felt this way since the day she started at the office and decided her name would be up on the sign next to Theo and Mateo's one day.

Isla grabs another oyster from the plate.

"Now you're getting it," Theo says with another laugh. Next to him, Mateo looks at her over his glasses and smiles, approving. The meat slides down her throat like the first, but the ache remains.

Isla slides against the smooth leather of Mateo's BMW and tries to find purchase as he tears around another sharp bend. They're doing seventy on the forest backroads—driving away from the restaurant—and she does her best not to think about what would happen if they wrapped themselves around one of the trees illuminated by his high beams. Instead, she tugs on her seatbelt to make sure it's secure and studies the interior.

"How do you like your car?" she asks, powering through her reluctance to distract Mateo from the road.

"She's a dream," he says, voice roughened from age and a smoking habit given up with great reluctance. He runs a hand through a thinning part. From her position, she can't see his face but can see the rim of his glasses and the moles along his bald spot.

"Better than some crappy Lexus," Mateo adds. He raises an eyebrow at Theo in the passenger seat. From her vantage point, Isla tries to build the features she can't make out. Theo has half of an easy smile, dark hair smooth and disappearing into the shadows of the other side of his face.

"You wish, Mateo."

She leans back against the seat, giving up on trying to see the men in front of her. Maybe she'll trade in her old Honda and get one of these now. In her mind, she pictures the check they'll be writing her next week. Mateo speeds into another curve, and the oysters rock low in her belly. She expects the motion to make her sick, but instead, it seems to allow space for that odd hunger again.

"Never trust his recommendations in cars," Theo says and glances at her over his shoulder. The lights blaze a trail down the dark, empty road; the tall pines press in around them. Theo's eyes catch the glow from the beams, sparkling as they absorb the gleam. She wants this car with its dark leather and expensive trim. She wants to straddle Theo in the back and worry about the cleanup later. The ache flares, and she crosses her legs, her dress cinching at her hips.

"You excited for next week?" Theo asks, and Isla pulls herself back to the present. He's smiling again and still staring at her. She tries to forget about the car and Theo's face so she can form a coherent response. Over the top of his head, fuzzy in the car's bright lights, a large animal wanders out of the forest onto the road.

There's something wrong with it.

They're coming up on it too fast, and the night blurs its detail, but she can see enough. Skin stretches over bone without muscle. It's too tall and too skinny, and there's something wrong with its head. There's something wrong. There's *something…*

"Watch out!" she screams right as Mateo sees it. He swerves, knuckles blanched against the steering wheel, and the car skids off the road. Her body jackknifes around the seatbelt, pain flaring through her spine. In the corner of her vision, the creature turns toward her. Then the car is skidding, and she can't see anything but the line of trees waiting to catch them.

A low roar swallows Isla's hearing as she blinks once, twice, to clear her vision. As the din quiets, she focuses on the burn where her seatbelt has cut across her collarbone and the dinging of the dashboard. Airbags fill the car with a white smoke and make the cabin foggy, ethereal. The front lights flicker, casting shadows against the tree trunk wedged into the crumpled hood of the car. She becomes aware of a choking groan; it emanates from Mateo slumped against his seat.

"Jesus!" Theo bats his airbag down, coughing around the powder floating in the cabin. "Mateo, you trying to kill us?" Then to Isla, "You okay?"

Isla nods and regrets it when her brain rattles loose in her skull. Mateo continues to moan, but he's picked up his head to hold a palm against it while she rolls out a sore wrist and unbuckles her seatbelt. She thinks he's being dramatic but doesn't say it aloud.

"What was that?" he says, finally dropping his hand and gingerly turning to look through the rear window. One of his lenses is cracked, the rim bent, and his glasses tip dangerously down the side of his face.

"What was what?" Theo asks and works to push his door open.

Isla remembers the thing in the road and whips around to look as well. Her vision sways and her neck stings. The road is empty.

"You didn't see it?" Mateo says, struggling to free himself.

"I saw you spin out." Theo pulls himself out of the wrecked car and stumbles to the other side.

"There was an animal in the road," Isla responds, but Theo isn't around to hear her.

Her door opens, and Theo bends down, offering her a hand. She shakes her head and gestures to where Mateo's still fighting. Theo moves to help him, and she slides out into the cool night air. Her heels sink into dead pine needles and dank soil while the hazards blink on and off in the aftermath of their abrupt stop, throwing the forest around them into strobing silence. Fear curls around the base of her neck, squeezing her already tight skull. She keeps expecting the animal to show up in between one of the flashes. That the road will be empty one moment and not the next.

"It was big," Mateo says, and she forces herself to turn and look at the two men. Theo has his hand under Mateo's elbow to help steady him. "Couldn't tell what it was, though."

"Okay." Theo's tone belies that he doesn't believe Mateo but also doesn't want to fight. "I think what's most important right now is calling for help." He looks around them. "I need to grab my phone."

As if the car was listening, a low pop sounds, and dirty smoke gushes out from beneath the hood. Within moments, the front half of the car is in flames.

Theo shouts and pulls Mateo away from the vehicle. The heat rushes over Isla as they retreat to the road. As she watches the inferno, she tries not to mourn the loss of her phone and the designer purse it rested in. She can buy a new one, a better one, once this nightmare is over. Maybe they'll bump up her bonus for this lousy evening. The hunger gnaws at her gut.

"Guess it's not as good as my car," Theo deadpans and drags Mateo into a slow pace. Isla follows, hugging arms around bare shoulders as the ice of the night pushes back against the heat of the fire.

"It didn't look like any animal I've ever seen," Mateo says, as if a car fire hadn't just interrupted the previous conversation. She wonders if he has a concussion.

"Sure," Theo responds and hikes Mateo's arm over his shoulder.

"It didn't look like anything I've ever seen at all." Mateo squints at the thick trees around them. Isla knows what bothered her about it, though doesn't know if Mateo saw.

The animal's head had been so emaciated it looked like a skull, but she won't say that aloud. Never.

"Jesus, you're heavy," Theo complains. He fists his hand into the back of Mateo's suit jacket and heaves him up higher in his grip.

Isla looks at the brown tweed and jealously studies the sweat starting to stain Theo's back as her own thin dress rides up around her thighs with every step. As if aware, the wind picks up and blows through her hair. She shivers and jogs to catch up.

"How far until we get out of here?" she asks, trying to keep her mind off of the goosebumps rubbing against her crossed arms. She feels like they've been walking all night. The car ride hadn't felt this long on the way to the restaurant, but she isn't sure how long it should be taking. Mateo was speeding, and yet still, the forest seems to stretch on forever.

"It can't be too much longer," Theo says. "We've been walking for hours, and this back road isn't that abandoned." He's trying to hide his breathlessness, but Isla can see the way Mateo sags closer to the ground.

She tries not to let his words bother her. But they've been on this road for so long, and they haven't seen any more cars or lights or even a break in these goddamn trees. They should be out by now—she *knows* they should be by the crappy gas station and the old school.

And now that she's paying attention, the moon hasn't moved in the sky, has it?

That's nonsense, utter nonsense. Her stomach clenches, reminding her she's been walking long enough to get hungry again. Cracked lips expose her growing thirst. It should be morning by now, that ache tells her. They should be out, she should be kicking her heels up in her new office, and the moon shouldn't still be right there above them.

Something moves through the trees—a flash of ivory among the dark greens and browns of the canopy.

Isla stumbles and goes down on one knee. The gravel pits into her skin, and she can feel her own blood steaming and cooling in the air. Stopping to look behind them, Theo sees her and pats Mateo's chest before letting his arm go. He jogs back to where she's still kneeling, and before she's even aware, he hooks hands around her waist and hauls her to her feet.

Startled, she gasps at the heat of his touch. She doesn't need his help, but when he lets go, she's acutely aware of the loss. Looking down, she sees he managed to smear some of Mateo's blood on the front of her dress. The stain will never come out of the fabric; she'll have to buy a new one. The ache low in her gut flares to life again.

"You wait here," Theo says, looking at both her and Mateo. "I'm just going to run up ahead and see if there's any cars coming."

He says it with a confidence Isla knows he's faking, but she just shrugs. Her ankles hurt, and they've been walking so long that she's glad for an excuse to stop. With one last look at them, Theo continues forward and soon disappears around a bend in the road, swallowed up by the trees.

"I keep thinking about that animal in the road," Mateo says behind her, and she startles, turning from her lookout position for Theo's return.

Mateo stares at the trees where Isla thought she saw the white earlier. He rubs at his temple with a shaking hand, and she wonders how bad his concussion is. "You saw it too, right?"

Isla thinks of stretched skin and an animal too tall to exist in these woods. She doesn't think of that head. No, not here in the dark forest when they're lost.

Mateo swipes at the mix of sweat and blood across his forehead and accidentally sends his glasses flying. "Damn it!" He takes an unsure step toward the forest, where he must think they've landed, but Isla sees the spectacles glint in the weeds beside them.

"I've got it," she says and walks over, stepping off the asphalt and onto the grass.

"What's that?" Mateo asks, squinting against his nearsightedness as he moves closer to the thick evergreens. Isla ignores the question, choosing instead to bend down and grab the abandoned glasses.

When she stands up, there is a skull watching them from the trees.

She shouts; Mateo screams. The creature unfolds itself, standing taller than some of the pines. It takes a step out from the woods, and it's too thin to have any organs. All Isla can think is that it must be hungry all the time. Five feet above them, a deer's skull smiles down, empty eye sockets tracking them.

"Oh God," Mateo whimpers, and he's too close, too close to this thing that can't be real. Yet, the creature is solid and they both can see it, and when it snorts warm air into the chill of the night, Isla can smell the rot carried on its breath.

The monster towers over Mateo, and suddenly he isn't the powerful head of the firm; he's cowering and frightened.

Move, Isla thinks, though she remains rooted in her own patch of earth. *Move*. He throws his hands over his head and bends down, and Isla pulls back in disgust. It's as if Mateo doesn't have the ache in his own gut—that drive to move and come out ahead.

A stretched, jointed hand flicks out and swipes at Mateo, but it misses. *Without eyes*, Isla thinks with a hysterical laugh bubbling in her throat, *depth perception must be hard.* At its blunder, the creature bellows in frustration and digs a hand into its own skull. It rips at the braincase, and the deer head collapses suddenly before new bone vomits upward and outward. A giant, grinning weasel skull studies them now.

Faster than before, the hand strikes again and grabs Mateo around the waist. As it snags its prey, that bony jaw unhinges in a silent laugh. It unrolls its tongue, and Isla is reminded of a mosquito. It keeps unfurling, as long as the weasel's head it's birthed from. The appendage is long and fleshy and sharp. Without warning, it pierces the top of Mateo's head, right over his balding part. He jerks once and locks up, eyes going wide. He stares at Isla, and she can only stare back, clenching his cracked glasses. The thing squeezes him with sharp claws and begins to drink.

Mateo folds in on himself, crumbles like tissue paper. The scaffolding inside has collapsed; the insulation is missing.

The thing that remains is so frail; it flutters like tissue paper to the road when the monster releases it.

The creature steps over Mateo's skin, now wrinkled and damaged by the loose dirt, and curls its long tongue back up its body. Back into its mouth. As it retracts, the weasel's long cranium collapses. A hog's skull grins at her now, nose almost as boundless as its tongue, tusks sharp and glowing as white as the moon above them. That tongue makes an awful slurping sound, making Isla think of Theo's lips against the oysters. The sound should make her nauseous—Mateo's empty *corpse* should make her nauseous—but that frozen smile turns toward her, and she is only reminded of that ache, of how tired and thirsty and cold she is from walking all night.

One of those tall legs slides forward, the beast bends down to her, and a hand reaches out. The nails are like talons, and she should be thinking about how it would feel to have her insides removed all in one violent go. Instead, all she considers is that she won't cower like Mateo. If she gives up now, then all the stress of the past few weeks, the past few *years*, was worthless. That hunger flares and drives her forward to meet the beast.

She grips Mateo's broken glasses in her fist and swings them up like a shiv. They jam into one of the empty eye sockets, and though there doesn't seem to be anything there, the creature still staggers backward and screeches. The head folds, consumes itself, and then explodes outward into an owl's skull. Beak clacking in anger and pain, the thing stumbles back into the tree line. Mateo's pelt catches under its retreating feet and flutters after the creature, and both disappear into the thicket. Isla retreats to the safety of the street.

Theo reappears around the curve of the road twenty minutes later. Isla almost doesn't notice him, too focused on watching the trees for any movement. When he draws near, he begins talking.

"Nothing up ahead that I could see. We'll have to try going farther." Theo stops and looks around her, finally noticing that there's decidedly fewer people than when he left. "Where the hell did he go?" He squints at the empty asphalt for a moment, as if Mateo sank into it.

Not quite, she thinks. The wind funnels through the trees and flutters under Theo's jacket. She thinks of Mateo's skin, empty and dry like a hunter's trophy.

"Isla," he says, sharp and impatient.

"The monster," she responds, as if that explains everything, and he shakes his head, angry.

"Goddamn it! Why'd you let him wander off? He's got a concussion!" His palms swing wildly in the air above him, and she remembers longer fingers, dirty nails, grabbing Mateo around the hips like he was a doll.

"Goddamn it," Theo shouts again, and then his shoulders sag. "We can't go after him—we'll just get lost ourselves." He starts forward and sharply gestures for her to follow. "Now we've gotta get out of here so the authorities can find him before he kills himself." He gives her another look, as if it's her fault he left them to be consumed by something terrible. Still, even if he doesn't know it, he's right. They can't stay here. She felt that creature's craving and knows that it will be back.

With no other option, she follows him down the road, her palm still bleeding from Mateo's lost spectacles. When she brings it up to suck at it, hoping to stem the bleeding, the copper tang reminds her how hungry she is.

Isla's sure they've been walking for days, even if the moon doesn't shift, even if the night still presses down against them. Her feet are a mess of blood and calluses, her dress stiff with sweat. A sharp ache—a mix of thirst and hunger and exhaustion—cramps her abs and her thighs, and she bites her lip until it splits. It's probably only making things worse, but the sharp metallic taste seems to quell the pangs for a bit. When she sucks on the cut, she pictures herself sitting in her new office, drinking one of the expensive coffees Mateo would show up with. She pictures a straw in his head, sipping him dry.

Gasping, Isla comes back to herself and looks over to Theo. After hours, days, his confidence has uncoiled on the pavement behind him. His shoulders hunch, eyes sunken deep, and he swings his head side to side, looking for some car that will never show. A rescue that will never come.

They round another bend in the road, and the forest presses closer. Isla nervously searches the gloom that wraps around the trunks for any signs of movement.

Theo suddenly grabs her arm, bruising her skin, and pulls them both to a stop.

"Did you see that?" he asks, pointing at the thick forest. "I'm pretty sure it's lights." Isla follows his hand, shaking from exhaustion and thirst. He's gesturing through the trees, pointing at the vast, cavernous eye holes of the monster as it watches them from in between the trunks. In the center of those twin abysses, something catches the moon and sparkles like a streetlight.

"No," she croaks. The creature shifts its head in a swaying motion. The reflections turn into car headlights.

"Let's go!" Theo grabs her hand and hauls her toward the trees. She struggles to yank them backward, away from the woods sheltering the monster.

That skull grins from between the leaves. It's a frog's head now— mouth wide enough to swallow her whole.

Yes, it seems to say, *come into the trees.*

Theo continues to drag her, her heels uselessly kicking up clods of grass and dirt. As they approach the tree line, the blank eye sockets are obvious as they loom over the two, and how does Theo not see them?

If they enter the woods, Isla knows they'll never find their way; they'll never get out. Leaning back against his grip, her fingers scramble to find purchase and stop their momentum.

"Stop," she begs. "It'll eat us both."

"You're going crazy," Theo snarls and yanks. She is desperate to stop. The frog's jaw unhinges and opens as they approach. Her hand closes around a sharp stone.

The monster is hungry, but she is hungrier.

The rock nestles perfectly in her palm, like it was always meant to rest there, and she swings it at the back of Theo's head. It catches in thick hair and drags along his skin. His bone feels like that of the monster, and then her rock is through and settling into something soft, deep inside his head.

Isla panics and rips the stone back. Without his anchor, Theo drops, and his grip goes slack. Tumbling backward, she rolls over the dirt, and pain flares across her back when she hits the sharp pavement. Everything hurts, and without Theo dragging her, maybe she just won't get up again.

The monster looks at her, but it seems to examine her now, even though she's not sure how a frozen skeleton conveys any emotion other than famine. Still, it cocks its head and considers her. A wave of nauseous hunger roils through her, and she groans against it, dropping the rock in favor of digging nails into her abdomen and squeezing her eyes shut. Rhythmic drumming starts in time with the throb of her dehydration headache. She looks up.

At the tree line, the creature taps a long finger against a rotten trunk, then again against its own exposed skull. The head shudders from bear to snake to elk—bones shifting and consuming themselves before belching out new anatomy. She is so tired that the fear bleeds from her, leaving only the hunger. The thing chatters the teeth in its wide jaw, as if it can feel the ache in her gut. The craving burrows deeper, and it's not her fault the others weren't hungry enough to survive. She wants to keep going; she wants *more*. She doesn't want to die here, not with so much promised to her. She wants food and water and a bed. She wants the nicer apartment, the new car, the flush bank account. She wants her name on the door. She wants to live.

She wants to feel full, just once.

The monster raps its head again, the sharp nail dragging grooves in stained ivory, and empty eye sockets look down past her. She follows its gaze.

Theo lies still and quiet on the bed of detritus. There is a defect in the matted hair of his crown; a crevasse gapes back at her through the gaps in his shell, something pink and soft sloshing back and forth underneath. Placing a finger to the hole, she brings it back to her mouth and tentatively touches it to her tongue. At the flavor, her hunger flares brighter. She wants more, always more. Over her shoulder, the creature turns its immortal smile toward her. She thinks it understands her ache.

Isla hunches over the gash, hunger and thirst driving her vision blurry, places her lips against the cracked bone, and begins to suck. The texture is awful, a wet, slimy feel, but she has to admit—as shards of ivory cut fine lines into the flesh around her mouth, shredding the skin from her own skull—the taste. . . .

The taste she could get used to.

About the Authors

A Terrifying Prize – J Neira

jneiraauthor.bsky.social

J. Neira is a cozy horror author & a passionate hicklib. Their YA novel releases next year from Graveside Press, the same publisher they slush for.

Apotheosis – David O Mahony

davidomahony.carrd.co

David O'Mahony is based in Cork, Ireland, and the author of two collections: The Ties That Bind and What Gets Left Behind.

Cornfield Gothic – Gabrielle Contelmo

gabriellecontelmo.com

Gabrielle Contelmo lives in Myrtle Beach, SC where she writes spooky short stories and character-driven romance novels.

Crack Open the Shell – AM Sutter

amsutter.com

AM Sutter works as a zoo and exotic animal veterinarian and enjoys hiking with her Shih Tzu, who fully believes he is a wolf.

Den Mother – Rey Revelli

reyrevelli.com

When he's not writing speculative fiction, Rey Revelli can be found gaming with his husband, arguing with their overly opinionated cats, and devouring curry.

Harbinger – LR Woods

LR Woods is a writer of speculative fiction, horror, and erotica. She lives in the Appalachian mountains with all the cool cryptids.

It Knows My Shape – Gio Clairval

gioclairval.blogspot.com

Gio's stories have appeared in The Dark, Fantasy, Weird Tales, and more. She translates fiction from several languages (The Weird, ed. Ann and Jeff VanderMeer).

Long Pig – A. Atkins

atkinswrites.com

A. Atkins is a serial genre straddler. When not writing genre-mash ups, she's at the barn trying not to fall off her bitchy red mares.

Lord of the Dance – Micah Giddens

linktr.ee/micah.giddens

Micah Giddens is a California Sasquatch currently living amongst the Moth People of Chicago. His fiction has appeared in Flame Tree, Spooky Magazine, and is forthcoming from Bannister Press.

Mimic: Breeding Season – R.R. Harrow

houseofharrow.org

Я.R. Harrow is a prolific on-spectrum reader and Graveside Press author originally hailing from the rural Adirondack regions of New York State. Я.R. Harrow currently resides in Western NY.

Mothman – Caterina Minezzi

linktr.ee/catminart

Caterina Minezzi was born in Bologna (Italy) in 1990. Self taught traditional artist, she paints horrors with ink. She likes skeletons, Star Trek, and jazz.

On the Nature of Grief and Ghouls – Hannah Birss

hannahbirsswrites.ca

Hannah Birss (she/her) is a writer and aspiring magpie based out of Ontario. She can usually be found in a nest constructed of books, writing journals, and shiny trinkets.

Out of the Woods – Jamie Churchman

jamiechurchman.carrd.co/

Jamie (she/her) has been a weird little horror gremlin all her life. She lives in Kansas with her husband and an odd assortment of sassy pets.

Pop Goes the Wasset – S.E. Howard

sehoward.com

S.E. Howard lives in Kentucky where she works as a registered nurse, certified in toxicology (a fitting field given her side-hustle writing horror stories).

Quarry – Liam Hogan

happyendingnotguaranteed.blogspot.co.uk

Liam Hogan is an award-winning short story writer, with stories in Best of British Science Fiction and Best of British Fantasy.

RIP Dag Gadol Diner – Laura Barker

Laura Barker's work appears in Apparition Lit, midnight & indigo, The Other Stories, Planet Scumm, Love Letters to Poe, FIYAH, Cosmic Horror Monthly, Riptide Journal, and Last Girls Club.

Separations – Aldrian Estepa

speculativereads.wordpress.com

During the full moon, Aldrian Estepa transforms into a speculative fiction writer. Previous work: New Maps, Flash Fiction Magazine, Symphonies of Imagination, and Mobius Blvd.

Skunkape & The Teague Thing – Terry Campbell

alittlewestofweird.com

Terry Campbell enjoys writing folk horror and weird westerns. His obsession with cryptids began as a kid when he discovered the cult classic "The Legend of Boggy Creek". What 70s kid didn't?

Split-Stone – Joshua Lim

joshualimwriter.wordpress.com

Joshua Lim is a medical student and speculative fiction writer from Klang, Malaysia. His stories have appeared in Fantasy Magazine, khōréō, PodCastle, The Dark and more.

The Beast of Always – C. Charles Knight

theknightwriter.com

C. Charles Knight is a horror author who has published short stories in magazines and anthologies. Upcoming stories featured in several anthologies, two novellas, and a short story collection releasing soon. He is currently working on a novel.

The Branches Look Like Antlers – Chrissy Gray

chrissygraywrites.com

Chrissy Gray is a writer from the Midwest who loves exploring her home region through fiction. She's obsessed with slashers, unlikable female characters, and a good love story.

The Cryptid in the Woods – Adrielle Reina

linktr.ee/adriellereina

Adrielle Reina is a spooky, kooky autistic lady from Appalachia. She studied biological anthropology and data engineering, but cursing her enemies and writing are her true passions.

The Guardian of the Forest – Marta Riva

intotheforest-illustrations.carrd.co

Marta is a dark medieval and fantasy illustrator specialized in book internal designs and fantasy art.

The Rattler – Alex Burnstein

alexburnstein.com

Alex Burnstein is a speculative fiction author who enjoys spending time with his wife, four cat children, and one snake child. He also loves coffee.

The Red Ghost – Frankie Regalia

frankieregalia.com

Frankie Regalia is a writer, an award-winning playwright, and editor of Folkloric. Her debut novel has been long-listed for the Lucy Cavendish College Fiction Prize.

The Sounds of the Forest – gaast

gaast.skin

gaast is a ghost currently haunting occupied Lenape land. It reminds all that Black Lives Matter and Palestine will be free.

The Spectergraph – Liddell Rayne

liddellrayne.com

Liddell Rayne writes haunting horror fueled by double-stuffed Oreos and whole milk. Their stories linger long after dark; sweet, chilling, and hard to forget.

The Windchime Witch – Brahn Smith

batwynn.carrd.co

Brahn is an artist who resides in a spooky shack in rural Maine and loves reading a good horror story with a nice lap cat.

The Winter Caretaker – J. Needham

j-needham.bsky.social

J. is a cryptid who lives with their fiancée and evil little dog. They love writing about queer people—both the heroic and morally grey kind.

Wampus – P. N. Harrison

harrisonhorror.wordpress.com

P.N. Harrison is a horror and dark fantasy writer from Western Kansas. His debut novelette, The Consort, is forthcoming from Baynam Books Press in November.

Wastes Beyond Wastes – Leon Saul

Leon Saul is the author of several short stories, appearing in NonBinary Review, Pulp Asylum, Max Blood's Mausoleum, and elsewhere. He lives with his family in Southern California.

Yamadhin – Z.D. Dochterman

zddochterman.com

Z.D. Dochterman writes dark speculative fiction, which has appeared in "Seize the Press," "Bone Parade" and elsewhere. He's also into hiking and doom metal.

Content Warnings

Please note: because this is a horror anthology, it should be assumed that the basic horror tropes will apply. These include death, gore, and violence.

- A Terrifying Prize - wild animal death and mutilation
- Apotheosis – burial, exhumation, issues with pregnancy, bugs, disrespect of the dead
- Cornfield Gothic – implied domestic violence and child abuse
- Crack Open the Shell - cannibalism
- Den Mother - alcohol use, dead wild animal, gun violence, infant illness, kidnapping, abuse of wild animals
- Harbinger - attempted ritual sacrifice
- It Knows My Shape - claustrophobia
- Long Pig – body horror, cannibalism, implied death of farm animals
- On the Nature of Grief and Ghouls - cancer, grief, human remains, eating of human remains
- Quarry - drowning, devourment
- The Beast of Always - implied interpersonal violence, risk to safety
- The Branches Look Like Antlers - animal death
- The Cryptid in the Woods – domestic violence, drinking, cheating, verbalizing animal cruelty
- The Teague Thing - children in peril, drug reference, abduction and death of transients
- The Winter Caretaker - internalized homophobia

Thank You!

Thank you for supporting Graveside Press and our authors. One of the biggest ways you can help is to leave a star rating or a review wherever you purchased your copy!

Stay spooky.

graveside-press.com

www.ingramcontent.com/pod-product-compliance
Lightning Source LLC
Chambersburg PA
CBHW030756310726
48969CB00005B/1428